Praise for *Adder in the Path*

"William Jensen engages us with some of the most extreme elements of behavior. He carefully credits several fictional characters that interact with historical figures in a way that develops the interest, sympathy and repulsion of the reader. Real and imaginary events push the complex story into an exciting and gripping conclusion. The reader is immersed in a dramatic and controversial historical period that few authors would attempt to portray."

—Blythe Ahlstrom, professor of history and former provost, Utah State University

"Bill Jensen's rousing tale of the early years of the church is a good read."

—Thad Box, columnist

"William R. Jensen's *Adder in the Path* is an accessible, often inviting introduction to the 1838 Mormon War, a bitter chapter in Missouri history. Wrapping much of the dry historical record in fiction, Jensen tells the story of two families—one newly arrived Mormons, one original 'gentile' settlers—caught up in the violence.

What makes it all work is good storytelling and the author's use of the key figures of the time, including the Mormon prophet, Joseph Smith. Through colorful dialogue, imagery and faithfulness to surviving historical fact, Jensen makes it easy for readers to imagine a tragic time that documents alone can never recreate."

—David Knopf, *Richmond News*, Richmond, Missouri

"William Jensen spins a fascinating tale... Intolerance by both the Mormons and the Missourians results in murder, intrigue, heartbreak and even suicide."

—Bruce Smith, publisher, *Herald Journal*, Logan, Utah

Adder in the Path

Adder in the Path

William R. Jensen

BELLE ISLE BOOKS
www.belleislebooks.com

ISBN 978-0-9849588-1-8

Library of Congress Control Number: 2012906282

Printed in the United States

BELLE ISLE BOOKS
www.belleislebooks.com

PREFACE

꧁꧂

As far as historical events go, the Mormon War in Missouri was little more than a blip, but it sent out ripples that greatly affect attitudes to this day. It is difficult to determine the truth of the Mormon War because the issues that led to the conflict were once white-hot but now have burned out and are ashes. Nevertheless, the progeny of both sides of the war continue to present conflicting accounts of the events that led to the conflict and the confrontation itself. This is especially true of the Mormons, or Church of Jesus Christ of Latter-day Saints, as they are formally known. To this day, the Saints like to portray their history as they wish it had been rather than how it actually was.

The Church of Jesus Christ of Latter-day Saints is unique in that it was founded and grew to maturity on the American frontier. The church was founded in the early 1830s in Palmyra, New York and incorporated much of the fanaticism and folklore of that place and time, including communion with God, seer stones, speaking in tongues and casting out devils. It is remarkable that this church, founded on the frontier, should suffer persecution there and eventually be driven to the isolation of the Great Basin.

This dichotomy, to my knowledge, has never been adequately studied or answered. Growing up in the church, I often wondered why the Mormons found only hostility and violence on the frontier that gave the church life. As an adolescent, I asked my parents and Sunday school teachers this question and received the standard answer: that the Devil incited the mobs to thwart the will of God and attack the Saints, because they espoused the only true religion.

Eventually, I found myself at Kansas State University, where I studied Western and military history. Manhattan, Kansas is only 150 miles from Independence, Missouri, the site of the Mormons' holy City of Zion, where they believe they will establish a world government based on righteous principles and where Jesus will come to usher in the Millennium. At Kansas State, I became deeply interested in the Mormon War in Missouri and studied it intensely, eventually writing a major paper attempting to answer the question of why the Saints suffered persecution in the very region where the church was founded and matured.

This book grew out of the ideas I formulated while writing that paper. I came to realize that Mormon doctrine is fluid and changes to meet circumstances despite the church's claim that truth is unchanging. Many changes in church doctrine came about because of opposition from non-members.

From the time the church was founded in 1830 until after the Utah War of 1857, the Mormons suffered a strange, recurring trend of hostility and expulsion. Each time the Saints were driven from an area and fled to another, they were received in the new area with compassion and support. However, within three years, the original residents tired of the Saints and insisted that they move on, often with violence. I believe there are several reasons for this persistent trend.

One major issue of contention between the Saints and the Missourians was the Missourians' belief that the Saints were encouraging free blacks to join the church and immigrate to Missouri, which was a slave state. In an attempt to defuse the animosity kindled by this issue, the church completely changed their doctrine regarding blacks.

Another bone of contention was the Saints' belief that Indians were actually descendants of Hebrews who migrated to the New World 600 years before the birth of Christ. As with most frontiersmen, the Missourians despised Indians and anyone they considered an "Indian lover."

The differing views on conformity versus obedience also caused friction between the two groups. Frontiersmen were generally individualists and suspicious of government and organizations that demanded conformity. Not so, the Saints. They were very close-knit and fanatical in their beliefs, especially regarding reliance on obedience to their church leaders and particularly to their prophet.

In its early history, the church was desperately poor, due to hundreds of disadvantaged converts pouring into its ranks. To finance its expansion, the church leaders developed a financial system known as the United Order of Enoch. This system was also known as the Law of Consecration. The Law of Consecration was a communistic scheme, modeled after the communal references in the Bible. It basically required members to consecrate all of their property to the church, which would allocate assets to the members according to their needs. The individualistic Missourians did not take kindly to the communal traits of the Mormons, nor to the hundreds of penniless members who poured into the area and squatted on any unoccupied land.

Due to its very nature and doctrine, the church demanded conformity. The Saints believed that until they established a righteous society, Christ would not come again. To ensure righteousness, the church leaders sought to control all aspects of the members' lives. They also tried to control local elections by ensuring the church members would vote as instructed by the church leaders. This attempt to control local politics infuriated the Missourians.

As resistance to the church grew on the Missouri frontier, the Saints attempted to protect themselves and stamp out apostasy and dissent in their own ranks by establishing a secret society known as the Sons of Dan, eventually referred to simply as the Danites.

This organization, forged in the crucible of persecution, became a pseudo secret police, dedicated to protecting the prophet and furthering the will of the church. It eventually became a feared shadow group and the very mention of the dreaded name, "Danite," was enough to stop a dissenter from questioning authority. The Danites were also used as "shock" troops in battles against the Missourians.

The Missouri experience helped forge the Mormons into the cohesive organization that they are today and is an essential element in their history. Nevertheless, it is difficult to get to the core of the Missouri experience because the Saints deny any blame in the atrocities of the war and the Missourians see the war as an embarrassment. Therefore, it is difficult to find a history that approaches the Mormon War in Missouri from an unbiased position. Although this book is basically fiction, I have tried to present the war and events leading up to it as reliably as possible.

The chronology of the story and most of the events related in this book are as accurate as I can make them. Many of the characters, such as Porter Rockwell, John D. Lee, and David Whitmer, were actual characters in the Mormon Wars in Missouri, but the main characters, such as the Evans and Devine families, are products of my imagination.

I drew most of the information for this book from original and secondary sources. It is difficult to find sources dealing with Mormon history that are unbiased. Anyone wanting to read a history of the Mormons that is well written and soundly researched should study Fawn Brodie's excellent biography of Joseph Smith, *No Man Knows My History*. I used this work extensively when writing this book. Another excellent source is Harold Shindler's biography of Orrin Porter Rockwell, *Orrin Porter Rockwell, Man of God, Son of Thunder*. Also, I relied on Joseph Smith's multivolume *History of the Church* for descriptions of events, people and church meetings. However, anyone reading this work should realize that Joseph wrote the compilation with an eye to his legacy.

In writing this story, I also consulted the standard works of the Church of Jesus Christ of Latter-day Saints: *The Book of Mormon, Doctrine and Covenants,* and *Pearl of Great Price.*

PART ONE

The Miracle

Chapter 1

T here is something about spring in western Missouri that touches the psyche and lifts the spirit. In 1831, the prairie was still largely unturned by the plow, and myriad wild flowers swayed on the rolling hills, filling the air with the subtle scent of the awakening earth. Although Missouri was still basically a raw frontier, the remnants of the once proud indigenous Indian tribes were scattered or totally banished across the rolling muddy waters of the Missouri to "Indian Territory." In fact, in 1830, the United States Congress, under the urging of President Andrew Jackson, had passed the Indian Removal Act that led to the infamous Trail of Tears.

Jake Devine sat on the low bluffs overlooking the Grand River Valley. The shallow valley was filled with a thin blue haze that muted the spring sun, but it was still warm on his cheek. Jake was whip-thin and appeared taller than his modest five-foot-six-inch frame. The responsibilities that had been piled on his young shoulders made him seem more mature than his twelve years. He lay sprawled in the lush bluestem grass, enjoying the spare warmth of the still-slanting sun.

Across his knees lay a long, thin Kentucky rifle that his father had acquired before they moved from the cane country of eastern Kentucky. The graceful rifle was Jake's prized possession and one of the few things he could actually call his own. The gun was made by one of the master gunsmiths of Pennsylvania and Kentucky, and the milled grooves in the barrel made it extremely accurate. His gaze shifted from the distant rolling hills to the graceful swirls of the curly maple stock. The curves of the wood grain always reminded him of the way the blue smoke curled up from his father's white clay pipe when he smoked it in the evening after supper. The gun was originally a flintlock, but some enterprising gunsmith had converted it to percussion after that much more reliable mode of powder ignition became popular in the 1820s.

Close to Jake's feet, a tricolor hound of dubious ancestry dozed in the spring sun. The dog, "Rufe," was a stray that Jake had persuaded his father to allow him to keep on the pretense that it would help him supply victuals for the family larder. Rufe displayed the characteristics of the English foxhounds and Talbot hounds of France. These dogs traced their ancestry to the rough hounds brought to England during the Norman invasion. Their lineage was first introduced to America through five dogs that George Washington received as gifts from the Marquis de Lafayette. Washington likened the baying of his hounds to the chiming of the bells of Moscow.

Jake had no inkling of the noble origin of the dog, but he felt a kinship with the animal from spending countless hours wandering the countryside in the company of the hound. The old dog looked up at his master with misty eyes that spoke of advancing age. In their brown depths was devotion rarely found in the human heart. Jake often felt a twinge of something primeval when the old dog looked at him in this way, something that spoke of an ancient bond between man and wolf, of a time when man was close to Mother Earth.

The Kentucky rifle was a relatively small bore, only thirty-six caliber, but it was adequate for any game that Jake was likely to encounter in Daviess County, Missouri in 1831. The buffalo had all but disappeared from the country east of the Missouri River. With the vanishing of the buffalo, the huge plains grizzly, which preyed on the great shaggy beasts, had also disappeared from the prairies.

Nor were the Indians a threat to Jake on his hunting excursions. The original tribes of the area were mostly Osage and Shawnee, but those who remained in the region were reduced to the state of ragged beggars. The United States government had officially seized the tribal lands of the Osage in 1808 and moved the tribe to eastern Kansas; however, a few straggling and starving members of this once-great people still wandered back to the valley of the Grand, where they subsisted on grass seeds and small game.

Lewis and Clark had encountered these people on their way up the Missouri on the great voyage of discovery. The noble explorers reported that the Osage were friendly to the Americans and provided them with much-needed supplies and information concerning the country along the Missouri near the mouth of the Grand River. Lewis and Clark described the Osage as a well-proportioned and handsome people of very large size. In fact, rumor had it that one Osage chief was over seven feet tall and weighed nearly three hundred pounds. Despite being formidable warriors, the Osage were usually friendly to the American and French trappers who traveled up and down the Missouri in the first half of the nineteenth century. They were even benign to the rough settlers who made up the cutting edge of the westward migration.

By the time that Jake lay on the bluffs overlooking the Grand, most of the Osage had been either killed or driven to reservations across the Missouri.

However, in 1831, a few roving bands still clung to their beloved homeland in the rolling prairie of Daviess County. Unlike his father and most of the local settlers, Jake bore no animosity to these pitiful, starving people. He occasionally met little bands of the Osage people as he wandered the countryside hunting game to supply his family with food. Many of the Osage could speak halting English, and because of his continued contact with them, Jake gradually learned to speak a little of their dialect. This, along with sign language, allowed Jake to haltingly communicate with the Indians.

As Jake looked out over the Grand River Valley, he reminisced over the events of the last year. Jake had struck up a relationship with an old tribal elder whose native name was Wazhozhe, meaning "Osage." Jake referred to the old man as Ozzy, which was much easier to pronounce and less proper than his formal name.

The day that Jake first met Ozzy stood out in his mind, and it was unlikely to ever fade from his memory. Jake first met the old man in an isolated cove off the Grand River. The cove was created by a short, spring-fed creek that headed in a limestone outcropping. The little cove was remote and thirty miles from a town of any size. The secluded spot had not yet been discovered by homesteaders and was teeming with waterfowl, deer and other game. The stream that began under the limestone outcrop was clear and cold and where it backed up before entering the Grand, it formed a deep pool that was swarming with fish.

Jake often came here when he was short of time to get "meat" for supper. Jake's father allowed him only so much time from his other chores to acquire fresh meat to supplement the meager rations supplied by the little homestead. If he failed to shoot or catch enough meat to satisfy his father or if it took longer than the "old man" thought it should, Jake would receive a vicious tongue-lashing or a violent beating, or both.

Habitually, when he dawdled or spent too much time just observing the captivating flow of nature, Jake would stop at the little cove, because he was sure to find either fish or game to satisfy his father's demands.

One warm fall day, Jake was in a panic. He had found an ancient Indian campsite and had spent two hours looking at the old fire rings and searching for arrowheads and other artifacts in the sandy soil. There was something about these primeval places that appealed to Jake and he felt a sense of mystery and longing. Now the sun was rapidly descending toward the western horizon. Jake knew this meant he had less than two hours to bag a deer or several ducks for the evening meal. Luckily, he was only a mile from his favorite hunting spot.

As Jake came over the low bluff separating the little spring creek from the main river, he froze in his tracks. Directly below him, along the banks of the clear little stream, were three people engaged in fishing for buffalo fish and chubs. They had built a smoky fire under a frame that was covered with cleaned and scaled fish. As Jake crested the rise, the old man either sensed his presence or heard a footfall, and he suddenly straightened up and faced Jake.

Jake vaguely knew this little band. He had met them once or twice along the Grand. He knew that the young brave and the Indian girl were the man's relatives, but he did not know how they were all related. He also knew that the old man had a strange name that sounded like "Ozzy" and that the girl could speak a little pidgin English.

The old man was tall and though the skin on his chest showed the spider web wrinkles common to old men, he was still lean and well muscled. The old man's head was closely shaved, except for a scalp lock that ran down the middle of his skull. In the center of this tuft of hair was an ornament made of dyed porcupine quills. At the back of his head was an eagle feather pointing down toward his shoulders.

His arms and chest were tattooed with intricate lines of dark blue and black, and his skin was bronzed from the sun and from the natural brown-red color of his people. Around his arm, he wore a soft buckskin armband decorated with beads and colored porcupine quills. The weather was still warm and pleasant and the old man was naked from the waist up. On his legs, he wore soft buckskin leggings, and around his waist and loins he wore a buckskin covering, decorated with more beads and porcupine quill embroidery. Jake had heard endless stories of the cruelty of Indians and how they were savages, not much better than the vicious beasts. Still, in the old man's face, Jake saw neither hatred nor hostility, but something akin to acceptance.

The old man quickly raised his hands and made the universal sign of peace or friend. However, shocked by the sudden appearance of the Indians, Jake had already begun to raise the muzzle of the long rifle. His action was instantly answered by the younger brave, who, quick as a puma, reached for a French tomahawk that hung at his waist. The old man spoke in guttural bark, and both Jake and the brave stopped their movement in mid-motion.

The old Indian faced Jake. "Hawey," he said.

Jake's blank look told the old man that he did not understand, so he tried again by saying "Wanon gue they."

Again Jake stood with the rifle gripped tight in his hands and stared at the trio. The old hound was strangely tranquil and just stared at the Indian and slowly wagged his tail. This was unusual for Rufe, who was often very protective of Jake. When he met some itinerant homesteader, Rufe would often growl deep in his chest and raise the hair along his back. However, even though Jake did not put his hand on the dog's head to restrain him, the animal was oddly calm, even though he had never been this close to Indians before.

When the hound did raise his ears and stiffen in alarm, the old Indian raised one hand, palm out, to the dog, and Rufe instantly wagged his tail in good-natured salutation. The group stood in awkward silence for what seemed minutes and the only sound was the distant cawing of the crows and the gentle lap of the water against the rocky shore. Finally, the old man broke the spell.

"Wa non bre gue they," he grunted.

A few months later, Jake would have instantly grasped his meaning, but now he had no idea what the old Indian meant. However, after much signing and gesturing, the Indian made Jake understand he was asking him to eat with the little group.

The young woman, who had been standing behind the two Indian men, gave a whoop and grabbed a rough stick that had been lying on the bank of the little stream. She gave a great heave and jerked a fat buffalo fish out of the depths of the backwater. Instantly, she sprang upon the fish and picked up a Green River knife that was lying in the clutter of the camp. In her excitement, she obviously intended to immediately kill and gut the fish.

Before she could kill the fish with the knife, the old brave stopped her with a sharp, guttural command. Her hand stopped in mid stroke and she looked sheepishly at the elderly man. He stepped quickly to her side and took the still-flopping fish and held it up to the east, while saying something in Osage in a sing-song voice. He then turned to the other three points of the compass and repeated the chant. Even to Jake, who at that time understood little of what the old man was saying, it was evident that Ozzy was thanking the spirits for the gift of the fish and expressing gratitude to the fish itself for the gift of its flesh. Jake would ultimately learn that the Indians had an elaborate system of beliefs concerning the natural world and how each creature fit into the fabric of life.

Jake eventually realized that the leader of the band wanted him to join them in a meal of buffalo fish roasted over the fire. However, he didn't feel at all at ease with the group and made an awkward attempt to decline and hurry home. Nevertheless, he was empty-handed and he felt fear rising in his gut as he contemplated what his father would do if he arrived home without fresh meat.

His assumed dilemma was resolved when Ozzy made a guttural grunt and indicated that Jake should take four of the cleaned and filleted fish. The blank look on his face told the old Indian that Jake had no idea what he had said. He turned to the woman and said something in Osage, and she immediately turned to Jake and said in halting English, "He wants to give you fish."

Jake had no idea how to thank the Indians or leave gracefully, but with the rising fear in his stomach, he grabbed the offering and turned south and east toward home and in an instant broke into a ground-covering trot. Rufe fell in beside him and seemed to pick up Jake's growing fear of what he would face when he reached the little dirt-floored cabin he shared with his parents.

Jake glanced anxiously toward the western sky and noticed with rising dismay that the sun was only an hour from dropping like a fireball into the western prairie. His father would be half drunk on corn whiskey by now and his mother would be terrified because she had nothing to cook but cornmeal, and when Sam Devine was drunk and hungry, he was ornery and mean. Jake picked up the pace to a grueling run and in his mind he mapped out the quickest possible route to the homestead.

As the shadows lengthened and the sun dropped toward the western horizon, Jake climbed a low ridge and dropped into a shallow draw, where a faint path led off to the southwest. His breath was now coming in labored gasps, and he had trouble maintaining his hold on the scaled and filleted fish. The closer he came to the familiar little homestead, the more panic rose in his insides. He had experienced his father's violent temper before and he didn't want to deal with what he knew was coming. His terrified mind searched for a suitable excuse or a way out of his predicament, but his feverish brain refused to deal with the situation.

Old Rufe had also experienced the wrath of Sam Devine, but the hound seemed totally oblivious to the panic that gripped his master.

Animals were not immune to the violent rage of the elder Devine. Jake had watched in horror and rage as his father beat one of their mules with a tug until the terrified animal screamed in pain and fear. The mule was lathered with foam and the muscles on its hindquarters quivered in exhaustion and terror. Sam Devine beat the poor creature to near death, because it balked while trying to pull a huge hickory stump from the black Missouri soil.

When he could no longer stand to see the black mule beaten and screaming in pain, Jake impetuously seized his father's arm to stay a savage blow. Jake had spared the mule further pain by turning Sam's fury on him. Jake had lain in bed for a day after that episode, recovering from angry blue-black bruises that covered most of his body. Sam hadn't stopped beating the boy until his son had lost consciousness and bled from his mouth and nose.

His mother had crept up the rickety old stairs on the outside of the cabin that led to the loft where Jake slept. She brought an old enamel wash pan full of warm water, containing crushed herbs to soothe Jake's bruised and ravaged flesh.

However, Bessie Devine didn't have the courage to stand up to Sam either, and the visits were made when the elder Devine was in the field or, as was more likely, had ridden one of the mules into Gallatin to drink corn whiskey in one of the saloons or attend one of the ubiquitous religious revival meetings.

In 1830, the frontier was aflame with revivalism and the second Great Awakening was searing the conscience of frontier America. Itinerant preachers roamed the raw edge of the settlement, holding revival meetings and performing healings and miracles and casting out demons and devils. New prophets and religious sects sprang up like mushrooms in the fertile soil of the frontier. One of these prophets made it a habit to cinch a leather girdle around his waist until his stomach swelled and he lost consciousness. In this semi-conscious state, he saw visions and other heavenly wonders.

Sam attended these revival meetings on a fairly regular basis and watched in fascination as the preacher worked the crowd into a state of religious euphoria. Men and women would whirl faster and faster until they fell in exhausted elation in a pile on the crude stage. While in a state of exhilaration, they would speak in tongues and cry out that they had dedicated their lives to the Lord Jesus.

Sam gradually began to understand that God was vengeful and cast sinners into a burning hell where they would suffer untold agonies for all eternity. Sam had no doubt that God enjoyed watching sinners writhe in exquisite agony as they paid for their sins for eternity. He understood that mankind was sinful by nature and could never refute their transgressions in their own right, but God in his infinite wisdom would forgive whom he would. Those lucky few who were forgiven manifested their status in outward signs of absolution.

Sam seized the emotional precepts he heard and saw in revival meetings and used those that fit his personal needs. He fervently believed that all men were basically sinful and unworthy of God's mercy, but those who perceived they were among God's chosen people would demonstrate their gratitude by attending revival meetings and church services, interpreting God's word in ways that were both dogmatic and merciless, praying publicly, and showing no tolerance for any behaviors that they perceived as sin.

Sam was inherently an intolerant man and believed wholeheartedly that because he was absolved he had the right to recognize and punish sin in others. He never viewed his drinking, womanizing, cruelty and fanaticism as sin, because he passionately believed he was saved and was one of God's elect. Besides, these failings were just the outward signs of his humanity. Yet anyone who had the audacity to disagree with him on any issue of religion, politics or social life was, in Sam's mind, either a disciple of the Devil or ignorant.

Sam believed that God created the world for man's use and gave mankind total dominion over the earth and all other living things that inhabited it. To Sam Devine, these included such godless heathens as blacks, Indians, Mexicans, Spaniards and others who exhibited the obvious curse of God. Sam constantly exercised his dominion and never hesitated to exhibit his superiority over any lesser creature he might encounter. Sam had no doubt that God was masculine and that his omnipotence was a powerful indication that women and children must be subservient to their husbands and fathers. Any perceived act of defiance on the part of Bessie, Jake, or any creature under Sam's authority was considered as blasphemy and was punished accordingly.

Jake was well acquainted with Sam's violent and intolerant brand of Christianity, and as he ran through the lengthening shadows he dreaded what he knew was coming. Even as he desperately tried to formulate some excuse or story to explain why he was late and had failed to bag something more acceptable than buffalo fish, he instinctively knew that it was futile and that Sam Devine would see his explanations and excuses as weakness. His heart sank as he saw the earth-covered roof of the ramshackle cabin rise out of the waving bluestem.

He noticed with some relief that there was a wisp of smoke rising from the stick and mud chimney, and he hoped that perhaps his father had killed a fat deer on his way home from Gallatin. If Sam Devine's gut was full of venison and whiskey, maybe his vicious temper would be calmed. Chickens squawked and scattered wildly as Jake ran into the cluttered yard leading to the splintery door of the log-and-sod hut. As he burst into the dark interior of the cabin, his eyes struggled to adjust from the still-bright light of the spring afternoon. Gradually, the shape of his mother, hunched over the rough stone hearth, became discernable, like a waif emerging from the gloom.

Chapter 2

H is heart sank as he realized that she was stirring something in the old iron
pot that hung from a wrought iron hook over the smoky fireplace. The only
thing Bessie ever made in that old iron pot was grits. Instantly, Jake knew that his
father was in a vile mood, because corn dodgers would never assuage his insatiable
appetite for red meat. As Jake opened the door wider, the rough plank scraped
against the stone that served as a step. His father and mother both turned toward
the slight sound of the opening door. Bessie's hand went to her mouth in fearful
anticipation of her husband's reaction to Jake's return. Obviously, Sam had been
brutally berating her about her sinful and slothful offspring.

As the sliver of light from the waning sun streamed through the opening door
and fell across his mother's stricken face like an accusing finger, Jake realized that
she was terrified. She was so frightened that she made no attempt to move or speak
in warning—only a stricken, high-pitched sound escaped from her constricting
throat, reminding Jake of the sound a mouse might make when crushed under the
heel of a boot.

Sam Devine's reaction was far different from his wife's. As he turned to face
Jake, his lips pulled back from his yellow and decaying teeth in an animal-like
grimace. Spittle flew from his brown lips as he screamed, "Where have you been,
you fucking little worthless whelp." Terror rose in Jake's chest like sour bile, and
he tried to stammer that he had brought some fish for supper. Sam's dark and
wrinkled face took on a red tinge from the uncontrolled rage that rose in his chest.

"I ain't eatin' no goddamn fish," he shrieked, his voice rising to an insane
falsetto. "I sent you out this marnin' to get some decent victuals and you bring that
fucking shit back!" he barked. "Where in the name of Christ have you been all this
time—probably playing with your pecker like some damn heathen, I suspect!" he
bellowed.

Sam's wild eyes fell on the cleaned and boned buffalo fish, and his rage increased like an over-stoked boiler. The black whiskers on his dirty, unshaven face stood out like lice against the crimson of his inflamed skin.

"Decent Christian white folks don't eat no slimy, shitty trash fish." He roared. A hint of realization spread over his face like a shadow cast by a passing cloud, and Sam grabbed Jake's wrist in a violent grip. He drew Jake against his face, and Jake could smell the rancid stench of moonshine whiskey and tobacco on his breath. "Where did ya get these trash fish?" he demanded.

Jake's throat closed in panic and when he tried to speak only small grunting noises escaped his lips. Sam Devine grabbed the front of Jake's shirt and jerked his face within inches of his snarling mouth and screeched, "Ya better tell me where ya got this shit."

Jake, nearly blacking out from the pressure of his shirt collar against his neck, managed to force the word "Indians" through his tortured windpipe.

His son's response only increased Sam's insane rage, and with his right hand, which still held Jake's throat, he violently flung him across the dim little room. Jake's head hit the rough logs of the back wall with a sickening thud and he crumpled to the rough plank floor. With a wild roar, Sam started toward the prostrate form of his son. Hearing the clatter inside the cabin, Rufe pushed through the still-open door. The dog sensed that his master was in danger, but his fear of Sam's wrath caused him to hesitate. Sam spun and viciously kicked the animal in the rib cage. Even above Sam's insane howling, Bessie heard the sickening crunch of the dog's ribs cracking.

Rufe howled in pain and turned yelping toward the door. As Rufe crawled toward the door to escape, Sam screamed, "Turn on me will ya, ya ungrateful son of a bitch," and stomped on the animal's back with his rough cowhide boot. Rufe yelped piteously and, dragging his hindquarters, he crawled toward the half-open door.

The violence of her husband shocked Bessie out of her fear-induced trance and she grabbed the back of Sam's shirt and screamed, "Don't kill them." Sam was shocked by Bessie's uncharacteristic act of defiance and he turned his fury away from Jake and the dog, toward his hapless wife.

"How dare ya defy yer husband," he shrieked. "Remember God's word, woman, obey yer husband!" In his insane rage, Sam totally lost control of his reason and he swung wildly at his wife. His balled fist caught her high on the temple and she dropped like a pole-axed ox. Sam grabbed the iron pot of bubbling cornmeal and tried to dump it on his terrified wife. Luckily, she saw his intention and evaded most of the cascade of hot corn mush. Despite her surprisingly agile move, some of the mush splashed on her face and hands.

Bessie cried out in pain and threw her spindly hands in front of her face in a futile attempt to protect her face from the hot pottage that had already burned her cheeks, neck and hands. Sam, his eyes blazing with righteous indignation, yelled down at her, "That'll teach ya to obey God's commandment to respect yer husband, woman! Ya best read the Bible and follow the Lord's word." With that, he turned on his heel and strode out the door.

Bessie listened to his retreating footsteps and eventually she heard him cursing the old black mule as he tried to force the bit between its teeth. After much cursing and kicking, Sam got the bridle on the frightened animal and Bessie heard the muffled hoofbeats heading southeast toward Gallatin. She knew Sam would not return for many hours and probably not until tomorrow afternoon.

Her burned face and hands smarted painfully, but she had avoided most of the mush and was able to rise with difficulty to her feet. Jake was also struggling to his feet, clutching his ribs, where Sam had smashed a boney fist into his chest. He struggled to his mother and was stunned to see the angry red welts rising on her neck and cheeks where the hot porridge had splashed on her body. Jake's own anger began to rise when he saw what Sam had done to his mother. He started to say, "Someday, I will kill that old bastard...." Bessie raised her fearful, tear-filled eyes to her son's and said, "Don't curse yer father, God commands ya to honor your father."

Jake was stunned. He looked into his mother's red, raw face and couldn't understand how she could possibly defend this man after he had constantly abused her. He looked into her stricken face and decided not to say anything more about Sam. Bessie gazed at her son with adoring eyes. "Come and sit down at the table. There is enough grits left for our supper and I'll cook some of the fish ya brought," she said.

After they had eaten, Bessie removed Jake's tattered linen shirt and put a poultice of hot water, wild onion and clay on the ugly blue bruises on his chest and ribs. After she had treated her son's injuries, Bessie soothed the burns on her own body with cool water and vinegar. Mother and son spoke little as she tended to their injuries, but they both understood what the other was thinking and neither wanted to broach the subject. Finally, Bessie said, "He's right, ya know, God commands us in the Bible to honor him as a husband and father." To Jake, the words were shallow and meaningless. How could God expect them to respect a man who had never shown compassion or love for either of them?

It was full dark when Jake climbed the rickety old stairs to the loft where he slept. The night air was cool on his feverish cheeks and the entire sky was filled with brilliant stars. It was a beautiful spring night—the air was warm and fresh as chokecherry wine, but Jake's mind was too filled with chaotic thoughts to notice. He pulled the rawhide string that lifted the latch and pushed the rough plank door open. Jake stepped to the battered old table, lifted the glass chimney from the cracked kerosene lamp and lit the ragged wick. Once the fitful flame had sputtered to life, he pulled the door shut behind him and sat on the bed. The ropes that were strung across the frame to hold the cornhusk mattress squawked in protest. Stiffly, he raised his arms to unfasten the bone buttons of his rough linen shirt. As he slid the shirt from his arms, he heard a faint scratching and whimpering sound from the vicinity of the door.

Jake was reluctant to raise his aching body from the bed, but the faint sound was persistent, so he stiffly rose and painfully hobbled to the door. As he pushed the door open, the faint wedge of light cast by the flickering lamp revealed Rufe lying on the top step. He looked up at Jake with pleading brown eyes and wagged his tail. Jake bent over and tried to pick up the hound, but Rufe yelped in pain. Jake took Rufe's front paws in his hands and helped the dog over the step into the room.

Once he was able to bend over and wrap his arms around the dog, he was able to put him on the bed without causing him to yelp in agony. Jake noticed the dog was bleeding from his nose and ears and when he touched his hindquarters and ribs, Rufe winced in pain. Jake struggled to pull off his heavy cowhide boots and slowly pulled down his stiff canvas pants. After undressing, Jake blew out the lamp, lay down next to Rufe and pulled the old rough quilt up to his chin.

Rufe nestled close to Jake and shivered while softly whining. The dog's breath came in ragged little gasps, and intuitively, Jake knew he was seriously injured. Jake gently placed his hand on the animal's head and stroked the soft fur. The boy stared into the darkness and reflected on the events of the day.

Despite the fact that Jake's father had constantly told him that only man had a soul and the only purpose of animals was to provide food, labor or pleasure for mankind, Jake could not help but feel closeness to the injured animal lying next to him. Despite his revulsion, Jake's feverous mind insisted on retrieving the image of Sam stomping on the helpless dog. Jake suddenly thought what it would be like on his rambles in the countryside without Rufe by his side. His throat constricted and hot tears coursed down his warm cheeks.

Jake's agitated mind dredged up images of him and Rufe lying in the sun on a grassy knoll, gazing out over the endless sea of the rolling prairie.

Hatred and anger flooded into Jake's chest like acid and he was surprised and frightened by its intensity. He hated himself for not protecting the dog from the insane wrath of his father, and shame and sorrow welled up from inside him as he realized the dog was hurt protecting him. Now Rufe might die because Jake was a coward. He thought back on the angry scene that had led to the dog's injuries and he cursed himself for not confronting Sam. Rather than face his father's wrath, Jake had cowered on the floor where he had fallen, unwilling to struggle to his feet and defend Rufe in his attempt to protect his master.

The more Jake reflected on the confrontation, the more he cursed himself for his cowardice and hot tears coursed down his cheeks in a torrent. He wished that he could call back that awful moment and in his imagination he pictured himself in a fury, throwing Sam into the corner like an empty wool sack and saving Rufe from the savage beating. Intuitively, he knew that given another chance, he would have acted no differently, for he didn't have the courage to confront his father. That realization stirred the emotional turmoil in his heart, like some ghastly hag's brew. His obsession was so intense that he felt as if he would explode like a firecracker. Despite the turmoil in his mind, Jake eventually fell into a deep slumber and didn't awaken until the morning sun was streaming through the dirty pane of the little window in his room.

Without thinking, Jake leaped from his bed, assuming that he'd overslept and his father would be screeching at him to get to his chores. As his feet hit the rough plank floor, a bolt of white-hot pain shot through his shoulders and back. His protesting body brought his mind to full awareness and he remembered the violent scene of the night before. Jake cautiously glanced out the window at the dilapidated pole corral where the mules were kept and gave a sigh of relief when he noticed the old black Mexican mule that Sam always rode was still missing from the enclosure.

Recalling Rufe, Jake hastily glanced to the corn husk mattress and was shocked to see the hound lying in the folds of the hand-tied quilt. The dog's muzzle was caked with dried blood and despite the warmth of the April morning and the warm quilt, he was shivering uncontrollably. The flood of emotion that had washed over him the night before came pouring back like a spring torrent, and he desperately searched his mind for a way to save the dog.

Jake ran down the rickety stairs that led to the tiny loft room and shoved the clapboard door to the cabin open with a bang. His mother was stirring the embers in the fireplace. Startled, she spun to face the door. She saw his stricken face and her hand shot to her mouth in fear. "What is it?" she stammered.

"I think Rufe is dying," he blurted out. "Please help him!"

Bessie touched her son's shoulder and replied, "Go do yer chores and bring in the milk fer breakfast. Mind ya, take that old wooden bucket with the leftover cornmeal to the hog, and I'll look after the hound."

Jake turned and strode through the door into the warm spring day, but he found no joy in the pleasant warmth of the sun. He walked quickly to the pole corral and rapidly milked the old red cow. After feeding the hog, he gathered the eggs, and carrying them and the milk, he hurried back to the cabin. His mother already had the fire going and had placed an old black cast iron frying pan on the fire. She put a generous dollop of lard in the pan to melt and broke the eggs into a porcelain bowl and stirred them briskly. She pointed to a piece of salt pork that was hanging from a hook in the corner and motioned to Jake to cut slices from the side meat.

While they were preparing breakfast, Bessie motioned with a toss of her head at Rufe, who lay by the fireplace on an old burlap bag. "I put a poultice made from comfrey leaves on him and gave him some willow bark tea and he seems a little better." Jake anxiously looked at the dog and noticed that his breathing seemed more natural.

"Thank you," Jake said, with a quaver in his voice. "I wish I would've stopped him from kicking Rufe," he continued.

His mother was putting steaming plates of scrambled eggs and fried side meat on the table and motioned for Jake to sit down. He pulled out a rough, bent-sapling chair and eased himself into it. Jake quickly shoveled a forkful of eggs into his mouth and, rolling the hot food on his tongue, he said: "Ya know, I hate that old son of a bitch and someday I'll kick his skinny ass."

Bessie gave Jake a shocked look and replied, "Jake, please don't talk that way about yer father. Ya know that God commands ya to honor your father and obey him."

Jake gave his mother a disdainful glance and replied, "He's my father, but I can't honor him, or respect him. It doesn't matter how hard I try to do the chores or put meat on the table, he's never satisfied. He beats me fer nothin' and what is worse he beats you, and all in the name of his God. Well I fer one don't believe in his God! Any God who would allow a man to act in his name, as Sam does, doesn't deserve respect either!" Bessie's eyes grew large with shock and fear and her jaw dropped open, but despite a few gurgling sounds, she couldn't reply to the harsh words her son spoke.

Finally, after several minutes of fighting for composure, Bessie was able to stammer, "But Jake, ya know that we must do what God commands or we're forever damned!" Jake was not especially well versed in the Bible, but his mother had used the book to teach her son to read and he knew it well enough to debate religion with her. His face softened, but he pressed on.

"Ya know, he's as much a hypocrite as the Sadducees and Pharisees. He pretends to obey the word of God, but he rides into Gallatin or Independence and spends days carousing with other women, drinkin' and gamblin' when you and I have no money and nothing to eat. When he returns, I hear him abuse you and afterwards, I hear you cry."

Bessie's face grew crimson and her hand went to her mouth in embarrassment. She wondered just how much her young son knew about physical relationships. Could he know that Sam took her violently after his two or three day binges in Independence or Gallatin? She knew Sam had been with other women, but she adamantly believed that, as a woman, it was her duty to submit to her husband. Afterward, she often cried herself to sleep, wondering if she was inadequate as a lover—why else would he seek other women? Now her son had implied that he knew Sam took her viciously after his debauchery. She desperately hoped that he only thought that Sam just beat her and didn't realize that he used her violently and made her do things that made her feel used and dirty.

Bessie looked into the bright, unlined face of her son. "He jest hits me because he's ashamed that he can't bring me a new dress or a pair of shoes. He really is a good, God-fearing man," she declared.

Jake decided not to pursue the subject any further, and in an effort to change the subject, he asked, "Is Rufe going to be all right?"

Bessie was grateful to move on to a less disturbing subject and eagerly replied, "I told ya I gave him some medicine and put some herbal poultices on his back and legs and he seems a little better. Ya better leave him in the house by the fireplace when ya go out huntin'. Indeed, I think ya better get ready and go see if ya kin kill a nice deer. We're out of fresh meat and ya know your father likes fresh venison. I suspect that he'll be home tonight."

Jake tried not to let the disgust he felt at his Mother's constant dutiful attitude toward his father show on his face when he replied, "Alright, I'll see if I kin find somethin' Sam might like." Bessie didn't seem to catch the sarcasm in her son's reply and turned to the table to clear the dishes. Jake gathered his things and touched his mother on the shoulder. She turned toward him and he kissed her lightly on the cheek. "Thank ya fer taking care of Rufe," he said and as an afterthought he murmured softly, "I love ya, Ma." Bessie was touched and somewhat stunned; her son had never before spoken to her in such a tender way. Embarrassed, she turned away from him and murmured, "Go get yer huntin' done."

Jake turned toward the door. Immediately, Rufe struggled to his feet and staggered to Jake's side. Jake half-heartedly scolded the dog and pointed to the old burlap sack in the corner, but Rufe showed no sign of obeying. Jake opened the door to a beautiful, warm spring day and didn't have the heart to force Rufe to stay home.

"Jake, please leave him home. Chasin' a rabbit or squirrel might mess up his guts worse," his mother said.

Jake reflected on the notion, but Rufe was pressing against his leg, wagging his thin tail with exuberance, and looking excitedly into his face, anxious to be wandering the prairie. Jake didn't have the heart to leave him, and the dog probably wouldn't stay anyway, so he slung the long rifle over his shoulder and yelled, "Okay, Rufe, let's go!"

Chapter 3

J ake decided he would head directly to the Grand River, which was not much farther than a couple of miles. The river bottoms were moderately wooded and the waters of the Grand attracted a variety of game. The bottoms near the Devine homestead were unsettled and the grassy bottomland still teemed with game.

Jake turned northwest and set a casual gait. Rufe didn't run far in front of him, as he usually did, but seemed content to stay close to his left leg. However, he seemed able to keep up with the ambling pace and though he showed signs of pain in his hips and a distinct limp, his behavior reflected his delight at being with Jake. The pristine land was aflame with wildflowers, cardinal and cone flowers nodding their bright heads in the gentle breeze. The bluestem and buffalo grass was nearly to Jake's knees and the balmy breeze sent rolling waves across the undulating plain, reminding Jake of the white tops he had seen on the Missouri when his father took him to Independence.

The sky held the puffy white clouds of spring and summer and had lost the cold, slate-gray look of winter. Two red-tail hawks rode the warm rising air and cut lazy circles in the azure blue spring sky. The soft breeze touched Jake's face like a lover's caress and carried the heady perfume of the awakening earth. Occasionally, he could hear the hawks scream a distant "skree, skree" as they rode the thermals and watched the grassy plain for ground squirrels, mice and voles. Jake glanced into the sun-bright sky and immediately picked up the light underwing color of the male red-tail. He often wondered how it would feel to ride the wind like a hawk and what the land looked like from their vantage point hundreds of feet above the prairie.

The gentle, mild breeze that blew across the grass and the occasional buffalo berry or chinkapin oak made a sighing noise. To Jake, it sounded like a muted, distant whisper, just low enough that one couldn't make out the words. Jake cocked his head and the wind seemed to murmur to him of primeval things, of secrets the earth had held for untold millennia, tantalizing, but not quite comprehensible.

Jake had always had an affinity for the rolling grasslands and wooded bottomlands of western Missouri. This was the only place he could really remember and since he had reached adolescence, he had mainly hunted alone. Once Jake became reasonably proficient at hunting, his father quit accompanying him on hunting excursions and spent his time plowing the homestead or, more often, riding the old Mexican mule to the nearest saloon or revival meeting.

It was only a mile or so from the cabin to the gentle bluffs that marked the flood plain of the Grand River. Jake stopped on the edge of the slope that led to the bottoms and surveyed the cottonwoods, willows and occasional burr oak that flourished along the stream banks. He didn't see any movement, except for a black turkey vulture sitting in a dead cottonwood snag. He glanced at Rufe, who had immediately lain down at his feet; the dog seemed uncommonly tired and lethargic. After carefully surveying the wooded valley, Jake checked his long rifle and, whistling at Rufe, began his descent to the river along a low ridge.

He hadn't gone fifty yards when he thought he detected movement out of the corner of his eye in the low gully to his left. He quickly sat on a little rise and studied the brushy ravine below him. The silence was almost stifling, and his ears rang with the effort to hear the faint whisper of the movement of a twig. Even the breeze seemed to have died, and the air hung still and oppressive around him.

Rufe's long, droopy ears were raised and gave his face a comical, framed look. The dog's attention was locked on something in the ravine, but nothing stirred. Jake was nervous that Rufe would throw his head back and give forth a long rolling bawl, for which his kind was famous, but the hound stood stiff and quivering, his eyes fixed on a spot about one hundred yards away.

Jake's straining eyes again detected a slight movement among the willows. What appeared to be a tree branch moved slightly, but there was not the slightest breath of a breeze. Focusing on the spot, Jake's eyes finally detected the outline of a little whitetail buck standing in the thick willows and brambles in the bottom of the hollow. The buck was alert, and his ears were facing directly toward Jake and Rufe, like an old man's ear trumpet. Jake knew that the buck had either heard him or picked up his alien scent and was poised to flee into the cottonwoods along the river. Slowly, he raised the long rifle and fixed the bead of the front site on the buck's neck.

He eased the hammer back, hoping that the buck would not hear the barely audible click of the trigger notch engaging the hammer. He set the rear trigger, took a deep breath and maintained the sight picture. Gently, he applied pressure with his index finger to the hair trigger and, as always, he was surprised by the report of the rifle. Through the blue haze of black powder smoke, he saw the buck throw its head up, stumble and fall. Instinctively, he knew it was a good shot and the buck would not move from where it fell.

Despite his previous lethargy, Rufe leaped to his feet and ran down the long ridge to where the buck lay, with Jake following at a more sedate pace. The dog, in his excitement to get to the deer, broke into a loping run and suddenly folded up like a wing-shot duck and hit the ground in a cloud of dust. Jake heard the dog's piteous yelps and ran to his side. Rufe was struggling to rise but couldn't, and blood was streaming out of his nostrils.

The deer, which was lying twenty paces away, was immediately forgotten as Jake rushed to where Rufe lay. Rufe was lying on his side, struggling to rise and yelping piteously. In desperation, Jake ran his hand along the dog's muzzle. Jake's touch did nothing to calm the pain and fear that consumed the hound. In desperation, Jake looked around wildly for something that might comfort the dog. Seeing nothing, he dropped on one knee and gently stroked Rufe's back and flanks. Jake was frantic but nothing he did seemed to relieve Rufe's obvious intense pain and fear. He kept struggling to rise and a fine mist of frothy blood came from his nose and mouth.

In his despair, Jake thought of the innumerable times when his father, seized by the spirit, would fall to his knees and, clasping his hands to his breast, implore God to plant the seed of righteousness in his wayward son, or ask that some sinful neighbor might be struck dumb for his transgressions.

Watching his father revel in self-obsessed prayer had soured Jake on the idea of communing with divinity. Now, with Rufe writhing in convulsions and obviously near death, desperation drove him to open his heart to whatever power might save the dog. He really didn't know how to throw himself at the mercy of a God, which he had been taught was a vengeful being and probably did not concern himself with smelly, slobbering old hounds.

Jake desperately tried to remember if there was any established protocol for prayer and, unable to recall any, he mimicked the antics of the revival preachers and his father. Standing and looking intently skyward, he threw his arms back and lifting his voice to a shrill falsetto, he shrieked into the spring sky, "Oh Lord my God, hear your humble servant, Jake, and grant me those things that I ask in religiousness. Bless your humble servant, Rufe, with health and strength and with your holy spirit, cast out this affliction, which seeks to keep your worthy follower Rufe from obeying your commandments." Jake never stopped to consider how ridiculous his words sounded, but he continued to spew out the expressions he associated with prayer.

As he spoke to the mysterious divine being, Jake heard or sensed that he was not alone. He turned with a jerk, and in the same movement, brought the rifle to his chest. Then, he remembered that he had not recharged the long rifle and he was essentially unarmed. Standing fifty feet away were the three Indians he had met by the spring creek. The old man again raised his hand, palm out, in the universal sign of peace. He said something in Osage to the young woman, who turned to Jake and said, "He want to know if you are performing ceremony to honor spirit of deer you killed."

Jake was shocked by the surreal appearance of the Indians and stood for what seemed minutes, staring at the trio in wide-eyed amazement. The woman again spoke. "He wonders if you're performing a rite to honor the spirit of the deer you killed," she repeated. Jake's feverish mind frantically searched the woman's words for meaning, and he finally realized she wanted to know if he was praying for the soul of the dead deer.

Jake looked into the woman's oval face and finally stammered, "No, I'm prayin' for my dog Rufe. I think he's dyin'!"

As if they had not noticed the yelping, bleeding dog, all three Indians turned in unison and looked at Rufe. The old man held up his palms facing Rufe with the thumbs splayed out and said something guttural in Osage. Almost instantly, the dog seemed to relax and the pitiful crying died in his throat. The old man looked at the woman and again said something in his native tongue.

She turned to Jake and with softness in her dark eyes she said, "He say for every birth a death is owed and we all must someday go back to Wakonda." Jake glanced at Rufe. Though the dog no longer yelped in pain, he was still bleeding frothy blood from his mouth and nose, and his eyes had taken on a filmy, dreamy look that Jake did not like.

There was something in the demeanor of the old man that told Jake he understood what was happening and if anyone could help Rufe, it was this old man. Jake looked again into the dark, almond eyes of the woman and pleaded, "Please tell 'im to help Rufe. I knows we all must die, but not now, I need him." The woman turned to the old man and spoke for what seemed a long time, but couldn't have been more than a few minutes.

After speaking to the old man, she turned back to Jake and said, "He is a holy man; he has completed the vision quest. He knows the ways of the Wakonda, above and below, the Earth and the Sky. He say he will try to speak to Wakonda and learn the wishes of the spirit of Earth and Sky."

The old man squatted on the ground by Rufe and reached into a buckskin bag that was decorated with ornate designs made of dyed porcupine quills. He removed a carved, brown stone pipe with a long stem, a pouch of aromatic, tobacco-like substance and an eagle wing feather. The old man began to chant in a singsong cadence and slowly filled, tamped and lit the pipe. He lifted his eyes toward the sky and continued to chant in a rhythmic tempo. His eyes took on a faraway look and seemed fixed on some distant object in the sky. As the blue smoke swirled upward like a rising mist, he fanned it with the feather, causing it to form little eddies and swirls as it rose on the warm air.

Jake was fascinated by the figure of the old man, squatting on the ground, his head wreathed in blue smoke. He couldn't help but compare the quiet dignity of the hunched figure to the pompous ranting of the revival preachers. The old man's eyes became milky and cloudy, like the eyes of a blind man, and his face became an impenetrable mask. He continued to chant for what seemed an hour, but in reality was only ten minutes or less. Eventually, the old man's eyes cleared as if a film had been stripped from their surface, like skimming scum from a stagnant pond, and the faraway look on his face gradually faded.

He grunted and glanced at Rufe with a look of genuine affection. He looked at the young woman and again spoke in Osage. As Jake listened to the old man speak in his native tongue, he was somehow reminded of the tinkling of flowing water, or the gentle murmur of the wind blowing through the bluestem grass. After the old man spoke to the woman for some time, she turned to Jake and said, "He say the dog will live for a time. He say dog is your brother and you are young, you having a bad time and need friend."

The old man turned and looked at the dead whitetail buck. He furrowed his brow and, glancing at Jake, he said something to the woman. She seemed to consider what the old man said, and finally, she turned to Jake and said, "He say that the deer is also your brother. He say, Wakonda not angry when brother deer is killed for food, but must honor the spirit of deer." Jake's face betrayed his bewilderment and the woman explained. "All animals are our brothers. The Wakonda gave them a spirit, like our spirit. He knows we must sometimes kill animals for food and skins, but when we do this we must thank the spirit of the dead animal for what it gives us." Jake looked at the girl with puzzlement and she continued, "I'll show you." The girl stepped to the carcass of the buck and, taking an old Green River knife out of a buckskin scabbard on her hip, she opened the abdominal cavity and deftly removed the still-steaming liver.

Jake watched in amazement and queasiness as she raised the organ above her head and faced the east. She lifted her eyes to the sky and murmured something in

Osage. She turned and repeated the strange ritual three more times for each point of the compass. When she had finished, she sank her teeth into the warm liver and ripped off a steaming chunk, which she chewed briefly then swallowed with gusto.

Turning to Jake, she held the raw liver out to him in an unmistakable gesture, inviting him to repeat the ritual. Jake took the liver and mimicked the actions of the girl, holding the liver to the four directions of the wind. Not knowing what to say, he looked at the girl, but she merely shrugged. Jake tentatively took a small bite of the liver and found that it had a pleasing texture and was surprisingly mild in taste.

Having completed the ritual, he turned back toward the woman, to find that all three Indians had left and were already disappearing over the lip of the bluff. Staring after them, Jake glimpsed a bony piebald pony hitched to a travois. Jake turned to where Rufe lay and found the dog sitting on his haunches, happily panting, his tongue dripping water like a leaf in a downpour. Rufe showed no sign of his previous convulsions, except for a little crust of dried blood around his nose and mouth. Jake bent and put his cheek against Rufe's ear and ran his hand over the hound's domed head. He received an enthusiastic swipe across his face with an amazingly wet tongue for his efforts.

Jake bent over the deer and began the task of gutting, skinning and cutting the carcass into manageable portions. He had performed this task hundreds of times and his fingers flew skillfully about the task of stripping the hide from the underlying connective tissue. The task was so familiar that his mind was free to wander, and he thought about what the old Indian had said about all life being sacred. Never again, he decided, would he kill anything without thinking of this moment and weighing the need for food with the responsibility of taking a life. Somehow the thought that all creatures were basically his kin or brothers, as the old man had put it, did not seem at all alien to his thinking. In fact, it seemed much more abnormal to consider other living things as "pests" or as living targets.

He remembered innumerable times when he had watched his father and other homesteaders shoot dozens of ducks or passenger pigeons in a killing frenzy, just to watch them fold and fall from the sky in a puff of feathers. His father had taken him on some of the wolf and coyote extermination hunts that the homesteaders periodically organized on the pretense that the predators were threatening their livestock or even their lives. During these slaughters, a line of men would advance across the prairie and shoot anything that they flushed from hiding. They never made any connection between the decline of the predators and the rise in number of destructive mice, rabbits, rats and other pests.

When he finished his task, Jake tied the meat and hide from the deer into a neat package and slung it over his shoulders. He knew that his father, if he were home, would be happy with tender young venison. Glancing at the sun, he was happy to notice that it was still relatively high in the western sky, so he had plenty of time to get home before his father demanded his supper. He turned and whistled to Rufe, who bounded to his feet, like a puppy, eager to be off. Jake turned his face toward home and set off in a ground-covering pace that only the young and robust know. All seemed right with the world, but nearly twelve hundred miles to the east, events were taking place that would drastically alter his life, for good and evil.

PART TWO

The Conversion

Chapter 4

J ohn Evans leaned against the rail of the steamboat *Arcadia* and watched
the roiling brown waters of the Missouri glide by the peeling white sides of
the vessel. Through the thin soles of his worn and battered shoes, he could feel
the powerful "thrum, thrum" of the single-cylinder steam engine as it drove the
huge paddlewheels of the old sidewheeler. The thick, black smoke and cinders
occasionally rolled past his face and stung his eyes, but he was reluctant to leave
the rail.

John glanced at his wife and daughter, standing a few feet away, and felt a
pang of fear. He was totally responsible to ensure the safety of his little family and
here he was traveling up the muddy waters of the River of the West toward the
raw frontier town of Independence, Missouri. John pulled his threadbare black
broadcloth coat closer around his neck to keep out the cold wind. It was February
5, 1832 and the weather was cold, but not bitingly, bitter cold as John would soon
learn the weather could be in western Missouri.

Again he glanced dolefully at his wife and daughter. His wife Agnes was a
spare, thin, severe woman, with a sour face that looked as if she constantly tasted
something unpleasant. His daughter Jennifer, on the other hand, was a pretty,
happy girl. Jenny stood several yards away, watching enthralled as the wooded
banks of the Missouri slid by. She was tall for a girl of fourteen, with thick, reddish
blond hair and high cheekbones that betrayed her Celtic ancestry. Despite her
good looks, she was a painfully shy girl and seldom spoke in a group, unless asked
a direct question.

Jenny's young body was just beginning to reveal the initial stages of
womanhood. Her waist was very slim, but her flaring hips were beginning to show
the influence of ongoing adolescence. Jenny was agonizingly aware of the changes
in her body, and especially embarrassing was the gentle swell of her small breasts
beneath her tight bodice. Agnes was a stern woman who saw the hand of God in

all things, including the changes in her daughter's body; however, she was loath to speak of these things with Jenny.

Thus, Jenny suffered through her first menstrual cycle in complete ignorance and without the support of her mother or anyone who would or could explain what was happening to her. When Jenny first noticed the beginning of bloodstains on her undergarments, she did not dare speak to her mother about the situation. She had heard her mother on countless occasions berate her father about the evils of lust and rebuke him viciously if she thought that he glanced at another woman with desire in his eyes.

Jenny knew that if she asked her mother any question concerning feminine anatomy it would be answered by a tirade concerning what happened to young women who entertained such vile thoughts. Agnes would demand that she purify her mind by reading the Bible and praying aloud for forgiveness and redemption for her wicked thoughts. Agnes fervently believed that the pain of childbirth and menstruation were God's punishment of women for their lack of self-denial when tempted by the serpent in the Garden of Eden. Jenny had heard murmurings among other girls about a woman's plight, but knowing her mother's religious fanaticism, Jenny suffered in silence and imagined that all kinds of horrible things were happening to her.

She eventually turned not to her mother but to her father, despite her mortification at discussing the blood flowing from her most private areas. She imagined she was dying of cancer, but her father gently assured her that it was part of the natural process.

John realized what this was all about. "Jenny," he said, "you're just becoming a woman. This is what happens when you mature and it is totally normal. It just means that one day you can be a mother." With sudden realization, Jenny looked at her father with devotion in her eyes. "I suspect that you best not tell your mother about our little discussion," he said.

"Don't worry," Jenny replied. "This isn't something I want to discuss with anyone, except you, and it's even difficult with you. If mother knew I talked to you about these things, she would make us both fall on our knees and pray for forgiveness for our debauchery." Both Jenny and John were greatly relieved and, true to their word, they never mentioned the event to Agnes.

As John reflected on Jenny's first encounter with puberty, he smiled inwardly. He glanced at Agnes's scowling countenance and noticed she was glaring at the ragged frontiersmen who swarmed on the deck. He knew the severe woman regarded these people as base sinners and the spawn of the Devil. She considered the journey they were on as a mission of God to establish a holy place in the

West, where Jesus would eventually return to usher in the Millennium. However, unlike Jesus, for whom she constantly expressed love and devotion, Agnes had no tolerance for those she considered as sinners or beneath her social status.

John looked away from the two women and contemplated the passing wooded shoreline. Like a fish swimming upstream to spawn, his mind and thoughts naturally returned to the event that had initiated this frightening journey. John had been a schoolteacher in Salem, Massachusetts and though it was a rather boring existence, it suited him. One evening, in the summer of 1831, he heard a light knock on his door. John opened the door and found himself face to face with a nondescript man of middle age. He was dressed in a top hat and coat that had once been fashionable, but were now shabby and threadbare. John immediately took the shoddily dressed stranger to be a beggar or traveling salesman.

As was her inquisitive custom, Agnes immediately came to see who was at the door and what they wanted. Before Agnes could speak, John rather brusquely addressed the man. "Yes, what do you want?"

The man was not very tall and his clothing hung on his thin frame. John was relieved that he was not in the least intimidating. "I am selling a holy book, which complements the Bible and answers many searching questions, including the origin of the American Indians," he replied matter-of-factly. He was an intense man and spoke quickly with the passion of one who believes he has an important message to convey. His eyes were rather dark and brooding and darted about like hummingbirds dart from flower to flower on a summer's evening. He also had the emaciated look of someone who was not used to eating on a regular basis.

John's first impulse was to send him away, but Agnes saw something in the man's haunted and flickering eyes that implied a fanaticism akin to her own. She turned to John and dismissed him with a disdainful wave of her hand. Turning to the strange, passionate man, she said, "Please come into the sitting room. Would you like a drink, or something to eat?"

The man eagerly replied, "Yes please, a drink of water would be nice, and if you have anything to eat, I would greatly appreciate it."

After they were seated in the dim little sitting room and Agnes had given him a glass of water and two slices of bread with butter and jam, the strange man poured out a strange tale.

"My name is Amos Eddings," he said, "and I am preaching the true Gospel of Jesus Christ."

That perked up Agnes's ears and there was no turning back. John knew that he was about to hear a long, tortuous tale, but by the enamored look on Agnes's face he knew better than to interrupt.

"The book I am selling," he continued, "is titled the *Book of Mormon*, and is a narrative of a people that left Jerusalem around six hundred years before the birth of Christ. The group eventually split into two warring factions, one who worshiped God and were righteous and the other who lived in iniquity and became a dark-skinned and war-like people. The Lamanites, as the wicked race was called, eventually destroyed the God-fearing Nephites, the white and delightsome people, who lived in righteousness. The Lamanites," Amos stated bluntly, "are the ancestors of the present-day Indians, who are actually a remnant of the Ten Tribes of Israel."

Hearing this, John glanced furtively at Agnes, because he had heard her say many times that the Indians were actually members of the Ten Tribes. She had gotten this idea after reading a book by Ethan Smith, entitled *View of the Hebrews*. Many of the itinerant preachers, who swarmed over the eastern states, expressed the same view that the Indians were actually descendants of Hebrews. Agnes was confident that if the Indians could be taught the truths of Christianity, they would lose the curse of their dark skin and become a "fair and delightsome people." Agnes also equated sin with the dark skin of the Africans and believed as well that once they forsook their sinful ways, their skin would become white.

John was dubious, but Agnes listened to the man's tale with rapt intensity. What he was saying coincided almost perfectly with her beliefs that she had developed from years of Bible reading and attending countless revival meetings.

John glanced at the book in Amos's hand and asked the obvious question, "Where did this book come from and who wrote it?"

Amos paused and took a deep breath as if to prepare for a long explanation and then launched into the most amazing part of the whole remarkable story. "This divine book," he said "was translated, if you will, by a young man, Joseph Smith, who lived in the Palmyra, New York area and was visited by an angel, who showed him a stone box on a hill close to the Smith farm. The stone box contained a sword of great antiquity and a breastplate with a pair of spectacle-like stones attached and a series of gold plates bound by rings.

"The plates," Amos explained, "were engraved with strange symbols and writings. At the sight of the golden plates, Joseph was so stricken by greed that the angel forbad him to remove the plates until he was sufficiently purified to carry on God's work. For four years Joseph returned to the site and finally on September 21, 1827, the angel permitted the young man to remove the plates from their hiding place."

Amos paused and looked at John and Agnes, as if to seek their permission to continue. John gave Agnes a furtive glance and decided to ask the obvious.

"You mean to say, that an angel picked this boy Joseph to approach with a holy book, out of the thousands of available people? Why Joseph?" John asked.

Amos looked at his feet and seemed almost embarrassed to continue. At last he took a deep breath and raised his eyes to look John in the eye. "Actually," he said softly, "Joseph went to a grove and prayed to his heavenly father and asked him what church preached the true Gospel of God and which one he should join. After pouring out his heart for several minutes, he saw a bright light in the sky and three personages descended from heaven. One of them addressed Joseph and said, 'This is my beloved son, hear him.'" John audibly sucked in his breath.

"Do you mean to tell me that God and Jesus Christ appeared to this man, Joseph Smith?" John said. Agnes turned to John and gave him a disdainful stare.

"Please show the courtesy to allow Amos to finish his story," she said witheringly.

Amos gave John an almost sympathetic look and continued. "Suffice it to say, God told Joseph that all religions were wrong and he, Joseph, was to be an instrument in the hands of God to bring forth the only true church. Later, Joseph," he said, "told his family about finding the plates and warned them that to look upon the plates meant death. Still, after several attempts were made to steal them, Joseph left the family farm and traveled to Harmony, Pennsylvania, to the home of his indifferent father-in-law, Isaac Hale. In a home owned by Hale, Joseph began the arduous task of translating the symbols on the golden plates.

John was so incredulous that he only partially heard Eddings' narrative. He wondered how anyone could believe the fantastic story Eddings described. According to Eddings, Joseph did not need the plates close by or even in the same building to translate. He merely stared into the stones on the breastplate, or as became his custom, into a black seer stone, which he placed in his hat to shield it from the light. He would then see the original symbols and a translation in English.

As Joseph's wife, Emma, who was pregnant, became frailer, Joseph convinced a wealthy and trusting farmer named Martin Harris to support the effort financially and take over as scribe. The translation was ponderous but eventually the two had managed to compile 116 pages of the manuscript.

Harris was elated with his part in this wondrous work and demanded to show the miracle to his doubting wife, Lucy. Lucy immediately stole the manuscript and taunted Martin and Joseph to duplicate it, if it were of God. Knowing that he could not, Joseph agonized for days until his vigorous mind found a solution.

Facing this dilemma, Joseph consulted God and received a revelation stating that there was another set of plates covering the same period of history.

John considered asking Eddings why God didn't just thwart the thief rather than provide such a complicated contingency plan, but after glancing at Agnes's mesmerized countenance, he decided against it, wondering if fanaticism precluded logic.

Chapter 5

At this juncture in the miraculous story, Amos paused for effect, and Agnes looked him hard in the face with glittering eyes and in a breathless voice urged him to go on with the tale.

"Wait," John shouted. "Before you go on I would like you to clarify a few things for me. First of all, I find it hard to believe that God would appear to Joseph and ignore the millions upon millions of people who must have sincerely sought his guidance. Secondly," he continued, "the Bible implies that God is so sacred man cannot look upon his face—even Moses could only look on his hind parts. Finally," John said without conviction, "I seriously doubt that the American Indian is a descendant of ancient Hebrews."

"You wait!" Agnes shouted. "You have always been a doubter of God's divine will and power and I will not have you question a man of God in my own house." John looked as if he had been struck across the face with a whip. His eyes immediately dropped to the floor and his contrite countenance told Amos this man would question him no more.

At the same time, Amos seemed shocked and almost embarrassed. The new religion he was preaching taught that women were subservient to men, but Agnes's outburst had silenced a troublesome query and for that he was thankful.

Agnes immediately grasped the importance of this new information. God had spoken to the righteous through this man Joseph, his prophet, and now God once more would make his will known to the people on earth. Agnes thought back to all the times she had sat in church or in revival meetings and listened to the preachers describe in intricate detail heaven and hell. She prayed incessantly to her God and asked that she be forgiven of her sins, but Agnes never really thought of herself as a sinner. She could always see sin in the teeming masses and in the dark-skinned races, but she never considered that she might also be guilty of the sins of arrogance, envy, pride, intolerance, and fanaticism.

Agnes always saw herself as one appointed to identify sin in others and to call those sinners to repentance. Now this man had told an amazing story of God communicating to his modern-day prophet. Agnes shuddered in ecstasy and looked at Amos with a beseeching stare, then asked the obvious question, "Where is this Joseph and how can I meet him?"

Amos gave Agnes an impatient look and said, "There is a little more I need to tell you about Joseph and the church, before I tell you where he is and how to join the church."

Joseph by this time had a new scribe, Oliver Cowdery, who also saw the spirit. The two men were visited by an angel, John the Baptist, who conveyed the keys of the Priesthood of Aaron and the authority to establish the true church of God. The two men quickly finished translating the "Golden Bible" and Martin Harris paid for the printing and distribution of the marvelous work.

On April 6, 1830, Joseph organized his church at Bainbridge and Colesville, New York with six members, but within a month, the church membership had grown to nearly forty. Later, Amos said, because of local persecution and lack of interest, the church was moved to Kirtland, Ohio.

Agnes immediately leaped to her feet and grabbed Amos's hands. She gazed reverently into his eyes and asked in a voice choked by emotion, "I want to go to Kirtland immediately and throw myself at the feet of the modern-day prophet."

Amos was shocked by the woman's passionate behavior, but he calmly said, "I suggest that you carefully read the *Book of Mormon* and then if you believe it is true, arrange your affairs so that you have money and clothing to sustain yourselves, for the church cannot support the people that are pouring into Kirtland."

Agnes never glanced at John, but continued to hold Amos's hands and look fervently into his eyes. "Then tell me how much you want for the book, because I cannot wait to be about the Lord's work!" she exclaimed. Amos informed her that he was only asking for the cost of printing for the book, which amounted to two dollars. The transaction was soon made and Agnes grasped the book to her bosom as if it were an adored child; without saying another word, she rushed from the room.

John turned to Amos and offered his hand; the younger man took it and gave him a firm, friendly handshake. "Thank you for coming," John said, without much enthusiasm. "I suspect that I better have another of those books, for I fear that I shall never pry that one away from my wife long enough to ever read it."

Amos took another book from a shabby valise that he had placed near his chair and accepted four dollars in change from John. He rose from the chair and walked to the door.

With his hand on the knob he turned and said, "Mr. Evans, I suspect that you are not as excited to hear about the true Gospel of Jesus Christ as your wife is, but rest assured that if you read this book with a pure heart, you will receive inspiration of its truth."

John nodded, but his thoughts were on the four dollars that he had paid for the two books. He thought how he could ill afford to squander even that paltry sum on his meager salary as a schoolteacher. Conversely, he knew that now that Agnes had heard the story about the "Golden Bible" and Joseph Smith's communication with angels and other divine beings, he could not oppose her.

After Amos left, John pondered the book in his hand and wondered where all this would lead him. He had a vague feeling of impending disaster, but he knew that he could never resist Agnes. Somehow, her imposing personality always intimidated him and he found it easier to acquiesce to her demands than to suffer the abuse that disagreement always brought. He was originally a member of the Unitarians, but Agnes had belittled his religious beliefs on the grounds that they were "worldly" and there was little structure in this religion.

Agnes wasn't one to tolerate what she saw as blasphemy in her mate. Rather than express his ideas and thoughts, or worship as he truly believed, John had given up and pretended to accept the strict Calvinism of his wife. Agnes had smugly pointed out to him that John Calvin had burned the Unitarian heretic preacher Michael Servetus at the stake, with his writings and books strapped to his body. Somehow she thought this act of barbarism was actually a work of rectitude.

Over the next two weeks, both Agnes and John pored over the "Golden Bible." However, they each saw the work in a much different way. Agnes nearly swooned as she pondered each word, for she believed that she was reading the revealed word of God. She hung on every syllable and when she wasn't poring over the book, she was in their cramped, dimly lit bedroom praying to God that she would understand what she read and be worthy to make the journey to Kirtland to worship at the feet of the man she had never seen but had come to adore.

John, being a teacher, was more analytical than his wife and he was skeptical of her steadfast belief that God revealed his will to one man. Unlike his wife, John read a wide variety of books and material and didn't select only articles and books that supported his opinion or some rigid dogma. In fact, he had read with interest an article that espoused the theory that the American Indian had originated in the steppes of Asia. He was excited about the commentary and mentioned it to Agnes, who derided him by mouthing stereotypes of the Mandarin Chinese and reiterating the widely held opinion that the Indians were savages.

As John studied the monotonous work, he was amazed to find that the language was much like that of the King James Version of the Bible. The pronouns *thee* and *thou* were used extensively as was "and it came to pass." John couldn't help but wonder if this was an intentional effort by the translator to give the book an air of credibility. Agnes, of course, believed that this was the language of Jesus and when John pointed out that it was actually Elizabethan English, she dismissed his comment with an arrogant toss of her head.

By nature, John was something of a scholar and he had an open mind. For much of his adult life, he had read and pondered scholarly articles and books and his methodical mind retained information like a sponge. He not only read, but he analyzed the information he read and compared it to what he already knew to decide what had value and what was propaganda. As he read the *Book of Mormon*, he found that there were whole passages in the work that were roughly direct quotes from the Bible, especially from the Book of Isaiah. The words were changed somewhat, but the basic intent was the same. John also found that many of the stories from the Bible were reiterated in the "Golden Bible" but again, in a slightly altered form. He read an account in the *Book of Mormon* of a woman dancing before a king, much as Salome had danced in the biblical story. Also, the *Book of Mormon* prophet Alma was miraculously converted in almost the same fashion as Saint Paul.

As John perceived these similarities between the two holy works, he couldn't help but wonder if the similarities were intentional. The *Book of Mormon* also included stories that seemed to mirror current events. In one case, the narrative described secret signs and passwords used by an insurgent group known as the Gadianton Band, which closely resembled signs and passwords used by the Masons, a group currently generating much controversy.

John and Agnes rarely talked on a personal level, but when they met during meals, they would occasionally discuss what they had read in the book and John would point out the inconsistencies that he had noticed. Agnes considered this a sacrilege and her eyes would glisten with rage. She would accuse him of deliberately trying to find fault with the divine truths she found in the work and would invariably quote from the Bible the words of Jesus: "Other sheep I have, which are not of this fold: them also I must bring and they shall hear my voice." This, she said, referred to Jesus's ministry to the Nephites in the Americas that was described in the *Book of Mormon*.

The battle between Agnes and John raged on for a fortnight. During this time Jenny quietly listened to the hostile debate. She rarely said anything, but she silently sided with her father. Though Jenny was a quiet and retiring girl, she shared her father's analytical mind and as she listened to the vicious arguments, she weighed each side and found Agnes's point of view long on emotion and short on logic and acumen. However, like her father, she was loath to defy her mother.

Jenny knew that her father never shared Agnes's bed because if she arose early or woke to use the little outhouse in the back, she saw her father sleeping on the little loveseat in the tiny parlor. Though she was naïve concerning sex and intimate relations, she did know that most married couples slept in the same bed. She had heard Agnes say many times that sex was a gift from God, to be used to procreate and not for pleasure. She often wondered what pleasure her mother was talking about, but knew better than to breach the subject with Agnes.

Soon after the visit by Amos, Agnes wrote a letter to the postmaster of Kirtland, Ohio and asked for the address of the fledgling Church of Christ. She received a brief letter in reply that contained the addresses of Sidney Rigdon and one Edward Partridge. The note stated that Mr. Partridge was something of a presiding bishop in the church and was steward over property held in common for the church, as well as administrator for the welfare of those wishing to join the church in Kirtland.

Ecstatic, Agnes wrote a long epistle to Bishop Partridge pouring out her heart. She described her long but joyous hours pondering the word of God that she found in the *Book of Mormon* and how her spirit soared and her bosom burned with the truths she discovered there. She told him that she longed to see the true prophet of God, who had translated this work and spoken with angels and that she would never rest or be satisfied until she joined the Saints in Kirtland.

Bishop Partridge answered her with an equally long and rambling letter, explaining that the church that Joseph had established was like the ancient Christian church that existed at the time of Jesus. He told her that the same titles and ordinances were used that were common in the primitive church. He went on to point out that like the early Christian churches, property was held in common in the restored church. He then described in detail how Joseph regularly received revelations from God, which were being collected in a holy book referred to as the Book of Commandments.

In glowing terms, Partridge described the church meetings, in which the Saints often rose to the Spirit and spoke in tongues, and how the prophet had cast out devils and healed the sick and afflicted, just as the faithful were healed in the time of Jesus. He went on to say that Joseph was constantly receiving revelations concerning the will of God and that eventually the Saints, as the members were called, would establish the New Jerusalem, where the righteous of the earth would gather. Once the New Jerusalem was founded, the Lost Ten Tribes of Israel would return from the north and then Jesus would return again in all his glory and would usher in the Millennium, said Partridge.

Agnes looked up from the yellow pages of foolscap and her face was glowing. She rolled her eyes toward the ceiling, as if looking into eternity. John looked into her radiant face and he knew that his days in Salem were numbered. He had experienced his wife's conversions before and he knew that the only way he could avoid being forced to tear up his roots and move to Ohio was to either leave his wife or divorce her, and he wasn't willing to do either.

Leaving Agnes would mean losing Jenny and John loved his daughter dearly, even though he had never established an especially close relationship with her. John was always painfully shy around women and he found it difficult to talk to any woman, including his daughter. Looking back, he never really knew how he and Agnes had come to get married, for he had never developed a loving relationship with her either.

John had thought of leaving Agnes many times during their married life, but he knew if he did, he would suffer the same grinding loneliness that he had suffered as a youth. He had always been agonizingly shy and despite the fact that he was intelligent, he could never think of anything to say socially. While attending a small college near Boston, he had tried to make friends with men of his own age, but he found that he had little in common with them. He was never comfortable around them and inevitably became the butt of their jokes. He learned that men usually talked about their sexual exploits, war or hunting, subjects that he knew little about. In fact, he was still a virgin when he met Agnes.

He had met Agnes in the library while studying English literature, his favorite subject. She was a nervous, plain girl, who shared his social ineptitude. She had been studying for an exam on Chaucer's works and somehow they found a common subject in the writings of the English bard. The attraction he found in her, if there was an attraction, was that she was also desperately lonely.

They had been married a year after the tentative discussion of Chaucer in the library. During their courtship, they never once engaged in anything that resembled passion and rarely engaged in hesitant, clumsy kissing and touching. Agnes's father was a Calvinist minister, who drilled a strict moral code into his daughter. She firmly believed that physical relations between a man and a woman were a moral sin, unless the sole purpose was procreation, and she used her beliefs like a club to keep John at bay.

Their wedding night was a total disaster; neither of them had any experience with lovemaking and they both sat on the bed in the little inn outside Braintree, Massachusetts and clasped their hands in embarrassment. John realized that it was his responsibility to initiate any action between the two and he was urgent and aroused. Rather than hold his new wife and gently fondle and caress her, he let his passion drive him. He pulled his clothes off and immediately lifted Agnes's long nightgown up to her neck. With no prelude, he had tried to enter her.

For her part, Agnes remembered the event with distaste and disgust. She remembered the blinding pain he inflicted on her, and the sight of his pale buttocks rising and falling in the dim light reminded her of a rutting bull. She could not get the image out of her mind, for she even thought that John's ragged breathing in her ear sounded like the breathing and bellowing of a bull. The whole event had been obscene in her mind and from that time on, any sex conjured up the nasty image of rutting cattle.

If John ever attempted to kiss her or touch her she would squeeze her eyes shut so tightly that she saw little stars and would say in a trembling voice, "Please, John, don't touch me now, I really do not want to be mauled and pawed." John overcame his frustration by turning to his work and studies and occasionally to masturbation.

Eventually, Agnes did get pregnant—John wondered if it was an immaculate conception—but neither of them looked back on the event with any pleasure. John could never tell if Agnes loved the little girl that had come into their lives. She was a good mother and took care of their infant daughter's needs. When she nursed the baby, she held it in the crook of her arm and gazed at it with something akin to love in her eyes. She often quoted from the Bible about a commandment to multiply and replenish the earth. John wondered if she saw the child as some kind of divine obligation.

John had tried to approach Agnes a time or two after Jenny was born, but she spurned him in such a humiliating way that he could never muster the courage to try again. Eventually, their relationship deteriorated into one of mutual tolerance, but they never shared physical or emotional intimacy. Despite the fact that he never shared intimacy or tenderness with Agnes, John allowed her to totally dominate him. For her part, Agnes could never see any inconsistency between her actions and the Christian faith that she so fervently professed.

They sold the little house in Salem in August of 1831, a week after John had resigned from his teaching position in the primary school there. John loved teaching. It gave him a captive audience with whom he could discuss the ideas that he gleaned from his reading and musing. He truly loved his students and, amazingly enough, he didn't become tongue-tied with them as he did when talking to his peers. He was loath to leave his work and their comfortable little home, but he couldn't conjure up the courage to defy Agnes, so when she firmly stated that they were going to Kirtland, John and Jenny sadly boxed their belongings and prepared to leave.

They packed and shipped their meager possessions in care of Bishop Partridge and purchased tickets to Kirtland on the local stage line. It was a hot afternoon in late August when the bouncing Concorde stage rolled down the dusty main street of the little town of Kirtland, Ohio. John leaned out of the narrow window of the rocking stage and looked in amazement at the neat and tidy little town.

John was used to the orderly and well-kept homes and lots of New England, but they paled in comparison to this immaculate little village. The picket fences were freshly painted in a blinding white and the small homes that lined the dusty street were all whitewashed to a blinding brilliance. As the stage rolled slowly down the street, John was amazed at the number of homes and businesses that were under construction. Everywhere he looked he saw the gleam of raw lumber and masonry as the walls of new buildings lifted their bony frames toward the Ohio sky.

Chapter 6

A s the stage slowed to a stop, the driver jumped down and opened the door
for the occupants. John noticed a small group of people milling around the
board sidewalk near a red brick hotel and one man left the group and walked
toward them as they disembarked. He raised his flat-crowned, wide-brimmed hat
in greeting. "I'm Newell K. Whitney," he said. "I apologize that Brother Partridge
isn't here to meet you, but he was called by God to accompany the prophet and
Sidney Rigdon on a journey to the church members in Independence, Missouri.

"I own a store here and maintain the bishop's storehouse," Whitney explained.

Newell Whitney was a stocky man with large, sad eyes that reminded John of
the guileless eyes of a puppy. He was quiet and reserved to the point of shyness and
spoke in a low voice that was difficult to hear over the constant hum of commerce
that the town emitted. Despite his apparent reticence, he grasped John's hand in
a firm grip and said, "I am acting in Bishop Partridge's stead until the good bishop
might return from Zion."

With a little sincere smile playing at the corner of his lips, Whitney continued.
"Brother Evans, you and your family are welcome in Kirtland. I'll make
arrangements for you to stay in my store, until more permanent accommodations
are found. Once you are settled, I'll meet with you and explain a little more about
the church and what we're accomplishing here in Kirtland."

John glanced at Agnes and saw irritation written on her face. He knew she had
desperately wanted to meet the prophet the minute that she arrived in Kirtland.
Agnes gave Whitney an irritated glance. "And just when do you expect the prophet
to return?" she demanded in a harsh voice. Whitney raised his eyebrows in surprise.

"I anticipate the prophet's party to return within a fortnight and, being an
amicable man, I am sure that Joseph will be wanting to meet with your family
then," he said. Whitney took John, Agnes and Jenny into the lobby of the little

hotel and introduced them to the clerk behind the desk and hurriedly left, after informing them he would meet them in the lobby in an hour.

The clerk, whom Whitney introduced as Edgar Sinclair, was a little, bald gnome of a chap with a constant grimace on his face, as if he were suffering from some ongoing discomfort. Edgar greeted them without any enthusiasm and showed them to a small dining room adjacent to the lobby. Immediately, an equally dour waitress appeared and with a suspicious stare she asked, "Would you like something to eat or a cool drink?" John glanced at the meager menu that was posted conspicuously on the wall and ordered lemonade for the three of them.

After the unsociable waitress had brought the drinks and marched sternly away, John remarked to Agnes, "Kirtland is an attractive town, but the residents seem less than amiable."

A fortnight passed very quickly. Whitney had provided comfortable but cramped accommodations for the Evans family above his store. He had discussed with them much of the workings of the church and had led them around the small but rapidly growing Kirtland. He had also explained the structure of the new revelation on tithing. Basically, he said, the head of a family provided ten percent of their income to the church to provide finances for the maintenance of the church and its leaders. He also told them that Joseph and his apostles handpicked those who would migrate to Independence to begin establishing Zion. Finally, he advised them that to become members of the church, they must prove that they were full tithe-payers and that they were worthy Saints. After being interviewed by a bishop or apostle and found worthy, they would be presented to the congregation during a church meeting and, if accepted, they would be baptized and confirmed members of the church.

Agnes was impatient for the process to begin and made it known to anyone who would listen that she wanted to leave as soon as possible for Missouri to begin the work of preparing for the coming of Christ.

One afternoon in early October, they finally met Joseph Smith. Whitney escorted them to a well-kept and quite spacious home. They knocked on the door and were greeted by a very attractive, dark-haired woman of around twenty-five, who escorted them into a cluttered study. A man immediately rose from his chair and in a warm and friendly voice said, "Welcome, I am Joseph the Prophet and I understand that you are the Evans family. The Lord has told me that you were coming and he has much for you to do."

Agnes sprang forward and clasped the man's hand in hers and gazed deeply into his eyes. "Oh Joseph, I have long waited for this divine moment," she said.

Smith seemed embarrassed by Agnes's adoration and, withdrawing his hand, he glanced at Jenny. "My, you are a beautiful young lady. What is your name?" he cajoled.

Jenny blushed, turning her face a fiery red, and, looking intently at her feet, she replied, "My name is Jenny Evans and I am here with my parents."

Agnes snorted through her nose in disgust, and immediately retorted: "Sir, we are here to serve the Lord and we want to know when we can be confirmed members of the church and interviewed by a church official to determine if we are worthy to travel to the holy site of Zion."

Joseph seemed to consider this as he sat down at his desk and indicated for the group to be seated.

While Agnes was speaking, Jenny gazed intently at the prophet. She thought that Joseph Smith came quite close to being handsome. She had heard those who adored him describe him as striking, but as she studied him, she saw him in less flattering terms. Joseph, she thought, had fascinating eyes; they were luminous and seemed veiled by spectacularly long, curved eyelashes, which gave him a mysterious and gentle look. The prophet's hair was thick and dark and swept back from his forehead in luxurious waves. However, his chin was weak and receding and when coupled with his markedly sloping forehead, his face took on an unpleasant, pinched effect; she thought his face resembled that of a weasel.

She found the prophet returning her look, and she flinched under his intense gaze. Somehow, she felt very uncomfortable under the stare of Joseph and she involuntarily shivered. Joseph appeared to sense her discomfort and he turned his eyes back to Agnes, who was asking the prophet if he would personally baptize and confirm her as a member of the church. Joseph hesitated and then reluctantly agreed to perform the ordinances the next Sunday. Agnes clasped her hands to her throat in an act of reverence and her eyes fluttered as if she were losing consciousness.

After a brief interlude, Joseph rose from his chair to inform his guests that their allotted time had expired. The little group rose in unison and, after they exchanged goodbyes with the prophet, Emma showed them to the door. As they were walking back to the Whitney mercantile, Agnes babbled incoherently about being in the presence of the prophet of God. Jenny, on the other hand, could not forget the sense of revulsion she felt under the intense stare of the cleric.

When they arrived back in their quarters above Whitney's General Store, Agnes immediately seized her Bible and went into the little bedroom, slamming the door after her. John and Jenny sat down at the rough pine table and neither spoke for several minutes. Jenny was reluctant to tell her father about her perception of

Smith. Finally, she said, "Father, I had a strange feeling when Joseph looked at me. He seemed to stare at me for a long time and it made me shiver."

"Well, Jenny, he is a famous man and perhaps that is why you felt uncomfortable in his presence," John replied. Father and daughter fell silent again and both mused over the strange meeting. John reflected on all he had heard and seen since meeting Amos Eddings and he felt misgivings rise in his chest like a gnawing worm. He couldn't help but think of the Inquisitor General of the murderous Spanish Inquisition when he heard talk of purging the iniquitous from the ranks of the church. He shuddered when he remembered Whitney describing Zion as a place where the Saints would judge nations and peoples.

John had never been a man to judge others regarding their religious beliefs. In fact, one of the concepts that drew him to the Unitarians was their devotion to tolerance. He felt a maggot of fear nibble at his heart when he remembered Agnes relating with delight the story of Calvin burning Michael Servetus over a slow fire. He had trembled when he recalled the passion in Agnes's eyes when she talked of judging the wicked. Now it seemed she had found a faith that, like her, reveled in its eagerness to stamp out iniquity.

John considered Joseph's role as a prophet and recalled that the seer had received a revelation that made him the sole recipient of God's will. It seemed to John any claim to know the will of God was enticement to punish those who didn't follow his "divine precepts." He reflected on his knowledge of the New Testament and remembered that Jesus had saved a whore from stoning with the admonition, "Let him that is without sin cast the first stone." In light of these words, all of the talk he had heard about chastising unbelievers seemed crass and meaningless.

The next three days passed quickly. The Evans family spent the time strolling around the vibrant city of Kirtland and talking to Saints that they met on these excursions. Agnes was exhilarated and whenever they stopped to talk to church members she bubbled with enthusiasm like an effervescent spring. John, on the other hand, found the Saints to be predictable and spurious. For her part, Jenny was lonely and bored. She was unable to make friends with anyone her age and found the church members clannish and aloof. She mentioned this to Agnes, but her mother informed her that once they had proven themselves faithful and were confirmed, that would all change. To Jenny, the concept of acceptance by association was duplicitous.

Saturday evening, Whitney came to their door and informed them that he was there to fetch them for their baptism. He had a little bag, which he placed on the table, and opening it he retrieved two white shift-like garments and a white shirt and trousers. He instructed the Evanses to put on the items and told them he would return in ten minutes. After dressing in the utilitarian clothing, John, Agnes and Jenny waited uncomfortably until Whitney returned. He led them to a small pool nearby, and with the assistance of two other elders, he quickly performed the baptism ceremony on each of the Evans family members.

John watched as his wife and daughter were baptized. He was surprised that Whitney mumbled the exact same prayer over each of the women. Once the incantation was spoken, the women were immediately and unceremoniously pushed backward and completely submerged. Whitney kept his arm in the small of their backs and once they were totally submerged, he raised them back to a standing position.

When Jenny was raised sputtering and coughing from the water, John was shocked to notice that her white shift had become almost transparent and her small, youthful breasts were pressing against the wet fabric. Jenny, too, immediately became aware of her erect nipples pressing against the damp, cold cloth. Instantly, her face turned a burning crimson and she immediately crossed her arms over her chest.

The appointed day of the Evanses' confirmation as members of the church dawned warm and sunny. John had satisfied the last hurdle for church membership by paying a tenth of his meager funds to Whitney as a tithe. When they arrived at the little church, not knowing protocol, they sat on the back row. After a long, boring prayer and equally long and boring meeting, they were called one by one to the front of the room, where three men laid their hands on their heads and confirmed them as members of the church. John and Jenny found the ritual mundane, but for Agnes it was sublime.

After the service, Newell invited them for lunch. During the meal, he informed the Evanses that they were scheduled to be interviewed by Whitney, the prophet and Sidney Rigdon to determine if they were worthy to immigrate to Independence.

The days passed quickly, and on the following Wednesday, Whitney's secretary, Bertha, stopped by the Evanses' living quarters to inform them that the prophet wanted to meet them in his study at one that afternoon to discuss their moving to Missouri. Agnes was delighted to hear the news and told John and Jenny to let her do most of the talking. Agnes had set her heart on traveling to Zion to aid in building the City of God. John knew that if they weren't selected to be in the vanguard of Saints pouring into Independence, there would be no consoling Agnes, and no living with her as well.

John knew from talking to Whitney and others that the poorer Saints were usually selected to build up the New Jerusalem, while the wealthier members remained in Kirtland to provide funds to finance the Holy City. He also knew that the more fanatic of the Saints were usually among those who were picked to go to Independence. This situation led to a division in the church between the poor, zealous members and the wealthy and more moderate Saints. Those who remained in Kirtland wore their wealth on their sleeves as a badge of their sanctity and constantly reminded the Independence Saints that the prophet had also chosen them to reside in Kirtland. Much like the Puritans, the Kirtland Saints believed that they were the elect of God, because they were generally affluent. John thought of the poverty of Jesus and wondered if the Kirtland Saints ever considered this paradox.

They arrived at Joseph's home punctually at five minutes to one. Emma opened the door for them and ushered them into the prophet's neat and comfortable study. The prophet immediately rose from his chair with a good-natured smile on his face, and extending his hand he said, "Good afternoon to you all and God bless you for choosing to become members of the church." He quickly turned to a man sitting next to him. "This is my counselor, Sidney Rigdon," he said solemnly. The man rose and shook hands with each of them while offering his congratulations to them for becoming members of the church.

Sidney Rigdon was immaculately dressed in a dark broadcloth coat with a silk vest and black ribbon tie. His clothes were perfectly pressed and tailored and his hair and beard were neatly trimmed. He was a man of medium height and was slightly rotund with a long, melancholy face. John studied him and noticed that his lips were narrow, compressed and turned down at the corners in a perpetual frown. In his mind, John thought that Rigdon's countenance was similar to most of the church elders he had met during the past fortnight.

"Now, Brother Evans," Joseph said gravely, "I speak to you as the head of this family. Have each of you paid an honest tithing and do you believe this is the true church of Christ?" Agnes snorted noisily through her nose, letting the prophet know that she could answer for herself. Joseph gave her a stern look and Agnes dropped her eyes in submission. "Brother Evans will soon be a priesthood holder," he announced. "In this capacity he is responsible for the actions of his family and may speak for them in these matters."

Joseph again gave Agnes a reproachful look and continued. "Are all of you willing to lay down your lives to build the holy City of Zion to aid the ushering in of the Millennium?" Agnes quickly answered in the affirmative, while Jenny and John considered the question for what seemed a long time. Agnes turned a stifling stare on the two and they each nodded and mumbled their agreement in unison.

Joseph turned his gaze to Jenny, which immediately caused her to blush a deep purple to the roots of her hair. The prophet didn't seem to notice Jenny's obvious chagrin and asked her in a gentle voice, "Jenny, are you sure of your decision?"

Jenny immediately looked at the toes of her shoes and answered in a timid voice, "Yes sir, I am sure." In her heart, Jenny was anything but sure, but she found that she couldn't look this man in the eye any more than she could tell him that she found his presence anything but revered.

Rigdon gave them a stern look and asked in a grating, high-pitched, nasal whine, "Does each of you promise to support the anointed of the Lord and to report any apostasy or speaking against the anointed that you may observe among the Saints?" Again, Agnes vigorously showed her agreement, while John and Jenny merely gave a slight nod of their heads. Joseph and his counselor then retired to another room for a whispered conference.

In a short time, they returned to the study and Joseph glowered at each of them. "Well, after considering you as a family, we have come to the conclusion that you will be a great asset in the blessed work of the Lord. We have asked the Lord for his inspiration and he has answered that this family will be a tool in his hands in building Zion."

Agnes exhaled noisily, as if she had been holding her breath during the entire meeting, and with a rare smile on her thin lips; she heartily shook each man's hand. John and Jenny stood in the background and mumbled their thanks as Emma ushered them to the door.

Over the next few weeks, Whitney kept the family busy. John was appointed to teach at the local school, while Jenny was assigned to assist in tending children and working in the Whitney General Store. Agnes insisted that she be appointed to study the Bible, the *Book of Mormon*, and the revelations of Joseph so she could identify any lack of faith among members. When she told Whitney what she wanted to do, he rolled his eyes, but agreed, rather than face her wrath.

Each member of the Evans family was paid a small stipend for their work, from which they were expected to pay a full tithe of ten percent of their gross income. They could also request vegetables, eggs and meat from the bishop's storehouse, but Whitney reviewed all allotments to ensure that only the truly needy received aid. The family continued to live above Whitney's store because they were scheduled to immigrate to Independence early in 1832. They were all kept very busy and the time passed swiftly.

During the last week of January 1832, Whitney approached John and gave him three tickets for the stage to Cincinnati, where they would board the steamship *Arcadia* for Independence. Whitney also provided the family with winter clothing and a little money to cover traveling expenses and food. The day they were to catch the stage, Whitney told John that he was expected to be familiar with the teachings of Joseph and the *Book of Mormon* and to preach the Gospel at every opportunity. He also said that the family would be expected to raise a sum of money to aid in building a temple in Kirtland.

The Evanses traveled by stage for three days to Cincinnati, followed by a month-long steamboat trip up the Missouri River on the old sidewheeler *Acadia*. Throughout the voyage, Agnes wavered between enthusiastic babbling about how wonderful it was to be living in the last days and angry complaining about the filthy, foul-mouthed men who were their fellow travelers.

PART THREE

The New Jerusalem

Chapter 7

It was a cold and blustery day when the Evans family trooped down the gangplank in the river port town of Fort Osage, or Sibley, as it later became known. The place was crawling with bullwhackers, teamsters and rough-looking frontiersmen. The huge prairie schooners plying the Santa Fe Trail bore an eerie resemblance to their namesake when they returned from the great sea of grass that was the Great Plains. As the wagons became visible on the horizon, their canvas covers billowing in the wind, they bore an uncanny resemblance to the sails of clipper ships. The little town was a favorite "port" for the prairie schooners because of the proximity of the river.

The wagon trains picked up manufactured goods and cloth from the boats for the run to Santa Fe and returned with mules, hides, silver and Mexican coins, which were either traded locally or loaded on the keelboats and steamships for delivery to the East. Because of the lucrative trade that developed between Missouri and Santa Fe, Independence and the surrounding area was crowded with buffalo hunters, teamsters, mountain men and other coarse border types.

As they walked down the narrow, swaying passageway leading from the *Arcadia* to the dock, the Evans family was greeted by a myriad of unfamiliar sights, sounds and smells. The main street was crowded with lumbering Conestoga wagons, pulled by four or six span of huge, long-horned oxen. Alongside these hulking beasts walked cursing bullwhackers, snapping their long rawhide whips. The rough plank walkway was crawling with tobacco-spitting, dirty, smelly, swearing men. Agnes stopped in her tracks and almost recoiled backwards at the sight of so many obvious sinners in one place.

As a great prairie schooner with a fluttering canvas cover came lumbering by, the lead ox, a huge red and white Durham bull, made a lunge toward the boardwalk, where a spilled sack of corn lay, and the teamster lashed the animal with a long bullwhip as he screamed, "Goddamn ye Brutus, ye old son of a whore, get the fucking hell back there where ye belong." Hearing this outburst, Agnes put her hands to her ears and stopped stock-still in horror. The teamster looked at her with amusement and shouted a few more favorite epithets to add to her shock.

Although there hadn't been much actual violence between the old settlers and the incoming Saints by the spring of 1832, there was growing friction. The frontiersmen and homesteaders along the Missouri Frontier were "dammed" up at the edge of the Great Plains. Andrew Jackson had temporarily halted the indomitable forward march of the frontier by declaring the lands beyond the Missouri River as Indian domain. The "backing up" of the frontier frustrated the footloose frontiersmen and added to the friction between the industrious Saints and the indolent flotsam of the frontier. Recognizing Agnes as one of the Saints who were pouring into Zion, the teamster gleefully goaded the uptight churchwoman.

The Evanses made their way to the town common, where Whitney had told them that someone would meet them and take them to Independence. The town common was nothing more than a large rectangle area in the center of Sibley. It was used as a wagon park and assembly area for the teamsters and was swarming with bellowing oxen and shouting, swearing bullwhackers. They stood on the boardwalk in front of a general merchandise store and surveyed the crowd of braying mules and bawling oxen, trying to spot someone who looked like a Saint in the sea of sinners.

Just as they began to think that their guide had not arrived, a nondescript little man driving a small black buggy pulled up to the boardwalk. The buggy was pulled by two of the ubiquitous Missouri mules, which the little man spoke to soothingly before he bounced happily from the buggy. He cheerfully extended his hand. "Good morning, I am Brother Charles Simmons," he declared.

For a small man, Brother Simmons had none of the little-man syndrome. He seemed genuinely happy to meet the Evans family and exhibited a sincere good nature. His pleasant face was split by a broad smile that displayed white but crooked teeth. He was dressed in the basic work clothes of the frontier: heavy denim trousers, a collarless linen shirt and rough cowhide boots with dangling "mule ears" to aid in pulling them on. Despite the fact that Charles was not wearing the dark coat and hat typical of the church leaders, there was something about his demeanor that branded him as a Saint.

Charles informed them he liked to be called "Chic," which was his nickname, and he much preferred it to the more formal "Charles." Chic demurely reached for Agnes's hand and helped her step into the buggy and turned to Jenny with a gleam of good humor in his eyes. "May I help you into the buggy, Miss Evans?" he asked cheerfully. Jenny immediately found that she liked Chic and, unlike some men, he did not make her feel uncomfortable or let his eyes drift down to her bosom. Once the women were aboard, Chic helped John load the luggage and then he leaped nimbly onto the spring seat next to John.

"Since it is still early in the morning, we have time to tour some of the outlying church settlements before going on to Independence," Chic announced. "Bishop Edward Partridge received three thousand dollars from the church in Kirtland to purchase land in Missouri for the Saints' inheritances. Partridge put the money to good use and purchased over nineteen hundred acres of land in and around Independence," Chic explained. "Partridge obtained the land in his own name as trustee for the church. As the Saints began to pour into Jackson County, Bishop Partridge parceled out their inheritances in ten and twenty acre lots for farmers and merchants or smaller parcels for those not dependent on the soil," Chic elaborated.

"God told Joseph that the City of Zion was to be a model city. Therefore, the streets are an unprecedented 130 feet wide and the houses are set twenty-five feet back from the street. Once a square is filled up, we are instructed to lay out another according to this visionary plan, until the shining city on the banks of the Missouri is a beacon for the entire world.

"However," Chic elaborated, "Independence and the surrounding area was settled by Missourians prior to our coming, which does create a problem, but we feel they will move on, once they see we plan to stay."

It was about six miles from Sibley to the outlying church settlements of Big Blue and Colesville. As they rode through the chilly late February morning, John could see signs of unprecedented growth. Raw homesteads were sprouting like weeds on rich bottomland and areas suitable for farming along the numerous streams and natural springs. Close to Sibley, most of the cabins were little more than a few logs stacked on top of each other, with dirt or sod laid on saplings to form a roof. Most of these cabins and homesteads showed little sign of pride of ownership or intention to establish a permanent home. The cabins were usually ramshackle, and hogs, cows, and mules wandered through the front yards untended and free. Garbage and refuse cluttered the yards and the surrounding land was still covered by brush and trees.

As they neared the Colesville settlement, there was a dramatic change in the milieu. The farms and cabins became much more compact and organized. The homesteads were no longer scattered, but were laid out in blocks with wide streets between them, and it was obvious that there was considerable cooperation among the residents.

The cabins were no longer ramshackle and hastily erected, but exhibited signs of pride and workmanship. The logs were laboriously and painstakingly squared using an adze or broadax. The chimneys were made of carefully laid rock or mud brick rather than the haphazard waddle and daub construction they had seen around Sibley.

The yards also showed signs of pride and hard work. Around each cabin the rocks and debris were cleared and the larger stones were piled up in neat rows to form the beginnings of fences. Behind the farm homes were tidy corrals and pens to contain the hogs, cattle and mules. Everywhere there were stacks of grass hay that the industrious Saints had gathered and stacked the previous summer and fall.

"It's easy to distinguish between the dwellings of the Saints and the Missourians, or 'old settlers,' because the Saints plan to stay in this area until the coming of Christ," Chic said. "Each Saint is dedicated to building a city that Jesus will be proud to visit, and they are always mindful that they are building a municipality where the righteous will establish a government based on religious precepts and judge the world," Chic said with a wave of his hand.

As they meandered along, marveling at what the Saints had accomplished in two short years, they skirted Colesville and headed west toward the church outpost known as the Big Blue settlement. "This outlying settlement was established by the Saints to control the crossing over the Big Blue River," Chic explained earnestly. "Bishop Partridge was divinely inspired to command the Saints to build a ferry on the Big Blue River, where they could raise much-needed cash by charging the teamsters a fee to cross the stream," he added.

As they drove up to the moored ferry in the black buggy, a short man with a great shaggy head stood up and shaded his eyes with his hand as he gazed at the buggy. He jumped nimbly from the deck of the roughly built craft to the shore and walked up to the buggy with a peculiar rolling bowlegged gait.

"Marnin', Chic," the man drawled good-naturedly.

"Good morning, Orrin," Chic replied. "This scallywag is Brother Orrin Porter Rockwell, operator of the ferry," he said good-naturedly to John.

Turning to Rockwell, Chic said, "These people are the Evans family, John, Agnes and their daughter, Jenny. They plan to settle in Independence." As John was introduced and shook hands with Rockwell, he studied the man and thought that he closely resembled a great shaggy dog. His eyes were friendly and without malice and his long hair cascaded from under his slouch hat, adding to his resemblance to a sheep dog.

Port, as he was called, seemed unassuming and gregarious, unlike many of the Saints that John had met. Shaking hands with John, Port said proudly, "I was raised in Palmyra, New York, and I was among the first of the Saints to settle in

Missouri. My marriage to my wife, Luana, was the first wedding celebrated by the Saints in Jackson County."

After talking to Rockwell for a short time, they asked him to ferry the buggy across the Big Blue so they could tour the settlement. They crossed the broad stream and drove the buggy onto a dirt track leading west. The area was captivating, with rolling wooded hills and a veritable thicket of cottonwood trees along the banks of the placid Big Blue. At the base of a high hill, covered with gamagrass and hazel bushes, Chic stopped the buggy. "Would you like to hike up to the top of that little hill? I think you would enjoy the view," he said.

Agnes brusquely declined and pulled her coat closer around her throat. However, both John and Jenny were enthralled with the countryside and were eager to climb the hill and get a panoramic view of the area. After a short but arduous climb, they reached the crest and looked out over the valley of the Big Blue. As Jenny gazed down at the meandering stream and the rolling, wooded countryside, she understood why the Saints had become so captivated with Jackson County.

The late winter sun shone weakly on the rippling waters of the river and gave the stark branches of the cottonwoods a dreamlike quality. She turned and gazed toward the west, and the immensity of the prairie took her breath away. It seemed as if she was standing on the last hill of any size between the Missouri River and the "Shining Mountains," as the Rocky Mountains were often called. She stared hard to try to differentiate where the slate-gray sky met the dun-colored prairie but the exact spot where earth met sky was indistinct.

As she pondered the immensity of the Great Plains, she remembered reading about the hundreds of starving and ragged Indians streaming west to the arid reaches of "Indian Territory." These people had been uprooted by the ruthless policies of Andrew Jackson, beginning with the Cherokee people and the infamous Trail of Tears. She strained her eyes to determine if the tiny black dots she saw in the distance were Indian ponies, buffalo or shrubs. Straining her eyes made them water and she also found that a lump was rising in her throat as if she were going to weep.

Something about the great expanse of land spread before her touched her heart and caused emotion to rise in her chest. "It is," she thought, "as if the earth is whispering to me." She reflected again on her mother's obsession that man was given dominion over the earth and all living things and, for some unexplained reason, the thought seared her soul and immense sorrow gripped her heart.

Her father called her name twice before she realized that someone was speaking to her. He must have realized that she had felt something profound, because he gently put his arm around her waist and pulled her to him, and she turned and stifled a sob against his shoulder.

After they had toured the little settlement of Big Blue, Chic clucked to the two black mules and turned their noses east, toward Independence. Agnes had stridently expressed her desire to see the city of the Saints and had complained loudly about the cold and the dawdling of her daughter and husband; she was completely oblivious to her daughter's spiritual experience.

Orrin Rockwell had left the ferry moored on the west bank of the Big Blue, anticipating their return. Chic whistled to the two amenable mules and they stepped gracefully over the lip of the dock and onto the deck of the gently rocking ferry. Porter Rockwell smiled good-naturedly and stepped forward to chock the wheels of the buggy. John helped him place the chocks and returned with him to the stern of the ferry as the slender boatman cast off and began to pole the rough craft out into the current.

Rockwell was a cheerful man, but he was not very talkative. To break the uneasy silence, John asked, "Port, how did you happen to join the Saints?"

Porter considered the question.

"I knew Joseph Smith when he was a youth of about twenty," he replied. "He lived on a farm a few miles from my pa's homestead. When he said that he had got the golden plates from the Angel Moroni and translated the *Book of Mormon*, I knowed it was true and I was baptized and confirmed. Shortly after my confirmation, I received the priesthood by the laying on of hands." He looked John directly in the eye. "Have ya received the Holy Priesthood of God, Brother Evans?" he asked.

John considered the question and replied, "No, Mr. Rockwell, no ritual was performed that conveyed the priesthood on me."

Rockwell gave him a strange look, as if John's answer was completely out of context with the question.

"Brother Evans, each male member of the church who has reached the age of accountability and is worthy should want to receive the priesthood," he said. "The priesthood," he explained, "gives man the divine authority to act in the name of God to further the Lord's work on the earth. Through the priesthood, man can perform the holy ordinances of God here on earth and actually help bring about the Millennium. With the coming of the Millennium, the Saints will once again establish the kingdom of God on earth that the prophet Daniel referred to when he saw the stone roll forth and cover the entire world."

Rockwell paused and looked at John as if to ensure that he was grasping all this. Then he continued, "Only the Saints can act in the name of God through his divine authority to establish his kingdom in the last days." A faraway look came into Porter's eyes and he concluded. "When the Saints have established Zion, they shall judge all men and nations, for this is the only true religion."

Porter's speech seemed rehearsed, and John felt a little shiver of apprehension touch his heart when he remembered that Calvin and the inquisitors had burned heretics in the name of truth. John looked at Rockwell, and noticed that his eyes had the glazed-over look of a blind man.

He cleared his throat to get Rockwell's attention. "Is it true that only men may hold the priesthood?" he asked.

"Yep," replied Port. "Women are not allowed to act in the name and authority of God." John considered this remark and wondered why a just God would relegate half of his children to a position of minions because of their gender. He wondered if Agnes understood the ramifications of this issue, but he kept his reservations to himself.

During the long ride to Independence, Jenny was even more withdrawn than usual. However, Agnes made up for any lack of conversation by the others. She incessantly babbled to Chic about Independence being the site for the New Jerusalem and the eventual second coming of Christ. John wondered if Agnes really understood that women were relegated to a subservient role in the "true church."

It was late afternoon when they rode into the compact settlement of Independence. Chic sat on the spring seat and looked intently between the long ears of the two black mules with the resolve of a man who knew where he was going. He kept the mules in the center of the wide dirt street until they came to a modest cabin, where he pulled the buggy up to a hitching post. He deftly jumped out and tied the halter of the right mule to the post; as Chic secured the mules, a dapper man dressed in frock coat and top hat walked jauntily out of the door.

He stood patiently as the Evanses climbed out of the buggy and then stepped forward with his hand outstretched to John and proclaimed, "I am Bishop Edward Partridge, welcome to Zion. I expect that you are John Evans and this is your family."

Chic interceded. "Bishop Partridge," he said solemnly, "this is Brother John Evans, his wife Agnes and daughter Jenny."

Partridge was a small, nervous man, who seemed to be in perpetual motion. He immediately spoke his mind, without the pretense of small talk.

"Brother Evans," he said, "I've received a post from Bishop Whitney and he informs me that you're a trained schoolteacher. He also informs me that you haven't yet been ordained an elder in the holy Aaronic Priesthood. I'll assign you a building lot and schedule a date for your ordination. Also, because of your expertise as a teacher, we have decided to assign you to teach at the church school here in Independence. In addition to your work as a teacher, you'll be expected to work with others in building a cabin for your family and to donate several hours a week to community projects such as the construction of the temple. As you know, you're also expected to provide any excess property or money you may have or earn in the future to the church in accordance with the holy Order of Enoch."

John felt overwhelmed by the rapidfire list of assignments and information that Partridge had thrown at him. He looked at the bishop and merely bobbed his head like a sandpiper in agreement. With his instructions stated, Partridge turned and strode back into his home. John turned to Chic, as if for clarification, but Chic simply shrugged his shoulders.

After they had climbed into the buggy, Chic turned to John. "I was going to introduce you to Bishop William Phelps, but it is getting late and we need to find you a place to stay and get you settled."

John became reflective and Chic looked at him out of the corner of his eye. "Bishop Partridge seems a little rude because he is probably upset," he declared. "The prophet reprimanded him and received a revelation from God that chastised him for lack of faith. It seems," Chic continued, "that Bishop Partridge complained about the quality of land that Joseph selected for purchase by the church. Members aren't allowed to criticize those in authority who receive inspiration from God."

Chic elucidated. "W. W. Phelps received a letter from the prophet that described the revelation pertaining to Bishop Partridge's transgressions, which was read to the congregations in Missouri." Chic repeated part of the revelation from memory: "Yea, for this cause I have sent you hither, and have selected my servant Edward Partridge, and have appointed unto him his mission in this land. But if he repent not of his sins, which are unbelief and blindness of heart, let him take heed lest he fall. Behold his mission is given unto him, and it shall not be given again."

John became quiet as he thought about what Chic had said. He was a man who believed that criticism of leaders was an indication of a free society and a necessary element in any democratic community. He was beginning to have serious misgivings about the theocratic quality of the Saints. John believed that man had the right to determine the nature of God in his own mind and had always believed that a just God wouldn't concern himself with ordinances and rituals but would judge mankind by their actions and what was in their hearts.

He had grave reservations when he considered the concept of God selecting one man as his mouthpiece and allowing that man to dictate to his followers. However, John also knew his limitations, and he was aware that despite his reservations he would continue to submit to the dictates of the Saints and his wife because he didn't have the moral courage to defy either. John could not face the wrath and condemnation of Agnes or the thought of being socially ostracized by the Saints. Intuitively, he sought the acceptance of his peers and frantically avoided the malice of his spouse.

The Evanses spent the night in a rather spacious cabin of one of the more affluent Saints. In the morning, Chic arrived to pick them up in the little buggy, pulled by the same faithful mules. It was a pleasant March morning, with a hint of spring in the light breeze. A pale sun shone, but did little to drive the late winter chill from the air. As they drove through the thriving town of Independence, John couldn't help but feel the tension that seemed to hang in the air like a noxious mist.

They passed several heavy wagons loaded with hides and trade goods, driven by dirty, ragged and malevolent-looking teamsters. The drovers didn't wave in greeting; rather, they glared at the occupants of the buggy with a surly stare. It was obvious to John that the old settlers didn't accept or particularly like the Saints. As they passed one especially dirty, greasy teamster, he looked directly at the group in the buggy with a belligerent stare and deliberately turned toward them and spit a long, brown stream of tobacco juice in their direction. As the lumbering wagon passed, John felt a twinge of dread that he couldn't dispel and in his heart he had a premonition that he would die violently in Missouri.

Chic stopped the buggy in front of a building in the process of construction. There were ten or twelve Saints toiling assiduously on the masonry walls of the building. Chic called to one of them and a rather tall man with a heavy mustache and prominent chin stood and wiped the sweat from his brow. As John and his family climbed out of the buggy, the man walked briskly into the street. He stopped in front of John and extended his hand in greeting. "Good morning," he said. "I am Brother William Phelps and this building we're so diligently working on is the office and printing room of the newest and only newspaper in western Missouri, the *Evening and Morning Star*."

John took the proffered hand and greeted Phelps in return. "And I'm John Evans and this is my family," he said. John intentionally left out the peculiar title of "brother." Phelps didn't seem to notice this affront and plunged on, babbling enthusiastically about the future mouthpiece of the Lord.

"The *Evening and Morning Star*," said Phelps, "will serve to provide the Saints with all the news and happenings within the church. In addition," he continued, "it will provide the Saints with the revelations and writings of the prophet. I foresee," he exclaimed, "that the *Star* will provide the Saints with the divine truths they need to carry out the work of the Lord in these last days."

John nodded in affirmation, but he couldn't help thinking that the *Evening and Morning Star* would be the only newspaper in all of western Missouri. He had no doubt that the Missourians would eagerly seek any tabloid that provided some local news. Despite the fact that many of the old settlers were illiterate, he knew they would become familiar with the newspaper, because it was common on the frontier for a literate resident to read the papers to their less-educated colleagues in saloons, general stores and other common meeting places.

This thought brought a little prick of anxiety to John's heart; somehow he didn't like the idea of the old settlers being familiar with the intimate ideas and beliefs of the Saints. He had seen firsthand how sanctimonious and self-righteous the Saints could be and he had no illusions about how the old settlers would react to their fanatical tirades. He didn't share his misgivings with Phelps, but as the man blathered on about the forthcoming trumpet of the angels, John knew trouble was coming.

"So when do you plan to have the building finished and the press up and running?" John asked casually.

"I hope to publish the first edition in April of this year," Phelps replied. John made a mental note of the time of the first edition; he realized that if the *Star* came to fruition, it would be a significant event and would profoundly affect relations between the Saints and the old settlers.

As bishop and administrator for the affairs of the church in Missouri, Phelps made arrangements for living quarters for the family. He also assigned each member of the Evans family a job and a position. John was appointed to act as headmaster and teacher at the church school. He was also assigned to work an allotted number of hours each week on public works projects and on erecting cabins for the incoming Saints.

After much discussion and arguing with Agnes, Phelps agreed to allow her to work some time each week at his office, reviewing and documenting church doctrine and information pertinent to church members from letters, newspapers and other documents received from the church hierarchy in Kirkland. Although Phelps saw this position as basically symbolic, Agnes took her new authority very seriously.

Jenny was too old to attend grammar school and there was no institution of higher learning in the area. Phelps deduced that Jenny was in a rather delicate position. She was too young to be involved in serious community matters, but too old to attend regular grade school classes. He decided she should help her father a few hours a day as a teacher's assistant. When she wasn't working with her father, he told her to report to Sister Abigail Sorensen, who was responsible for overseeing the sisters making quilts, blankets and items of clothing for the poor Saints swarming into Independence.

Phelps turned to John and lowered his voice, as if discussing some clandestine subject. "Brother Evans," he began gravely, "your ordination as a deacon in the Aaronic Priesthood is scheduled for the next sacrament meeting, at 4:00 P.M. on Sunday. After you've proven your worthiness and faith, you'll be ordained an elder in the Melchizedek or higher priesthood." Phelps cleared his throat as a signal that he was through discussing confidential priesthood matters and informed the Evanses that a cabin had been rented for them from a wealthy Gentile named Lilburn W. Boggs. With that, Phelps mumbled good day to the Evanses and turned on his heel back to the task of laying the masonry for the *Evening and Morning Star* office.

That afternoon, Chic delivered them to the small but comfortable cabin they would be renting until their own home could be built with the help of the Saints. "Bishop Phelps has paid the rent to Mr. Boggs, who happens to be the lieutenant governor of Missouri," he said. "Boggs owns large tracts of land in the Independence area and is active in land speculation. In fact," he added, "the great influx of Saints has already caused some consternation between Boggs and the church."

The next few days were a whirlwind of activity for the Evans family. They spent several days moving into the cabin that would be their home for the next few months and arranging the living quarters. John met several times with Phelps to develop a schedule for teaching, working on the family cabin, and other duties assigned to him by the church officials. Agnes reported daily to Phelps and pored over letters and newspapers searching for any bit of information that she believed related to the Gospel or the imminent coming of the Messiah.

Even though the *Evening and Morning Star* office and printing press weren't ready for publication, Agnes fell into her new responsibility with the fervor of a fanatic, which she was. She spent long hours analyzing documents. Every earthquake, famine, or natural disaster she noted as a harbinger of the day "when the wicked would burn as stubble." Agnes loved to savor the thought of the wicked burning in eternal torment.

John quickly settled into his role as teacher and mentor to the myriad children who attended the grammar school. Phelps cautioned him to be ever mindful of the Gospel when he taught his little charges. According to Phelps, the minds of little children were easily swayed to the ways of the world, and, therefore, he expected John to teach only spiritually enlightening subjects. John wasn't quite sure what Phelps meant by this strange statement, but he couldn't imagine anything more enlightening than the study of literature, mathematics and history.

When John wasn't teaching, a priesthood member would assign him tasks for the building of Zion. This usually involved helping poor members erect homes, including his own, and surveying and laying out streets and public works according to the prophet's plan for the City of Zion.

After attending to their responsibilities each day, the Evans family came together every night in their little rented cabin. Only Agnes seemed energized, while John and Jenny conveyed a need to recharge. Whether the rest of her family was listening or not, Agnes spoke loudly of the discoveries she had made in her research and continued reading of her holy book. John had found a little cranny in the cabin where he could store his books and he created a sanctuary to shut out the tension that surrounded him. Jenny would often close herself in her room, reading John's books or writing in a journal she had brought with her. Agnes had found her paradise, while her husband and daughter struggled with the new world around them.

Chapter 8

⌇⌇⌇

Jenny loved helping her father teach the schoolchildren. They ranged in age from six or seven to nearly her age. They arrived each morning at the little log school, dressed in ragged overalls and homespun shirts of linsey-woolsey. They usually carried a little tin lunch box and a bottle of milk. The girls wore homespun dresses and heavy work shoes, much like their male counterparts. They sat on rough-hewn log benches and wrote their lessons on small individual slate chalkboards.

Jenny found that she was much more sophisticated than most of the children who attended the school. Many of them came from desperately poor families and had received little if any prior education. To Jenny it was refreshing to interact with adolescents rather than the stuffy old "brothers" and "sisters" that she had been forced to associate with for the last fortnight. She loved to discuss the works of Milton, Jefferson, and James Fenimore Cooper. Despite the fact that many of these adolescents were barely literate, she found that they were eager to learn and loved to discuss academic subjects.

However, Jenny wasn't enthusiastic about her work with Sister Abigail Sorensen. She reported to the home of Sister Sorensen every Monday and Thursday afternoon, where she was expected to help the sisters with quilting, knitting sweaters and sewing clothing for the poor. Jenny wasn't fond of handiwork and, worse, she found that the sewing sessions turned into discussions of the revelations, miracles and rapture of the Gospel.

Abigail was very fond of saying that women in the church received their great blessings through the priesthood of their husbands. Jenny once asked her how single women would receive these blessings and Sister Abigail responded by insisting that Jenny get down on her knees and ask forgiveness from God for her scurrilous attitude. Abigail later informed Jenny that true daughters of the church sought marriage to a righteous man and any woman who desired to remain single must be immoral or decadent.

One of Sister Abigail's favorite subjects was the *Book of Mormon* and its assertion that American Indians were actually descendants of the Ten Tribes of Israel. She was fond of saying that Indians who accepted the Gospel would became "white and delightsome." Jenny knew better than to question this dubious claim, but she wondered why the white race was considered delightsome, when they enslaved blacks and slaughtered or drove the original inhabitants of the land from their homes.

Sister Abigail never tired of relating fantastic stories of the prophet and other apostles of the church. She told Jenny of an incident during a meeting of the church hierarchy. Brigham Young, a popular church authority, had been asked to address the group and was so overcome with the spirit of God that he spoke in tongues. Later, Brother Joseph told the group that Brother Brigham was speaking the pure language of Father Adam. Jenny pondered this "miraculous" event and wondered why God would inspire Brigham to speak this ancient language if no one understood what he said. However, she remained taciturn because she had no desire to spend forty-five minutes on her knees asking for forgiveness for her derisive attitude.

In one of her more cavalier moments, Jenny asked Sister Sorensen to explain the essence of the Gospel. Abigail gave her a stunned look, as if Jenny had asked her to describe some intimate sex act. She then rolled her eyes toward heaven as if to seek divine inspiration and launched into a patronizing, brief description of the Gospel. "God," she said, "after centuries of silence, now spoke directly to man through his mouthpiece, the prophet." She explained, as if to a slow child, "God has given the keys to his kingdom to his prophet and church members can now act on earth through the authority of God."

Finally, she described the "gifts" of the Holy Ghost and the authority to heal the sick and cast out demons that each priesthood member received through the ordinance of the laying on of hands. Sister Sorensen assured Jenny that no one would be saved in the celestial kingdom or even the terrestrial glory unless they were baptized and confirmed members of the church and testified to the truthfulness of the Gospel.

It seemed illogical to Jenny that God would require membership in some arbitrary organization before even a gentle and caring person could receive his love and guidance. Nor could she understand why God would withhold his love and counsel from an honest, compassionate and moral person just because they hadn't undergone some ritual such as the laying on of hands. Jenny had an open and searching mind, much like her father's, and she adhered to his liberal beliefs concerning the nature of God. She was very much a child of her father, for she found more logic in the uninhibited ideas of Unitarianism than the conformist dogma of the Saints. But, like her father, she lacked the audacity to stand alone according to the dictates of her heart and she couldn't defy Sister Sorensen or her mother.

All members of the Evans family were very busy that late winter and spring and time passed at an astonishing pace. John was walking to the little school one morning and noticed that the sky had lost the dreary slate-gray hue of late winter and was beginning to display the subtle blue of spring. He was amazed to see a faint twinge of green on the rolling hills to the west that suggested the earth was awakening. The hint of spring lifted John's spirits and he felt happier than he had in weeks.

He had never really been comfortable with the principles of the church and as time went on he found himself questioning the teachings of the prophet. However, he kept his reservations to himself and never voiced his doubts to either Agnes or his associates in the church. He had not become close to any of the church members because he could never share the intimacies of his mind and soul with them. He knew if he did voice his doubts, he would be immediately chastised and dragged before a bishop or apostle to answer for his lack of faith.

He knew the story of Sidney Rigdon, one of Joseph's most trusted counselors, who warned the Saints at a meeting in Kirtland that he feared that the authority to act in God's name was being withdrawn because of the wickedness of the members. Rigdon was publicly rebuked by the prophet for this imprudent remark and shunned by the members until he begged for forgiveness during a church meeting. Rigdon wasn't rebuked so much for the audacity of his statement, but because he circumvented the prophet's authority. Joseph publicly delivered Sidney to the buffetings of Satan, claiming he couldn't be forgiven until he underwent this trial, and many claimed that Sidney was violently thrown about in his private chambers by the Evil One. John believed the story reflected an arrogant and autocratic attitude on the part of the prophet and of the church. He wanted to speak out on the matter in public, but when the opportunity arose, he found he was rooted to his pew.

One beautiful warm morning in June, John was walking to school through the growing metropolis of Independence. He marveled at how fast the little frontier ͞ ͞ since he had arrived. The Saints had continued to pour in from ͞ ͞ ͞ ͞ ere 1,300 of them in Independence in the spring of 1833. ͞ ͞ ͞ members was a growing irritation among the Missourians, who began to grumble about the Saints settling on the best land. The Saints didn't only settle on the land owned by the church, but the poorer members were too impatient to wait until the church could purchase more land and they "squatted" on unoccupied property.

John noticed this growing tension between the old settlers and the church members. It reminded him of the "electric" feeling that permeated the air before one of the violent thunderstorms common to the Great Plains broke over the city.

John had forgotten his misgiving about the imminent publishing of the first edition of the *Evening and Morning Star*. As John walked by the building that housed the printing press and office of the Star, he nearly collided with Phelps, who came dashing down the steps.

"Brother Evans," Phelps called out. "Stop a minute; I have something exciting and wonderful to show you." John stopped and turned to face the eager Phelps. "Look at this," he exclaimed, holding out a freshly printed newspaper. Instantly, John realized that the long-awaited first edition of the *Evening and Morning Star* had finally seen the light of day. He felt a pang of fear as he took the paper that Phelps insistently pressed into his hands.

John arrived at the little school before any of the students and he walked quickly to his battered pine desk at the front of the room and laid the paper out on the marred wood surface. As he looked through the printed columns, he inwardly groaned and an icy cold fist of fear squeezed his heart. The first page of the paper reiterated national and world news, gleaned from other papers and publications. However, each account of a natural disaster or calamity was followed by an editorial affirming that the Four Horsemen were riding hard and the last days were imminent. An article on the first page immediately snagged John's eye. It was titled "From the *Book of Mormon*" and it cut to the heart of the matter.

It began: "Harken, O ye Gentiles, and hear the words of Jesus Christ, the Son of the living God, which he has commanded me that I should speak concerning you: for behold he commandeth me that I should write, saying, Turn all ye Gentiles from your wicked ways, and repent of all your evil doings, of your lyings and deceivings, and of your whoredoms, and of your secret abominations and your idolatries, and your murders, and your priestcrafts, and your envyings, and your strifes, and from your wickedness and abominations, and come unto me, and be baptized in my name, that ye shall receive remission of your sins, and be filled with the Holy Ghost that you may be numbered with my people, which are of the house of Israel."

John's practiced eye noted that the entire statement was made up of one long rambling sentence. However, that was not what chilled John's soul. He realize that in the very first edition of the mouthpiece of God, Phelps had cast down gauntlet to the Missourians: join us or be cast out. John realized that with these indiscreet words the first step was taken toward bloodshed and war in western Missouri, and he knew implicitly that his wife had played a major part in setting the stage for the impending calamity.

Despite John's misgivings, there was no outbreak of violence following the release of the first edition of the *Star*. To be sure, there were incidents that reflected the growing hostility between the Saints and the Missourians, but for the most part, resentment simmered just below the boiling point. Port Rockwell reported that a Brother Edwards was awakened one night by wild yelling and found his haystack on fire. Some of the other Saints in the outlying regions like Big Blue heard insults hurled from the night and in some cases rocks were thrown as well as epithets. But only a few windows were broken, not the fragile peace that prevailed on the rolling prairies of bluestem.

As the warm days of summer rolled pleasurably by, John began to feel a deep sense of relief. The publication of the *Star* hadn't increased the instances of harassment and occasional violence between the Saints and the old settlers. However, he couldn't shake the gnawing feeling that a gathering storm was about to descend on the people of western Missouri.

One day as summer began to wane and the days grew cooler and more comfortable, John borrowed Chic Simmons's buggy and team of docile Missouri mules and drove out to Port Rockwell's ferry.

As John drove up to the ferry, Rockwell was bent over the side of the rustic, cumbersome craft mending a line or checking the planking. As he heard the crunch of the buggy wheels in the gravel, he raised his shaggy head and squinted at the little buggy and team. He raised his arm in salutation when he recognized the rig and its driver. As John climbed down and approached the landing, Port greeted him.

"How air ya, Brother Evans," he proclaimed good-naturedly.

"Very well, thank you, Porter," replied John. "I was out for a little drive and I thought I would go by Wilson's store for a cool beer, since the sun is warm today."

Port looked at John out of the corner of his eye and exclaimed, "I dunno, Brother Evans, if that is a good idea. I was over there the other day and them old boys that hang out there seem a mite surly these days. Besides," said Port, "I hears that some o' the Saints is sayin' that the prophet is against drinkin' liquor."

John smiled matter-of-factly at Port and replied, "Oh, I don't think they will bother me. I really am not the fighting or arguing kind."

"I know that," replied Port, "but them guys is a little fussed up since they's been reading the *Star* around the cracker barrel over there. I'd feel better if ya didn't go, but if ya insist on stopping there, maybe I should go with ya."

John drove the little buggy onto the ferry and climbed down to talk to Port as he poled the craft across the Big Blue, which was narrow and low this late in the summer. "There's no need for you to leave your business and go with me," replied John, "I will be just fine. I just want to see for myself how the old settlers feel about the Saints these days. Besides, I really do want a cool beer."

Port gave him a jaundiced look and said, "Wull, watch your back and if ya ain't back in an hour, I'll come a-lookin' fer ya."

John waved at the grizzled ferryman as he drove the rig off the deck and onto the dirt track leading to Big Blue and Colesville. Port squinted into the lowering sun and watched him go with a definite feeling of misgiving in his gut. Twenty minutes later, John turned onto a side road and drove through a grove of huge cottonwoods, which cast a pleasant shade on his sweaty face. Soon he pulled up in front of Wilson's General Store and tied the team to the hitching rail. He noticed that there were several saddled mules and horses standing patiently in front of the rough log building.

He pushed the rough plank door open and stepped into the cool, dim interior of the log building. As his eyes became accustomed to the dim light, he noticed a large table toward the back of the store where several men were playing cards. Along one wall there was a bar of sorts made by placing a plank across two whiskey barrels. He walked up to the bar and faced a short, stout, bald man, who was trying in vain to wipe a glass clean with a very dirty towel.

The little bartender reminded John of a newt, with his moist, shiny skin and yellow reptilian eyes. He looked at John with a churlish stare and gruffly inquired, "What ya want?"

John smiled at the little gnome of a man and pleasantly asked, "Good afternoon, may I have a beer?"

The bartender looked at John with his snakelike eyes and snarled, "We only got beer from Saint Louis, what is shipped in on the steamboat, and it's twenty-five cents a glass." John winced at the price, but he was thirsty and had not tasted a beer for some time. His heart was set on the bitter flavor of hops and he dug into his watch pocket and pulled out a Spanish 8 reales piece, which had been quartered. He tossed the quartered coin on the bar and smiled again at the little troll with the apron.

The bartender glared back and took a dirty glass from a shelf on the dusty wall and tipped it against a spigot protruding from a barrel. He pulled the handle, quickly filling the glass with the amber brew. John eyed the glass thirstily, with its half-inch head of frothy foam, and smacked his lips. Just as the bartender placed the glass in front of him, John was aware of someone standing next to him. Before he even noticed the bulk of the man in the corner of his eye, John detected the strong, pungent odor of an unwashed body.

He turned his head and his breath caught in his throat. Standing next to him was a giant of a man, who must have stood well over six feet. He had huge shoulders and the muscles in his forearms knotted like writhing snakes. John looked up into the leviathan's face and was greeted by a sneer that revealed three or four long yellow teeth jutting from puffy gums. The big man wore a shaggy, untrimmed beard and the slouch hat on his head was stained with sweat and dried blood. John noticed dried blood smeared on the man's hat and clothes and surmised he must be a professional buffalo hunter. He was wearing a buckskin shirt and trousers that were rancid and stained with sweat. A huge knife in a beaded buckskin scabbard hung from the stranger's belt.

He glared down at John from under shaggy eyebrows and grunted, "Ain't seed you 'round here before, has I?"

John extended his hand and replied pleasantly, "No, I've never stopped at Wilson's before. My name is John Evans." The man eyed John's hand, but made no effort to reach for it.

The hunter looked down his bumpy, blotchy nose at John and grunted, "Ya looks like one of them Saints—is ya one of them Bible-thumpin' idjits?" John knew before he spoke that this man meant to force him into a fight and he felt fear rise in his stomach like bitter bile.

"If you are asking if I am a member of the Church of Jesus Christ," John said amiably, "yes, I am, but I don't believe in forcing my opinion on others."

"Angus there has been readin' that *Star* to us, and we don' like bein' tol' that God is goin' ta' drive us out so's ya kin' have inhairtances." The man snarled in John's face. "Sides, ya think them Injuns is human, and think they is like white men. What is ya, squaw humpers? Besides, ya is nigger-lovin' Northerners—first thing ya knows, y'all have them niggers thinkin' they is like white folks and they'll cut our throats in our sleep."

John had just opened his mouth to speak to explain that he didn't want any trouble and he didn't see the vicious blow coming. The behemoth smashed him in the side of the face with a fist the size of a Virginia ham. John heard a loud humming in his ears and bright points of light swirled before his eyes. The force of the blow lifted John's feet nearly off the floor and the back of his head hit the rough plank floor with a sickening thud. The huge man bent to grab John by the coat and hoist him to his feet, but he froze in place when a shrill voice from the door ordered, "Hold it there, hoss."

Out of the corner of his eye, the hunter saw a dim figure standing in the door holding a huge horse pistol. Porter Rockwell could feel his heart beating in his throat and he knew that he was in a precarious position. The place was crowded with eight or ten mean-looking men who turned in unison when Porter spoke.

The hunter turned toward Rockwell and snarled, "Ya better drop that hog leg, 'cuz ya's outnumbered, and y'all will only get one shot off 'fer we git ya."

Porter stared into the face of the huge, greasy hunter and said in an even voice, "That is probably true, friend, but you're the one that is gonna stop this slug."

The hunter stared into the fifty-caliber bore of the big horse pistol and his face blanched. "Ah don't want no trouble with ye," he stammered.

One of the men around the table slowly rose to his feet. "You git 'em, Lem, he ain't goin' to shoot ya," he said. However, as Lem looked into Porter's eyes, he knew for sure that if he made any hostile move, Port would, in fact, shoot him. Lem's eyes darted toward the men in the back and then returned to Porter like two circling blowflies. Porter could read the intense fear in the man's eyes and for the first time since he stepped in the door, he thought he and John had a chance to escape from the place with their lives.

Porter flicked the barrel of the heavy pistol toward Lem menacingly.

"Now then, Lem, you just pick that man up and bring him here," he commanded. Lem thought about pulling the huge bowie knife from his belt, but something in Rockwell's eyes and manner told him that if he did, Rockwell would shoot him. Lem had seen what a fifty-caliber ball could do to a man and he didn't want his lungs and other vitals splattered against the wall. He bent down again and almost gently picked John up by his shoulders. John was dimly aware of someone lifting him and he felt his feet touch the floor.

He tried to walk, but he could do little more than shuffle his feet. Lem almost tenderly lifted John and, holding him around the waist, he half carried and half dragged him to where Rockwell stood. The toes of John's boots made a screeching noise as they scraped across the floor and the men around the table watched in astonishment. One of them made a slight move toward Lem and John, and Rockwell shifted his dark eyes toward the dim form. "Make a move and I'll blow Lem's guts all over you," he hissed. The man froze with his hand spread at his waist, as if reaching for something under his coat.

Lem gave a furtive look toward the table and said in a strangled voice, "Don't do nothin', Abe, ah know he'll kill me."

Port slipped his arm around John. "Can you stand, Brother Evans?" he asked. John was aware of a splitting headache and suddenly realized that he couldn't open his left eye. He tried to stand and swayed back and forth precariously. His stomach heaved and he felt as if he would lose the contents of his guts at any moment.

Gradually, his head cleared and he carefully put his weight on both feet. "I think I can walk if I lean on you, Porter," he mumbled through puffed lips.

Porter slowly backed out of the door, with John leaning heavily against his shoulder. He kept the big horse pistol leveled toward the plank door, which was hanging ajar. When they reached the buggy, Rockwell leaned against the spokes of the wheel and allowed John to slowly and painfully ease himself into the seat. Rockwell quickly untied the team and leaped into the seat next to John, all the while keeping the big bore of the pistol aimed at the door. He had tied his own mule to the back of the buggy, anticipating the need for a quick departure.

As he clucked to the mules, he kept his eyes glued to the dark wedge of the half-opened door, but he noticed with relief that the door remained motionless. As they drove away, he kept glancing furtively over his shoulder, expecting to hear the sounds of pursuit, but he heard nothing but the crunch of the iron wheels in the gravel and the distant, whimsical song of a meadowlark.

Rockwell kept the mules at a fast trot and they soon arrived at the Rockwell cabin. As they drove into the yard, Porter yelled loudly at the cabin. Almost immediately his wife, Luana, appeared at the door, holding their year-old daughter Emily in her arms. She rushed out and helped Porter get John down from the buggy and into the cabin. They laid him on a cornhusk bed and Luana examined his face. She was appalled to find that John's left eye was swollen completely shut and a trickle of dried blood ran from the corner of his eye and down his jaw. The huge, angry, purple bruise covered the entire left side of John's face from his eyebrow to the point of his jaw.

Porter and Luana were relieved to find that John could talk rationally and answer their questions quickly. After forcing the lid of John's left eye open, Luana found that the eyeball was basically undamaged and no facial bones seemed to be broken. She went to the well and wet a rag in cool water and laid it on John's face. Despite the fact that she laid the rag gently on his cheek, John winced in pain and jerked his head away from her tender hands. Porter asked John how he was feeling, and he replied in a hoarse voice, "I feel terrible, I have a dreadful headache, it feels like someone is sharpening a knife on the inside of my skull and I feel very nauseous, my stomach is churning."

"I think you may have a concussion," replied Luana. "I believe that you better stay here until you feel better."

John tried to sit up too quickly and groaned softly in his throat. He lay back slowly on the pillow and said, "I can't stay, I have to get home. Jenny and Agnes will be very worried and I have to get ready to teach in the morning."

"Don't worry," replied Porter, "I will ride to Independence and tell 'em what happened and tell 'em ya will have to take the day off tomorrow. Those kids will get along without ya. Besides, ya are in no shape to ride in that buggy all the way to Independence."

John stayed at the Rockwells' cabin for three days before he felt well enough to ride the eight miles back to Independence in the jolting, swaying buggy. He profusely thanked Rockwell for rescuing him from the Missourians at Wilson's store. He was amazed that Port had followed him to Wilson's so soon. When he asked Rockwell why he checked on him so quickly, Porter considered the question for a moment and then matter-of-factly attributed his timely appearance to the still, small voice of the Holy Ghost.

When he finally felt well enough to get up and sit in the spring seat of the buggy, Porter drove John to Independence. During the long ride, John sat on the rough seat, holding a cool, wet rag against his cheek. When they arrived at the Evanses's cabin, the door sprang open and Jenny rushed out and ran up to the buggy with tears in her eyes. When she saw the huge, purple-green bruise on the side of John's face, she could not hold back her emotion, and hot tears burst forth in torrents. After John had slowly and painfully climbed down from the buggy, she rushed to him and gently laid her head on his chest, sobbing softly into his coat.

Agnes came to the door as John hobbled up the steps and gave him an insensitive look. With a pious toss of her head, she said, "If you would stay away from liquor and the places where it is used, this would never have happened. You need to associate only with God's chosen people and then the Devil won't have sway over you. Besides, if you took your priesthood ordination seriously, the Holy Ghost would guide you away from such evil places."

Jenny gave her mother a withering look, but John said nothing and painfully walked into the house. Jenny turned to Luana and Porter with shining eyes. "Thank you so much for taking care of my father. I don't know how to repay you," she said.

"You're welcome, child; your father has thanked us at least twenty times for taking care of him," Luana replied. After Jenny turned and walked back into the house, Luana and Porter took the buggy back to Chic and then both climbed onto the back of Porter's sturdy mule. On the long ride home, Luana broke the silence and said emphatically, "Port, that woman has no feeling for poor John at all. It is a good thing that he has a loving daughter, or he would have no one who loved him."

Physically, John mended quickly. The headaches went away in about a week, and after a fortnight the great bruise had faded to a slight, yellow tinge on his left cheek. However, the damage to his psyche went much deeper. At night, he frequently dreamed of the confrontation and in his recurring nightmares, he saw the naked hatred in the greasy hunter's eyes. In his heart, John knew that violence was brewing on the Missouri frontier like the ugly black-green clouds that brought tornadoes.

He revered Porter Rockwell for the courage and spirit he had showed by striding into the hostile atmosphere of Wilson's store to rescue him. He knew that if the roles were reversed, he would never have summoned the courage to go into that place to save Rockwell, and he cursed himself for his lack of spirit. Though he pushed it from his mind like something distasteful, he knew that something much worse was coming and he prayed that he wouldn't falter when his time came.

The last days of summer passed quietly and pleasantly by, and soon the nights turned chilly and the leaves on the cottonwoods blazed in brilliant yellow. After the attack on John in Wilson's General Store, relations between the old settlers and the Saints settled down to a festering hatred that rarely exploded into physical violence. The harassment of the Saints in the outlying areas continued on a sporadic basis, but only involved a few broken windows and an occasional burned haystack. With the coming of winter and cold weather, the old settlers seemed to hole up and things settled down to nothing more than a few surly looks and muttered oaths as Saint and Gentile passed on the streets of Independence.

PART FOUR

Expulsion from Eden

Chapter 9

J ohn spent the winter teaching, finishing the family cabin and working on community projects that were assigned to him by the priesthood presidency. Despite his work and church membership, John never felt accepted by the men of the priesthood, probably because he lacked their zeal for the Gospel and was a free thinker. He never really believed that devils and disease could be cast out of a suffering body by the laying on of hands and his half-hearted attempts to appear as one of the faithful lacked credibility. On several occasions, Bishop Phelps had asked him to remain after a church meeting and berated him for his lack of conviction.

Phelps repeatedly told John that he had a sacred trust in his position as teacher and he must instill in the children a love of the prophet and the Gospel of Jesus Christ. John had no problem with instilling the principles of Christianity into the children that he taught, but he balked at teaching them values that he considered intolerant and bigoted. He never really believed that God would favor one person over another because they had undergone some seemingly ludicrous religious ritual. He inwardly cringed when a dedicated Saint rose in a sacrament meeting and derided the Gentiles as ungodly and called for their eviction from Zion. In his heart, John ardently believed that tolerance and acceptance were the key principles of Christian theology.

John was acutely aware that he wasn't totally accepted by his brethren in the priesthood. As time passed, this became even more evident when John wasn't selected to be ordained to the higher priesthood and remained a lowly deacon, while others who were recent converts were quickly ordained as elders and promoted to higher offices. John never mentioned this rebuff, but Bishop Phelps told him during one of their meetings that until he showed more passion for the Gospel, the Lord wouldn't see fit to select him for the Melchizedek priesthood. Although John never wanted a higher office or advancement in the church, he became lonely in his isolation.

John longed for someone with whom he could discuss religion, philosophy and politics. Agnes had become even more fanatical in her convictions than many of the more ardent Saints. She seemed to sense John's skepticism of the Gospel and eschewed him even more. In his exile, John turned to his daughter for comfort. He found that he sought her conversation during meals and in the long evenings. Agnes rarely spoke to him unless he asked her a direct question, which she answered in single words. John tried to develop a more intimate relationship with her, but when he laid his hand on her shoulder in a gesture of affection, she shrugged it off as if it were a disgusting insect. Jenny was aware that Agnes and the community at large regarded John with blatant aloofness and she compensated by showing him the love and compassion that she actually felt for him.

With the coming of spring, Independence began to buzz with activity like a beehive. Converts continued to pour into Zion and most of them came from the northern states, Canada and northern Europe. On one hot July morning, John strolled by the newspaper office and, on a whim, stopped by to see if Phelps had the latest edition ready for circulation. As he stepped into the office, Phelps looked up from his desk and said, "Good morning, Brother Evans, on your way to school?"

John acknowledged Phelps's greeting and inquired if the most recent edition of the *Star* was printed.

Phelps smiled and handed John the paper. John thanked him, tucked the paper under his arm and hurried off to the school so he would have time to review the news before his students arrived. He sat down at his desk and spread the paper out on its battered surface. Under the familiar masthead he noticed an article entitled "Beware of False Prophets." He glanced through the article and observed that it contained Phelps's usual harangue against Gentiles and other religions, including a diatribe against false prophets who come in sheep's clothing. John skimmed the bombast and then scanned on down the page until he came to an article headlined "Free People of Color."

The first paragraph of the article suggested the topic. "To prevent any misunderstanding among the churches abroad, respecting free people of color, who may think of coming to the western boundaries of Missouri, as members of the church, we quote the following clauses from the Laws of Missouri."

John's heart leaped into his throat because he knew that Phelps had inadvertently thrown down the gauntlet to the Gentiles of Missouri. Unlike Phelps, John was acutely aware that one of the issues that festered in the flesh of the old settlers like a poisonous thorn was that most of the Saints were from the northern states and the Missourians suspected they were abolitionists at heart. He knew that

Phelps's words would appear to the Missourians as an invitation for free blacks to immigrate to the region.

John shivered as he thought of Lem; he knew that the hunter had intended to seriously injure him, basically because he considered him an Indian lover and an abolitionist. In the border states like Missouri, slavery was an even more volatile issue than in the South and the despised abolitionists were often dealt with violently. As John stared at the headline, he knew that the Saints would pay in blood for Phelps's indiscretion.

John leaped to his feet and, gripping the paper like a club, he ran out the door and down the street to the office of the *Star*. As he was running up the steps, he nearly collided with Phelps, who came striding down the stairs with a self-satisfied smile on his face. "Well, good morning, Brother Evans," he said, tipping his stylish top hat. John ignored the greeting and, unfolding the paper, he thrust it into Phelps's face.

"Do you know what you've done?" John shouted at Phelps.

Phelps gaped at him as if he were insane, and stammered, "What do you mean, Brother Evans?"

John gave Phelps an incredulous look and replied, "William, don't you see? The article in the *Star* will appear to the old settlers as if you are encouraging Negroes to migrate to Missouri. This is a slave state, and a border state. The old settlers will interpret your article as an attempt to overrun this area with free Negroes and destroy the institution of slavery."

A light of understanding slowly dawned on Phelps's face and his jaw dropped as he realized the damage he had done. He stared at John for a moment as sweat beads grew on his brow like little mushrooms. He exclaimed, "I will print a retraction and I will state that we don't want Negroes to join the church." With that Phelps turned and ran up the stairs and into the door of the two-story brick building.

As promised, Phelps immediately published a retraction of the previous inflammatory article, in which he said that the original article had been misinterpreted and the intent of the article was to actually discourage blacks from immigrating to Zion and to prevent them from becoming members of the church.

John was appalled at Phelps's reply and considered it a feeble attempt to deny his mistake, one that smacked of racism. When he had first heard the term "fair and delightsome" applied to the Caucasian race, he saw it for what it was: an attempt to justify racism and glorify one ethnic group over all others. The prophet actually preached that when a Saint accepted the Gospel and received the Holy Ghost, the spirit of the Holy Ghost purged out the old blood from his veins and the convert essentially became of the blood of Israel. John had always found this idea humorous, for he knew that the seed of Abraham were actually Semitic people and relatively dark skinned. The prophet later received a revelation saying that blacks were the descendants of Noah's son Ham, who carried the curse of Cain, and that they had refused to take a stand in the War in Heaven between Lucifer and the followers of Christ, therefore they were cursed with a dark skin and were denied the privilege of holding the priesthood. This became the policy of the church.

W. W. Phelps's attempt to defuse the situation by printing a retraction, however, did nothing to placate the Missourians. The day after the article appeared in the *Star*, hand-printed flyers appeared all over town. They announced that a citizens' committee had been formed to deal with the "Mormon Question," and urged the Gentile citizens to meet at the courthouse on Saturday evening to draw up a list of demands to be presented to the Saints.

That Saturday evening, John stood at the doorway to his little cabin and watched dozens of rough men wending their way toward the courthouse. He knew that they were meeting to discuss the problem of the Saints in Missouri and he knew that they would draft their demands for the Saints to move on. John understood that the local leaders of the church couldn't make a decision and give the Missourians an answer without consulting the apostles in Kirtland. He also guessed correctly that they would never give up Zion without a struggle and he dreaded what he knew was coming.

That night, John watched from his front porch as hundreds of pinpricks of light danced around the courthouse square like fireflies. He knew they were torches carried by the old settlers, who were discussing what to do about the Saints pouring into Jackson County like locusts. The old settlers complained bitterly that the Saints would eventually control the political system of the county and elect their own representatives. The thought of abolitionists and religious fanatics controlling the political offices of the area terrified them.

At the courthouse that evening, the old settlers drew up a manifesto and a list of five demands. The Missourians stipulated that no more Saints should migrate to Jackson County and that those Saints that had already settled there should sell their property and move on. They also demanded that the *Star* cease publication and all church-owned businesses should close immediately. Finally, they alluded to the Saints' love of the gift of tongues and implied that if the demands weren't met, the Saints could discern through this gift what the future would bring.

During the dialogue, the Missourians fortified themselves with cheap whiskey, and by the time the manifesto was hammered out, they were ready to take action. John was sitting on his porch listening to the whippoorwills when he heard a vociferous shout from the area of the courthouse and watched the flickering lights of the torches converge and then suddenly move north on Main Street. He knew by the deep roar that the mob had turned ugly and he jumped to his feet and ran in the general direction the throng was moving.

Breathing hard, he found himself in the shadows, across the street from the home of Bishop Edward Partridge. Once more, John's courage failed him and he slunk into an alley between two buildings and watched from the shadows. Two men from the rabble detached themselves and, mounting the steps of Partridge's little home, they beat on the door, demanding that the church leader come out.

A shaft of light illuminated the faces of the two men as Partridge opened the door. John heard him ask in a quavering voice what the men wanted, and he heard someone reply that they wanted Partridge to agree to the freshly written demands of the citizens' group. There was some low murmuring and then he heard Partridge say in a loud voice, "I cannot agree to these stipulations until I have consulted with the church apostles." A woman screamed and the men grabbed Partridge and dragged him into the center of the street.

John felt his heart beating fast and sweat stood out on his forehead. He slunk back farther into the sheltering darkness of the alley, but he couldn't take his eyes off the terrible scene that played out in the wide street. The moon was at its zenith and the street was bathed in a surreal light. To John, the struggling figures in the center of the dirt street resembled actors from a Shakespearean tragedy, acting out a scene under wavering gaslights.

He heard Edward Partridge scream again. "Please do not strip me naked before my family and here in the street!" he begged. One of the men muttered something that John couldn't make out and then several more figures converged on Partridge. John could hear the hapless bishop shriek above the shouting of the mob and he heard the distinct sound of ripping clothing.

A man yelled, "Goddamn, Angus, git over here with that tar an' them feathers." A dim figure holding a bag detached from the mob and ran to the struggling figures in the road.

John heard Edward Partridge beg, "No, no, please, for the love of God, do not defile me so!" Someone let out a loud guffaw and Partridge's screams became muffled and unintelligible.

Through the din, someone yelled, "That's enough with him; let's go take care of Phelps and that fuckin' newspaper." Like some grotesque beast, the mob abruptly left the figure lying in the street and assembled itself into an undulating black mass and rushed off down the street toward the office of the *Evening and Morning Star*.

As the shouting of the rabble died down, John cautiously crept out of his sanctuary in the shadows and walked slowly over to the moaning figure of Bishop

Partridge. As he reached the spot where the bishop lay, Partridge's wife, Lydia, leaped from the porch of their cabin, where she had watched the humiliation of her husband, and ran shrieking up to the form of the bishop, who was struggling to rise. In the pale moonlight, the feathers and tar that besmirched Edward's nearly naked body looked like blood and ragged skin. Lydia placed both hands over her mouth and began to moan like a phantom.

As John reached Partridge, he was on his knees struggling to rise to his feet. John took his arm and helped him rise on wobbly legs. Mrs. Partridge lost her paralysis and seized her husband's other arm. Between the two they finally got the bishop into the little cabin. As they entered, six children of assorted ages gawked at their father with wide, frightened eyes, but they said nothing.

In the flickering light of the oil lamp, John could see that the other man's body was liberally smeared with black, sticky tar and generous dollops of chicken feathers. As they lay the moaning Partridge on the floor, several Saints rushed in to the crowded cabin to assist their bishop. John quickly examined Edward and couldn't find any obvious injuries. He asked him if he was hurt, and Partridge replied, "Oh, Brother Evans, it burns so, I cannot stand the pain." John suddenly realized that his hands were stinging as if they were on fire and he quickly realized that the tar had been mixed with acid or some caustic substance.

He looked around wildly and shouted at the little group of Saints that had gathered in the cramped room. "Get some turpentine; we must get this tar off his body before it eats his flesh."

Someone rushed from the room to retrieve the turpentine and others went to get soap, hot water and rags to wipe the gooey mess from Edward's body. After he determined that Partridge was not seriously injured and others had gathered and were cleaning the tar from him, John quickly left the little cabin and slunk out into the night.

As he walked up the street, John could hear the mob yelling and screaming in the vicinity of the newspaper office. He reflected on his ostensible cowardice and he realized that he had been emotionally unable to confront the mob that was tarring and feathering Bishop Partridge. He thought back to the bone-chilling fear he felt when Lem confronted him and he suffered a searing sense of shame because he didn't stand up to the hulking thug. As John considered the situation, he cursed himself for his inability to stand up to his domineering wife and find the moral courage to express his personal beliefs and core values. He knew that he didn't belong in a conformist society, but he couldn't find it in his heart to defy his wife or tell the Saints that he didn't share their dedication to the Gospel.

John cursed his weakness and almost wished that he could feel the passion that Port Rockwell felt for the Gospel. Although it wasn't in his heart to trust the prophet as Orrin did, at least if he shared Port's passion perhaps he wouldn't feel the guilt that ate at his heart like a maggot because of his lack of moral courage.

John ran toward the newspaper office with no true purpose in mind. He knew he couldn't challenge the mob or its leaders, but he felt driven to do something to protect the gentle Phelps. As he neared the corner where the press was located, he again slid into the shadows to take stock of the situation. He was appalled at what he saw. A rabble of over one hundred men, with black painted faces and mostly naked from the waist up, were ruthlessly sacking the Star building. They carried furniture, papers and the press machinery into the center of the street, where a huge bonfire was burning brightly. With unrestrained glee, they threw everything they could carry onto the all-consuming fire. John learned later that nearly every copy of the Book of Commandments, a collection of Joseph's revelations, was burned.

John searched the mass of flitting shadows to detect any sign of Phelps or any other Saint who might have fallen into the hands of the lawless mob. He was relieved to see that most of the Missourians were occupied in destroying the contents of the building and smashing the windows and doors of the structure itself. He strained his eyes to make out any sign of a captive Saint, but it seemed the mob was absorbed with the destruction of the press.

John found some solace in the fact that no other Saint appeared to challenge the mob and were obviously content to hole up in their homes or other sanctuaries while the Missourians sacked the *Evening and Morning Star*. John stood against the wall of a building, hidden by the dark shadows, and watched the wanton destruction. He felt a deep sense of loss when he realized that the only press within four hundred miles was being smashed. In his heart, however, John realized that the Saints had partially brought this calamity upon themselves with their self-righteous attitudes, intolerance and hypocrisy.

John watched the mob until they lost interest in smashing the remnants of the press and furnishings of Phelps's office and began to drift away in little groups. He was relieved to see that Phelps was nowhere to be seen and hadn't confronted the mob to save his beloved *Evening and Morning Star*. The night was cool for July in Missouri and sound drifted like a leaf in a stream, but after a few moments, the cries of the mob completely died away.

John stepped out of the gloom of the alley and quickly surveyed the damage to the *Star*, and he knew that Phelps wouldn't be publishing more contentious articles for some time. The mob had ripped the press machinery from its moorings and hauled it into the street, where they had smashed it with sledgehammers and thrown the remnants into the flames. The lead type was cast whole into the searing flames and had melted into a great glop of gray-silver metal.

John stepped into the doorway of the newspaper building and caught his breath as he looked at the damage inflicted by the vengeful mob. Desks, furniture and supplies were smashed and scattered throughout the building. Chairs and tables had been thrown through the windows into the street below and the entire interior of the sturdy brick building was a shambles. Hardly a stick of furniture was still in one piece and glass crunched under his feet like ice shards as John walked aimlessly about the office and pressroom. As he turned to retrace his steps to the door, John saw the outline of a man standing by one of the arched windows in Phelps's office. His heart raced in his chest like a cornered wild creature and he tried to speak, but his voice came out in a hoarse croak. "Who's there?" he finally managed to stammer.

Relief washed over him like a summer thundershower when he heard William Wines Phelps answer in a trembling voice, "Brother Evans, thank God it is you. Look what they have done to my beautiful newspaper. Why would God allow this travesty to happen—what have I done to deserve this?" John quickly walked to the dim figure of the editor and found that he was dejectedly leaning against what was left of his rolltop desk, running his hand across the smashed and splintered writing surface.

"Why would they do this to me, to the mouthpiece of the Lord?" asked Phelps despondently. A beam of moonlight slanted through the shattered window and bathed Phelps's face in a vaporous light. The tears in his eyes glistened like diamonds and John felt a wrenching pity for the man. He reflected on the past issues of the *Star* and knew that Phelps had brought this destruction upon himself and the Saints with his intolerant and sanctimonious editorials, but he didn't have the heart to tell the man.

John put his arm on Phelps's shoulder and said in a sympathetic voice, "Don't worry, William, we will rebuild it better than before."

Phelps turned to him with a strange glitter in his eye and said, "That's it, Brother Evans, we'll contact the prophet, he'll know what to do. That's it, we'll ask Joseph and he'll commune with God. He'll tell us what we should do." To John, Phelps appeared like a small child, pleading with his father to tell him what he wanted to hear.

John looked at him with more contempt than pity and replied, "That's it, William, you ask Joseph." With that, John turned and strode out the door into the moonlit night.

As he walked back home, John thought about all that had happened that night. He understood that the Saints' belligerent attitude had caused much of this destruction, but he was appalled that the Missourians had reacted with such unfettered violence. John abhorred violence and much preferred to discuss issues rather than resort to hostility. He felt out of place on the Missouri frontier, where he had seen Indians shot on sight because some local believed his land claim was challenged. He wondered why these rough men were so prone to resort to brutality rather than compromise. He looked into his soul and considered if his attitude toward aggression was an indication of what he perceived as his lack of moral courage.

As he opened the door of their little cabin, Jenny ran to her father with tears in her eyes. "Father, thank God that you're all right. We heard that Bishop Partridge was assaulted and that a mob was ransacking the newspaper office," she said.

Agnes was standing in the bedroom door and said with a sneer, "You don't need to worry about your father, Jenny. He doesn't have the guts to stand up for the Word of God or the truth, and he was probably cowering in some dark corner while those filthy cowards destroyed the *Star*."

John looked at Agnes and for a brief fleeting moment he hated her for her arrogance and self-righteous, demeaning attitude. He looked at the sneer on her thin lips and for the first time in his life, he wanted to smash his fist into someone's face. Jenny leapt to her father's defense and shouted at her mother, "No solitary man could confront that wild mob and you know Father did what he could." Agnes arched her eyebrows in surprise at her daughter's insolence and she hesitated as if she were going to confront her daughter, but she shrugged her shoulders and turned back into the darkened bedroom.

Jenny put her arms around her father and said, "I am so glad that you are home safe. I was worried sick about you."

John put his arm around Jenny's shoulders and kissed her cheek, wishing Agnes would show him the same love and concern. John knew better than to enter the bedroom that night, so he waited until Jenny had gone to her little gable room and then he crawled onto the little loveseat and spent a very uncomfortable night.

Chapter 10

During the next few days, things seemed to settle down, and John began to think that the crisis had passed. Then the mob reassembled and demanded to meet with representatives of the Saints. The church leaders meekly met with the agents of the old settlers and under duress, they agreed to meet their demands. The Saints in Missouri were trying to buy time until they could get word to their prophet and church leaders in Ohio of the disaster in Zion. Phelps and Partridge immediately dispatched Oliver Cowdery, a missionary to the Indians and confidant of the prophet, to Kirtland to discuss the situation with Joseph. In the meantime, they had no recourse but to agree to the demands of the Missourians.

They signed an agreement with the Missourians that stated that the Saints would begin moving out of Jackson County by January 1, 1834, and that they wouldn't attempt to publish any other church newspaper or publication in the meantime. They also agreed to close all church-owned businesses and begin selling their property in western Missouri.

When John heard the news of the agreement, he inwardly breathed a sigh of relief, but he knew the zeal of the Saints, and he didn't believe they would give up the holy City of Zion so easily. He had heard the Saints say innumerable times that once they had established the New Jerusalem, Jesus would then come trailing clouds of glory and the Saints would establish a world government based on the Gospel and judge nations and peoples in the last days. He knew that this belief was the centerpiece of their Gospel and in his heart he understood that the chosen people would fight for their moment of glory.

The summer passed in relative peace. The Saints made no obvious effort to republish the *Evening and Morning Star*, and they kept a low profile, waiting to hear from their prophet. When word finally came from Kirtland, Joseph was noncommittal. He issued his customary revelation in which God made vague references to constitutional rights and commanded his people to abide by their covenants or they wouldn't be worthy, and finally he instructed his people to renounce war and bear indignities with fortitude.

When Phelps publicly forgave the mob that had abused him, the Saints proclaimed him a martyr and it became fashionable in Zion to suffer for righteousness' sake.

One morning at breakfast, Agnes stood and dramatically declared, "I wish that vile mob had stripped me naked in the streets so I could have stood exposed before them and proclaimed that Joseph is a prophet of God."

John stared at her incredulously, and when she saw the look of shock on his face she added, "Through martyrdom I would be assured of eternal life."

Joseph admonished the Saints to follow the word of the Lord, turn the other cheek and wait until the animosity died down. He was sure that if the Saints didn't antagonize the Missourians further, the crises would blow over. He also instructed Phelps and Partridge to petition Governor Daniel Dunklin for protection from the mobs and reimbursement for the loss of property from mob violence. After hearing the Saints' grievances, Dunklin advised them to obtain legal council, and they eventually retained the firm of Reese, Atchison, Wood and Doniphan.

The Saints took Joseph's counsel to heart and basically ignored the agreement to leave Jackson County by the first of the year. During the pleasant days of late summer, John would often borrow Chic Simmons's buggy and take long drives in the Missouri countryside. He loved to be alone with his thoughts and he found the rolling green countryside a soothing balm for his tormented soul. During these excursions he was amazed to find that the Saints went about their business of farming and worshiping their God as if nothing had happened. There was no indication that they were preparing to leave Missouri. In fact, it appeared to John that most of the Saints had become even more fanatical in their conviction that Jackson County was a sacred place that God had rightfully given to his chosen people.

The days began to drag for John and he longed for the unpretentious and honest company of his friend Porter. One pleasant Indian summer day at the end of October, John borrowed Chic's buggy and rode out to the Big Blue settlement to spend some time with Rockwell. He felt a twinge of fear building in the pit of his stomach. Little beads of sweat were breaking out on his forehead, despite the fact that the day was cool. Chic seemed to notice his reluctance. "Well, Brother Evans, if you would like me to ride along with you today, I don't have much to do and it is a nice day, I would be glad to go," he said.

John seriously considered accepting Chic's offer, but he wanted to confront his demons on his own terms and he replied, "No, Chic, I know that Bishop Partridge has things for you to do and I need to do some serious soul searching, so I think I'll go alone."

John clucked to the two mules and they started off at a brisk pace. He found that he had grown very fond of Chic's gray Missouri mules. He searched his mind and couldn't remember what Chic called them, but they were gentle and affectionate beasts and John had an affinity for all creatures. He loved the way that they nuzzled him with their velvet-soft noses and raised their long ears in greeting as he approached.

As he rode, John thought about how he had in many ways become a prisoner of his own fears. He decided he was more timorous than most men, as he had rarely observed any other man allow a woman to dominate him as Agnes dominated him. In fact, on the frontier it was not unusual for a man to beat his wife or woman in public. Even among the Saints, women were considered subservient to men and weren't allowed to perform any of the church ordinances. As he thought about his submissiveness to Agnes, he felt a wave of shame roll over him and he was glad no one could see him, because he knew his face must be glowing like a jack-o-lantern.

John wondered if a man could be courageous and still be kind and tolerant. He searched his mind for an example and decided that if all that he had read about Thomas Jefferson was true, then it was possible for a man to stand up for his principles but have a gentle and loving nature. He had read excerpts from Jefferson's letters and diaries and he had developed an impression that the great man was fascinated by nature and was kind and caring toward other creatures. Although Jefferson believed that women weren't suited for politics and should maintain home and hearth, John couldn't put his finger on anything Jefferson had said that would imply he believed a man should be brutal to a woman. He also admired Jefferson's spiritual beliefs, as they closely resembled his own humanist ideals.

John roused from his musings and was amazed to find that he was in sight of the Big Blue and Porter's ferry. He squinted into the slanting October sun and could just make out the ferry tied to the landing on the opposite bank of the river. The Big Blue was low, even for this time of the year, and John could hardly see the water for the willows and brush along the banks. As he approached the little wharf where Porter tied the ferry on the east side of the river, he noticed that the figure on the rough little craft had straightened up and appeared to be looking in his direction.

By the time John reached the spot where the dirt track stopped at the high water mark, Porter had cast off and was poling the ungainly craft toward the east bank. John tugged on the reins and called "whoa" to the two mules. He bounded out of the buggy and snapped a line attached to a cast iron weight to the bit of the left mule. That done, he ran down the sandy bank to the edge of the water. Porter was still thirty yards from shore, but he waved his free arm in greeting. "Hey, Brother Evans," he yelled across the muddy water.

As the ferry grounded itself on the sandy bank, Porter leaped off the rickety vessel and ran up to John, extending his right hand in greeting. He clasped John's hand firmly and vigorously pumped it in a sincere and good-natured salutation.

"It is great to see ya, Brother Evans; I have been wonderin' where you was. I haven't seed you since that little ruckus in Wilson's store; I was hopin' they didn't scare ya off." A look of embarrassment crossed Porter's face like a shadow from a passing cloud when he realized what he had said.

"I'm sorry, Brother Evans, I didn't mean to imply you were skeered," he said quietly.

John realized that Porter didn't mean to hurt his feelings, but the words cut like a knife. He dropped his eyes and for a fleeting moment he felt inadequate in the company of Porter Rockwell. Rockwell immediately realized that his words had hurt John and he flung his arm around his shoulder and smiled broadly to minimize the awkwardness of the moment.

"There is many kinds of courage, John," he said, "and I admire yer determination to find God in yer own way, despite what others think." John gave Port an incredulous glance, for he couldn't imagine that a man who obviously feared no one could think that John had any admirable characteristics.

He turned away from Rockwell so the other man would not see that he was embarrassed. "John, I am glad ya rode out today," Rockwell said softly. "I seen a lot of rough-lookin' men riding through here and one group, who used the ferry, was armed to the teeth. One of them shoved a Harper's Ferry horse pistol inta my face and tole me to keep my mouth shut and mind the ferry, then he tole me that they wasn't payin' no money to cross the river." Porter paused and considered the situation and added, "I am very worried about Luana. She and the baby are home alone and my parents and sister also live nearby."

John was incredulous: how could Porter stay here on the Big Blue and tend his run-down ferry when his family members were possibly in danger from marauders? He considered remaining silent—the safety of Porter's family wasn't his concern— but then he reconsidered. Actually, in John's mind, Porter's problems were his problems because Port was a friend and even if that weren't so, John felt strongly that it was a human obligation to offer help, advice or solace to anyone in need.

He looked into Porter's worried eyes. "Port," he said, "why are you minding this ferry when there are no paying customers. Why don't you go home and check on your family?"

Porter looked away from John and gazed intently up the river across the glass-smooth water. For a moment, John thought he wasn't going to answer, and in the ensuing lull he heard a crow call hoarsely from a huge cottonwood snag on the west bank of the stream. A fish or muskrat made a sudden splash on the placid surface of the Big Blue and John was suddenly aware of the soft drone of insects in the balmy autumn air.

Finally, Porter turned back to John and with downcast eyes he replied, "John, the elders and apostles of the church assigned me the business of mindin' this ferry and I took an oath that it would be open fer travelers to cross the river from the time the ice went out in the spring, until it froze agin in the fall and by damn, I'm a'goin' ta carry out my obligation. I took an oath to mind this ferry and turn over all the profit to the church fur the building of Zion."

"But Porter," retorted John, "the river is low enough for anyone to cross on horseback or even on foot and hardly even get their feet wet. Besides," he continued, "you said no one but those marauders have used the ferry in a week, and they refused to pay for their passage."

"Doan' matter," Porter said curtly. "Ah accepted the responsibility and ah gave my word to the apostles of the church that ah would mind this ferry fer fourteen hours a day and I'm gonna do it."

"But Porter," John exclaimed, "there is no reason to man this boat when it is not used and the water is low enough that travelers can easily cross the river without your help. Besides," he said, raising his voice, "you have an obligation to care for your family as well as for the church elders."

Porter stuck his chin out obstinately and replied, "Ah love my family, John, but they cain't attain my salvation fer me. That's up to me, and the only way ah am ever goin' to get inter the celestial kingdom is to show steadfast obedience to the laws of God and the words of his appointed leaders."

John was exasperated; he couldn't understand why a man would follow the dictates of the church officials when they made no sense at all, especially when that man's family might be in danger.

"Porter," John yelled in the man's face, "can't you see how ridiculous this is? You can't do anything here, but you might be able protect your family from harm."

Porter fixed John with a stubborn stare and merely shook his head.

John decided that he couldn't change the obstinate man's mind and he may as well stay with Porter until he decided that his ludicrous sense of honor was satisfied. He looked up through the naked branches of the leafless cottonwoods and was surprised to notice that the sky was darkening. The western horizon had already lost the red glow of sunset and was now bathed in the pale, almost luminous glow of the autumn twilight. The evening was calm and peaceful, and the rhythmic call of whippoorwills reverberated across the still water. Their plaintive call sent a shiver up John's spine and he couldn't help but feel a sense of foreboding as the darkness deepened.

John wished he had stayed in Independence; he didn't want to drive all the way home alone in the dark, but he hadn't told Agnes or Jenny where he was going and he knew they would be worried—or at least Jenny would be. The thought of the long dark road back to Independence and of the marauding nightriders sent an uncomfortable surge of fear through his gut. Anxiety seized him and he couldn't think clearly. He cursed himself for losing track of time and letting the deepening darkness catch him far from his comfortable cabin.

He turned to the brooding face of Rockwell and noticed the man seemed to be in deep thought. "Porter," he said, "I think we need to ride over to the Big Blue settlement and check on your family. It is dark now and no one is going to use the ferry anymore tonight."

Porter lifted his eyes to John's and seemed to consider the suggestion.

"I guess you're right, Brother Evans," he replied. "Go get your rig and drive it on the ferry and I'll take it across."

The crossing was uneventful and John leaned on the rickety railing and listened to the dark water hiss past the rough planks of the ferry. As the lingering twilight turned into a velvety darkness, lit only by the pale twinkling stars and a baleful sliver of a moon, he again wished that he were home, sitting by the rock fireplace with a good book. He thought he would rather be anywhere than here in the middle of the Big Blue on a cool, dark, fall night. He thought again about the marauders that Port said were roaming the countryside. He looked at Porter's broad back and sinewy arms as the man pushed hard against the long pole and he knew he would stay with Rockwell until dawn.

They tied up the ferry and climbed into Chic's tidy little buggy and, without asking, Porter seized the reins and slapped the mules on the rumps with the slack. Porter kept his eyes on the pale road rising up between the mule's ears and remained silent. John wondered what the stoic man was thinking. As if in answer, Porter took the whip from its post and popped it on the rump of the left mule, while clucking and urging the team into a ground-covering trot.

As they crested a gentle rise and began the descent into the Big Blue settlement, John strained his eyes for any sign of trouble, but he could see nothing in the ghostly light of the waning moon. Porter urged the mules into a lumbering lope and soon they pulled up in a cloud of dust in front of his cabin. In the darkness they could hear a woman sobbing and moaning as in fear.

"Luana, is that you?" Porter shouted into the night. They heard a choked reply and Porter, placing a hand on the wheel, vaulted out of the buggy and onto the dusty road in one graceful movement. John cautiously felt for the iron step and carefully stepped down. In that instant, a cloud moved from the face of the moon and in the pale light, John could see that the roof was torn from Porter's cabin.

Luana burst through the doorless frame of the cabin and ran sobbing into the arms of her husband. "Porter," she moaned. "It was awful, a dozen men, stripped to the waist and hideously painted, come riding up to the cabin and demanded that you come out. When I told them that you weren't home, they threatened to cut my throat if I didn't tell them where you were. They dragged me out of the cabin and threw our bedding and furniture into the corral and then tossed ropes over the ridgepole and tore the roof off. They said they were going over to your parents' place and they were going to kill any male Saint that they could find."

"Is the baby safe?" Porter demanded.

"Yes, thank God," Luana replied. "They didn't harm her and she is sleeping in her cradle."

Porter clenched his teeth until John could see the outline of his jaw muscles even in the dim light of the moon. "Damn," Porter exclaimed, "I'm sick and tired of being pushed around by these fucking pukes, and I am gwine git a gun and do the pushin' myself!"

He turned on his heel and commanded, "You two git the baby and git in the buggy. We is goin' to my pa's place, now!"

Luana ran into the ruined cabin and scurried about, wrapping the baby in a blanket. She rushed out of the doorless entry out of breath and leapt into the buggy. Porter whipped the mules into an ungainly lope. The elder Rockwell's homestead was less than a half a mile from Porter's and in less than ten minutes they came clattering into the dark yard. Even by the pale light of the moon, they could see that the elder Rockwell's cabin had suffered serious damage. The roof lay on the ground and the door hung forlornly by one hinge. As Porter reared back on the reins and halted the rearing, lathered mules, Porter's mother rushed up to the buggy.

"Thank God you're here, Porter," she sobbed as Porter jumped down from the rocking buggy. "I tried to stop them."

Porter threw his arm around his shivering mother. She buried her head in his chest and let a deep sob escape from her throat, then the words kept pouring out of her. "One of them jerked a bowie knife out of his scabbard and pointed it toward me and said that if I didn't get out of the way, he would draw it across my throat. I tried to stop them."

Porter tried to comfort his mother but his words only increased her fear.

"Those sons-of-bitches," he exclaimed. "Never again will I be unarmed, and anyone who tries to run me out of my own home or threaten my loved ones agin will pay the ultimate price!" Porter glanced around at the furniture and clothing scattered in the dirt and yelled, "Where the hell is Pa? Is he all right?"

Porter's mother, who was terrified to the point that she couldn't even blubber, found her tongue. "Yer pa went to check on the others," she choked out between sobs, "since we was not hurt."

Porter didn't reply, but gave her a patronizing look. As they stood in the moonlit yard, they became aware of the pounding of approaching hoofbeats and suddenly a lumbering wagon, pulled by two lathered horses, came careening out of the darkness. The sound of the pounding hoofs threw a bolt of fear through John's chest and he expected to see the Four Horsemen bearing down on them. As the wagon stopped next to his buggy, John was relieved to see the wizened face of George Coleman, a devout Saint, peering over the rumps of the excited horses.

As Coleman jumped down from the high wagon, he yelled at the little group, "Come quickly, they've shot Brother Hickman and beaten Brother Beebe near to death."

John and Porter ran to the wagon, which was rocking back and forth as the agitated horses reared and stamped in fear. As John reached the wagon bed, he saw the bodies of two men partially covered with a blanket. John and Porter quickly helped to carry the two men from the wagon into the shattered cabin. They found an unbroken lantern and laid the two men on the floor in the circle of light cast by its wavering flame.

Even though they distrusted him for not being one of them, the Saints looked up to John as an educated man, who had some skill as a self-trained physician. Coleman turned to John. "Brother Evans, will you look at Brother Hickman? I think he is dead. He was confined to bed because of sickness and they demanded that he get up. When he couldn't they shot him in the head."

John felt the blood drain from his brain and he swayed on his feet.

"I cannot treat a gun shot wound to the head," he exclaimed. "I am not a doctor!"

"But you're all we have got right now," Porter stated flatly, "and if you don't help him he will die."

Though he felt totally inadequate, John cleaned the men's wounds as best he could. He was relieved to find that Hickman's injuries were not as serious as expected; the ball had just grazed his scalp. As he was finishing, Porter stated that he was taking the lone horse from the corral and going to check on his father and neighbors.

John felt a bolt of fear tear through him at the thought of being left alone to guard the women. Forcing his mind to function, he directed the women to barricade the door and found an old corn cutter, which gave him a spurious sense of security. Despite his apprehension, he eventually fell asleep and woke with a start at a crashing noise and opened his eyes to see Porter impatiently kicking the boards out of the doorway.

"There air about ten cabins that is unroofed and six or seven men was whipped and beaten last night," declared Porter. "But thanks be to the Lord, no one was kilt," he added. He went on to explain that most of the Saints had fled the wrath of the Missourians and were homeless but relatively unscathed. The few men who were unfortunate enough to be caught by the raiders had escaped with a whipping or beating, but no one was seriously injured.

Port nodded at the injured men and the little group sprang into action, loading them into the wagon.

The ride to Independence was uneventful and John gave a sigh of relief when he saw the dome of the courthouse rise in the distance. It was a beautiful Indian summer day and the sky was an azure blue with hardly a cloud casting a shadow on the rolling prairie. However, the mood of the little group of travelers in the buggy and lumbering farm wagon didn't match the beauty of the day.

As the buggy neared Independence, John could sense that something wasn't quite right there. As they entered the outskirts of the bustling frontier town, he noticed broken glass littering the board sidewalks and scattered about in the dirt road. Several cabins were unroofed and demolished like the Rockwell cabin. The street was swarming with little groups of people talking animatedly and pointing and gesturing. John slapped the mules on the rumps with the reins and clucked them into an awkward trot. As he saw the destruction about him, John felt a bolt of fear constrict his chest. He saw the loving face of his daughter and silently he prayed for her, but he knew he must get help for his charges first. He pulled up in front of the two-story frame building that housed the doctor's home and clinic.

He pulled the mules to the boardwalk and ran into the little foyer that served as a waiting room for patients wanting to see the busy doctor. John glanced around quickly and spotted a nurse bustling through the crowded foyer. He grabbed her by the arm. "I have two seriously injured men in a wagon out front!" he exclaimed.

She turned and gave John an unsympathetic look and replied, "As you can see, sir, the doctor is inundated with injured and wounded people. The pukes attacked the Saints in Independence last night."

John glanced around the packed little anteroom and for the first time became aware that it was full of men, women and children with a myriad of injuries. "Then could you find someone to help us get the two men into the waiting room?" he implored.

The burly nurse gave John an impertinent glance over her shoulder as she bustled off. "Find someone on the street to help. I am busy," she replied.

John rushed back out into the street and spotted a knot of men he recognized as members of his congregation. He ran up to them and grabbed one by the shoulder to get their attention. They turned in unison and looked at John with apprehension.

"Please, help me," he implored. "There are two seriously injured men in that wagon and I need help getting them into the doctor's office."

One of the men stepped forward and looked John directly in the eye, "I know you—your name is Evans, and the word is you are an apostate!" he barked.

John looked back into the belligerent eyes of the speaker. "My beliefs don't matter now," he said, with more conviction than he felt. "There are two men who need medical attention. Please help me get them out of the wagon."

The men looked at him sullenly, but followed him to the wagon and lifted Beebe and Hickman out of the wagonbed and into the crowded waiting room.

As they turned to leave, the obvious leader of the group intentionally rammed a burly elbow into John's ribs and muttered, "There is a meeting scheduled for tonight at eight in the Ward Meeting House. If you are one of us, be there!"

John gaped at the man in astonishment. He hadn't always agreed with all of the tenets of the Saints, but he didn't realize that he was viewed with such suspicion and distrust because of his liberalism.

After thanking Porter and asking him to drop Chic's buggy off, John dejectedly turned and began walking toward home. The further he went the more apparent it became that the Saints in Independence had suffered as much as the residents of the Big Blue settlement. John had to step into the street several times to avoid broken boards and logs sprawled across the sidewalk from the roofs and walls of cabins that were demolished. Glass from broken windows twinkled on the board sidewalk and in the dust of the street and eerily reminded John of Christmas decorations. Men, women and children wandered aimlessly about in a daze looking for loved ones or trying to gather belongings scattered in the dirt.

Fearing the worst, John began to run through the littered streets. As he rounded the corner leading to the narrow lane where he lived, John breathed a great sigh of relief. None of the cabins along the street showed any sign of serious damage. As he ran up the path leading to his home, the door burst open and Jenny ran down the steps and into his arms. She buried her face in his chest. "Where have you been, Daddy?" she sobbed. "I was terrified that the Missourians had got you and whipped you or worse," she moaned into his vest.

He lifted her chin gently with his index finger and looked into her brimming eyes. "I am fine," he assured her, "but it touches my soul to see you cry for me."

He placed his arm around her shoulder and they walked through the open door into the little living room. Agnes stood in the door to her bedroom and looked at him through hooded eyes.

"It is just like you to stay out all night and never tell me where you are or what you are doing," she said through clenched teeth. "When the Saints are attacked by the legions of Satan, we can never depend on you to stand on the side of righteousness, can we?" She spat at him venomously. John stared at her, but did not try to explain, for he knew it would do no good.

Jenny turned to her mother. "Let Daddy explain. I am sure he would have come home last night if he could."

Jenny looked at her father imploringly and John began to stammer out his story, but before he had begun, Agnes gave him a contemptuous look and spun on her heel, slamming the door behind her. "By the way," she said through the door, "Bishop Partridge has called a meeting at the Ward Meeting House for tonight at 8:00 P.M."

John turned toward Jenny with his arms outstretched beseechingly. His daughter looked at him with eyes brimming with tears and her chin quivering, but she couldn't bring herself to speak.

That night, at 7:30, Agnes abruptly opened the door to her bedroom and stepped into the living room. She was dressed primly in a black dress with a high ruffled collar and cuffs. She didn't speak to John, who was sitting dejectedly at the rough pine table, but gave him a glance that let him know she expected him to follow her. Jenny had long since retired to her loft room, where she buried her face in the pillow and wept for her father.

Agnes took the lead as they marched out of the door and into the darkening street. The rough board sidewalk was crowded with grim-faced men and women all heading in the same direction as Agnes and John. John caught up to Agnes and tried to slip his arm through hers, but she jerked her arm away and clamped it tight against her body to signify that she didn't want him to touch her. She did, however, walk by his side, but John knew that the reason she allowed him to walk close to her was so that the other Saints wouldn't know how she despised him.

As they neared the little meetinghouse, the throng grew thicker. John was amazed; it appeared to him that every church member in Independence was crowding into the ward house. As they pushed through the doors and found a seat on one of the rough pine benches that served as pews, John noticed that most of the local church leaders were already seated on the rostrum.

His eyes roamed across the group of men seated at the front of the room and he noticed, among others, Bishop Partridge, W. W. Phelps, Lyman Wight, A. Sidney Gilbert, and David Whitmer. John was surprised to see Gilbert at the rostrum. He knew that Gilbert had written a letter to the church leaders in Kirtland complaining bitterly about lack of support for the Independence Branch and the poor quality of the land that was purchased for the Saints. Gilbert had been chastised publicly for "blind insinuations, pretensions to holiness, and covertness," but obviously he had regained favor with the leaders in Kirtland.

Precisely at eight o'clock, Bishop Partridge rose to the pulpit and called the meeting to order. "Brothers and Sisters," he began, "I can feel the presence of the Savior with us tonight. We must seek his Holy Spirit to aid us and to guide us through these perilous times. The evil one is trying desperately to thwart the work of the Lord. We are meeting here tonight to ask for God's guidance in continuing his holy work. Now I will ask Brother Enos Thatcher to offer the invocation."

John cringed inwardly when he heard that Brother Thatcher was offering the opening prayer. Thatcher had a reputation of being fanatical and long-winded. Thatcher lived up to his reputation; he asked the Lord to bless each church apostle and then called on God to destroy the evil Gentiles and sweep Jackson County free of unbelievers. He spent twenty minutes importuning the deity to aid the Saints in establishing Zion and preparing for the day when the Saints should establish a holy city in the wilderness to serve as a seat of power for the righteous to judge the wicked.

Thatcher finally mumbled "amen" and took his seat; Partridge again rose and walked to the rostrum.

"Brothers and sisters," he gravely said, "I've called you together this evening to discuss the crisis that confronts us. Those whom we have called neighbor have chosen to attack us and are striving to drive us from our homes and this holy land that was given to us by God as our inheritances. Our Prophet, Seer and Revelator has unequivocally said that we aren't to sell our land or leave Zion, but we face multitudes and we are few.

"I stand before you," he continued, "to ask you to look into your hearts and seek the inspiration of the Holy Ghost to help us resolve this dilemma. We have signed a citizens' agreement to leave this area by April of next year. What must we do to inspire those who hate us to allow us to live in peace? I will now open this meeting to suggestions."

John sat quietly and listened as six or seven Saints rose and berated the Missourians as evil men who were under the influence of Satan. All the speakers hit on the theme that because the Saints were doing the Lord's work and establishing the holy city in the last days, they were attacked by the godless. Most of the speakers demanded that the Saints stand and fight and then God would come forth from his hiding place and fight their battles.

John listened to one fanatic tirade after another calling for the Saints to purify themselves before God so that he would destroy their enemies. Finally, he could stand it no more and he rose and waited for Partridge to acknowledge him. Partridge seemed reluctant to call on John, but no one else seemed anxious to speak and finally Edward Partridge turned toward John and curtly pointed at him to acknowledge that he had the floor.

A murmur went through the crowd as they saw Partridge acknowledge John. John suddenly realized that he faced a hostile audience. He began to tremble and beads of sweat popped out on his forehead like condensation on a cold glass. Agnes glared up at him and impatiently tugged at his hand, indicating for him to sit down. John desperately wanted to settle into his seat and become anonymous in the confines of the uncomfortable pine bench, but he thought of all the times he had turned away from his convictions and he took a deep breath, cleared his throat and looked over the sea of sullen faces.

"Ladies and gentlemen," he said, fully aware of the breach of protocol that his choice of words indicated, "I know how vicious the nightriders can be, but before we seek to claim the high road in this dispute, perhaps we should look for the mote in our own eyes. I don't condone violence and I don't believe the Missourians have the right to attack this people and destroy their homes, but perhaps we should consider their point of view. How many times have you said to your neighbors, 'God has given this land to us and if you don't leave he will destroy you?'

"I have heard all of you tell your neighbors that if they did not accept the word of the prophet and become baptized, they would burn in hell for all eternity. How do you think you would feel if someone told you this? Editor Phelps constantly published accounts of disasters in the *Evening and Morning Star* and implied that they were precursors of the coming of Jesus and that at his coming the Gentiles would be burnt as stubble."

Agnes reached up and grabbed John by the shoulder and angrily jerked him toward his seat. An angry murmur ran through the crowd like a tremor on a horse's back at the bite of a deer fly. John could feel the antagonism in the room like a blast of hot air from the door of a suddenly opened oven. He fell heavily into his seat and allowed Agnes to restrain him.

Lyman Wight jumped to his feet. "Be careful, Brother Evans," he declared, "you're dangerously close to apostasy and the cardinal sin of speaking against God's anointed! It is said," he continued, "that the only way one can atone for certain sins is through the shedding of their blood."

The blood drained from John's face as he looked into the wild eyes of Wight and realized that this man was deadly serious.

The room grew deathly quiet, and a hundred pairs of eyes turned to John. He physically shrunk into his skin like a slug touched by a finger and he knew that if Partridge crooked his finger, he was a dead man.

The Bishop rose to the rostrum. "Brothers and Sisters," he said, "we've importuned before the feet of the judges and been denied; we've importuned before the governor and been denied; now I say we must defend ourselves. Three Saints are being held in a Gentile jail on false pretenses; I say let us arm ourselves as best we can and rescue our brethren.

"Tomorrow let all priesthood holders arm themselves and gather at the town square. We are going to take back what is rightfully ours!"

He looked directly at John. "It would be in your best interest to be there also, Brother Evans," he said pointedly.

Chapter 11

November 3, 1833 dawned clear and cold in western Missouri. Even before the sun lightened the eastern horizon, rough men began arriving at Wilson's store a few miles west of Independence. They weren't Saints and they were gathering for a sinister purpose. Missourian spies had picked up the word that the Saints would try to storm the jail and release the three Saints held there. As the leaders stomped onto the plank entrance to the store, they were muttering about the fanatics being on the march.

As the men gathered around the store in the predawn light, Bill Turner stepped up on the rough pine planks of the porch. Standing next to him, John Keck blew an old bugle to get the mob's attention. Turner was a tall, skinny man who resembled a scarecrow in his ill-fitting open-necked shirt and baggy canvas trousers.

"Men," he yelled in a high-pitched voice that cracked with exertion, "we have news that the fanatics is gathering to release the prisoners that we hold near Independence. Ya is all armed and ya know what we must do."

With that a thunderous shout burst from the throats of three hundred coarse men and as one they raised their muskets above their heads toward the waning moon. "We have word that they is marchin' an hour after dawn and will take the old Post Road outside of Independence. Now, mount up and les' go."

Again a ragged yell burst from the throats of the mob and they turned and ran to the picket line, mounted and thundered out of the yard in a cloud of swirling dust.

Ten miles to the east, David Whitmer stood before a similar but much smaller group of desperate men. They had gathered around the Ward House in Independence as they had been told to do by Partridge the night before.

"Brethren," yelled Whitmer, "may the spirit of God be with you and protect you this day. We'll march out the old Post Road and surround the jail and release our brethren. Are there any questions?"

Whitmer's question was answered by a rousing "Hosanna!" that burst from the mouths of a hundred Saints.

"Then may the strength of the Lord dwell in your arm today. Forward!"

John Evans purposely maneuvered so that he was toward the back of the little force. He noticed that only a few of the men were armed with muskets or pistols. Most of the group clutched corn cutters or sickles, but what they lacked in armament they made up for in fanaticism. He had heard many of the men exclaim that the cloak of the priesthood would protect them from any Gentile bullets and many fully believed that should they confront the Missouri mob, God would appear to fight their battles.

Despite the veiled threat that Partridge had thrown at him the previous evening, John had fully intended to stay home today. After the meeting, however, Agnes had berated him unmercifully for his criticism of the Saints and she demanded that he redeem himself by marching with them to confront the Gentiles. John found that the resolve he had felt the night before when he spoke out in the meeting fled in the early morning hours when confronted by his shrewish wife, and he left the house with an old sickle in his hand rather than stay and face her wrath.

He was grateful that Jenny did not appear when they got home from the meeting and wasn't awake when he left in the predawn dark. The morning was cold but clear, and John pulled his old broadcloth coat tighter around his shoulders. Few of the men had military experience and the little group struggled along, stepping on each others' heels because no one called cadence and they couldn't manage to stay in step. As they straggled through the streets of Independence, a few women gathered on the side of the dusty road to cheer them off.

As they left the outskirts of town, someone in their midst began singing "Come All Ye Sons of Zion" and the entire group joined in at the top of their lungs. John inwardly cringed, for he knew that any Missourian within a mile could hear the Saints coming. After a rousing chorus of "How Firm a Foundation," Whitmer passed the word back that he wanted silence. After that, they marched in relative quiet, except for the clanking of makeshift weapons and the buzz of muted conversations.

As the sun rose, they found themselves traveling at a brisk pace along the Post Road. As they neared the intersection of the road leading toward the Big Blue settlement, they heard a scattering of musket fire. At the urging of Whitmer, they turned toward the sound of firing and broke into a ragged run. As they topped a low rise and descended toward a little settlement, they saw a group of men milling around a little cluster of cabins. As they approached, the men turned and stared at them and they heard someone yell, "Fire, goddamn ye, fire." There was a scattering of musket fire and John heard the whistle of musket balls pass overhead.

One Saint, who was in the front of the little group, screamed and fell writhing onto the dusty road; Whitmer urged the men to spread out into a skirmish line and attack the Missourians. There was much confusion as the Saints tried to arrange themselves into a battle line, but finally they were able to unleash a ragged volley and several Missourians fell thrashing onto the dirt. The Missourians took one look at the cheering Saints bearing down on them and they mounted their horses and fled.

As the Missourians disappeared over a little rise, the Saints went wild with elation. They threw their arms into the air and split the air with three "huzzahs." Once David Whitmer had got the rabble under control, they checked on the casualties on both sides. Two Missourians lay in the dust with their lifeblood pouring onto the black soil. One Saint had been hit in the chest. The big fifty-caliber ball had effectively ripped his lungs from his body as it exited his back.

John avoided looking at the dead, but as he walked toward the shade at the side of the road, he nearly stumbled over the body of one of the Missourians who had been dragged there by the jubilant Saints. His foot hit something soft and wielding and he inadvertently looked down into the lifeless face of John Keck. The corpse's eyes were still open as if in panic and the mouth hung open in a silent scream. A trickle of blood ran out of the corner of the mouth and spilled into the dry dust of the road. John retched involuntarily and covered his mouth in horror. He stumbled to the porch of a little cabin and sat down with his head in his hands and stomach churning.

Through a haze of nausea, John felt the boards creak under him as someone stepped up on the porch near him. He looked up through blurry eyes and saw the reproachful face of David Whitmer looking down at him. Whitmer gave him one more critical look and turned to face the cheering Saints.

"Brethren!" He yelled at the top of his lungs to be heard. After several yells and much arm waving by Whitmer, the crowd quieted and turned to face Whitmer. "Brethren," Whitmer repeated, "God has granted us a great victory here today. These pukes had ambushed a group of our men and were in the process of hunting them down in the cornfields when we arrived. You see how they flee from the Army of Israel! Let this day be a lesson to you all. With the spirit of the Lord, we can establish the City of Zion here in the heart of the continent."

John listened to the brave words, but he realized that the Missourians had the strength of numbers on their side and that the old settlers controlled the government and judicial systems. He gave the corpse lying in the dust a furtive glance and wondered how many more would die on both sides before this insane conflict was over. He gave an apprehensive glance to the west in the direction the

Missourians had gone and wondered how long it would be before they returned at the head of the militia.

John had no idea just how accurate his fears were. As the triumphant Saints dispersed, the defeated Missourians reported their misadventure to Lieutenant Governor Lilburn W. Boggs, one of the signers of the citizens' ultimatum demanding the Saints leave Jackson County. Possibly at the urging of Boggs, the nightriders spread the word throughout Jackson County that the Saints were in collusion with the Indians and intended to lay siege to Independence. Boggs then approached Governor Daniel Dunklin and requested that he call out the Jackson County militia under Colonel Thomas Pitcher to maintain the peace in western Missouri.

Although Governor Dunklin had been supportive of the Saints' request for protection, he also realized that to give the Saints arms or militia protection would precipitate a bloody civil war in Missouri. He finally agreed to call out the militia, but suggested that both sides in the conflict be disarmed to prevent further hostilities.

John was well aware of these events; they were announced shortly after they took place at the myriad meetings the Saints held to keep abreast of the movements of their perceived enemies. The evening following the clash outside Independence in which Keck was killed, John was notified by a runner from Bishop Partridge that his presence was requested at the meetinghouse. He dared not decline, because he realized that his standing with the Saints was in jeopardy because of his ill-advised remarks at the previous gathering. John had a vague feeling of uneasiness that the Saints might resort to more than just shunning him if they saw him as an apostate.

That night, John and Agnes entered the meetinghouse shortly before eight, the time he was told the meeting would begin. Agnes had rebuked him before they left home to keep his opinions to himself and follow the counsel of the elders. With piercing eyes she had stared into his very soul and informed him that it was moral suicide to reject the guidance of the Lord's anointed. She demanded that he read the scriptures and the writings of the prophet and then seek the advice of the bishop and his counselors and do as he was told. John wondered if God demanded strict obedience and no independent thought, why had he given man intelligence and creativity? But he wisely kept his thoughts to himself.

Precisely at eight, Bishop Partridge rose and asked Brother Hendricks to offer the customary opening prayer. After old man Hendricks had droned on for nearly a half an hour, he finally sat down and Partridge asked one of the sisters to lead the congregation in singing a modified Baptist hymn, "How Firm a Foundation." Following the hymn, Partridge rose again and announced that he would turn the time over to Brother Lyman Wight, a high priest and church apostle. Wight was a huge bear of a man with a thick, black beard and hair that added to his wild look. He had a reputation to go with his appearance and was known among the Saints as the "Wild Ram of the Mountains" because of his fanaticism and devotion to the Gospel.

As Wight stood to speak, John realized what an imposing man he was. As Wight grasped the podium and stared intently at the congregation, his eyes glistened with intensity.

"Brothers and Sisters," he bellowed, "if only ten of you who trust the Lord will follow me, I will drive the pukes from Jackson County. This land was given to us by the Lord to establish his holy city and by God we'll do it! I want every able-bodied man who has a gun to join me at dawn tomorrow on the town common and march against the Missourians to take back that which God has granted us."

Instantly, as one, the congregation leaped to its feet and cried "Hosanna!" John was swept to his feet by those sitting next to him, but inwardly he gave a sigh of relief, for he didn't own a firearm. Agnes was standing next to him with her right arm over her head as a sign of support. The blaze in her eyes matched the shine in Wight's eyes and her breath came in ragged gasps. Stunned, John glanced at her from the corner of his eye and shuttered when he saw the fervor in her face.

When they returned home that evening, Agnes walked by John's side but stridently refused to allow him to take her arm in his. Jenny was nowhere to be seen when they walked in the front door and John assumed that she had retired to her little loft room. He turned to Agnes and asked, "Just what is it you would have me do?"

"Live your religion and follow the word of the church leaders," she said callously.

John looked at her with defiance in his eye. "I am living my religion," he replied, "I just am not living yours." With a shriek, Agnes rushed at him and raked her nails across his face, cutting deep red furrows down his cheeks. Without thinking, John grabbed her by the shoulders and flung her across the room.

John put his hands to his smarting face. "Why did you do that?" he yelled.

"Because you are a spineless coward who doesn't have the gumption to stand up for your prophet and your God!" she screeched. John stared at her with blood running down his face.

Just as he was going to shout back at her, the bedroom door burst open and Jenny stood in the doorway with her eyes blazing. "Stop it, stop it right now!" she demanded.

John spun around to face his daughter and when he saw the tears glistening in her eyes and running down her cheeks, his heart broke to think what he and Agnes had done to this innocent girl.

"Oh, sweetheart," he said, "we were just arguing about what was said at the meeting tonight."

"No you weren't," she shouted. "You were quarrelling about religious beliefs. Why can't you let Daddy decide what he believes for himself, Momma?"

Agnes stood defiant and glared at her daughter. "So," she screeched, "you have turned against me and God, too?"

"No, I haven't, but what makes you think you know what God wants?" Jenny demanded. Agnes stared at her with red-rimmed eyes. For a moment, John thought she was going to attack her daughter as she had attacked him, but Agnes spun on her heel and stormed into the bedroom, slamming the door behind her.

Jenny ran to her father and threw herself into his arms. She buried her tear-stained face into his chest. "Oh, Daddy," she said through trembling lips, "why is she such a witch? Why can't she be content to believe what she wants and let others decide what they will believe?"

"Because," said John, "when people think that God speaks directly to their leaders, or themselves, they believe they have the divine right and anyone who believes differently is not only wrong, but deluded. I am going with Wight in the morning," John announced, "if for no other reason than to keep peace in this family."

As dawn broke, John quietly shut the door of the house. Jenny had begged him not to join Wight's men, but he knew if he didn't make an appearance, the Saints would think him a coward and a skeptic. When he told Agnes that he was going to join Wight's mercenaries, she pursed her lips and finally gave him a rueful smile. However, when he rose and dressed in the gray light, just before dawn, neither of the Evans women were anywhere to be seen. He had hoped that Agnes might come out of the bedroom and wish him well, but nothing stirred in the house as he rose from his uncomfortable bed on the horsehair sofa and dressed.

The morning of November 5, 1833 was cold and the sky was streaked with pink-tinged cirrus clouds. John glanced at the sky and decided that the red streaked clouds would bring rain or snow before long. He hurried along the nearly deserted streets of Independence as the new day gradually lightened the eastern sky. As he neared the common, he met little knots of men hurrying in the same direction he was going. Most of them were dressed in coarse clothing and carried a possibles bag slung over their shoulder to hold lead bullets, powder and patches.

Most of them also carried a long gun of numerous types, including old Brown Bess muskets, fowling pieces and more modern percussion plains rifles.

As they neared the common, John could hear someone bellowing orders and shouting instructions. He found himself pushed along by the crowd until he was standing on the common with nearly two hundred men. He was surprised to see that many of the men were armed with makeshift lances and homemade swords fashioned from old scythes and other discarded farm tools. Lyman Wight was standing on a little rise that was just high enough for the milling mob to see him.

Wight was armed with a Model 1822 Harper's Ferry musket. In addition to the musket, Wight also carried a brace of .59 caliber Harper's Ferry horse pistols across the pommel of his saddle.

Once he got the men's attention, Wight flung his arms skyward in a supplication and shouted at the gray sky, "Oh God, hear our entreaty, and bless this, thy army, with the courage to destroy thy enemies. Bless us in this holy endeavor to regain the sacred soil of Zion and drive the ungodly from this blessed place. Help us to establish thy holy city and hasten that day that thy son returns to earth and establishes thy government in this world. Bless us that we may rescue our brethren from the clutches of the heathens and smite the ungodly with thy holy sword."

With that, Wight signaled that he was through speaking to God by lowering his arms and pointing toward the crowd. "Brethren," he bellowed, "let us behave as Saints of the one true God and go forth and smite the wicked who strive to thwart the work of the Lord. Our spies tell us that the pukes are holding three of our brothers, Sidney Gilbert, John Corrill, and Isaac Morley, and are threatening to hang these Saints. Know this," he bellowed to the gray sky, "the Lord is with us and our cause is his cause. Forward!"

The rabble surged forward to follow Wight and redeem Zion. John looked into the shadowy faces of the men around him and he saw unbridled fervor reflected in the pale light of a gray dawn. John felt the familiar twinge of fear gripping his groin and in an instant he knew that these people were heading for disaster. In panic, he looked around wildly for a way out, but the surging mob forced him forward. In the faces of the men around him he saw such a passion that he knew if he tried to turn back, he would be torn to pieces as a traitor.

Wight's lieutenants tried to form the rabble into some semblance of a military organization, but the men had no idea of dismounted drill and shuffled along in ragged and disorganized lines. Brother John Moore was assigned as captain over the pack that constituted the "group of fifty" that John found himself a member of by default.

The mob straggled along for nearly an hour and John found himself nearing exhaustion.

Dust rose in choking clouds from dozens of shuffling feet and irritated John's throat and lungs. His eyes watered from the stifling, swirling dust and he could hardly see the feet of the man in front of him.

Just as John thought he could stand it no more and began looking for a way out of the milling mob, a cry of "Halt!" came from the front of the column. Brother Moore repeated the command in a comic falsetto voice that was meant to convey authority. From where he was in the rabble, John couldn't see what was happening, but word was quickly whispered from man to man from the front of the column. The man in front of John, Brother Joshua Lewis, whispered over his shoulder, "We have run face-to-face into the Missouri militia," he murmured. On hearing this, John's heart fluttered and his chest constricted until he felt as if he were suffocating.

The order came for the Saints to break formation and disperse to the side of the road. Twenty minutes passed and neither side stirred. John Moore, who had left to see if he could find out what was going on, returned with the news that Lyman Wight was negotiating with the commander of the Missouri militia, Colonel Thomas Pitcher, and Lieutenant Governor Lilburn Boggs. According to Moore, Lieutenant Governor Boggs had suggested that the hostilities were basically a mistake caused by inflammatory statements by Joseph Smith. He recommended that the Saints and the old settlers surrender their arms to the militia, who would then preserve the peace between the two groups.

Colonel Pitcher, a signer of the citizens' manifesto requesting that the Saints leave Jackson County by January of 1834, readily agreed to this truce. Lyman Wight took Pitcher at his word and ordered the Saints to surrender their arms. Wight ordered his officers to form the Saints into ranks and stack their weapons. Once the command came down, Moore ordered his company to stack their weapons and be prepared to turn them over to the Missouri militia. A massive groan rose from the throats of the entire company, but Moore quickly explained that the order had come from Lyman Wight, who was acting on the promptings of the Holy Ghost.

Once the weapons had been gathered and loaded into the militia's supply wagons, Lyman Wight addressed the Saints. "Brethren," he shouted, "Lieutenant Governor Boggs and Colonel Pitcher have requested that we surrender our weapons. We have agreed to do this and Colonel Pitcher agreed to seize the weapons of the pukes and to use the Missouri militia to protect the Saints. Governor Dunklin has also said that we could apply for militia arms and protection if we are attacked. To bring peace to Jackson County, I have agreed to surrender the arms of this army. May God be with us. You are dismissed."

Josh Lewis turned to John. "I hope that Brother Wight knows what he is doing. I don't feel very safe knowing that we are basically disarmed and that we must rely on the likes of Pitcher to disarm the pukes and protect us."

John didn't reply, he was so relieved that there was not going to be a battle and he wouldn't see any mutilated bodies today like that of John Keck.

The little army of Saints immediately began to break into small knots of men, who began to wander off while talking among themselves and shaking their heads in doubt.

Josh Lewis was livid. "I didn't walk five miles out here in the dark just to turn my gun in and walk home," he lamented. "I really wanted to smite a sinner today and hasten the coming of the Savior."

John looked at him with disbelief; he couldn't fathom how a man could profess to love Christ and want to kill others because of their beliefs.

John arrived home at noon and as he entered the cabin, he found Jenny and Agnes sitting on the horsehair loveseat. Agnes rose and glared at John through gleaming eyes.

"So," she demanded, "did you stand and fight with the others or did you run like a frightened rabbit? Tell me, did the Army of the Lord destroy the heathens or did you all turn tail and run?"

John just looked at her with sad eyes and wondered why everyone seemed bent on killing each other over issues that neither side truly understood.

"I am too tired and hungry to discuss this matter now," he replied.

"If you are hungry, then you can fix something yourself or you can see if your puke friends will feed you," Agnes angrily exclaimed. Leaping to her feet, she fled to her bedroom and slammed the door. Jenny rose from the couch and went to her father.

She looked up at him tenderly. "Come in the kitchen," she said. "I gathered some eggs this morning and I will scramble some for you." John looked into the blue-gray depths of the girl's eyes and his heart melted from the heat of the love he saw reflected there. In his mind he wondered why his wife couldn't be as kind and understanding as his daughter.

The news that the Saints were disarmed and helpless spread like a prairie wildfire among the Missourians. In the long afternoon following the confrontation between the Missouri militia and the army of the Saints, virtually every old settler in Jackson County knew what had happened. Once they knew that the Saints were disarmed, the cowards among them rose like mushrooms from cow shit and headed first for the outlying settlements of Big Blue and Lee's Summit.

The first warning many of the Saints had that disaster was about to befall them was the sound of pounding hoofbeats as a mass of men with blackened faces or masks covering their features surrounded their cabins. They destroyed every cabin and homestead belonging to the Saints they could find and drove the inhabitants into the teeth of a November gale. The dark night was dotted with the glow of burning homesteads across the rolling grasslands west of Independence. The women and children were rousted out of their homes with the threat that their cabins would be burned down around their ears, then they were driven before the mob like a herd of despondent cattle, clinging to what meager belongings they could carry.

The men were treated even worse, and many were lashed with bullwhips or quirts or run over with horses if they tried to resist or protect the women and children. One old man cursed the mob for cowards and was rewarded with a fifty-caliber ball through his head. The mass of refugees was systematically herded toward the Missouri River and the border with Clay County. As evening fell, the wind picked up until it became a moaning banshee rushing through the bare cottonwoods bordering the creeks and ponds. The dark overcast skies opened and rain poured down in blinding torrents on the miserable refugees.

Women with babies in their arms looked up and cursed the dark skies. As if in answer, the rain turned into a blinding sleet storm that blanketed the prairie with a glaze of ice. The tracks of those who had been driven out without shoes were rimmed with blood. The wretched refugees headed in the only direction open to them, north and east toward the Missouri bottoms.

Lyman Wight was warned of the gathering storm by one of the brethren and he saddled his black Morgan and fled into the gathering gloom. He realized that if he were caught, the Missourians would hang him as a traitor and a radical without bothering with the niceties of a hearing or trial. As he thundered across the old wooden bridge over the Blue Branch, a group of masked horsemen saw him and, with a whoop, they gave chase. Wight spurred the big Morgan in the ribs and, leaning over the horse's withers, he whispered imploringly in its ear to run like the wind and save his life. As if the magnificent animal understood, it suddenly stretched out to its full stride and with nostrils flaring, the big black gelding gradually pulled away from the nightriders.

When he could no longer hear the pounding of hoofbeats, Lyman finally reined the big horse in and allowed it to blow and get its breath. Lyman would spend a week on the prairie hiding in the timber along the myriad creeks and branches before he finally joined the Saints on the Missouri bottoms, ragged and emaciated, but safe to fight another day.

Chapter 12

John and Jenny sat in the little kitchen of their cabin and watched the fire crackle and pop. John had just finished eating the eggs and salt pork that Jenny had prepared for him after he returned from the ill-fated campaign. He didn't realize he was so hungry. Jenny filled the old cast iron fry pan full of eggs and pork and John devoured every morsel and mopped up the grease with a bit of cornpone. After eating, he was stuffed and contented and in that dreamy netherland when the mind teeters on the brink of sleep.

He was telling Jenny about the day's adventure when he glanced at the window and was amazed to see the mauve tinge of approaching evening coloring the pale light of the overcast sky. He was about to rise and tell Jenny that he was going to retire when he heard the rhythmic drumming of dozens of galloping horses' hooves. John leaped to his feet and despite his tranquil state he knew instantly what the racket meant. His first thought was to protect Jenny, but before he could speak, the front window broke in a mass of glittering glass shards. A huge rock went skittering across the rough pine boards of the floor and thumped solidly against the leg of the horsehair loveseat where Jenny sat clutching her knees.

Before John could move, the door burst from its hinges with a crash and the entire door landed flat on the floor. The dust was still swirling when a huge man stomped into the room, wearing a slouch hat and a grotesque mask made from an old bed sheet with eyeholes and a slit for a mouth. "Git the hell outta here ye fuckin' fanatics," he screamed, "'afore I beat the shit outta ye with this here bullwhip."

A shock of terror went through John like a lightning bolt. He faced the apparition and tried to speak, but his throat closed like a clenched fist and all that came out of his mouth was a whiny squeak.

Jenny leaped to her feet. "What is the meaning of this?" she demanded. "How dare you break into our home like this? Get out or we will have you arrested."

The huge man turned and leered at her through the eye slits of his mask like some smirking gargoyle.

"Wull missy," he hissed, "seems ye got more guts thun yer ol man. If ah didn' have more pressin' business, ah would teach ya a few things."

John's paralyzing fear suddenly turned to rage when the nightrider threatened Jenny. With a wild shriek he rushed at the huge man with fists flailing like a runaway steam engine. The man grinned in his mask and brought the butt of the bullwhip he was holding down on John's head with a sickening thud.

John slumped to the floor like a windblown scarecrow and flopped over on his back. Jenny screamed and rushed at the big Missourian, shrieking like a banshee. He flicked his huge wrist and flipped her away like a bothersome fly. At that second, the bedroom door flew open and Agnes burst into the room with her hair in tangles and her eyes flashing in anger and insanity.

"You ungodly heathen," she screamed, "git out of my house, you defiling piece of shit!"

The big Missourian grabbed her by the wrists and lifted her off the floor as if she were a rag doll.

Just then, another man stepped through the door and spoke in a commanding voice. "Luke, goddamn ya, git them Bible thumpers outta this cabin and let's get on with it." At that Luke threw Agnes against the log wall with a nasty-sounding thud. She slid down the wall and crumpled onto the floor. Luke turned as if to leave the house, then he spotted the coal oil lamp burning on the table. He grabbed the lamp by the base and flung it against the far wall where it smashed with a tinkling of glass and a flash of igniting coal oil.

With a smirk he looked at Jenny. "Okay missy," he said, "if ye kin get that cute ass behind ya enough to drag them two outta here maybe they won't fry in hell just yet. If ya git them outta here alive, ya better git outta Jackson County and never come back."

With that he turned and followed the other man out of the door. Jenny glanced at the rapidly spreading flames licking hungrily at the dry pine planks of the flooring and realized that she had little time to get her parents out of the cabin before it was entirely engulfed in flames. She rushed to where John lay sprawled on the floor by the loveseat.

"Daddy," she tearfully implored the motionless figure of her father, "please wake up! We have got to get out of here."

John moaned slightly and his eyelids fluttered like moths, but he did not move.

Jenny looked around her wildly and her heart sank when she saw that the fire was crackling and roaring like a wild animal and had nearly doubled in size in the two minutes since the Missourian threw the lamp. She grabbed John by the collar and tried to drag him across the floor, but to her horror, she found she couldn't even move his torso. She cast a terrified glance at her mother and realized in an instant that Agnes was even more insensible than her father.

Jenny jumped to her feet and ran to the door, nearly colliding with William Ingram, a staunch Saint and elder in the local church branch. "Jenny," he yelled, "you have to get out of here! The entire cabin is going to be engulfed in a second."

"I can't leave until I get my mother and dad out," she answered pleadingly. Ingram looked wildly around the cabin and instantly realized that John and Agnes were unconscious. Ingram was not a big man, but the panic that rose from his groin sent a flood of adrenaline coursing through his body. He grabbed John and flung him over his shoulder like a sack of meal and, running for the door, he grabbed Jenny by the arm and dragged her with him.

Ingram dropped John in the mud of the street, and looked Jenny in the eye.

"Stay with your father," he demanded. Ingram turned and ran into the now-blazing cabin. Jenny watched him in horror. The entire cabin was now in flames and the sparks were streaming skyward like an insane swirl of fireflies. In terror, she covered her mouth with one white hand. She could not visualize anyone entering that blazing inferno and returning alive.

To Jenny's amazement, seconds later, Ingram emerged from the now-collapsing cabin with Agnes flung across his shoulders. Jenny could not help but notice that Agnes's skirt had hiked above her waist and her spindly legs were showing below her billowing bloomers. For one fleeting second, Jenny pictured a scrawny chicken plucked for the boiling pot. Horrified, she flung the image from her mind, but she couldn't completely erase the comical image from her psyche, and she silently chuckled in spite of her fear and dismay.

Jenny ran to her father and looked into his pale face. She was relieved to see his eyes flutter open and a shadow of a smile flicker across his lips like lightning flickering on the horizon. She suddenly became aware that the street was full of mounted men with blackened faces or masks. Several of the Evanses' neighbors rushed up and began to comfort Agnes and John. Brother Ingram straightened up and looked at the mounted mob. The leader was sitting astride a big buckskin horse a little in front of the rest of the rabble.

Ingram strode toward the rider and stopped a few yards in front of him. "Why have you done this?" he asked in a pleading voice. "We have done nothing to you."

The mounted man looked at Ingram with eyes flashing beneath his long hood.

"You tell us God will destroy us and that we are sinners," he said in a muffled voice. "You tell us that this land was given to you by God, but we were here long before you came. You say that we are sinners, but we worship God, too. You invite niggers to come into our country, but we are slave owners, and then you wonder why we want you to leave. You are fanatics and we cannot abide to live with you as neighbors. I am sorry it has come to this, but you will leave or we will drive you out with a bullwhip."

Ingram put his hands on his hips in a gesture of defiance and replied, "Our prophet has said that this is holy land given to us as a birthright and we shall not leave just because a bunch of pukes threaten us."

The Missourian rose in his stirrups and urged the big horse forward with a nudge of his knees. Jenny caught her breath because she thought the man was going to ride over Brother Ingram. Instead, he reined the horse in a few feet from William and flicked the huge bullwhip to its full length; with a flip of his wrist, he sent the pleated leather whip hissing forward like a monstrous snake. It wrapped around Ingram's shoulders and back like a boa constrictor, cracking like a rifle shot.

Ingram gave an agonized scream and fell writhing into the mire of the street. Jenny was amazed to see that the whip had cut Ingram's coat and shirt like butter and laid the flesh of his back open in a great, gaping wound. Ingram was squealing like a stuck pig and thrashed about in acute agony. The Missourian who had lashed Ingram deliberately coiled the deadly whip and, sitting straight in the saddle, looked down on Ingram with distaste.

"You people have poured into our county without money or support and have squatted on land that isn't yours. You have suggested that the Indians are actually Hebrews and have encouraged them to farm the land and stay where they are not wanted. You have told us daily that we are sinners and that God will destroy us so you can take our land as an inheritance. Now it is time for you to leave this county or you will suffer the same fate as this man or worse. Now all of you must go!"

John looked at the tall figure sitting on the big horse and he felt the familiar bolt of fear, but despite his panic, he ran to where Ingram was still thrashing about and screaming at the top of his lungs. He took the agonized man by the shoulder and tried to speak to him, but Ingram's pain was so intense that he couldn't stop writhing and shrieking. John threw his arms around Ingram and held him to stifle his maniacal threshing and spoke soothingly into his ear.

Eventually he stopped squirming and screeching and slowly got to his feet. John was shocked to see his coat and shirt were soaked with blood and the heavy fabric of the coat hung open, revealing a long gaping wound that made John think of a loose, moist mouth hanging open like an idiot's smile. He helped Ingram hobble to the sidewalk and turned toward the leader of the mob.

"Please," he pleaded, "this is a terrible night—the wind is blowing hard and it is beginning to sleet. Before the night is over there will be snow on the ground. You can't drive these people from their homes on a night like this."

The leader of the Missouri mob continued to sit casually on his big buckskin. The horse seemed to reflect its master's nonchalance and stood hip-shot with its ears back and head down.

The Missourian looked at John through the hideous eye slits of his mask and said in his muted voice, "You fanatics should have thought of that back in July, when we burned your newspaper and told you to leave. Now the time has come to go and we will not hesitate to whip or shoot anyone who doesn't leave now, so git!"

Bishop Partridge suddenly stepped forward. "Let me address the people and then we will leave," he said.

The man on the pale horse looked at him with impatience. "Be quick about it," he said curtly.

"Brethren," yelled Partridge to get the milling Saints' attention. "All of you gather at the bishop's storehouse and bring any burlap sacks you have; we'll give out all the flour and cornmeal that we have in the store as well as clothing so we'll have some supplies to support ourselves until the Lord sees fit to help us regain our homes."

With that, the bishop marched off down the street without a backward glance. He knew that the faithful would follow him without question.

John looked around for Jenny and Agnes. His head was throbbing like a drum and a bolt of pain shot through his shoulder and arm when he moved them. He gingerly felt his forehead and found a huge knot forming just above his eyebrow. He found Jenny sitting in the muddy street next to Agnes, trying to comfort her as she watched the remains of their cabin crash down on itself in a shower of sparks. John looked at Agnes and was shocked at her appearance. Her left eye and face were grotesquely swollen and the flesh around her eye and cheek was already beginning to turn a dark, angry purple.

When Agnes saw John's boots stop in front of her, she looked up and John involuntarily recoiled when he saw her left eye was entirely bloodshot and had hemorrhaged from the vicious blow she had received. "Why didn't you protect us?" she shrieked. John said nothing, but hung his head in humiliation. Jenny suddenly stood and put her hands on her hips in a pose of indignation.

"Mother," she barked, "Dad did try to protect you and that huge brute hit him with a whip and knocked him unconscious."

Agnes gave her daughter a furtive glance and curled her upper lip in a sneer that clearly indicated she didn't believe her husband had the guts to stand up for anything. Agnes's sneer cut John's heart like a knife and he wished for once in his life he could stand and fight like other men.

He reached down to help Agnes to her feet, but she jerked her arm away and got unsteadily to her feet without his help. Jenny took her mother's arm and tried to steady her, but Agnes gave her a withering glance and shook her arm off.

"I have learned to rely only on myself and the Lord," she spat, and turned and shuffled off in the direction Partridge had gone. Jenny gave her father a sympathetic look and took his hand. Together, they set off in the direction of the bishop's storehouse.

When John and Jenny arrived at the storehouse they found a long line of Saints, but they had no alternative, so they took their place at the end.

John glanced warily at the sky and noticed that it was as black as sin. The rain had stopped for the moment, but the wind had turned cold and the air had the feel and smell of snow. He shuddered when he realized that he and his family had no shelter or food and the wind on his face had the feel of a coming blue northern. His heart sank when he realized that Jenny and Agnes depended on him for survival. Feeling overwhelmed, he desperately wanted to retreat into his psyche and let someone else take this awesome responsibility, but there was no one else.

His agitated brain frantically searched for some solution. Lost in thought, he involuntarily jumped when someone touched him on the shoulder.

"Brother Evans, perhaps we could pool our resources," Port Rockwell said in his booming voice.

John looked into the genial blue eyes of Rockwell and his fears dissolved like a spring snow. He admired and trusted Porter Rockwell; he knew that Port was an experienced frontiersman and knew how to live off the land. His desperation dropped from him like an old coat and he felt a glimmer of hope. For once, he thought that perhaps God had come to his aid in his time of need and sent this shaggy, kindhearted man to save him from failure.

"Port, what will we do? We don't have any shelter or warm clothes; we'll freeze or starve if these men drive us from Independence," John implored.

Porter looked at him with sympathy rather than the disdain that he had come to expect from self-assured men like Rockwell.

"Don't worry, Brother Evans," Port said in a confident voice, "we'll go to the Missouri bottoms where we'll be protected from the wind un we kin build shelters from the cottonwoods. It's no problem ta start a fire and make a suitable shelter from cottonwood logs and bark. Don't worry, Brother Evans, we won't die out there."

Two hours later, John, Jenny and Agnes sat on the rough board sidewalk and took stock of their situation. They were able to get two sacks of cornmeal, two quilts, items of winter clothing and a heavy canvas tarp. Port Rockwell had told John to stay in front of the bishop's storehouse and he would meet him there. As they waited, John noticed that the wind had picked up in intensity and a few pellets of sleet stung his cheeks as he sat on the rough plank boardwalk.

As usual, Agnes was admonishing John over his shortcomings. "Just how do you expect us to carry this food and clothing?" she wailed. "You should have found us a buggy."

John gave her a tired glance and sighed. "From the reports that I heard while getting supplies, I think we're quite well off," he said. "They say that most of the Saints from the outlying settlements weren't allowed time to prepare at all and the Missourians whipped them and drove them out on the prairie without giving them a chance to gather any belongings."

Agnes raised her eyebrows and was about to say something when they heard the clatter of hooves and a lumbering buckboard came around the corner. As it drew nearer, John recognized the squat figure sitting on the spring seat as Port Rockwell, with Luana and the baby. Rockwell drew the team to a stop in front of them and quickly sprang from the seat of the wagon.

John looked at the stock of supplies in the back of Port's wagon and whistled. "Port, you really thought ahead."

"We moved our stuff inta the wagon after the pukes tore off my roof and I kept it supplied, in case they came back. When Brother Wright gave up our guns, I hitched up the team and came inta Independence fer protection. Load yer stuff in here and we will head north ta Clay County. I hear they is welcomin' Saints that is drove outta Jackson."

The two big draft horses stamped their feet, shook their heads and blew through their nostrils, seemingly as anxious to be away from Independence as their master. John anxiously began to load their supplies into the back of the buckboard. Agnes, her eye now nearly swollen shut, glared at John out of her good eye and he instantly thought of the witches from *Macbeth*.

They headed north and east from Independence toward the Missouri bottoms and the border with Clay County. Being a ferryman, Port knew that a ferry operated on the Missouri near Sibley. Port slapped the reins across the rumps of the two Conestoga horses he called Don and Dime. The slap was not meant to cause any sting, but just to let the two big draft animals know that their master was in charge and alert.

Port had a deep fondness for Don and Dime. He admired their shining coats and huge fetlocks with long, curly white hair. The horses seemed to have a sense of pride in their handsome appearance and massive power, for they loved to prance, especially when they had an audience. Port was unaware of the heritage of these great animals, and he would've been surprised to know that their ancestors originated during the Ice Age in Europe.

Agnes and Jenny sat in the back of the wagon with Luana and her baby. They wrapped themselves in two heavy quilts and pulled the canvas tarp over their heads to protect them from the driving sleet. John wrapped himself in an old wool blanket and sat on the spring seat next to Port. Port handed him an old German flintlock horse pistol and told him to keep it under the blanket and ready in case they were accosted by one of the groups of omnipresent nightriders who kept the Saints moving north out of Jackson County.

John felt a stab of guilt as they passed groups of men, women and children on foot, trudging across the frozen prairie. Most of these refugees had only what they could carry. Many had wrapped old blankets around their shivering shoulders to ward off the biting wind and driving sleet. The ragged blankets flapped around them in the wind, giving them a forlorn look like lonely forgotten scarecrows flapping in an empty autumn cornfield. To his shock, John noticed that many of these destitute refugees had wrapped burlap bags and pieces of blanket around their feet in a futile attempt to ward off frostbite. As the wagon rolled past these poor waifs, they looked up at its occupants with unbridled envy in their eyes.

"Port," John said, "Perhaps we could pick up some of these poor people and give them a ride in the wagon?"

"Naw," Port replied. "The wagon is 'bout full and if we pick up two or three of these people, it will make little difference to the hundreds that is fleein' Jackson County."

Some of the fugitives were lucky enough to have horses or oxen and wagons or buggies, but for the most part, Zion trudged north on the feet of the Saints.

As they rolled through the dark night, the wind continued to rise and the sleet turned into a driving wet snow. The big draft horses didn't seem to mind and kept their noses turned northeast and their rumps to the south in the direction of the wind. From time to time they would violently shake their bodies and stamp their huge hooves to dislodge the snow from their wet coats, but they didn't seem to suffer from the wind and driving snow. Agnes, on the other hand, kept up a constant whining about the weather, the pukes and the loss of her home, which Port and John let slide by like the sleet.

The long night passed slowly and John frequently dozed, but as soon as he drifted off, a wagon wheel would hit a hidden rut or badger hole and he would wake with a start. By the time the sky began to lighten perceptibly in the east, his body ached and he was groggy from lack of sleep. As dawn broke, they saw the sky was a leaden gray and the wind continued to rise until it rushed across the sullen prairie like a phantom. With the dawn, the driving snow turned back into a hard, cold rain that came down in torrents. John couldn't ever remember being as miserable as he was now. He looked past the sodden rumps of the big draft horses and all he could see was a gray curtain of rain and fog that descended to the very top of the dry, brown gamagrass. He marveled that Port could find his way in this gray wilderness, but Rockwell pressed on without any outward sign of doubt.

The rain continued to come down in torrents and the howling wind drove it almost horizontal to the ground. Nothing could keep the streaming water out and it ran down John's neck in a rivulet. As he stared straight ahead, he found that he couldn't see more than a few yards until the landscape disappeared into a gray curtain. Water poured off his hat in a torrent and ran into his eyes and finally splashed into his lap, soaking him to the skin. He glanced at Port, who stared straight ahead, water pouring from the brim of his hat, ostensibly oblivious to the weather.

About midmorning, Porter suddenly reined in the steaming horses and dismounted from the wagon onto the sodden prairie. John looked at him quizzically.

"Got to scout the trail inta the bottoms," Port said tersely. John had no idea how he knew that they had arrived at the bluffs overlooking the Missouri, for he could see nothing but swirling gray mist. John climbed out of the wagon and stepped onto the spongy grassland and instantly leaned against old Dime to steady himself on the soft, wet soil. He followed the disappearing back of Rockwell, who stopped suddenly. John stepped up beside Rockwell and was amazed to find that the land fell away in a steep slope. John could hear the soft murmur of running water in the distance and realized that they had arrived at the Missouri bottoms.

"How did you know where we were?" he asked Rockwell.

"Ah jus' watched the horses, and when they sensed the bluffs, they hesitated and begun ta shy and throw their heads."

Port walked along the brow of the hill for a short distance until he found a fairly well-used track winding down the bluffs toward the unseen river.

Port instructed John to hold Dime's bridle and he held Don's and they led the horses down the treacherous trail. Though the wagon nearly slid off the track, Porter dug a trench for the upper wagon wheel and got it back on the trail. Shortly they arrived in the bottomlands.

They found a few Saints were already camped in the willows, burr oaks and cottonwoods bordering the Missouri. These people informed Rockwell that the ferry between Jackson and Clay counties was no longer running because the Missouri was at flood stage and the ferrymen considered it far too dangerous to operate the little craft with the river running high and full of sawyers and debris. Their escape to Clay County was cut off until the weather improved and the river became passable.

Rockwell immediately went to work to establish a livable campsite. Despite the rain that continued to come down in torrents, he retrieved a big double-bitted ax from the wagon and began to cut down some medium-sized cottonwood poles. John hurried to Port's side to offer any assistance, but he had no idea what Porter was going to do and just stood and watched. Porter sensed John's feeling of inadequacy and sent him scurrying off on errands.

"While I cut a couple of good-sized cottonwoods with a fork, you kin take an adze and strip some good-sized chunks of bark offn' them cottonwoods yonder," he instructed.

Soon Porter had constructed the framework for two small shelters and a pavilion to provide cover for the little group while eating or just discussing their plight. Rockwell covered the framework with bark slabs that John stripped from the cottonwoods and soon they had cramped but comfortable shelters.

The little group quickly unloaded the wagon and piled their belongings in the three shelters. Porter hastily unharnessed Don and Dime and rubbed them down with an old burlap sack. He then led them to a cottonwood thicket where they would be partly sheltered from the rain and could gnaw some nourishment from the cottonwood bark. When he had finished getting the group settled, he walked down to the river to see if there was any possibility of the ferry running. He returned dejected and reported that the river was still rising and was full of floating sawyers. "Ain't no chance of the ferry runnin' until it quits rainin' and the river drops a spell," he said.

That evening, the rain stopped and the skies cleared. After eating a spartan meal of corn meal porridge and a duck that Porter had shot and after Luana had suckled the baby, they sat under the little brush arbor and shivered in the cold north wind. Porter looked heavenward and pointed out the myriad of stars that glittered frostily in the black sky.

"It 'pears that the storm has passed and if another one don't come in the next few days, we kin probably get across to Clay County," he surmised.

Over the next two days, the weather held and the Missouri bottoms filled up with destitute and freezing Saints. Most of them had little or no food or bedding and only the clothes on their backs. Porter and John helped the other men erect rough shelters, but they could do little or nothing to help them find food or warm blankets. There were many women and children among the refugees pouring into the lowlands along the Missouri and the crying of hungry children filled the air day and night. The destitute Saints were reduced to trying to rub corn ears that they gleaned from surrounding fields on the perforated bottoms of old tubs to produce a gritty corn meal.

Porter knew that if they didn't soon get across the Missouri to Clay County, many would die, and if they remained in the filthy camp much longer, cholera was bound to explode among the starving Saints. The apostles and leaders among them constantly held prayer meetings and cried out to their God for relief. Each night, Agnes would kneel in front of their little bark shelter and in a loud voice cry to her God for justice, vengeance and a sign that he heard her plea.

There was no rain for three days and the river began to recede. The area along the Missouri where the Saints were bivouacked was a squalid and fetid cesspool. The refugees had little knowledge of hygiene and had not dug latrines or other facilities for the disposal of waste. Already, the signs of dysentery and typhoid were beginning to rear their ugly heads. John knew that unless the Saints quickly moved on, disease would destroy them.

The evening of November 13, 1833 was cold and clear. Luana and Jenny had prepared a meal of glutinous porridge made from moldy corn meal. They ate the unappetizing stuff under the shelter of their little bowery. Agnes was in her usual foul mood and glared moodily at her bowl of corn meal mush. Her lips moved incessantly in a silent prayer and sporadically she would throw her arms wide in a silent supplication to the heavens. The others were making small talk and trying not to listen to the cries of hungry children that wavered constantly in the cold air. There was no moon and as twilight faded, the night became velvety black. The only light was from the glittering stars that sparkled coldly in the dome of the sky and the flickering light from the dying fire.

Suddenly Agnes leaped to her feet with her arms outstretched and stared with rapture into the heavens. "Look!" she screamed, "my prayers are answered! God has given me a sign: it is the end of the world. Jesus is coming!"

The others looked skyward and were shocked to see thousands of meteorites streaking across the dark sky. It was as if every star in the heavens was torn from its place and went streaking across the firmament. The Saints didn't know it, but they were witnessing one of the most astounding meteor showers of the nineteenth century.

Agnes was in ecstasy. She stood in the mud with her arms outstretched and watched the streaking meteors flash across the heavens. Her eyes were wide and her lips moved in a silent prayer of thanks. She was sure that God had provided this glorious sign to her alone for her untiring devotion and prayer. As she watched the flaming trails across the dark sky, she was convinced that God meant this dazzling display for her personally. She was sure that it was a sign that she was to help purge the church of all the unworthy and drive the ungodly from the sacred land of Zion.

John looked at the sky in wonder, but as his gaze came to rest on Agnes he shuddered in dread. He knew that her fanaticism and intolerance would now climb to new heights because she had seen a sign of God's pleasure.

PART FIVE

The Sons of Dan

Chapter 13

M ost of the residents of Clay County, Missouri welcomed the Saints and charitably provided them with food, clothing and shelter. The local newspapers, such as the *Far West* and the *Jeffersonian Republican*, decried the vicious actions of the mobs in Jackson County and encouraged the old settlers in Clay County to provide succor to the Saints.

After they crossed the river in late November, the Evans family found shelter with an old farmer and his wife near the town of Liberty. The man and his wife generously opened their humble home to the Evans family. John breathed a sigh of relief once he crossed the roiling river and put his back to Jackson County, but little did he realize his troubles were just beginning.

The Missouri Saints sent Parley Pratt and Lyman Wight to Kirtland to meet with the church leaders and explain their predicament. The prophet directed the people to stay close to Zion and not to sell their properties. At first, Governor Dunklin was sympathetic concerning the plight of the Saints and allowed them to apply for public arms to defend their property. However, the Saints knew that even if they were armed, they were vastly outnumbered by the old settlers and animosity toward the Saints in Jackson County did not wane.

The Prophet Joseph received his accustomed revelation concerning the plight of the Saints and God explained that they had brought the wrath of the Missourians on themselves because of their lack of faith, obedience and devotion. Lyman Wight implored the prophet to assemble an army of God to return to Missouri and retake Zion from the infidels. Joseph, in a moment of recklessness, leaped to his feet and shouted that God would fight the Saints' battles, and set about assembling an army among the church members in Kirtland. Zion's Camp, as the rag-tag army became known, was a dismal failure. When they arrived in Missouri, they were greeted with fear and distrust. In fact, the old settlers of Clay County viewed the coming of Zion's Camp as a hostile invasion and much of the good will toward the Saints there was squandered. The army did not dare cross the Fishing River into Jackson County and camped on the prairie, where many were stricken with cholera and other diseases.

Joseph tried to negotiate an agreement with the old settlers to allow the Saints to return to Independence, but the presence of the armed band of Saints precluded any agreement. When negotiations with the Missourians broke down, Joseph was forced to disband the army on the banks of the Fishing River and allow the foot-sore soldiers to melt into the refugees in Clay County and the surrounding areas. However, before he returned to Kirtland, Joseph again prophesied that the Saints would return to Jackson County in three years and "there would not be a dog to open its mouth against them."

The members remained in Clay County and the surrounding area until the summer of 1836, when the residents of Clay County also began to tire of the sanctimonious Saints. In June of that year they publicly asked them to move on. The Clay County residents decorously suggested that they would provide funds and supplies for the poor among the Saints, but rigidly demanded that they leave.

The Saints, through their lawyers Doniphan and Acheson, petitioned the governor to intercede on their behalf, but Dunklin was upset by the incursion of Zion's Camp and feared that any attempt to aid the Saints would plunge Missouri into a bloody civil war. He harshly replied, "The vox populi is the vox dei"—"The voice of the people is the voice of God." Eventually, the Saints petitioned the Missouri legislature to set aside a sanctuary for them in the essentially uninhabited land in northwest Missouri. In December 1836, the Missouri legislature organized a new county, Caldwell, out of the upper half of Ray County. This new county was to be used exclusively for the settlement of the Saints.

Jake Devine sat next to the fireplace on a cold, blustery evening in January 1836 and soaked up the warmth of the fire. His stomach was agreeably full of venison roast and he began to fall into that pleasant ecstasy that comes just before sleep. His father was reading a copy of the Liberty newspaper, the *Far West*. Jake could hear him mumble over the words and stumble over the pronunciation of any word of more than two syllables. Sam had learned the rudiments of reading, but he found it frustrating and difficult. Sam's reading was always accompanied by a constant barrage of curses as he struggled to decipher the meaning of the text.

Jake knew better than to say anything when his father was making the extreme effort to interpret the printed page, be it the Bible or some frontier newspaper. Sam did not often make the effort to read, but if some issue arose that interested him or if he wanted to consult the Bible to prove a point, he was often motivated to stumble through a few paragraphs. Jake knew that his father had followed the story of the coming of the Saints to Clay County with extreme interest, if only because he viewed them as heretics and usurpers.

Now, intermingled with Sam's profanity, Jake heard Sam curse the Saints and the Jackson County residents for not killing all of the heretics.

"Says here," he said through a wad of chewing tobacco, "that them pests has settled in Clay, and the old settlers is feedin' 'em and givin' 'em a place ta live. Whatta ya think, boy!" he shouted, looking directly at Jake with red-rimmed eyes.

Jake swallowed hard and tried to decide what his pa wanted him to say. "I dunno,'" he answered noncommittally, "I haven't seen one of 'em yit."

"Wull, if ya do, I expect ya to plug 'em same as ya would an Injun. I 'spect it won't be long till they is in the Grand River country. In fact," he continued, "says here that the decent residents of Clay County is itchin' fer 'em to move on now and that the legislature is a'thinkin' of settin' aside a place fer 'em close to Daviess County. Ah guess if they comes here, we will be ready fer 'em, huh, boy!"

Jake was afraid that his father would hear his sharp intake of breath at the mention of shooting Indians, but the old man went on mumbling as he tried to read the newspaper article. Jake found his mind uncontrollably pulled back in time like a whirling leaf carried in the teeth of a November gale.

During the warm days of the past summer, Jake had often found himself drawn to the springfed pond on the Grand River, near where Ozzy had miraculously healed Rufe. On those trips he had often met the little Indian band. He gradually learned enough Osage words that he could communicate with them. He also learned that the muscular and surly brave's name was Ahowi, or Deer, and the slim, shy girl's name was Adsila, or Blossom.

Over time, Jake learned that Ahowi was not really as malevolent as he seemed, but his manner reflected the natural Indian suspicion of whites and resentment of the loss of the Osage lands and the Indian's freedom to roam. The girl, who spoke broken English, was gentle and shy. For reasons he couldn't understand or explain, he felt a deep attraction to her. It was more than the warmth he felt for Rufe or his friend Buck; it was almost a pain or an ache.

One warm early fall day, Jake, accompanied by Rufe, found himself climbing the little hill that bordered the pond. As he neared the top, Jake heard the musical trill of feminine laughter. Rufe was twenty yards ahead of Jake, happily snuffling through the tall bluestem looking for sharp-tails. As Rufe topped the rise, Jake heard sudden splashing and a startled yell. He ran to the top of the rise and was shocked to see Adsila, standing in the water up to her waist, looking at Rufe.

What shocked him more than suddenly seeing the girl was the fact that she was naked. Jake had never seen a woman naked before. He had seen his mother from time to time, bathing in a little tin tub before the fire. However, she had always been careful to cover herself with an old towel before she got out.

Despite his mother's efforts to keep him from seeing her naked body, Jake had seen enough to know that women were basically different from men. Seeing his mother in the tub had never had any effect on Jake except to embarrass him. Now as he stood on the little rise looking down at the rippling blue water of the pool, he felt paralyzed. His mouth fell open and his eyes were glued on the most sensual sight he had ever beheld. Adsila had heard Rufe as he ran through the dry buffalo grass. She naturally turned toward the sound and was standing with her arms at her sides with the water just below her navel.

Jake was about twenty yards from her and the scene was burned into his mind. The slightly slanting sun of early autumn was at her back, but the light reflecting off the rippling water illuminated Adsila's body with subtle undulating light and shadow. Jake's eyes went immediately to her dusky breasts, which, though relatively small, stood out proudly from her body. Around each erect nipple was a dark circle, which mysteriously intrigued Jake. Her stomach was flat and slightly rippled with well-toned muscle. Her navel was elongated and deeply dished, yet there was no excess flesh on her stomach or sides.

She made no effort to hide her nakedness and returned Jake's stare, but it was much more demure than Jake's open-mouthed gape. She gazed back at Jake, frozen on the little rise with the sun shining on his smooth cheeks and the wind rippling the shock of hair peeking out from under the battered old felt hat. Gradually a shy smile spread across her face like the shadow of a cloud moving across the prairie on a summer day.

"Hullo, Jake," she said in a soft voice that sent shivers up Jake's spine.

Jake realized that his mouth was open and that he was staring at her in rapture. His mouth snapped shut with a click and he stammered, "I didn't expect to see ya here."

She giggled and her small breasts jiggled. For some reason this simple movement sent exquisite waves through Jake's stomach. He tried to speak, but nothing came from his lips but some idiotic grunting noises. With the same sensual smile playing across her lips, Adsila walked gracefully out of the water with her fingertips trailing lightly across its rippling surface.

Jake stood rooted to the spot where he stood. He stared at the girl as she walked toward him. For the first time he noticed that her skin was a luxurious brown, not the pasty white of his mother's where it was protected from the sun. Her hair glistened with water and seemed as black as a crow's feather. She reached the edge of the water and stopped, looking into his face with the same little smile still playing at the corner of her mouth.

As if they had a mind of their own, Jake's eyes swept downward from her breasts to her swelling hips. He shuddered as if from fear or cold, but actually the emotion he felt was more akin to ecstasy. His wide eyes came to rest on the dark triangle of hair between her legs, glistening with water beads and curling luxuriantly against her smooth skin.

"Hullo, Jake," she repeated, now standing less than five feet from him. Finally Jake managed to stammer out a greeting.

"Ahowi and Ozzy fishing," she said simply. With that, she turned and walked gracefully down the bank in the direction that she had indicated.

Jake watched her go and noticed how gracefully her hips swayed and how intriguing her smooth brown buttocks were. As Jake stood there watching her walk down the shoreline, he suddenly became aware that he had an erection. His rough denim pants stuck out in the front like a pitched pup tent. He felt the blood rush to his cheeks and knew that they must be glowing red. He cursed himself for standing there like an idiot, stammering and gawking at the girl, unable to return her greeting. He wanted to turn and run and never face her again, but he was irresistibly drawn to her and he turned and walked slowly down the beach in the direction she had taken.

Rufe seemed to sense the turmoil in his master and he stopped hunting for sharp-tails and walked close to Jake's right leg, occasionally looking up questioningly into his master's face.

In perplexity, Jake slowly walked in the direction that Adsila had gone, and as he rounded a gentle curve in the shoreline, where the beach bent around a little promontory, he saw the Indian camp. Adsila was nowhere in sight, but Ozzy and Ahowi were doing something in the water a few yards from the shore. The old, sway-backed, piebald pony was standing patiently near a canvas-covered lean-to. A fire smoldered under a rack, consisting of four corner poles and covered with willow branches, and Jake knew the Indians were drying and smoking fish.

As he drew nearer to the camp, Deer looked up from the fish trap he was tending and raised his arm in a greeting. He said something in Osage that Jake couldn't quite make out and punched the old man on the arm and gestured in the direction of Jake and Rufe. The old man stood up stiffly and waded to the shore. Ozzy brought his clenched right fist quickly to his chest and looking into Jake's eyes he grunted "Hawe" in a guttural tone. Jake inwardly breathed a sigh of relief. He wondered if Blossom had said something to her father about Jake's reaction to seeing her naked, but the old man greeted him warmly.

As they were standing facing each other, Deer splashed out of the water and slapped Jake on the shoulder in an affectionate greeting. Obviously, Adsila had said nothing to her brother and father. Jake needn't have worried, for she thought nothing of bathing naked in front of the men of her tribe. However, she did find it strange that Jake seemed to lose his ability to speak when she walked out of the water.

In the Osage tongue, Ozzy patiently explained to Jake that the little band was smoking fish and waterfowl for an upcoming journey. He tried to explain the purpose for their journey, but Jake couldn't understand the unfamiliar Indian words. Frustrated, Ozzy tried to clarify his point using what few pidgin English words he knew, but he was unable to make himself understood. As the three men stood on the bank gesturing and waving their arms in exasperation, Blossom emerged from the lean-to and walked toward them. Jake involuntarily turned toward her as he caught sight of her from the corner of his eye. He suddenly realized that he would never look at this woman in the same way again.

She was dressed in a light-colored doeskin dress that seemed to cling to her slender form. As he watched her walk toward them, Jake again saw her standing naked in the shimmering waters of the Grand. His heart leaped into his throat and he was certain that he would again become mute and stammer like an idiot. With more self-control than he thought he could possibly possess, Jake managed to greet her without mangling his words.

Blossom looked at Ozzy and said something in rapid Osage. The old man replied and she turned to Jake. "He says that he was trying to tell you why we are leaving and where we are going," she said in halting English.

"Yes," Jake replied simply. Blossom lowered her eyes as if to gather her thoughts and then lifted the brown orbs and looked directly into Jake's soul. Jake found that he could not break the bond of Blossom's gaze and her misty brown eyes seemed to look into his very being. Jake's chest constricted with an emotion that he had never before felt and he wondered if this girl possessed some of the mystical powers that Ozzy had exhibited.

"The old man had a vision three moons ago," she finally said. "In the vision, he saw this land run red with blood. He saw two bands of white men and they fell upon each other with knives and guns and many were slaughtered. Earth Mother showed Ozzy this land in the future and it was burning; many of the white man's houses lay in ruin and cattle and horses were slain for no other purpose than to deny them to the other band. Earth Mother told him that this war between the two tribes of white men came about because they disagreed with each other about how to honor the Great Spirit."

Jake tried to say something, but Blossom put her finger to her lips in a sign that she had more to say. "Earth Mother told the old one that if the Osage stay here they will be caught between these two groups of warring white men and destroyed. She whispered to Ozzy, who is a holy man, a medicine man to the white man. The old one heard Earth Mother murmur to him in the wind, and she said that something evil was coming, so he built a sweat lodge and sat in it for many hours, until he journeyed out of his body and saw a vision. In the vision, he saw the Osage fleeing the white man's war and crossing the river of muddy waters. Earth Mother told him that we must seek our brothers in the treeless land across the muddy waters and there we will be safe for a time."

Jake looked at her and a thousand emotions that he couldn't explain swirled through his mind. "Can't you just stay here? Nobody comes here and you'll be safe."

"No," she admonished, "it was made clear to the old one that we must leave our homeland or we will be killed. Even though Earth Mother gave us this land, we can no longer stay here. If you want to find us, we will be on the plains in the land of the Cherokee and Kansa." With that she turned and began gutting fish.

Jake sensed that he'd been dismissed and she had finished speaking to him. Actually, Blossom had told Jake what was in her heart and she now waited to see if he would offer to go with them. To her disappointment, he looked soulfully in her direction, but turned on his heel and called to Rufe. He and the dog climbed the hill above the pool and soon disappeared from view as the waving prairie grass seemed to rise up and cover them as they crested the hill and dropped from view down the other side.

Jake didn't worry about not having bagged any red meat for the larder. His father had set out that morning on the old black mule for Gallatin to attend a meeting of the old settlers to discuss the problem of the Saints. Sam Devine constantly fretted about the myriad Saints in Clay County. After they were driven out of Jackson, they still flooded into Missouri and the disbanding of Zion's Camp had further swelled their ranks. Sam feared that if the Saints continued to pour into Clay County, it wouldn't be long before the old settlers asked them to move on, and the logical place for them to go would be the sparsely settled Grand River region of northwest Missouri.

Sam naturally joined the other struggling homesteaders and teamsters who were on the bottom of the social structure of the frontier and who feared the coming of the Saints because they would be pushed further down the hierarchy. The frontiersmen also didn't understand the Saint's obsession with the Indians and feared their constant efforts to convert the red men. To the flotsam of the frontier, Indians were less than human and anyone who saw them as otherwise could not be trusted. Although most of the lower class Missourians weren't slaveholders, they supported the slave system and feared and mistrusted anyone who opposed slavery in any way. The average frontiersman didn't know or care that after the burning of the *Evening and Morning Star* Joseph had changed his views of the Negro and now denied them the priesthood because they were the seed of Cain.

Jake knew that his father would harangue against the Saints in some saloon until he was drunk and then he would probably shack up with some whore until he slept off the effects of the rotgut whiskey. The boy was confident that he wouldn't see his father today and probably not for two or three days. It was a warm and pleasant September day, and Jake and Rufe meandered slowly home. Jake wasn't much interested in hunting and unbidden, his mind returned again and again to the image of Blossom standing in the shimmering waters.

The old dog ran in front of him with his nose to the ground, joyously snuffling the delicious scents that lingered in the damp grass. Occasionally, he would discover the fresh trail of a cottontail or a prairie chicken, but Jake didn't respond to the hound's delighted baying. After discovering an especially warm trail of a prairie chicken, Rufe joyfully leaped clear of the grass and, lifting his long nose, he gave tongue to let Jake know that he had discovered game. The old dog couldn't understand why Jake didn't react to his primeval call, and leaving the trail he dejectedly followed his master toward home.

Jake usually relished the soul-stirring bawl of the hound on a fresh trail, but today his mind was on weightier things. For some reason the thought of Blossom and her band leaving the area lay heavy on his mind. He especially found the thought of never seeing the girl again depressing. As he neared the cabin, he was surprised and unnerved to see the old black mule that Sam always rode tied to the pole corral. The animal's flanks were covered in lather and it was standing with its head down panting piteously.

Jake could see that the mule had been ridden nearly to death from its heaving sides and dripping muzzle. He untied the mule from the rickety pole fence and got a bucket of water from the well. While he was getting the water, the mule stood in place with its head between its front legs. Jake glanced up from the well from time to time to ensure that the animal did not lie down. He was sure if the mule went down, it would flounder and die. Jake pulled the old wooden bucket from the dark well and ran to the heaving mule. He put the bucket of cool water near the animal's muzzle and eventually it lifted its head and began to drink in great slurping drafts. Jake allowed the mule to drink about half the bucket and then took the water away.

He led the critter into the minimal shade of the straw-covered shelter and then, taking an old burlap sack, he dipped it in the remaining cool well water and then rubbed the overheated animal all over with the wet sack. Eventually the mule quit shaking and slobbering and Jake gave it the rest of the water. He slipped a halter over its head and tied it to one of the uprights under the old straw-covered lean-to. Once he was sure the mule had partially recovered, he filled the bucket with corn from the crib and gave it to the exhausted animal.

After milking the cow and finishing his other chores, he walked reluctantly toward the little cabin.

As he entered the door, he noticed that a fire was burning in the fireplace and his mother was standing with her back to him, tending something cooking over the fire. Sam was sitting at the table with a bottle of corn whiskey in front of him. From the half vacant look he gave Jake, the boy knew that the old man was drunk. The door scraped across the warped flooring and Bessie automatically turned to see who had entered. Jake was stunned to see that one of her eyes was nearly swollen shut, and the flesh around it was a violent purple. She looked at Jake with the eyes of a rabbit caught in the talons of an eagle that beseeched her son not to make an issue of her injuries.

Instantly Jake knew that the old man had not found a whore to shack up with in Gallatin and had returned and taken his wife violently. Jake didn't understand the particulars of the matter, but he knew when Sam returned early from town because he couldn't find a woman, his mother invariably suffered. Sam gave him a defiant look and Jake knew that any word from him would initiate an immediate truculent reaction from his father.

Jake realized that he couldn't stand up to Sam, so to avoid a confrontation, he muttered, "Gotta go git muh gun and possibles bag."

With that he turned and walked out of the door into the waning sunlight of the early autumn evening. In that instant, an impression came suddenly into his mind like the shadow of a vulture flying over the grass, and he knew that one day he would kill Sam Devine.

Chapter 14

In June of 1836, the residents of Clay County met in Liberty and issued a proclamation officially asking the Saints to leave. They offered to raise money to support the poor among the Saints to obtain food and supplies to support their move, but they were adamant that the Saints should go. The Saints briefly considered moving to Wisconsin, but their overtures there were met with opposition.

The spring of 1837 found the Evans family involved in a mass exodus of Saints, all moving north. The vanguard of the migration began the previous year and had located a site in Caldwell County for the new City of the Saints. The location was in the rolling country in the north section of the county. The embryonic city was dubbed "Far West" and, nurtured by the industriousness of the Saints and the great flood of land-hungry immigrants, the fledgling city grew like a mushroom in the fertile soil of Missouri. John had been in no great hurry to leave the comfort of settled areas of Clay County and by the time that he assembled a dilapidated wagon and sway-backed team to haul their belongings to Far West, the spring had evolved into summer.

The trip to Far West took them three days. Porter Rockwell and his family had caught up to John's aged, slow-paced nags on the first day. John, ever aware of his own inability to tackle wilderness chores, had been relieved to have Port's skilled companionship. Agnes had been pleased not only for Port's skills but also to have a companion who shared her narrow views of God and religion. She used the opportunity to verbally chastise John both for his incompetency and for what she perceived as his tolerance of sin.

Jenny was happy for the extra company, though she did not share her mother's attitude. She recognized that her father possessed qualities that Porter didn't and that the traits that John enjoyed were as valuable as Porter's. She didn't have a critical nature and she did not judge her father for his lack of ability to start a fire or build a shelter out of natural material, and she respected John for his knowledge of human nature and the classics.

On the last day of the journey, as the raw little city of Far West became visible in the distance, John felt his old nemesis, fear, squeeze his guts. Although the Evans family and the Saints were arriving in a new home, John knew that the intolerance was coming with them and would continue to cause problems.

Agnes had become even more fanatical after her experience in the Missouri bottoms. She was convinced that the dramatic meteor shower was a sign from God, directed to her personally to assure her that she was doing the Lord's work. After receiving this amazing sign, Agnes had redoubled her efforts to study the work of the prophet and to maintain a list of commandments, prophecies and writings that spewed forth from him.

In 1833, Joseph had received a revelation that he referred to as the "Word of Wisdom." In part, this bleak revelation forbade the use of alcohol, tobacco, coffee, tea and other hot drinks and the use of meat except in winter and times of scarcity. Joseph received the revelation during a time when temperance was running rampant among American churches, and Joseph obviously felt pressure to bring his church in line with other sects by adopting a policy of temperance. Emma had also complained bitterly to Joseph about the smoke and tobacco juice on the floor of their home after the meetings of the Apostles.

By nature, Joseph was not a long-nosed temperance preacher, but he knew when to bow to the inevitable. For several years, Joseph didn't enforce the Word of Wisdom and considered it more good advice than a commandment. Joseph enjoyed the things of this world too much to embrace an ideology of self-denial. However, Sidney Rigdon and the high council, in an effort to stamp out sin and ensure that the Saints became worthy to inherit the New Jerusalem, forced the issue and made the Word of Wisdom a commandment in 1834. After that time, failure to abide by the Word of Wisdom was reason to deprive a church official of his office and deny a Saint access to the Holy Temple.

Agnes heartily embraced the Word of Wisdom and relished it as a club she could use to chastise the wicked. She also looked upon obedience to the Word of Wisdom as a badge worn proudly by the righteous. She became so fanatical about it that she frequently embarrassed John by loudly denouncing strangers whom she saw drinking or smoking as unrighteous sinners. Agnes became a self-appointed enforcer of the Gospel and was sure that through her intolerance she was hastening the redemption of the Saints and the coming of the Savior. It never occurred to Agnes as she read the New Testament that Jesus had a much more tolerant approach to the "sin" of drink than she did.

Once she had decided that it was an affront to God to smoke or to drink alcohol or tea or coffee, Agnes constantly reproached John for his occasional glass of wine, sour mash whiskey, or aromatic pipe. John greatly enjoyed smoking his pipe in the evenings with a glass of sherry. He resented Agnes's efforts to force him to give up the few simple pleasures that life still afforded him. To avoid Agnes's constant nagging, John took to hiding his pipe, tobacco pouch and a bottle of sherry in some secluded spot where he could be alone and relax with his depravity.

As Far West drew closer, John couldn't help but think about what might await them in the new city. His agitated mind dredged up all that had happened over the past two years and he looked forward to establishing a new City of Zion with dread. To John, it seemed that the Jackson County experience had made the Saints even more fanatical and intolerant. He had often heard them say that those who rejected the Gospel were evil because they couldn't recognize the truth when they heard it.

Agnes constantly lectured him to deny the way of the world and live the word of God. Since they had embraced the Word of Wisdom, the Saints appeared even more sanctimonious to the flotsam of the frontier. Now the Saints believed that baptism into the church and devotion to the teachings of the prophet caused the blood coursing through the veins of the righteous to change into the actual blood of the Hebrews. John realized that this arrogance would only lead to more troubles with the Missourians and in his heart he believed that the coming storm would be far more furious than anything the Saints had seen yet.

As they had camped overnight on the journey across the grasslands, Port had talked of a new development that could lead to other issues. John's mind carried him back, as if through a dark tunnel, to the discussion. They had been sitting by the fire after camping one night and Porter had glanced at John and noticed a melancholy expression on his face. "What are ya thinkin', Brother Evans?" he asked.

"Oh, I was just wondering what awaits us in Far West; I don't think I can endure the violence that we experienced in Independence."

"Wull, Brother Evans," drawled Porter, "ya gotta remember that we is the chosen people and evil men will always try and thwart the will of God. But if we persevere, eventually the Saints will rule the world and we will have riches beyond belief. Our prophet has said that once we has learned to live the Gospel and never question his appointed, we will establish the City of God and the Ten Tribes will come from the north carrying gold and untold riches."

John couldn't tell Porter that he didn't care about riches and that he seriously doubted the Saints were going to rule the world or that the Ten Tribes would return from the north with gold and jewels. He often wondered how the Saints could profess to follow the teachings of Christ, who refuted riches, power and wealth and espoused tolerance. John couldn't get their destination, Far West, out of his mind. He envisioned a desolate, barren wasteland that would require the very frontier skills that he lacked. He didn't relish the thought of trying to scratch the tough sod-covered soil with an iron-shod plow or sweat in the hot sun trying to build a suitable home for his family.

With these reservations on his mind, he turned to Porter. "Porter, what can we expect in Far West? Is it still raw wilderness with no sign of civilization and no homes or cabins?"

Porter gave John a curious look. "No, John," he replied. "The prophet sent William Phelps to Caldwell County some time ago with fourteen hundred dollars to purchase land. As ya know, land prices has been a'risin' fer some time and ya kin buy land on credit. Many Saints moved to Far West when trouble first started in Clay County. They bought land on credit and the risin' prices was enough to pay fer their land."

Porter stopped and stared into the dying fire to collect his thoughts and continued. "That is, until that heathen Andrew Jackson passed his Specie Circular, which stopped land agents from acceptin' credit fer land and required anybody buyin' land to pay hard money, gold and silver, fer it.

"Joseph had a vision," he continued, "that required all Saints in good standing to sign their property over to the church and to give ten percent of their increase to the church. Those who didn't have property or money to contribute gave their labor. In Far West, the population was divided inta farmers, artisans-mechanics, shop-owners, and laborers. Everyone works, or they don't eat or take the fruit of the industrious. I think ya will be pleasantly surprised when ya see Far West."

Chapter 15

The sun had set and twilight was beginning to fall like a dark blanket when the tired travelers finally rolled into the bustling town of Far West. For once Agnes showed some interest in her surroundings and she displaced Jenny on the spring seat next to John. As they slowly rolled down the main thoroughfare, she looked out over the dynamic town with sparkling eyes.

"I understand Brother Phelps is in Far West," she declared.

"Yes, I think he is," replied John.

Agnes sighed. "He helped establish Joseph's School of the Prophets here in Missouri. I must talk to him and continue my work in documenting the words of the prophet," she said simply. John glanced at her sitting raptly in the seat next to him and he shuddered inwardly, for he knew that Agnes had taken another step down the road of fanaticism.

Porter pulled up his team at the town square where the industrious Saints had already laid the cornerstone of another temple. Porter jumped down from his wagon and approached a well-dressed man walking along the board sidewalk.

"'Scuse me, kin ya tell me where we might find the bishop?" he asked.

The man turned to him and doffed his top hat. "I'm not sure where you might find Bishop Partridge," he replied, "but if you are Saints wanting to settle here, go to the end of the street and ask at the meetinghouse. They will provide you with a place to stay and you can meet one of the church leaders tomorrow." With that he brusquely turned and continued down the street.

John and Porter tied up their teams and told the others they would return shortly. With that they walked down the bustling street in the direction the man had indicated. The meetinghouse was a low, clapboard building, with a small belfry above the entrance. John pushed open the door and found himself in a tiny foyer. A slender, gray-haired man was just picking up his coat and hat from a hook on the wall. He turned and smiled at John.

"Good evening," he said, "my name is John Whitmer. Can I help you?" Whitmer was a soft-spoken, almost shy man who radiated a demeanor of vulnerability. His gray eyes were soft and gentle and his smooth face looked almost boyish. His suit was stylish, but it hung on his gaunt frame and accentuated his awkwardness.

John immediately liked this unassuming man and felt comfortable in his presence; taking Whitmer's hand, he introduced himself. Whitmer fixed his gentle eyes on John. "It is late, Brother Evans," he said. "I own a small hotel immediately across the street. I suspect that there is room there for you and your family and Brother Rockwell and his family. Tomorrow is Sunday. The Saints will gather to worship in this meetinghouse in the morning at ten o'clock. Please be there and the bishopric will give you instructions then. By the way, there is a livery stable next to the hotel where you can stable your animals." With that, Whitmer doffed his hat in salutation and turned and left.

The hotel proved to be rustic but relatively comfortable and John slept well. Agnes and John were forced to sleep together in the large bed that dominated the room and Jenny slept in a small trundle bed that was stored under the large bed. The large bed was a huge, hardwood affair with an ornate headboard. It was wide enough for four adults to sleep comfortably in it, and Agnes slept as far from John as she could, curled up in a fetal position.

When he awoke in the gray dawn, John felt a pang of something akin to loneliness and he looked at the piteous lump on the far side of the bed that was his wife. He felt a longing to snuggle against her and hold her in his arms, but he knew that if he nestled against her she would forcefully shove him away and rebuke him for lust. It wasn't sex that John hungered for but human acceptance and respect, and then John realized why he abhorred Agnes's fanaticism.

He climbed quietly out of bed and, finding a bowl and pitcher of water on the nightstand, he washed his face and shaved. Checking his watch, he found that it was only seven in the morning and both Jenny and Agnes were still sleeping soundly. He thought how nice it was to sleep with his wife for the first time in many months. Even if she was cold and indifferent, there was something soothing in the rhythmic sound of her breathing and he didn't feel so alone when he awoke.

At a quarter to ten, the Evans family walked briskly down the board sidewalk toward the meetinghouse. Despite the fact that their clothes showed the effects of being packed in a trunk and transported a hundred miles over the dusty prairie, the family still looked freshly scrubbed and combed. Even Agnes had a coy smile on her thin lips and greeted other pedestrians on the rough boardwalk with a nod and murmured greeting. They soon arrived at the meetinghouse and were welcomed at the door by the bishop and stake president of Far West. The president, David

Whitmer, was a distinguished-looking, gray-haired man. When he placed his hand in John's in greeting, it felt limp and dead; impulsively, John looked down at the offending hand to ensure that he wasn't touching something disgusting.

Whitmer had a long face and his lips drooped at the corners in a perpetual frown.

"Good morning, I am President Whitmer," he said to John in a voice as limp and dead as his handgrip.

"Good morning," John replied, trying to make his voice friendly and cheery. As John moved on into the meetinghouse, he heard Agnes lecturing Whitmer about her dedication to the Gospel and her self-appointed position as scribe of the church in Missouri. The murmur of the congregation partially drowned out Whitmer's reply to Agnes, but to John it appeared that he was trying desperately to dismiss Agnes without wounding her.

John filed into the crowded chapel and found a pew that had three empty seats. He slid down and made room for Jenny and Agnes, who shortly joined him. Soon the room was filled to capacity and people were standing along the walls for want of a seat. The room was filled with the hum of muted conversation and reminded John of the gentle buzz of bees around an apple tree in the spring. Whitmer rose and strode to the pulpit. Instantly, the murmur stopped like crickets when they sense a footfall. Whitmer cleared his throat and gazed out over the throng.

"Brothers and Sisters," he began, "we have much to discuss this morning concerning the work of the Lord. To begin, we will ask Brother Levi Anderson to offer the invocation." John thought he heard a barely audible groan rise from the congregation. An old man rose from the midst of the crowd and, with the aid of a cane, he hobbled to the pulpit.

When the old man finally said "amen," the congregation gave a little sigh of relief and repeated "amen" in unison.

A rotund, gray-haired woman rose from her seat and pompously marched to the front of the room. She was carrying a baton, which she wielded like a miter. She raised her hands and in a whiny voice she announced, "Brothers and Sisters, let us begin this service with a hymn to cleanse our hearts and help to ensure that the Holy Spirit will be with us this morning. We will sing 'Hail to the Man.'" With that she swung her plump, short arms in an arc and the congregation burst forth with "Hail to the man who communed with Jehovah." John Evans cringed when he heard the words and he wondered in his heart if this was blasphemy to pay homage to a man who claimed to have face-to-face discourse with the Almighty.

After the Saints had finished paying tribute to their prophet in song, David Whitmer rose from his seat with dignity and, straightening his coat, he grasped the podium with both hands and leaned forward toward the audience like a cat stalking a mouse.

"Brothers and Sisters," he began, "I must enlighten you as to what is happening in the kingdom of God. First of all, the prophet has clarified the revelation on the Word of Wisdom. Brothers and sisters, this is now a commandment, a commandment for the weakest of those who would call themselves Saints. The prophet has said that those who break this commandment will be cut off from the church. In fact, twenty-two Saints were disfellowshiped in Kirtland recently. Some of them were cast out from the church for not obeying the Word of Wisdom, but others were cut off for shameless behavior such as dancing with their arms wrapped around another as the Gentiles do. The prophet has made it clear that we as Saints must obey the dictates of the Lord and his appointed leaders.

"Brothers John Whitmer, Martin Harris and Oliver Cowdery were called before the high council in Kirtland for not supporting the brethren. These men actually witnessed the Golden Plates from which the *Book of Mormon* was translated, but they succumbed to the wiles of Satan. They were chastised for speaking out against the prophet and accusing him of sordid crimes. These men actually filed charges against the prophet for fraud involving the Kirtland Safety Society Anti-Bank. As you know, this bank, owned by the Saints, failed because of actions by the government. We know that Joseph has prophesied that those who would come forward and forgive notes issued by the bank and other transactions would be blessed by the Lord with riches unimaginable."

To John, this sounded like a desperate attempt by the church leaders to escape the crushing debt that they had incurred through the ill-fated Kirtland Safety Society Anti-Bank and land speculation ventures. He gazed about him to see how the others were accepting Whitmer's message but every face he could see was raptly intent on his every word.

"Brothers and Sisters," Whitmer continued, "if we're to avoid the temptations of the adversary, we must follow every word and every commandment that issues forth from the prophet and his counselors. We were driven out of Jackson County because we didn't live the Gospel to its fullest. There were whisperings, dissension, fornications, and consorting with the Gentiles. We're a chosen people and we must stand apart from the world if we are to receive the blessings that the Lord has promised.

"The Saints are also commanded to give their surplus to the bishop and to deed their property to the church to help relieve the brethren of their debt. Those who do this will be blessed with riches and blessings that they can scarcely contain. However, those who don't follow the teachings of the prophet and who transgress will be cast out and they'll lose their possessions to the Gentiles. If we remain faithful, the Lord will fight our battles and the Gentiles won't be able to harm us. Now let's go forth and build here in Far West a city unto God. Hosanna!"

The crowd rose to its feet as one and, thrusting their right hands into the air, they shouted "Hosanna! Hosanna! Hosanna! To God and the Lamb."

Once the crowd had sat down and the babble gradually died out, Whitmer seized the pulpit until his knuckles turned white. He looked out over the congregation and said in a low, stately voice, "Before we close with song and prayer, Brother Lyman Wight would like to address the Saints."

He turned and took his seat behind the podium. John recognized Wight's bear-like frame as he rose from the front row and strode to the stand.

"Brothers and Sisters," he roared in a bull-like voice, "we're a chosen people devoted to doing the Lord's work. Therefore, we cannot tolerate any dissension in our ranks." He stopped speaking and glared out over the silent ranks to let his words sink in. "In Kirtland," he continued, "men who've witnessed the hand of God have turned on the prophet and accused him of adultery, deceit, and of being a false prophet. He's been accused of preaching a system of spiritual wifery and of adultery. In fact, Brother Heber Kimball said there're hardly twenty men in Kirtland who would acknowledge that Joseph is a prophet of God. We'll not allow this type of dissension in Far West. If one of you speaks against God's anointed, you'll be driven from this place. Remember, there are sins that can only be forgiven by the spilling of the sinner's blood."

Again, Wight fell silent and glared out over the spellbound congregation and shook his shaggy head like an old bull buffalo. "We're engaged in a great work and a wonder and we cannot allow any disparagement. Therefore, anyone who condemns the leaders of the church will be driven from our midst. Anyone breaking the Word of Wisdom or using vulgar language shall be cut off from the church and driven from among us. Also, we're engaged in building a city to which all the righteous shall come to see the return of the Savior and anyone who doesn't work won't eat the bread of the industrious." With that Wight again shook his bushy head for effect and turned and left the podium.

John knew that the simple joys he loved so much—his pipe, a cup of tea or coffee, an occasional glass of wine—were now taboo, and he wouldn't dare to imbibe, even in private. He didn't want to incur the wrath of Agnes, whom he knew would report him, nor did he relish being dragged before the high council court for enjoying personal pleasures. He wondered if leaning back in his chair on his porch and enjoying the morning sun for an hour would be considered sloth in this society. He felt smothered and instinctively knew that he would never be happy in such a structured environment, because it stifled his sense of freedom. He was far too much of a free spirit to be intimidated by such a regimented milieu, but he was bound to it by an iron bond that was Agnes. To John it was ironic that he was bound by his marriage to Agnes, a woman who used the teachings of the church to coerce her husband, based on a system that demanded that women obey the men.

The rest of the meeting was a blur for John. After Wight had implied that sinners might pay with their blood, his ears were roaring and he felt as if he could not breathe. He looked around him at the mesmerized people hanging on every word and he wondered if these people were capable of murdering those who didn't believe in their Gospel and prophet. A thought came to him as if whispered in his ear: he would die here and, oddly, he thought of the Holy Ghost.

Fall quickly passed into winter and the Evans family fell into a comfortable routine. Because of his background, John was again appointed as headmaster of the local school. It was a job that he loved, for he enjoyed inspiring young minds. However, he also realized that it was a dangerous position. He knew that members of the priesthood would keep a close watch on him, and anything he said or taught that could be construed as contrary to the Gospel would be duly noted and disciplined. He didn't relish being called before the brethren to answer for some supposed sacrilege. He cherished free thought and he realized that the only way to open young minds was to teach them to explore all avenues of an issue. However, Far West wasn't a place that encouraged such free thought. After leaving Independence, John had acquired a few classical books to replace the ones lost in the fire, but he knew that the Saints wouldn't look kindly on the ideas discussed in these treatises. He worried that Agnes would report his books to the Bishop so he kept them out of sight and never discussed the ideas they contained in front of Agnes.

The Evans family was assigned a lot and a cabin and once they were settled, Agnes marched over to W. W. Phelps's office to offer her services as scribe of the Gospel. She wouldn't take no for an answer, even when Phelps pointed out that responsible church positions were always held by men, who were members of the priesthood. Phelps finally gave up with a sigh and let Agnes have a battered desk in a musty corner of the meetinghouse. Every morning, Agnes set off to her duties with a self-satisfied air.

Jenny, who was nearing the age of seventeen, was considered old enough to marry and most girls her age actively sought a mate, lest they be considered a spinster. Joseph had instructed his people to be fruitful and go forth and multiply and replenish the earth and most Saints took this teaching literally. They believed that there were multitudes of spirits in the pre-life that were waiting to receive a body and be born; therefore it was the duty of every married couple to have as many children as possible and Far West gradually became filled with children. Many families had ten or twelve offspring.

Jenny shared her father's belief in free thought and had no desire to become involved with a man who considered women subservient and a fertile garden for producing children. Her young mind was still searching for an identity, but, like her father, she had no inclination toward fanaticism and conformity. She attended church because she didn't want to incur the wrath of her mother and she realized that in the regimented society of Far West it wasn't good to draw attention to oneself by appearing to question the dictates of the Gospel. However, she didn't mingle with the Saints of her own age, and when she attended church meetings she remained aloof.

Agnes constantly rebuked Jenny to show some interest in the young men of the church, especially those who, in her mind, showed exceptional zeal. Jenny felt unfulfilled. She loved to discuss philosophy with her father, but they couldn't do this in their home if Agnes was present. Father and daughter began to make a habit of walking in the rolling prairie that surrounded Far West and letting their minds wander where some thought led them.

Chapter 16

Around the middle of January 1838, word came that the prophet had fled Ohio because of pending lawsuits and accusations from the dissenters. The dissenters, including Oliver Cowdery, had accused the prophet of fraud, lying, cheating and adultery. Cowdery had heard rumors of a liaison between Joseph and a young woman named Fanny Alger. He referred to this matter as a "dirty, nasty, filthy affair."

With his church in Kirtland falling apart around his ears, lawsuits pending and creditors demanding payment, Joseph fled Kirtland for the more accommodating milieu of Missouri. Agnes immediately proclaimed the prophet's expulsion from Kirtland and arrival in Far West as an act of God. With the prophet in their midst, they could press on to found the perfect society and stamp out any dissension that reared its ugly head in the Holy City. Agnes was ecstatic that the prophet was now in their midst and had fled the Babylon that was Kirtland.

Agnes was elated and incessantly babbled at the dinner table that the coming of the prophet was the beginning of the Millennium. She had always known that Missouri was the centerplace for the gathering of Israel and she believed wholeheartedly that Independence was sacred and sanctified ground. When they heard that Joseph was coming, the church leaders assigned choice lots and homes for him and his brother Hyrum. When they finally heard that the prophet's entourage had arrived at the little river port of De Witt, they sent an assemblage of wagons and buggies to carry the prophet and his brother into Far West in triumph.

It was a cold and raw day in early February when the Saints of Far West lined the streets of their proud city to welcome the prophet to the Promised Land. Agnes had risen early to ensure that she would have a choice spot to pay homage to the man she revered. She was already gone when John and Jenny rose and took time to eat breakfast. By the time they arrived on the main street, it was lined with an exuberant throng and they were forced to stand far back from the street under the overhang of a hardware store. However, neither of them was disappointed and the portal gave them shelter from the biting wind and sleet.

The unruly crowd suddenly grew silent as the first buggy, carrying their prophet and his bodyguards, came into view. It was drawn by a matched team of shining black horses and the buggy itself was a magnificent black, fringe-topped surrey. The prophet was sitting in the back with his brother Hyrum and was immaculately dressed in a black broadcloth frock coat and top hat. In unison, the throng raised their arms in greeting and a throaty "Hosanna!" rose from several thousand throats. John got a glimpse of Agnes; she had run into the street and stood with her arms raised above her head as if welcoming a conquering hero. To John, the whole affair reminded him of the Caesar's triumphant entry into Rome.

After the excitement of the prophet's arrival, the Evans family settled into a daily schedule. John essentially taught all grades in the little clapboard school. Agnes spent her time annoying the bishop, stake president and members of the Twelve Apostles asking questions about church doctrine and nagging them for copies of letters, revelations and other relevant documents. Jenny helped her father by tutoring children and was dragged against her will to church youth events and women's gatherings where the ladies knitted socks and other garments for the poor immigrants pouring into Far West. Invariably at these meetings some well-meaning woman would suggest an eligible young man to Jenny.

Jenny was perceptive enough to understand that her father was not happy in his relationship with Agnes and she also understood that most of the resentment between her parents was caused by their differing opinions on religion. She shared her father's liberal attitude and she had no desire to become a wife and lackey to a member of the priesthood. Even at her young age, she believed that two people who shared a relationship could still cherish their individuality.

Jenny also shared her father's fascination with nature and loved to wander the rolling countryside around Far West alone. Her mother forbade her to leave the town unaccompanied because she feared that some godless Gentile would rape her or something worse. Actually, the Saints' relationship with the Gentiles was fairly benign during the early spring of 1838. There was an occasional clash over land or squatter's rights but there was no real violence between the two groups.

The prophet's flight from Kirtland left a void in that town and the church set up by the dissenters soon fragmented. Many of the apostates became disillusioned with the radicals in Kirtland and eventually came straggling into Far West, half contrite and half unrepentant; among them were Luke Johnson and Oliver Cowdery. These men were greeted with suspicion and downright hostility in Far West. Some of the city leaders who had offered support for the dissenters after the collapse of the Kirtland Bank and the schism in the church in Kirtland, were cast in the same lot with the dissenters. These people were considered a "stench" in the nostrils of those who had never questioned "God's anointed."

Chic Simmons had migrated to Far West in 1837 and had established a little livery stable close to the Evanses' home. Jenny would often sneak down to Chic's stables and coax him to let her borrow a gentle mare to ride on her exploring excursions. Chic knew that Agnes frowned on her daughter wandering beyond sight of town, but he found it difficult to resist the girl's charm. Jenny refused to wear a skirt or ride sidesaddle on her outings. When Agnes was at Bishop Phelps's office, busy compiling references to the Gospel, her daughter would dress in an old shirt and pants belonging to her father and sneak down to the livery stable, where Chic would cringe when she swung straddle-legged into the saddle.

Spring came early to northwest Missouri in 1838, and one beautiful morning in late March, Jenny rose and found her parents gone. She hurriedly dressed in boots, baggy pants, a loose-fitting shirt and a floppy slouch hat and crept down to Chic's stable. She avoided the few pedestrians that were on the sidewalks early in the morning and from a distance no one would recognize her in her riding garb.

After much persuasion, she finally convinced Chic to lend her the old gray mare, whom she called "Molly." She quickly saddled the mellow horse and, gracefully swinging into the saddle, she pulled the old slouch hat over her eyes and headed north out of Far West. The morning was one of those rare times in early spring when the breeze feels balmy and promises that spring will soon arrive in earnest. The meadowlarks called in their melodious trill from the tops of the few scattered burr oaks. She rode past a little springfed pond and a red-winged blackbird announced, "Cheer up, cheer up, spring is here" from the catkin of a dry cattail stalk.

Coneflowers and black-eyed susans were already in bloom and nodded good-naturedly at Jenny and Molly as they rode by. The bluestem and gamagrasses were by now showing green, and distant rolling hills took on a misty emerald aura. Jenny impulsively took a deep breath and found the spring air as intoxicating as heady wine. In fact, she felt lightheaded, as if she had secretly shared a glass of Merlot with her father. She felt strangely exhilarated and she suddenly dug her heels into Molly's flanks and clucked to the old mare to urge her into a gallop. For an old horse, Molly had a surprisingly smooth gait and seemed as full of life as Jenny. She eagerly broke into a gentle gallop and they charged up a grassy hill and drew to a halt at the top.

Jenny looked out over the rolling grassland dotted with distant trees and brush-lined creeks all waking to the gentle urge of spring. As she gazed into the distance, she realized she was witnessing the miracle of rebirth. She suddenly felt as if she were a part of this wonder, and she spread her arms wide to as though to embrace the awakening earth. She felt the horse stir beneath her thighs and she felt erotic warmth in her loins. Whenever she was alone in the embrace of nature she experienced a strange sensation of exhilaration and belonging as if she were a part of the great renewal. She placed her hand on Molly's neck and felt a kinship with the animal that reminded her of meeting a dear friend that she hadn't seen for a long time.

Jenny sat for what seemed a long time on Molly's back, surveying the exquisite beauty of the endless rolling grassland. In the distance, she could see wandering lines of cottonwoods and brush lining the distant springfed runs that crisscrossed the well-watered prairie of upper Missouri. A coyote suddenly broke cover from a clump of buffalo berry not ten feet from Molly's nose. She watched enthralled as it gracefully darted away on dancing feet. The sudden appearance of the coyote broke the spell. Jenny clucked to the horse and they ambled off in the direction the coyote had taken. A sharp-tail grouse flushed in front of Molly's hooves and the clatter of wings startled Jenny completely out of her reverie.

Jenny lost all track of time and had no idea what direction they were traveling. She just sat straight in the saddle, engrossed in the countryside. As she topped one of the many rolling hills, she spotted something moving in the little valley in front of her. She squinted and recognized it as a large dog, which had its nose to the ground busily snuffling in the emerging bluestem. As she stared at the dog, a distant figure suddenly came over the little rise above the valley. Jenny felt a little pang of fear rise in her gut. Panicky, she quickly looked around her and found that she didn't know in which direction Far West lay. She glanced again at the distant figure and saw the flash of the sun reflecting off of what appeared to be a gun barrel.

She thought of kicking Molly in the ribs and riding away from the advancing figure, but Molly raised her head and pointed her ears at the figure and gently whinnied as if in greeting. Jenny was naturally a gregarious person and something in the way the figure moved reassured her. With the grace of youth, she threw her leg over the horse's neck and jumped to the ground. She watched the shape below her slowly cross the valley. Whoever it was, their interest was centered on the dog and they followed the general direction of its meanderings, which was directly toward Jenny. She watched intrigued as the figure drew nearer.

Jenny could now tell that the stranger was probably a man by the way he was dressed and moved. He stopped stock still as if he sensed her presence. He raised his head and looked directly at the spot where she and Molly stood. He raised the gun diagonally across his chest and tilting his hat back he looked intently in

Jenny's direction. He slowly raised his arm and yelled loud enough to be heard, "Howdy."

He whistled to the dog and, springing into a graceful trot, he quickly covered the ground to where Jenny stood holding the horse's reins. As the figure grew nearer, she realized that it was a young man of about her age. He was wearing ragged trousers and a well-worn linsey-woolsey shirt. The dog reached her first and gently sniffed her leg. He was an old hound and his muzzle was totally gray, but he appeared friendly and quietly licked her hand that she held out to him.

The young man stopped about ten feet away and tilted his slouch hat back from his forehead, revealing a shock of unruly black hair. He was painfully skinny, but something about his whip thin body spoke of strength, stamina and agility.

"'Scuse me, sir," he said, "I thought ya was Luke Benson, 'cept he always rides a mule, not a nice horse like that. My name is Jake Devine, and ah live over near the Grand. My pappy is Sam; maybe ya has heard of him?"

Jake didn't often meet people in his wanderings and most of those he did meet were homesteaders and neighbors whom he knew on sight. This stranger appeared to be close to his own age, but his face was soft and smooth and strangely appealing. He was wearing baggy pants and a shirt that was too large, but despite the ill-fitting clothing, there was something also peculiarly alluring about the boy's body. Jakes eyes dropped to the stranger's chest and it appeared that under the loose-fitting shirt, there was a gentle swell and he noticed that there was also a captivating swell to his hips and buttocks.

Jenny blushed a bright crimson and the ghost of a smile played at the corner of her mouth like a kitten plays with a string. She looked at her feet and stammered, "I'm not a *sir*. My name is Jenny Evans and I was out for a ride, but I think that maybe I'm lost."

Jake's mouth dropped open and he stood there with his eyes wide and his mouth hanging open like a baby bird. Jenny looked at him and couldn't help but giggle.

"I'm sorry," she said, "I didn't mean to be rude, but you look so funny with your mouth gaping open like that."

With that she took off her battered gray hat, and her auburn hair cascaded to her shoulders and shone in the sun like burnished copper. The sight of Jenny's hair falling about her shoulders confounded Jake even more, and though he tried to speak all that came out were incessant grunting noises.

Jenny realized that Jake was embarrassed and tongue-tied, so she tried to change the subject to ease this poor boy's embarrassment. "I'm sorry," she entreated, "but I didn't pay much attention to the direction I was traveling and I think I'm lost. Could you tell me how to get to Far West?"

The question broke Jake's stupor and his mouth snapped shut with an audible click. He looked down at his feet for a moment to gather his wits and then looked up directly into Jenny's expressive blue-gray eyes and he thought for a moment he would lapse into a daze again.

Once more he looked away and cleared his throat. "Far West is about ten mile south," he said, pointing in that direction.

Jenny glanced at the sun and surmised that it was near noon.

"I have some bread and sliced ham in my saddlebags and a canteen of water. Would you like to eat with me?" she invited.

At the mention of food, Jake suddenly realized that he was ravenous, and as if in answer his stomach growled audibly. Jake flushed a bright crimson.

"I will take that as a 'yes,'" Jenny said with a stifled giggle. With that she turned and opened her saddlebags and retrieved an oilskin pouch. She spread it on the grass and opened it, retrieving a package wrapped in brown paper. She sat down on the soft bluestem and indicated with her hand for Jake to join her. Jake hesitated, then with a self-conscious awkwardness he settled in the grass a few feet from Jenny.

Jenny pulled her canteen from the saddlehorn and set it next to the oilskin pouch. She unwrapped the sandwiches and handed one to Jake. Jake accepted the sandwich in silence, but then he thought of all the times his mother had told him to say thank you when offered something and he murmured, "Thank you."

Jenny raised her eyebrow in a gesture of surprise. "You're welcome," she replied. For some reason, her simple act of raising an eyebrow sent a tremor down Jake's spine. Jake was very uncomfortable. He didn't know what to say or if he should look directly into this girl's eyes. He stared at the remains of his sandwich and murmured, "Is ya one o' them Saints, what's been takin' over the land and claimin' that God is goin' to drive us out?"

At that moment, Rufe nuzzled Jenny's hand and drooled at the sight of her sandwich. She looked into the hound's misty eyes and broke a piece of her sandwich and held it out to the dog. Rufe took her entire hand into his mouth and sucked the bread out of her fingers.

Jenny laughed and Jake thought her laughter sounded like the trill of a meadowlark.

Jenny turned her attention to Jake and said, "You can look at me when you talk." She added, "And yes, I guess I am a Saint, but not really by choice." She went on to explain to Jake that she didn't really like the regimentation of the Saints and resented being told what she could read, think and say. She tried to explain to the boy that both she and her father didn't speak out against the authoritarian nature of the church because of her mother's control over them both. Jake thought of his father and he knew how a strong-willed and manipulative person could control another, especially one who lacked the confrontational attitude to resist.

Jenny went on to elucidate some of the Saints' beliefs, such as how a person could only be saved if they underwent the accepted rituals and unquestioningly obeyed the dictates of the prophet and twelve apostles. She explained that only those who accepted the Gospel would be saved, and that a woman could only be saved through tacit membership in the priesthood and through her husband. Only those, she explained, who were baptized and confirmed as a Saint could receive God's guidance through the Holy Ghost, and this was typically reserved for male members of the priesthood.

As she spoke, Jake felt much more comfortable in the presence of this girl. In fact, he felt much as he did when he talked to Blossom. "Are you a member of any church, and do you believe in God?" Jenny asked him.

Jake considered her question and replied, "My Pa is a Bible thumper, and he beats my ma and me. I met an Indian band and they taught me about Mother Earth. Their medicine man saved Rufe after Pa nearly beat him to death, so I guess I am more comfortable with their beliefs."

Jenny listened intently as he told her that the "People" believed that they were the children of the Earth. They called their Earth God "Wakanda," and she asked her people to respect their brothers, all the creatures that dwelt in the land. He told her that if one showed respect to brother creatures and each other, when they died a horse would come and carry them home to the bosom of Wakanda.

Jenny was amazed to learn that the Osage didn't believe in killing others, but were duty bound to exact revenge for a serious wrong committed by another. She was especially enthralled with the Indians' respect for nature and all living things. Although Jake spoke with a frontier drawl, he expressed himself well when discussing something he understood and cherished.

They sat in the grass talking for hours, oblivious to the passage of time or the slow descent of the sun toward the western horizon. Jake's quick mind reminded Jenny of her father's. Jake, for his part, was enthralled with the amiable girl. The only other woman of his own age that Jake had even spoken to at any length was Blossom and he willed the day to go on forever. Molly was content to drag her reins and munch the succulent bluestem while her mistress sat in the grass, and Rufe wandered across the little valley looking for rabbits and sage hens. Jenny sat spellbound listening to Jake talk about his association with the Indians. She even felt a little pang of jealousy when he described how Blossom had explained Osage beliefs to him. Impulsively, she bent over and lightly kissed him on the lips.

Jake was stunned and gazed back at her with his eyes open wide in shock. At that moment, a spider ran across Jenny's hand, which was splayed in the grass when she leaned forward toward Jake. She quickly looked down and shook her hand, breaking the reverie. Jenny glanced up at the sky and realized that the day was almost gone. Panicky, she leaped to her feet. "My mother will be home soon, I have got to go!" she exclaimed.

She hastily gathered her bag and canteen and, throwing them in the saddlebags, she turned to Jake. "What is the fastest way to Far West?" she said breathlessly.

Jake was as shocked at the passage of time as Jenny was and as he glanced at the sun, low in the west, he hoped that Sam was spending the night in some brothel. Though he knew that he should head for home now, he was loath to leave this girl.

He grabbed the cantle of the saddle with one hand and vaulted on the horse's rump behind Jenny. Putting the gun across his thighs he settled in on the saddle skirt. Pointing, he said, "Head in that direction and I'll show you the best way."

Jenny clucked to Molly and as if she sensed Jenny's anxiety she broke into a gentle, rocking gallop. Rufe leaped to his feet and loped along happily behind the horse.

Jenny was amazed at Jake's knowledge of the lay of the land; he seemed to intimately know every gully and tree. In less than an hour, the outline of Far West appeared on the horizon. As they neared the outskirts of town, Jake leaned over the saddle and spoke into Jenny's ear. "Stop and let me off here," he said. Jenny reined Molly in and Jake slid over her rump to the ground. He looked wistfully at Jenny and then turned as if to go.

"Jake, wait!" Jenny called out. Jake turned and looked at her, sitting tall and straight on Molly's back. "Meet me on the hill above the little hollow where we met today on Tuesday about noon," she said pensively. Jake stared back at her, but she could not read his eyes under the floppy hat, then he slowly nodded, turned and broke into a ground-covering trot with Rufe at his side. Jenny gently kicked Molly in the ribs and turned her head toward Chic's livery. She was intent on getting home before her parents and she didn't see the man standing in the shadow of a box elder tree.

As Jenny rode away, he rose from a crouch and looked after her with a cunning gaze in his eye. He was a lean man, and as he took off his broad-brimmed hat to mop his head, his bald pate gleamed in the slanting sunlight. His skinny wrinkled neck and bulging Adam's apple gave him the appearance of a vulture eyeing his prey. He gave Jenny an appreciative glance as she rode away, and the shadow of a smile curved the corners of his mouth.

Jake broke into a run and glanced anxiously behind him at the lowering sun. He judged that it was nearly 4:30 and nearing the time he was expected to milk the cow and take care of the stock. In his heart he offered an entreaty to Wakanda that Sam was swilling rotgut in some saloon or drunk in the arms of a whore. He maintained an amazing pace and Rufe began to fall behind with his tongue lolling out of his mouth like a huge, wet ribbon.

As Jake neared the cabin, he gave a long sigh of relief and eased off the grueling pace he had maintained for several miles. The old black mule that Sam always rode to town was not in the corral and a welcoming wisp of smoke rose out of the wattle-and-stick chimney. He hurriedly milked the cow, fed the stock and gathered the eggs. With a bucket of foamy milk in one hand and a little wooden pail of eggs in the other he walked to the door of the hut. He kicked the door open with his foot and slid his lanky frame through the half-opened door. His mother turned from the fireplace and, seeing her son, she smiled brightly. Jake returned her smile, bounced to her and put his arm around her waist and kissed her lightly on the cheek. Bessie put her hands against his chest and gently pushed him back. Looking into his face she said, "If'n I didn't know better, I would think ya had a special girl."

Jake was shocked that his mother had read his mood so accurately. His face turned scarlet and he turned away from her to keep her from seeing his embarrassment, but she knew by her son's reaction that her assessment was accurate. She said nothing, but she was delighted to see her son so happy.

"Where's Pa?" Jake asked, trying to change the subject.

"Don't know," she replied. "He rode outta here this mornin' on that ol' black mule and he ain't been back since. He was near apoplectic 'cause he heard that them Saints was a homesteading land over 'round Grindstone Fork and Millport."

Jake's heart leaped into his chest.

"But Ma, I thought them critters was not supposed to settle outside of Caldwell County, and them places is in Daviess, and not ten mile from here."

"I know," she replied. "Yer Pa took his rifle and says he was a'goin' to Gallatin to get some militia boys and run them Saints off."

Jake thought of the fanatics settling the prairie along the Grand and his heart sank. He wondered if some Saint would decide that the little springfed pond was his God-given inheritance and settle near it, filling it with cow and pig shit. He thought of the beauty of the spot and of the day he saw Blossom bathing nude in the clear, springfed waters and he didn't think he could bear to see the land he loved in the hands of a pious fanatic.

"Never ya mind," his mother said. "Set the table and I will serve up some o' this cornpone and boiled chicken."

Jake's mood became somber and Bessie knew that he was worried about the close proximity of the Saints.

"Don't ya worry 'bout them Saints," she intoned. "Folks round here ain't goin' to let them idjuts drive us off our land in the name of God."

The situation in northern Missouri simmered like a kettle on a hot fire, and was finally brought to a boil in April of 1838 by the arrival in Far West of the bombastic and vindictive Sidney Rigdon. Rigdon didn't believe in the right of free speech or free thought. To him, anyone who questioned the prophet or any other officer of the church in good standing should be excommunicated or worse. When he found that Cowdery and others who had questioned the authority of Joseph in Kirtland were now living with impunity among the Saints in Far West, he flew into an apoplectic rage. He immediately called a meeting of the high council and insisted that the nonconformists be cut off from the church.

John, as a member of the priesthood, was invited to attend the meeting to railroad the backsliders. Porter called at John's home one evening and informed him that the high council under the leadership of Rigdon was going to deal with the deceitful and faithless men the next evening at seven in the Ward House. John wanted none of it, but Porter's belligerent mood gave him to know that he had best be there or be counted among the unrighteous.

John was glad that Agnes and Jenny couldn't attend since they weren't priesthood holders. He knew that if Agnes were there, she would lend her voice to chastise those whose only crime had been to speak their mind, question the church authorities or seek to control their own finances and property. John didn't know Oliver Cowdery, but he knew that the quiet and gentle John Whitmer was among those who would be tried for heinous crimes against the truth. John had taken an immediate liking to Whitmer, who had provided his family with a place to sleep when they had arrived in Far West and who had treated John with compassion and kindness. John also knew that William Wines Phelps was under suspicion, and he felt that Phelps had suffered enough for the church.

The next evening after dinner, John dressed in his broadcloth coat and hat and sat on the dingy, worn loveseat and watched the Regulator clock count off the minutes until the allotted hour. Each tick of the big clock sounded like the muffled drums of doom to John. He dreaded the affair and searched his mind for some justifiable excuse to not attend, but he knew that his presence was expected and if he weren't there, his absence would be duly noted. He also knew that Porter was convinced that the high council and Rigdon were acting in the name of God and were only carrying out the dictates of the most high. Porter was nearly as fanatic in his beliefs as Agnes and John knew that any reluctance on his part in carrying out his responsibilities as a priesthood holder would be noted by Porter and the council.

John watched the hands move toward seven with a deep dread. At exactly 6:45 there came a firm knock on the cabin door, and John's heart leaped into his throat. Agnes sprang to her feet and opened the door with a flourish. A light breeze was blowing and the cool spring air rushed in, cooling John's feverish brow. He thought how pleasant it would be to sit on the porch with his pipe and a glass of wine and read a few pages in *A Midsummer Night's Dream* rather than go to this bullying.

Porter strode into the little sitting room, dressed in rough boots and a shabby duster. "Good evenin', John," he announced, "air ya ready to go? We don't want to be late."

Without speaking, John rose from the loveseat and, picking up his hat from a small table, he nodded to indicate his readiness. His throat was so tight that he felt that he couldn't speak and his palms felt greasy. Agnes gave him a piercing look as he stepped toward the door, covertly warning him to show no mercy in the name of the Lord.

Jenny rose and hugged her father. "Follow your heart. I love you," she whispered in his ear.

The two men strode down the tidy plank sidewalk without speaking. When they arrived at the meetinghouse, the doors were open and Bishop Edward Partridge was welcoming the men as they streamed into the little church. John nodded to Partridge and, looking around the crowded chapel, he spotted two vacant seats on one of the pews near the front of the chapel. John took his seat and slid over to allow Porter to sit next to him. His heart was hammering and he didn't even glance to his right to see who was sitting next to him. Instead, he stared at the stand and saw the glowering countenance of Sidney Rigdon staring self-righteously back at him.

Tearing his eyes away from Rigdon's scowling face, John noticed that other church officers were sitting on the stand, including the Prophet Joseph, Brigham Young, Thomas Marsh and David Patten. John knew that these were the prophet's counselors and a representative of the high council.

Patten was a tall, raw-boned man with a perpetual scowl on his face. At exactly seven o'clock he rose and strode to the podium. "Brethren," he began, "it is a blessing that we have in our midst the only true prophet of God." With that he turned and nodded to Joseph. "We are gathered here tonight," he continued, "to determine the fate of certain church leaders who have questioned the word of the prophet, denied the word of God, and disobeyed the dictates of the only true Gospel. Before we begin this somber task, let us pray."

Patten looked into the audience as if to choose one to offer the prayer. His eyes momentarily met John's and fear rose in John's chest like sour bile. To John's relief, Patten's eyes shifted on. "We will ask Brother Peck to offer the invocation," he said. John was sure that those around him had heard the audible sigh of relief that escaped his throat when Patten chose another, for he knew that whoever offered the prayer was expected to beseech God to give this eminent body the gumption to castigate others for showing independence and he knew he couldn't do this.

Reed Peck rose from the congregation and strode to the front of the hall. Rather than offer the usual rant, he merely asked God to give the brethren inspiration to guide them, which surprised John and lifted his impression of Peck.

After Peck had taken his seat, Patten again rose and, gripping the podium with his large, bony hands, he paused for effect. "Brethren," he began, "we are gathered here tonight to hear charges against men who have been appointed by God to positions of authority in this church and who have deceitfully denied those holy callings. The men who you are about to righteously judge have committed heinous crimes against their brethren, against the true prophet of God, and against the true and everlasting Gospel of Jesus Christ as revealed by our latter-day prophet.

"We will first consider the cases of Oliver Cowdery, Lyman Johnson and William McLellin. These men were among the most rabid of the dissenters in Kirtland. They accused the prophet of thievery, lying, fraud and being a false prophet. For these reasons alone, they should be cut off from the church, for no man may speak out against God's anointed.

"This is especially true of Brother Cowdery, for he was Joseph's scribe when translating the *Book of Mormon* and he was with Joseph when John the Baptist returned and conveyed the keys of the holy priesthood on them. Now this deceitful man has accused Joseph of adultery and of being a false prophet. Brothers Johnson and McLellin were accomplices to Cowdery in this heinous crime against righteousness."

John glanced around the meetinghouse and noticed that none of those who were accused were present. He wasn't surprised. Patten stood ramrod straight at the podium.

"Are there any present who wish to speak in defense of these brethren?" he demanded. No one in the audience stirred.

"Then let it be shown by the sign of the square, those who support considering these men no longer members of the church."

Everyone in the audience raised their right hand even with their shoulder, forming a square in the accepted method of showing approval of the actions of the church authorities. John considered asking for someone to elaborate on the alleged crimes or at least to allow the accused to speak in their defense, but he knew this would be considered as unfaithfulness and he cursed himself for his lack of moral principles.

"Next we will consider the justification for denying membership and fellowship in the church to Brothers David Whitmer, John Whitmer, and William Wines Phelps," announced Patten. "These brethren have criticized the high council for giving the prophet a lot in Far West. They have also spoken out against the prophet for his handling of the bank in Kirtland. Finally, they have refused to provide funds for the building of the Temple and haven't consecrated their property to the church as required by revelation from God. It is reported that these men have stated that they wish to have control of their own property and they have sold their inheritances in Jackson County, despite being forbidden to do so by a revelation from the prophet of God.

It has also been brought to our attention that these men have been seen disobeying the Word of Wisdom by using coffee, tea, and tobacco. One who has accepted the truth and then denies it commits the most heinous of crimes and is not worthy to associate with God's chosen people, therefore it is proposed that these men be cut off from the church and no longer be considered members.

"John and David Whitmer witnessed the Golden Plates, which the Prophet Joseph used to translate the *Book of Mormon*, yet they choose to deny the holy word of God. Please show your accord by making the sign of the square."

Again, every man in the audience raised his right hand to his shoulder to demonstrate his loyalty and agreement with the predetermined decision of the church presidency and the high council.

Patten surveyed the audience with a self-satisfied air. "Thank you, brethren, for doing your duty as Saints and members of the chosen people," he declared. "We will now ask Elias Higbee to offer the closing prayer."

John didn't hear anything that Higbee said. He couldn't get his mind off the fact that a man he liked and considered a friend had been denied a hearing and had been stripped of membership in an organization he cherished because he questioned some of the dealings of the church.

John Whitmer had treated him with kindness; now he was dishonored because he chose to deal with his personal property as he saw fit. He thought about Phelps, and his chest constricted when he remembered the night the man was tarred and feathered and abused by a mob for his devotion to his religion—now the members of that religion had terminated his association for nothing more than a rumor.

How could a man like Cowdery, if he had actually seen an angel of God, accuse his friend and prophet, Joseph, of adultery with Fanny Alger, a young girl who lived with Joseph and Emma, if there was not a germ of truth to the matter?

The night was dark when they left the meetinghouse and the velvet sky was a mass of glittering stars. However, John's mind wasn't on the beautiful spring night, for he couldn't get the proceedings of the evening out of his mind. Porter sensed John's preoccupation. "Don't ya worry, John," he consoled. "Those men was guilty of criticizing the prophet, and that's a grave sin." John didn't reply but walked on in deep reflection.

At that point, John made a pact with himself and whatever divine force created the universe and all living things that he would never again deny his convictions, no matter what the consequences. John couldn't know then, but his decision would have grave consequences. As they arrived at the door to his cabin, John mumbled a good night to Porter and without another word he turned and entered the little cottage.

Agnes looked up from her Bible with sharp eyes. "I hope that you did your duty tonight," she said.

John was so full of emotion that he didn't reply but turned away from her so she would not see his misty eyes. Jenny, who had been sitting at the table reading, quickly rose and walked to her father.

She looked into his troubled face and, putting her hands on his shoulders, she leaned close to him and said, "To thine own self be true."

PART SIX

The Adder

Chapter 17

J ohn had expected the apostates to leave Far West, but they didn't. He noticed
that John Whitmer's business at the hotel and the livery stable, which he had
purchased from Chic, dropped off to the point that it was almost nonexistent. He
also noticed that the men that Patten had singled out were ostracized on the streets
of Far West and many residents would actually cross the street rather than pass
one of these outcasts. One day John stopped by Whitmer's livery to discuss any bill
that he owed for Jenny's covert renting of the little gray mare. He found Whitmer
in the stable diligently cleaning the stalls and covering the floor with fresh straw.

"Morning," John said cheerily. Whitmer jumped, for he hadn't seen John enter
the dark stable. He turned and, seeing John, he gave a little sigh of relief.

"Good morning, Brother Evans," he said. "What can I do for you?"

"Well," John began, "I was wondering if that daughter of mine had stopped by
to rent that little mare again and if her bill was paid up with you for all the times
she has taken that horse. I really don't know what has got into that girl; all she
seems to want to do is ride out on the prairie. I worry a little, what with the friction
between the Saints and the Gentiles."

Whitmer looked down at the tines of the fork he was holding and seemed to
give the question deep thought. "You don't owe me anything, Brother Evans," he
said. "Jenny has more than paid for the use of the horse by cleaning the stable
and currying the horses. She is a gentle, kind girl and she loves animals, especially
horses."

"I want to pay you for the use of your animals," John said. "And as for Jenny
working off her debt, I know her and I suspect she is getting the best of the deal."

Whitmer again looked at the stable floor as if in reflection and his eyes misted
over. "I want to thank you, Brother Evans, for treating me with kindness. I believe
you are the first person who has spoken directly to me since I was disfellowshipped.

I was just going to hitch up a team to this wagon and ride over to Grindstone Fork to purchase some flour."

"Why don't you buy it here, rather than drive ten miles out of your way?" John asked.

Whitmer sat down on a bucket and began to sob. "I don't know what to do," he said. "I love the church, but I want to control my own property. I was corresponding with the presidency in Kirtland, and I questioned the revelation from Joseph demanding that we consecrate everything we own to the church. I also questioned his revelation that God would lead him to treasure that was hidden in Salem, Massachusetts to allay the debts of the church. I don't believe that God reveals hidden treasure through revelations and especially to pay for expenses brought on by poor financial decisions. For questioning revelations and drinking a cup of tea I'm denied membership in this church, which I've served since it was founded. Now men and women I've known for years treat me as if I were a leper."

Whitmer covered his eyes and his shoulders shook with stifled sobs. John looked down at the pitiful figure and, not knowing what to do to comfort him, he laid his hand on the weeping man's shoulder. Whitmer reached up with his left hand and squeezed John's hand in reply. John stood and looked down at the back of Whitmer's head for a moment and, feeling extremely uncomfortable, he turned and walked out of the dim stable.

Jenny was aware that her father knew about her clandestine rides away from Far West, but she didn't think that he knew she was meeting Jake. Her mother was far too busy with her compiling of the word of God to even know that her daughter was missing from time to time. However, Jenny had an eerie feeling that someone was watching her and she wondered if her mother was involved. Jenny had met Jake three or four times and each time she had packed a light lunch of fruit and sandwich for them. The next day, after John had spoken to John Whitmer, Jenny rose and, finding herself alone in the house and the sun shining, she quickly dressed in her riding togs and, putting a lunch in the canvas bag, she left the cabin. She walked quickly to the livery and was surprised to find John Whitmer there instead of Chic.

"Good morning, Brother Whitmer," she said, "where is Chic?"

Whitmer turned and looked at her with affection. "I can't afford to keep him as a stable hand anymore," he replied. "By the way, "he added, "your mother asked me not to let you take the horse."

Jenny blushed and looked at the toes of her heavy boots.

"Don't worry," Whitmer said, "I know you like to ride that little mare, and I'll not tell your mother. Just go saddle her and when you get back, rub her down. I really don't worry, Jenny, because I know you will take care of her. You can curry the horses or clean the stable to pay for the rent."

Jenny hardly heard what Whitmer said. She was impatient to meet Jake at the little valley where they always met. She found that she was strangely attracted to the boy and was fascinated with his description of Indian religious beliefs. She, in turn, told him about the Saints and explained to him that she found their beliefs too restrictive to be appealing to her inquisitive nature.

He didn't have deeply held preconceived notions and he seemed to evaluate each new idea on its merits. She had never kissed a boy before she gently kissed Jake on the lips when she first met him. They had grown accustomed to kissing goodbye when they parted and occasionally during their long talks. She couldn't describe her feelings for Jake, but each time she set out on Molly to meet him, she found her heart hammered in her chest like a drum and she felt strangely excited to see him.

Today was no exception. The sun was shining brightly and a gentle, balmy breeze blew across the blooming grasslands. As she rode along, a mourning dove called from a cottonwood tree. The soft sensual call sent a little shiver down her spine. It was early April and the grasslands were in bloom. Bluebells dotted the hillsides and buttercups nodded bright yellow among the burgeoning bluestem. A killdeer sprang from in front of Molly's hooves and quickly darted a few yards to the left of the horse. There it stopped and spread its wing in a charade that it was injured. Jenny was amazed that the bird would go through such pretense to lead her away from its nest. It even called in a rapid "chee, chee, chee," as if it were injured and in pain.

Jenny was fascinated by nature and the beautiful spring day seemed almost sensuous. She nudged Molly in the ribs to urge the horse into a ground-covering trot. Jenny had never been so anxious to meet Jake and she asked herself what it was that drove her forward. As she crested the little hill that bordered the shallow valley where they always met, she saw him lying in the bluestem, with Rufe lolling in the grass by his side. A little thrill went through her as she saw his lithe body sprawled in the grass.

He heard the beat of the horse's hooves and raised his hand in greeting; she returned the wave and gracefully sprang from the saddle before Molly came to a complete stop. She took a set of hobbles from the saddlebag and secured the horse. Jake lifted his lanky frame from the grass and helped her unsaddle the horse and get the groundcloth and lunch out of the saddlebags. Rufe, with wagging tail, greeted Jenny in dog fashion by snuffling at her crotch. Jenny flushed and gently pushed Rufe's head away while rubbing his ears. Jenny flapped the groundcloth to rid it of crumbs and let it settle on the ground, then they both sat in the fragrant grass and Jenny handed Jake a thick sandwich.

They looked into each other's eyes at the same moment and each saw something there that touched their souls. To Jake, it seemed as if he could see into the very essence of the girl's psyche and what he saw there made him catch his breath. He could not describe it, but he felt an attraction for her that seemed almost painful. Jenny returned the devoted look and a little shiver of ecstasy ran down her spine.

For reasons beyond her understanding, Jenny slid closer to Jake, until their shoulders were touching. She explained to him what was happening in Far West and how the dissenters were ostracized. She told about her father's quandary and how he had begun to fear for his safety. As she talked, Jake looked at her lips and they were pink and moist. He tried to remember what she was saying, but he found himself distracted by the warmth of her body and her closeness.

Jenny must have sensed Jake's rising passion that matched her own, for she placed her hand gently on his thigh. A thrill shot through Jake and his breath caught in his throat; an indescribable feeling rose in his belly and he wanted to touch her and take her in his arms. Myriad thoughts swirled through Jenny's mind like a summer dustdevil. Though she had never had any experience with physical love, she knew where this situation was heading. The words of her mother spun through her agitated brain: "Sex is evil and men are perverted. God has reserved relations between a man and a woman for procreation and nothing else. Those who imbibe in physical love for pleasure are no better than the drunkard who gives in to the wiles of wine, and they renounce the blessings of the Lord."

Yet Jenny found Agnes's religious ranting ludicrous, and besides, if God didn't want his children to indulge in physical love to show affection, why did he plant this irresistible need in her soul? She remembered something her father had said when she had asked him about love: "You will know when it is right, Jenny, and if you have commitment to another, nothing is more satisfying and beautiful." But was she committed to this boy and did she love him?

She opened her eyes and looked at Jake. His face was flushed and reflected the passion that had consumed him. He too opened his eyes and looked into hers.

"Jake, we can't do this unless you love me more than any other and feel you want to spend your life with me," Jenny implored. Jake continued to gaze into her cornflower blue eyes and nodded almost imperceptibly.

"I knew what you were thinking," he whispered, "and I don't want to hurt or defile you. My father uses my mother when he can't find a whore and I hate him for that. I've never been with a woman, but I've seen my mother strip herself of her self-respect because she thinks it is her duty as a wife, and it ain't right. I want you, Jenny, but not if ya don't want to, and if I give you my heart I won't give it to another."

She knew he was struggling to express to her what he felt in his heart. She touched his lips with her finger and whispered, "It's okay, Jake, I want to." Somehow the dam of their passion broke and ecstasy overwhelmed them. She moaned and clamped her lips to his. She didn't have any experience in lovemaking, but instinctively she thrust her tongue between his lips and searched his warm mouth. He moaned in response and his hand went to the baggy shirt that she wore. He fumbled with the buttons and impatiently she brushed his hand away and deftly snapped the offending fasteners through the buttonholes.

Her shirt fell open and Jake was amazed at how white her skin was in the direct sunlight. Disappointed, he saw that her breasts were contained in some sort of garment and he had no idea how to free them. Again Jenny eagerly brushed his hand aside and undid the catch to her brassiere. The garment fell away and Jake involuntarily gave a little gasp. Jenny's breasts were small but firm, and they stood out proudly from her chest. Jake was amazed that they were so white and the aureole was almost pink. He thought of Blossom and how dark and dusky her breasts were and how dark were the circles around her nipples. He felt a stab of guilt that he should think of another woman while holding Jenny, but unbidden the image of Blossom had burst into his mind.

He looked at Jenny's unfettered breasts and instinctively bent down and placed his lips on the alluring pink nipple. Jenny felt as if she would explode or pass out from ecstasy and a little cry of pleasure escaped from her throat. Jake felt driven on and his hand fumbled for the fly of Jenny's baggy trousers. Jenny realized that Jake was about to discover the core of her being and she grasped his wrist with surprising strength. He looked into her flushed face and whispered, "I won't if you don't want me to, but I want you so much."

Jenny looked into the depths of Jake's brown eyes and she saw no guile in them. She felt a bond with this boy that she had never felt with anyone before, and she remembered her father's admonition that she would know if it was right when the time arrived, and she did. She slowly reached down and unbuttoned the buttons of her trousers and then unbuckled the belt. To Jake it was the most sensuous thing he had ever witnessed and he grasped her belt and attempted to pull her pants down. Jenny lifted her hips to allow him to slip them off and they fell into each other's arms, nearly suffocating as they gasped for air in their passion.

Jake placed his hand between Jenny's legs and was disappointed to find that she was wearing some sort of undergarment. He had no idea what women wore under their clothes and he was thwarted by the seemingly voluminous folds of

Jenny's bloomers. Again, Jenny reached down and helped him, by lifting her hips and slipping the offending garment down to her ankles and kicking it off. Jake glanced at the curly, light brown hair and, unsought, the image of Blossom sprang into his head and he remembered the thick, black mass of curls that had so intrigued him. Like a stab of a knife he felt a pang of guilt for thinking of Blossom again.

He slowly placed his hand on the intriguing mound and Jenny squirmed seductively beneath his hand. She was deluged with emotion and possessed by passion; she gently placed her hand on Jake's crotch. She was amazed at the size of the bulge beneath her trembling hand and she felt a pang of fear when she realized what the end result of this would be. She needn't have worried, because despite the fact that both achieved a thundering orgasm they didn't consummate their lovemaking. Driven by youth, hormones and passion, Jake shuddered in climax and Jenny cried out, "Jake, don't stop, don't stop," and intuitively, if awkwardly, he brought her to her climax.

They both realized that what they had just experienced was not the ultimate, but Jenny knew that she had avoided possible pregnancy and pain. They embarrassedly dressed and sat silently for a few moments.

"Jenny, I am so sorry," Jake lamented.

Jenny looked at his crestfallen face and giggled. "Don't be," she said. "I enjoyed it and now I realize that I love you, Jake Devine, and someday we'll be together. The Saints would probably stone me if they knew what we did, but they don't realize that love is not a sin, but lust is."

Jake gave her a quizzical look as he tried to make sense of what she had said.

"Never mind," she said, "as long as we love each other and are faithful to each other, then we can show our love and I know that God won't consider it a sin."

She rose and picked up her things. "Jake, I have to go and I can't see you for at least a fortnight. My mother is suspicious and she has told Mr. Whitmer not to let me borrow the horse for a while. I have to work things out. Please don't think I don't want to be with you."

"How will I know when ya want to see me agin'," he asked despondently.

She looked at him and realized that he thought she was leaving him forever. The look on his face broke her heart and she bent over and kissed him gently on the mouth.

"Jake," she said, "I'm not saying goodbye; I'm saying take care, until we meet again, and we will. There are strange things happening in Far West. My father says he has heard rumors of a secret organization that is dedicated to purging the Saints of sinners and dissenters and who will fight to drive the Missourians out of upper Missouri so it can be a holy site for the Saints. My father is terrified and doesn't know what to do. I think he fears for his life and I need to find out what is happening."

"How'll I know when I can see you again?" he asked.

"You pointed out where your cabin is," she said. "When things calm down and they don't watch me so much, I will come there."

Jake's face went pale. "What if my pa is there? Never come around if he is there. Stop on the little hill above the cabin and if the black mule is in the corral, pile several rocks on top of each other and I'll know you were there. If the mule is gone, come and knock on the door."

She kissed him again and, putting her foot in the stirrup, she swung lightly into the saddle and turned Molly toward Far West. Jake sadly watched her go and wondered if he would ever see her again.

Jake turned and wandered aimlessly across the awakening prairie. He couldn't bear the thought of going home and his heart ached to be with Jenny. Through a blur of tears he watched Rufe trying to interest him in hunting prairie chickens. He knew that his father was meeting with the Daviess County militia to discuss the issue of the Saints expanding beyond the established boundaries of Caldwell County. He knew that Sam would be in Gallatin and once he met his cronies in the saloon, he was not likely to leave for a couple of days. Besides, he had shot a big whitetail buck yesterday and the meat would last them several days. If he got home before dark to take care of his chores, his mother wouldn't worry. Bessie was the one reason that Jake stayed on the little homestead. He realized that if he left, his mother would be at the mercy of Sam, and he couldn't desert her.

Without realizing where he was going, Jake suddenly found himself on the ridge over the springfed pond, where he had first found the little Osage band and where he had seen Blossom bathing. As he topped the hill, he was astounded to see smoke rising from the wooded hill across the clear pond. He sat down on the top of the ridge and squinted across the dazzling water and could make out several cabins among the cottonwood trees on the distant hill. The grassy plain near the sparkling pond was plowed and several oxen were wading in the pond. The waters of his pristine springfed pond were muddy from the hooves of the animals and he noticed a green tint to the water where the beasts were ambling through the mud.

Jake felt as if something precious had suddenly been defiled. He ran down the slope to the pond and noticed that the water was no longer clear as it once had been, but was an ugly coffee color and chunks of cow shit were floating in it. He pulled his old slouch hat further down over his eyes and made out a figure near the cows on the other side of the pond. Calling to Rufe, he broke into a run and quickly circled the pond to where the figure was standing. As he drew nearer, Rufe lifted his head and bayed at the dim shape and as it turned, Jake noticed it was a man and he was armed with a long gun.

The man was large and dressed in rough workclothes. His head was covered by a wide-brimmed black hat and his beard was long, black and wavy. As he drew near, the man pointed a double-barrel shotgun at Jake's face.

"Hold it right there. You better announce yourself and your intentions or I'll blow yer head off," he challenged.

Jake looked at the man and found him intimidating. He was a huge bear of a man and his shoulders were massive. There was something about the way he held the gun unwaveringly pointed at Jake's head that told him this man was not to be trifled with.

Jake was carrying his Kentucky rifle low by his knee and he knew that if he made any movement to bring it to his shoulder, this man would kill him. Jake stopped dead still. "My name is Jake Devine. I live near here and I want to know what you're doin' letting them shitty cows ruin this pond."

"Ain't none o' your concern," the man replied belligerently. "My name is Lyman Wight and I'm an apostle in the only true Church of God. The Prophet Joseph found this place and God revealed to him that on this very spot Father Adam will come to minister to his people in the last days as foretold by the Prophet Daniel. In fact," he continued, "this is the very place that Adam dwelt after he and Eve were driven from the Garden of Eden, which was in Independence."

Jake stood wide-eyed and tried to comprehend what this huge man was saying. Impulsively he began to raise his rifle and Wight responded by nudging the stock of the shotgun closer to his cheek and tightening his finger on the right trigger. Jake instinctively let the rifle hang loose against his thigh. The barrels of the shotgun looked as big as oak whiskey barrels and Jake noticed that both hammers were back and cocked. "This land ain't your'n," Jake exclaimed. "Ol' Bob Miller filed on it and uses it fer a spring pasture."

"Don't matter," Wight replied. "God has given this land to his chosen people and he's revealed to us that he will send angels to fight our battles against the ungodly. Any man or woman who denies the truth doesn't deserve this land or to live and God's chosen will see to it that we end their miserable lives. No man can deny the truth and enter the kingdom of God."

Jake began to tremble. He wondered if this man was insane and capable of blowing him in two with the shotgun because he wasn't a Saint. "I am leavin'," he said in a soft voice. "Don't ya shoot me in the back." With that Jake slowly turned and started to take a step away from the burly man. Rufe had been standing straight up and tense at his side with his hackles raised.

Jake became aware of the low rumble emulating from the dog's throat and he realized that if Rufe lunged at this man, both of them would be killed. As he turned he reached down and grabbed the old leather strap that he had put around Rufe's neck as a collar. "Rufe, come!" he exclaimed and half dragged the big dog after him.

Jake turned his back on the man and felt a burning itch between his shoulder blades. At any moment he expected to feel the sledgehammer blow of a buckshot charge tear his chest apart, but it never came. As he topped the rise above the pool, he looked back and the huge, dark figure was still standing, staring at his retreating figure. He whistled to Rufe and the dog ran happily to him, his tail wagging joyously. The hound sat in front of him and looked up at his master with devotion in his soft brown eyes. He waited patiently for Jake to give him a command. Jake looked at the dog and in that instant it seemed that the only living thing that loved him and wanted to be with him was this old hound. Jake looked at the graying muzzle and he knew that Rufe wouldn't be with him much longer. He fell to his knees and threw his arms around the dog's neck. Tears flooded down his face and he wept into the wet fur of his soulmate.

Chapter 18

Ｉt was nearly dark when Jake finished his chores and pushed open the door of the cabin. Bessie looked at him and she knew that something was wrong, for anguish was evident in his face. "Jake, what's happened, is it Rufe?" she implored. Jake raised his red eyes and knew he couldn't tell his mother everything.

"Ma, there's a bunch of them Saints, what's homesteaded down by Spring Hill, and they's running they's cows in the pond. One of 'em run me off with a shotgun." Bessie's face blanched and her hand sprang up to her throat impulsively.

"Jake, don' tell yer pa 'bout this, cuz he is just lookin' fer a reason to get up a bunch of them no goods in Gallatin and go fight them fanatics."

"Maybe we should run 'em off before they burn us out," he said, remembering what Wight had said about the ungodly.

Bessie cut Jake a huge venison steak and fried it over the stove with some potatoes. Jake loved potatoes fried in venison grease and his mother knew it. When they sat down to eat, she cut a piece from her steak and tossed it to Rufe, who was lying near the table. Jake knew his mother was trying to manipulate him. She didn't like him feeding the dog at the table. His father, had he been there, would have kicked the dog out of the door and knocked his son off the chair for feeding the dog good meat. Jake knew there was something on his mother's mind and he had a good idea what it was.

"Don't worry, Ma," he said. "I aint goin' to tell the old man that them Saints is building a town down by Spring Hill, but you know that he'll find out soon enough."

"I know," she replied, "but if ya don't tell 'im he won't demand that you and him go out and run 'em off. I really don't care iffen him and them drunks in Gallatin does it, but I don't want you git'n hurt or killt in the fracas."

John Evans could feel the change in the air in Far West. The dissidents remained in Far West, but they were social outcasts. The only social life that existed in any town settled by the Saints was directly tied to church membership. John often saw

John Whitmer and the man looked like a whipped pup. John habitually wondered why he and the rest of the apostates didn't leave Far West and then he considered his own situation and found he couldn't condemn the apostates for not severing their ties with the church when they had once believed the Gospel was the road to salvation and all of their friends and family were still members.

One warm, sunny Sunday in June 1838, John received word from a neighbor that church services would be held in the town square because the weather was warm and Brother Sidney Rigdon was slated to speak. Rigdon had a well-deserved reputation of being a great orator and he could keep audiences spellbound for hours. He was also first counselor to the president of the church and next in power to the prophet himself. A huge turnout was expected. However, Brother Sidney also had the reputation, even among the Saints, of being somewhat tyrannical in his beliefs and fanatical in his devotion to the prophet and the church.

The meeting was scheduled for evening to avoid the heat of midday. When John, Jenny and Agnes arrived a little before seven, the town square was already filled almost to capacity. A raised stand had been built, with a podium for the speaker. At exactly seven o'clock, Brother Sidney strode triumphantly to the podium.

"Brothers and sisters," he began, "before I address you, we will have a word of prayer and then we shall sing the hymn, 'The Spirit of God Like a Fire Is Burning.'" Amazingly, the old brother who offered the prayer only droned on for ten minutes. After the prayer, a huge woman rose and lumbered to the podium to lead the congregation in the hymn; following her lead, the audience sang lustily, if a little off key.

Following the hymn, Rigdon again rose and strode pompously to the stand. Grasping the podium he gazed out across the rows of Saints. In that moment, he looked to John like a great turkey vulture looking greedily at a pile of buffalo guts. Rigdon was a small, withered looking man and his head seemed to sit back on his neck like a buzzard's.

He was dressed immaculately in a fine pulpit coat with a ruffled shirt and black tie. He cleared his throat. "Brethren and Sisters, I've chosen for my theme 'Ye are the salt of the earth.'" Rigdon launched into a tirade that was understood by all as a threat to the dissenters, apostates and unbelievers in their midst. "Ye are the salt of the Earth," he screeched, "but if the salt has lost his savor wherewith shall it be salted? It is thenceforth good for nothing but to be cast out, and to be trodden under the foot of men."

Rigdon then threw himself into a vitriolic rant about how the Saints had been chastised and persecuted for their beliefs, which, he said, were true and were derived directly from God. Any person who had embraced the Gospel and then denied the truth and turned away from the church should be trampled under the feet of the just.

Living among the Saints in Far West, he said, was just such a set of men, who where doing everything in their power to thwart the work of the Lord in establishing the kingdom as prophesied by the Prophet Daniel. It was the duty of the Saints, he declared, to trample these men into the earth. Breathing hard as if physically exerted, Rigdon stopped speaking and glared out over the sea of faces for effect and then launched into the last of his bombast.

"I tell you one thing, Judas did not hang himself—he was hung by Peter. If this country cannot be freed from them any other way, I will assist to trample them down or to erect a gallows on the square of Far West and hang them as they did the gamblers at Vicksburg, and it would be an act at which the angels would smile with approbation."

With that Rigdon glared at the congregation and turned with a toss of his head and stepped down from the stand. There was a hush over the crowd for a minute, then from a thousand throats burst the cry "Hosanna."

John knew exactly what Rigdon meant and he knew he must warn John Whitmer and the others. He glanced at Agnes and her face was mesmerized. He knew that she agreed with every word Rigdon had uttered and she would never knowingly let him warn the dissenters.

Jenny looked at her father with eyes wide with fear. She had never realized how vindictive and vicious men could be when they assumed they knew the will of God. "Dad," she whispered imploringly, "this thing has gotten totally out of hand and I fear people are going to be murdered. I worry about you, because you question things and believe in freedom of thought."

John looked at her and saw the fear in her eyes and realized that he too was frightened, but he had denied his conscience before because of fear and now he felt he must warn the dissenters. He spotted John Corrill and an idea sprang into his mind. He touched Agnes on the shoulder. "I must speak to Brother Corrill," he said quietly.

She glared at him with venom in her eyes. "I have heard that he has questioned the prophet and apostles," she spat.

"Oh," he replied, "I merely want to ask him a question about where to rent a horse now that we don't deal with Whitmer."

Not waiting to hear her reply, John turned and confronted Corrill. John knew that Corrill had refused to vote against John Whitmer when he was called before the high council to answer for questioning the prophet. Corrill was also the church historian and was acquiring a reputation of questioning some aspects of the Gospel.

"Brother Corrill," John said in a low voice, "may I have a word with you?"

Corrill looked at him with anxious eyes and indicated with his head that they should step to a more secluded spot.

"Brother Corrill," John repeated. "After what has been said here tonight, I think it would be wise to inform John Whitmer and the others that they may be in danger." Corrill's eyes shifted about like darting swallows; when he felt they wouldn't be overheard, he fixed John with his gaze.

"I have already decided to warn them," he said. "I know that if anyone finds out, my life will be in danger. Rumors are flying that a secret society has been formed to stamp out any dissension and questioning in the church. It's whispered that this group is led by fanatics who believe that anyone who questions the prophet or apostles should suffer blood atonement. So, if a Saint denies his faith he can only atone through the shedding of his blood. These are dangerous times, Brother Evans; watch what you say and to whom. I will warn Brother Whitmer and tell him to inform the others about what was said here tonight." With that Corrill turned and walked away without another word.

That evening, John sat on the little horsehair loveseat in the tiny living room of their cabin and his mind was in a quandary. He couldn't believe that he had become ensnared in a society that threatened death to anyone who didn't follow its dictates or who practiced free thought. The whole situation ran counter to his cherished ideals of self-determination and freedom of religion. John had always believed that God's greatest gift to man was his intelligence and that man should use it to the ultimate and go wherever his mind led him. He longed to open his heart to someone, but he remembered Corrill's warning that anyone who questioned the prophet or his apostles would pay with their life.

He looked at Jenny, sitting quietly at the kitchen table, seemingly busy with some studies. He would've liked to talk to her about his dilemma, but lately Jenny had become very withdrawn and reclusive. He had asked her if anything was bothering her and she had averted her eyes and murmured that she was just busy. This was so unlike his usually gregarious daughter, who loved to discuss anything in her heart with her father.

Since the rumors of the secret society that ensured complete devotion to the church apostles had became rampant in Far West, Agnes had embraced the principle of a closed society wholeheartedly. She believed that through the Gospel she could know the will of God and anyone who denied this truth was unworthy to live among the Saints and even unworthy to live. Agnes viewed John as one too weak to live up to the dictates of the true church and undeserving to take part in establishing the kingdom of God in the last days. To her, the great work of building the kingdom of God and establishing the ecclesiastical government that would support it would only be carried out by those strong enough to resist the temptations of the flesh. She held John in utter contempt, and if the men of the secret society saw fit to spill his blood because of his weakness, then so be it.

John cursed himself for becoming trapped in an unloving relationship, but he still couldn't bring himself to tell Agnes that he wanted to leave her. He had always avoided confrontation at all costs and he knew if he told her he was going she would berate him for his cowardice and weakness and in his heart he knew she was right. Then again, there was Jenny, and even though he knew Jenny didn't respect her mother, he didn't want to submit her to the turmoil that would erupt if he asked for a divorce.

As he sat on the loveseat and pretended to be engrossed in a copy of Montesquieu's *Spirit of the Laws*, he thought he must be the most miserable man in the world. As he spiraled down into a sea of despair, an almost inaudible knock came at the door. For a moment, he thought it must be the wind, but then it came a little louder. Agnes had secluded herself in her bedroom and Jenny seemed to be in deep thought and oblivious to anything. He rose and walked quietly to the door. Opening it, he was shocked to see John Whitmer standing in the dark with his hat in his hand. His eyes were downcast and he looked morose.

"Brother Evans," he said with a meek voice, "I'm sorry to bother you, but I must speak to someone. Sidney Rigdon has written a manifesto demanding that the dissenters leave Far West within three days or suffer grave consequences.

"My brother, David, spoke to the prophet and asked him what we could do to alleviate the ill will against us that pervades this city. The prophet said that we should put our property into the hands of the church and never again speak ill of God's anointed. David told him he wanted to control his own property and he had a God-given right to speak out when he saw men acting against the principles of justice and the law. The prophet replied that David wished to pin him down to the law and terminated the meeting. The manifesto demands that we leave Far West in three days. What shall we do?"

John looked at the meek, kindly man before him and anger welled in his heart at the injustice of it all. "I think that you, your brother, Oliver Cowdery and the others should go to Liberty in Clay County and retain a lawyer to protect your property and your lives!" he exclaimed. Whitmer looked at him with large, frightened eyes.

"Do you know how hard this is for me to deny my church and the prophet I once revered?" he asked.

"I think so, but you have your reasons, which I think are justified."

"John," Whitmer said in a soft voice, "I fear for your life and safety as well. The declaration that Rigdon sent to us demands that we leave Far West, or we suffer the consequences. The letter leaves no doubt what the consequences will be if we don't pack up and leave in three days.

"Rigdon said that a secret society was organized to deal with any dissension toward the church leaders or any free thought whatever. According to Rigdon, the members of this society will kill anyone who they hear questioning the church, the prophet or the twelve apostles. John, you must come with us. I have heard things and I don't think that you are safe here anymore. People in high places have marked you because of your free thinking, your scholarship, and because you have questioned some of the precepts of the church. Please come with us."

John despondently looked at Whitmer. "We are trapped by this situation," he said. "Agnes is caught up in the fervor that is sweeping the Saints, that is to stamp out all perceived wickedness so they can usher in the Millennium, and she won't leave. My daughter needs me and is not old enough to be on her own."

Whitmer looked sadly into John's eyes and gripped his hand firmly. "Good luck, John," he said. "You're a good man and a good friend, I wish you well, but I fear for your safety and the safety of your family."

John placed his hand on Whitmer's shoulder. "Don't worry," he said without much conviction. "We'll be fine. I'll see you again in better times."

With that Whitmer turned and walked slowly into the deepening darkness.

John's fears were soon realized. The Whitmers, Lyman Johnson and Cowdery rode to Liberty to retain a lawyer. The Far West underground immediately spread the word and their families were cast out into the street with little else than the clothes on their backs and a little bedding. When the dissenters returned from Liberty, they found their families on the road carrying what pathetic belongings the fanatics had left them. With nowhere else to go, they fled to Richmond in Ray County and told their sad tale to the *Missouri Press*.

The rumors of the secret society that was formed to protect the Saints spread like wildfire. When people spoke of this secret organization they did so with fear in their eyes and in whispered voices. After seeing what the shadowy and feared enforcers had done to the dissenters, John decided he must know more about them for his own security. No one he knew would speak of the group or, when asked, pleaded ignorance of them. Then, he thought of Porter. Porter was a fanatical Saint and a confidant of the prophet. If anyone knew what was going on in Far West, Porter would know.

One day in late June, John called on Porter at his cabin. He knocked on the rustic door and Luana quickly opened it. She greeted him with reserve and when he inquired about Porter she curtly replied that he was out back tending to the stock. John found Porter currying one of his draft horses. Rockwell didn't see him approach, so John whistled softly to alert Porter and the horse of his presence. Porter lifted his head and looked over the withers of the huge draft horse he was grooming. When he saw John, he grunted and went back to work.

John made a wide detour around the nose of the horse until he was on the same side of the animal as Porter. "You seem a little aloof," John declared.

"Maybe I is, but I don' know whut that is."

John looked at the shaggy man with affection in his eyes.

"I mean you don't greet me like a friend."

Porter seemed to weigh John's words for a moment, "It ain't that I'm not your friend, its jest that you seem bent on getting throwed outta Far West."

"I don't know what you mean, Porter," John replied.

"Well, most folks around here believes that the prophet's words are the truth and the word of God, when he says 'Thus saith the Lord.' The Lord has said that there is only one true church and all others is an abomination in his sight. Those who deny the truth are not fittin' to live with the Saints and must be driven out."

"Is this why the Saints have driven some of the old settlers off their land and seized it for their own?" John asked. Porter gave him a baleful look.

"Yah, that's why, and we mean to raid the Gentiles and take they's property and wear 'em down, and this way build up the kingdom of God."

"Porter," John said beseechingly, "can't you see, each man has a right to make up his own mind what's true and what's not. Each man must have the right to find God in his own way, and if he is a good man and treats his fellow man with respect and respects the earth and all the creatures that dwell on her, then God will open his arms to him when he dies and he will go to heaven, or wherever good people go when they die.

"However," John exclaimed, "that is not what I wanted to talk to you about. People in Far West are talking about a secret organization and they are frightened. Do you know anything about this?"

Porter leaned against the big horse and considered what John had said.

"Well," he began, "they is a group of devoted men who have taken an oath to support the prophet and his apostles in all things and to protect the Saints from mobbers. They is led by Brother Sampson Avard, and they is called the Sons of Dan. They is called that because they is likened to the snake referred to in Micah 4:13: 'Dan shall be a serpent by the way, an adder in the path, that biteth the horse heels, so that his rider shall fall backward.' The Sons of Dan are like an adder in the path to those who fight agin' the true Church of God and the mouthpiece of the Lord."

John shivered, even though the sun was warm on his back. He knew how fanatical these people were and this organization could easily get out of hand and harm those they saw as traitors to the cause. Porter gave John a sidelong glance that seemed to John to be devious.

"Brother Jared Carter is the military leader of the Sons of Dan and he has expressed an interest in seein' you," he said quietly. "They is a'meetin' in the grove just outside of town on Honey Creek tomorrow night 'bout seven. Would ya like to come and meet the brethren?" he said almost under his breath.

John caught the covert look in Rockwell's eyes and he felt a bolt of fear go through him. He wanted to say he would forgo meeting the Sons of Dan, or Danites as they were known in the rumor mill in northern Missouri. But he'd promised himself that no more would he allow his lack of courage to keep him from living up to his convictions. There was something in the way the Porter acted that worried him, but he liked Porter and considered him a friend. He didn't believe that this benign man would ever harm him.

When he arrived home, John would have liked to discuss his misgivings about attending the meeting, but he knew better than to criticize anything about the church to Agnes and Jenny seemed totally lost in her own world. He made a mental note to talk to his daughter and see if she would tell him what it was that so obsessed her. He glanced at Agnes, who was poring over some document dealing with church doctrine. She was so engrossed that she was oblivious to everything around her. Her lips moved in silent recitation and her eyes gleamed. He suddenly had a horrible thought; he despised this woman and their relationship was nothing more than mutual neutrality.

He looked at his daughter and felt a rush of affection. She was sitting in a shabby, stuffed chair in the corner, pretending to read, but her eyes didn't move and they glistened moistly. Her face was flushed and her brow was furrowed with thought or emotion. He knew he must live to see her reach adulthood. Her mother was dedicated to her prophet and would sacrifice her daughter to her newfound God in a heartbeat. John felt a wave of depression and desperation wash over him. He wanted to speak to Jenny, but he knew Agnes would hang on every word. If he asked her to go for a walk in the gathering gloom, Agnes would accuse him of incest, or something else equally disgusting. Seeing that there was no chance to empathize with Jenny, he decided to go to bed.

He rose from the horsehair loveseat and gathered his reading glasses and book. Turning toward the little lean-to where he slept, he hesitated. "Good night," he said. Looking directly at Jenny, he said, "I love you."

She looked up from her book and gave him a wistful smile. "Good night, Dad, I love you too," she murmured.

John looked at Agnes sitting at the table. He expected to see her at least glance at him, but she never raised her eyes from the copy of the *Book of Mormon*.

John realized that he had told his daughter he loved her and had ignored his wife. He felt a pang of guilt, for he realized he had intentionally done it to hurt her. On the other hand, he understood that Agnes knew he was retiring and refused to even acknowledge that he was leaving the room. He wondered if she noticed that he didn't tell her he loved her. He decided that Agnes was probably so engrossed in the mysteries of the kingdom and assuring her salvation that she was incapable of loving another human being.

That she didn't love him didn't really bother him anymore. He had tried to establish an affectionate relationship with her, but even before she had become engrossed with Joseph's teachings, she had never returned his affection. John wasn't an exceptionally corporeal man, but he understood that emotional love between a man and a woman is rare without a physical relationship. During their entire marriage, Agnes had considered sex disgusting and turned aside his advances by insinuating that he was sordid.

John's agitated mind turned away from his frigid wife to the issue of the Sons of Dan. The Saints had always been clannish and fanatic in their beliefs and anyone whom they thought didn't share their exuberance for "the truth" was generally shunned and socially ostracized until they willingly left the community and the church. Now, however, it seemed that the Saints had put together a militant band whose sole purpose was to stamp out nonconformity and candid thinking among the Saints. To John it was such a paradox that the Saints believed that they represented the true Church of Christ, but they denied the principles of tolerance, acceptance and love that Jesus taught.

His mind wandered to Sidney Rigdon, and he didn't doubt that the bellicose Rigdon would support a band to stamp out dissension among the members. Nor did he doubt that Rigdon would condone murder to rid the community of unbelievers who questioned the word of the prophet. Rigdon was an intolerant bigot and he coveted the power that he wielded as a counselor to the most influential man in the church. John had heard Rigdon speak frequently and he trembled when he thought of the tirades he had heard Rigdon preach. He knew this man was fully capable of using whatever method came to hand to stamp out any heresy that might rear its ugly head in the church.

John didn't care about the purity of the Gospel or how to browbeat the backsliders into submission, for he had never believed that Joseph received revelations. The accounts he had read in the *Book of Commandments* were far too trite, self-serving and mundane to be credible. John remained in the City of God because he was ensnared in a web woven by his own inability to deal with confrontation. However, he didn't want to see an insidious secret organization gain power in the church that would stamp out freedom of conscience by intimidation, force or even murder.

He wondered if Joseph, the prophet, was aware of the Danites and he decided that he probably was. It seemed that nothing occurred in Joseph's realm without his permission and knowledge. To the Saints, there was no church without the prophet and they didn't embark on any scheme without the implicit approval and sanction of Joseph. After all, he was the only pipeline to God and he alone communicated with the most high. Therefore, without his approval, nothing in the church had the endorsement of the Lord. Besides, Porter Rockwell was devoted to the prophet and had grown up on a farm close to where Joseph spent his boyhood years, and they were friends. It was unthinkable that Porter would become involved with a clandestine church organization if it didn't have the full support of his beloved prophet.

To John, it seemed that his life was crashing down around his head. His wife was cold and indifferent and he couldn't break through the hard shell that her uncompromising faith had formed around her inner sanctum. His daughter was desperately unhappy and he suspected it was because the unbending beliefs of the Saints smothered her perceptive mind. He toyed with the idea of packing up his daughter and their belongings and fleeing Far West in the night like thieves. Somehow, this went against his morals. Agnes was Jenny's mother and he couldn't take her daughter and steal her away without saying a word. And again, Rigdon had said that the last backslider had left Far West that was going to, the next one who threatened to leave would be killed, "And the only burial they would get would be in a turkey buzzard's guts." As he considered his dilemma, he decided the only option he had was to attend the meeting with Porter and convince these people that they couldn't gain conformity in the church through coercion and fear. Once he had finally come to a decision, John's mind seemed to find peace and soon he was snoring softly.

The next day was Saturday and John didn't have to teach school. He slept late, and when he arose, the sun was shining through the wavy glass window in the little lean-to where he slept. He rose and quickly dressed and went into the kitchen. The house seemed empty; he knew that Agnes was probably at the stake president's office, working at her self-appointed job of church scrivener. Jenny was nowhere to be found either, and this made John uneasy for some unknown reason.

He went into the kitchen to see if he could rustle up something for breakfast. There was no evidence that either Jenny or Agnes had eaten anything before they left. He desperately wished he had a cup of coffee, but he suspected that there was no coffee to be had in Far West and with rumors of the church enforcers running rampant, he didn't think any residents of the holy city would dare imbibe in the brew. He found some grits and he warmed a cup of water and sweetened it with sugar and cream. He sat down and grimaced at his cup of "Saint's tea" and picked at the lumpy grits. His mind turned to the upcoming meeting of the Danites and he wondered if it was safe for him to attend.

Chapter 19

I f John had known where Jenny was, he would have been justified in being uneasy about her. Jenny had intended to wait until things settled down to see Jake again, to wait until she felt safe in talking John Whitmer into lending her a pony; yet she couldn't get her mind off Jake, and she decided she had to see him or she would go crazy. She found that she couldn't think, she couldn't eat, she couldn't sleep and her heart literally ached to see the skinny youth. Over the few times she had met Jake, she had gradually come to enjoy his company; but after they had made love on the hill overlooking the little valley, her mind would not let her rest.

She wondered if it was just lust and passion that drew her to Jake. She thought about what her mother incessantly said about lust, that it would pervert one's soul, and she considered if that was what was tearing her apart. Then she thought of the emotions she felt when she looked into Jake's adoring eyes and she decided that physical love was just a normal extension of emotional attraction. Her father, unlike her mother, had frequently told her that when one commits to another, physical love is beautiful, not degrading.

Whatever the case, she awoke that morning and decided she must see Jake. When they had last parted, she had been confused and her mind was in turmoil after he had touched her in secret places. She had ridden away, her emotions in a quandary. Now she longed, even hungered, for his touch and she knew she couldn't go on without him.

Jenny knew that Whitmer and the other dissenters had been driven out of Far West. The gentle Whitmer had understood Jenny's wanderlust and love of horses and he even suspected that Jenny might be seeing someone, but he understood the passions of youth and helped her covertly sneak away from Far West. Now Whitmer was gone and she didn't have a confidant to secretly supply her with a horse. With her mind in a whirl, she left the house and aimlessly wandered. She was amazed to find herself at Whitmer's livery stable, but she didn't remember making a conscious decision to go there.

She walked out of the glare of the sun into the cool barn, smelling of fragrant grass hay, oats and horse odor. Her eyes were dazzled by the sun and she could scarcely make out the shapes of the horses standing in their stalls, but she was familiar with the stable and headed directly for Molly's stall. Just as she reached for the latch, a strong, sinewy hand grasped her wrist in a painful grip. She cried out in pain and fright. She squirmed around until she faced her unseen assailant and the first thing she was aware of was the stench of fetid breath in her nostrils. As her eyes became accustomed to the dim light in the stable, she looked up into the leering eyes of Luke Rasmussen, Whitmer's stable hand.

Despite the fact that Luke was supposedly a Saint and lived the stringent rules of the church, she had always known that he kept a chaw and whiskey in the livery. She had often smelled it when he had brought Molly at Whitmer's orders. Now, at close quarters, she could smell stale tobacco and whiskey on Luke's putrid breath.

She looked into his yellow eyes. "You are hurting me, Brother Rasmussen," she cried.

"Yah, well old man Whitmer is gone now, and ya gotta deal with me. The Bishop appointed me to manage this here stable, and what I says goes."

"I just want to borrow Molly for a little while. I will pay for the rent," she stammered.

"Maybe ya will and maybe ya won't. Like I says, I decides who rents horses and who don't. Iffen ya wants to rent this horse, ya better be nice to me," Luke leered. "They's now folks what watches who comes and goes in Far West, and ya will find it ain't so easy to sneak out like it was when old man Whitmer was here. Tell ya what," Luke said, smiling and showing yellow teeth covered with a disgusting, greenish film. "Ya remember that ol' Luke was nice to ya and maybe I'll let ya take the hoss."

Jenny was frantic to get away. Luke didn't slacken the iron grip on her wrist and all she could think of was to get away from that leering face and foul breath that threatened to smother her.

"I will remember," she beseeched. Luke smiled at her again and, letting go of her wrist, he turned toward the stall. She stood there in the cool dim stable and suddenly realized that she was trembling and her breath was coming in gasps.

Rasmussen returned with Molly, already saddled and bridled.

"There ya go, missy," he sneered. "Don' forget ya owe me fer lettin' ya take this here hoss. Remember, they is people watchin' what goes on in Far West, and if ya wants to stay healthy ya better be nice to ol' Luke. Them apostates what left the other day reported to the Gentiles on what's goin' on 'round here and Brother Rigdon says the last 'oh yes man' has left that is a goin' to."

There was no mistaking Luke's meaning and Jenny shivered with disgust. She just wanted to get away from this loathsome man. She thrust her left foot into the stirrup and bounced on the toe of her right foot to give her a little momentum for springing into the saddle. As she turned away from Rasmussen, she felt him place his hands on her buttocks as if to help her into the saddle. Even through the baggy men's trousers, she could feel his boney fingers tighten on the soft flesh of her cheeks. She nearly flew into the saddle and, turning toward Luke, she gave him a malevolent look. He grinned at her again and she noticed his red, puffy gums surrounding rotting stumps of teeth. Her only thought was to escape and she turned Molly's head toward the stable door and dug her heels into the mare's flanks. The startled horse lunged forward and almost ran over Luke, who stood leering after her.

The warm June sun seemed to cleanse Jenny of the repulsion that she felt from Luke's touch. As she rode, she gradually began to feel calm. The gentle, balmy breeze on her face and the fragrant air full of the perfume of the blossoming prairie seemed to calm her soul. She wasn't sure where she was going; she knew that Jake wouldn't be at the little valley where they had always met. She remembered that he had described where he lived and had indicated with a sweep of his hand that the Devine homestead lay north and east of the basin where they met.

She felt numb and her heart was hammering in her chest like a drum. She knew that Rasmussen would spill his guts to the bishop and high council and he would probably embellish what little he knew about her frequent wanderings. She knew her father was worried about the restrictive atmosphere that was rampant in Far West and now she wondered if she were doing the right thing to ride out looking for Jake.

She kept her eyes glued to the endless prairie in front of her, looking for a speck that might be Jake. When she had ridden for what seemed miles, she began to consider turning around. She felt vulnerable and exposed on the rolling grassland. Just as she was about to rein Molly in and start back, she saw the top of a little clapboard house surrounded by ramshackle corrals. The house was nearly a half-mile away, but she could make out a thin blue ribbon of smoke spiraling up from the wattle and stick chimney. She remembered that Jake had told her never to come if his father was home and she could tell if Sam were around because the old black mule would be in the corral.

She turned Molly to the left and dropped down into a little swale where she couldn't be seen from the house. She followed the swale until it opened up into a little basin where the cabin stood. From there she surveyed the homestead. She was relieved to see that there was no black mule, only what appeared to be a young gray animal. As she sat on Molly, staring at the corrals and outbuildings, she saw a familiar figure come out of a rickety straw-covered shed that probably served as a barn. Her heart jumped when she recognized Jake, followed closely by his old hound.

Jenny nudged Molly in the ribs with her heels, more vigorously than she meant to, and the little mare lunged forward. Jake heard the sound of hooves and spun around; he immediately recognized the mare and raised his hand in greeting. Rufe ran joyously toward Molly, violently wagging his tale and baying.

Jenny jumped from the saddle before the horse stopped and hit the ground running. She sprang into Jake's arms and buried her face into his chest. Lifting her face, she looked into his eyes. "I cannot live without you," she murmured and mashed her lips against his until she tasted the coppery hint of blood.

They stood wrapped in each other's arms and were unaware that the door to the shack had opened and Bessie was standing in the doorway, staring at them with her arms folded. She had a quizzical look on her face, but it wasn't malicious.

"Jake," she finally called, "would ya like to bring the young lady inta the house?"

Jenny pushed away from Jake and spun toward the sound of the voice. She had been totally oblivious to anything around her and didn't even think about being seen.

Jenny's face turned a bright scarlet. "I am sorry," she stammered.

"Don't be," Bessie answered from the doorway, "jest come in and have a cup of coffee."

Jake had no experience with the social graces or with women for that matter, and he had no idea what to say or do. He stood there with his mouth gaping open and looked at his mother. Bessie smiled at the two awkward figures. "Please come in," she repeated.

Obediently, Jake started toward the door, forgetting Jenny. She reached out and took his hand and they walked self-consciously toward the house.

Jake entered first and kept his eyes turned toward the floor. Jenny walked in with a little more grace, taking Bessie's hand. "I am Jenny Evans. I am glad to meet you," she said.

After an awkward introduction, they all sat down at the rough plank table and Bessie set the table with battered and chipped cups and saucers. Once she had served coffee, they sat in an awkward silence until Jake blurted out, "I am sorry, Ma, but we met one day by the little spring in Simpson Holler and I guess we like each other."

Bessie looked at him and her eyes shone; a little smile played at the corners of her mouth like a kitten playing with yarn.

"Well," she remarked, "from the look of things y'all do like each other and ya have met a very nice gal."

Jenny lifted her eyes to Bessie's and she saw understanding and hope there. Immediately she liked this unpretentious woman.

"Tell me," Bessie said, "where y'all from, Jenny, and what are you two plannin' to do?" Jenny looked at Bessie in shock; she had no idea what to say.

Finally, she exclaimed, "I am from Far West and I hate it!" Tears filled her eyes and she looked down at her coffee. "Do you know if they knew I was drinking coffee, they could call me before the high council and rebuke me and my mother would go to the prophet and ask him to pray for my soul?" Jenny covered her face and her shoulders shook with stifled sobs.

Bessie rose from her seat and put her arms around the girl. She had always wanted a daughter and she felt a deep affection for this young woman.

"Don't cry," she said. "Tell me what is bothering you, maybe I can help."

As if a dam had burst, Jenny told the whole sordid story of her mother's fanaticism and the nightmare of living in an oppressive society. Once the floodgates opened, she couldn't stop and she recounted her father's loveless relationship with her mother. She described being driven from Independence and how stifled she and her father were by the trap that they found themselves in.

She told them about the Saint's beliefs that they would set the stage for the return of Jesus by establishing the City of God and maintaining a sinless society. She talked about the fear that walked the streets of the Holy City where neighbors viewed each other with suspicion lest they be reported to the high council for some breach of the Gospel. She described how her father had hidden his cherished pipe and his books on philosophy and religion lest he be branded a heretic. And lastly, with tears in her eyes, she told how her friend, John Whitmer, was banished from Far West for questioning the prophet's business dealings.

Bessie listened to all this with rapt interest. She hardly took her eyes off of Jenny as the girl spilled the contents of her soul. When Jenny was done, Bessie sighed and, rising, she left the room without a word. They heard her moving things in the little bedroom, and presently she returned.

She held out her hand to her son and said, "Take this and use it to git you and Jenny out of Missouri. Go somewhers else where ya kin be happy. I fear that before this is over, the prairie will be aflame with killin' and death."

Jake looked into her palm and saw a twenty-dollar gold piece glittering against the red and calloused skin of her hand.

He and Jenny gasped in unison. "Ma, where did ya get that kind o' money?" he asked incredulously.

She looked at him with shining eyes and murmured, "My pa give it to me afore I was married. He never liked yer pa, and he tole me if things get bad, use it to leave him."

"Then do it now!" Jake exclaimed.

Bessie looked at him with incredible sadness in her eyes. "Naw, it is too late fer me. I wouldn't know where to go or what to do. Besides, I got this feelin' that I ain't gonna be around much longer. I suspect that they's gonna be a nasty conflict round here 'fore this is over, and I got this hunch I ain't gonna survive it."

Jake looked at his mother and his eyes brimmed with tears.

"Don' say that, ya kin leave today. The ole man always beats ya and treats you like one o' his mules. Take the money and go to Saint Louis."

"Jest how long do ya think this money would last there," she asked, "and what would I do when it ran out?"

"You could find someone else to marry," he replied.

Her laugh was a cynical bark. "And who would have me? Look at me, I is bent and haggard and I look like a ole woman. No, you younguns has got your whole lives before ya, mine is over—take the money and run. My pa would want you to do that."

Jake closed his hand over the double eagle and looked at Jenny with questioning eyes.

She knew what he was thinking. "I have to tell my dad. I won't leave him in Far West or with that fanatic, my mother. Let me go back and talk to him. He has some money put away, too, and I know he is desperately unhappy among the Saints. He is stifled there, and my mother treats him like a lackey."

"Them people sound as nutty as a squirrel's nest in a hazel bush," Bessie said.

"But, Ma," Jake said, "yer life is like that too. He comes home and beats ya if there is nothing to eat. He uses ya like a whore and he never shows ya any love; ya is no better'n a black slut."

Jake suddenly realized what he had said, and his eyes dropped and his face flushed a bright red. He looked at Jenny, but she didn't appear to be shocked by his words or the comparison to a slave woman. The only thing he could read in her eyes was compassion for this maligned woman.

"I won't leave ya here with that worthless pig!" Jake exclaimed, looking at Bessie.

She returned his poignant look. "Jake, can't ya see, I am an ole woman before my time. It's too late fer me, but not fer you and Jenny. Now make yer plans and leave here while ya kin."

Jake turned and looked questioningly into Jenny's expressive gray eyes.

"She is right, you know," Jenny said quietly. "We can go somewhere and get a job. My dad can teach and when we get a house, we can send for Bessie. I'll go back and tell my dad about you and what we have decided. I know he will want to go and will help us. I will meet you at our special place in Simpson's Hollow a week from today at nine in the morning. Oh, Jake, can't you see this is the only way?"

Jake looked at his mother and she gave him a sad smile and a slight nod. Tears sparkled in her eyes. "I will miss ya Jake, but it's the only way. I know if ye stay, Sam will kill ya one day."

Jenny rose from the chair and, stepping around the table, she put her hand on Bessie's shoulder and kissed her gently on the cheek.

"I wish you were my mother," she said softly. "You are a remarkable woman, and God, or whatever divine being created this Universe, will take you to his bosom one day. Don't worry; you won't need some ritual or words mumbled in a temple to be saved. If there is a just God, your good works will ensure that you'll go to heaven, or wherever good people go." With that she took Jake's hand and led him out the door into the bright Missouri day.

They walked to where she had tied Molly to a rickety fence. She turned and stepped into Jake's arms. Lifting her face she looked into his troubled eyes. "It'll be alright Jake," she said easily. Then she pressed her lips against his. Her tongue slipped between his teeth and intertwined with his. Jake's breath immediately began to come in gasps and he cupped his hands around her firm buttocks.

"No!" she said. "I love you, but we don't have time now; it is getting late and I have to get back and talk to my father."

With that she turned and mounted Molly. Both of them were too enthralled with each other to notice the flash of the afternoon sun on metal and glass on the hill overlooking the Devine homestead. As Jenny swung into the saddle, a tall man in a light-colored pulpit coat watched the couple through a brass telescope. As he watched Jake grasp Jenny's butt and lock her in a passionate embrace, his lips curved behind his beard in a malicious smile.

It was dusk when Jenny rode into Far West. She nudged the sweating horse into a trot and stopped in front of the big swinging door at the livery stable. She opened the door and hesitated as she looked into the gloomy interior. She called out, but no one answered. She breathed a sigh of relief. Obviously Luke had gone home. She hurriedly unsaddled Molly and slipped the bridle over her ears. She found a currycomb and gave the horse a few quick swipes. She would've liked to spend more time grooming Molly, but she was anxious to get home. Putting the horse in its stall, she found a bucket of oats and poured some in the manger. She checked to make sure the animal had water; giving Molly an affectionate pat on the nose, she turned and left.

She broke into a ground-covering jog and soon arrived at the door of their little clapboard home. Opening the door, she called out, "Dad, are you home?"

"No, he is not; he left some time ago with Porter and didn't say when he would be back," said Agnes. "I would think you would want to see your mother after being out all day dressed like a man. How dare you dress in britches? You know it is immodest and violates our vows of chastity? May I ask where you've been, and who you've been with?"

Jenny stared at her mother. "I've been out riding and that is why I wore pants—they're more comfortable. I asked about dad because I am worried about him and yes, if you must know, I feel more comfortable discussing things with him, because he's not a religious fanatic and he's not judgmental."

"How dare you question me?" Agnes screamed. "I am doing the Lord's work and you would do well to learn more about the Gospel."

"Not likely!" Jenny retorted and went into her little room, slamming the door after her.

About half an hour before Jenny came home, Porter had stopped by to take John to the mysterious meeting of the Danites. John had been waiting in the tiny drawing room of their cabin when the knock came on the door. To him, it sounded like the knell of doom.

For some reason, he couldn't relax and little beads of sweat stood out on his forehead. His heart was pounding and when the knock came on the door, he felt a bolt of fear shoot through his gut. He couldn't imagine why he was so anxious. He'd been to dozens of church meetings and though he found them oppressive, he never felt threatened.

He opened the door and found Porter standing on the porch. Again, Porter avoided his eyes as if there was something he was hiding. He mumbled a greeting under his breath that John couldn't make out. Turning on his heel, he walked out to a buggy, which was standing next to the sidewalk. John walked around the vehicle, noticing that Porter had his team of matched blacks hooked to the little black surrey. John wondered if Porter considered the meeting special enough to use his fancy rig. He swung into the seat next to Porter. "Nice evening," he said, trying to ease the tension that seemed to rise between the two like a caustic fog. Porter glanced at him and then averted his eyes again like a chastised child.

"John," he said solemnly, "I think that it would be wise for you to just listen tonight. I told ya I would take ya to this meetin', but you must never tell anyone what ya hear and don't antagonize anyone tonight. It could be dangerous fer ya."

John gave Porter a covert glance to see if he was serious and decided he was. They rode the rest of the way in awkward silence. It was getting dark when they topped a little rise and saw a huge bonfire burning in a little opening in a grove of large sycamores. The scene was almost surreal. Porter reined in the horses some distance from the bonfire and tied up the team to a large sycamore. They dismounted from the surrey and Porter laid his hand on John's arm. "Brother Evans," he said grimly, "remember to hold your tongue; I cannot protect you if you incite these people."

John looked at Porter and saw that he was deadly serious, and he wondered if he should turn and walk home. Then he remembered his promise to himself, never to deny his principles again out of fear. Porter seemed very pensive and they walked in silence toward the fire. When they entered the ring of firelight, they found a large gathering of rough men. John couldn't help but notice that they didn't so much resemble Saints as they did nightriding Missouri brigands. The dancing flames cast long undulating shadows across the faces of the men, making them unrecognizable and radiating an eerie atmosphere. John felt a sudden chill, which he tried to attribute to a night wind, but in his heart he knew there was evil here.

As they approached the fire John saw that a low stand had been constructed out of rough lumber. It was about three feet high, and a set of steps had been built on one side to provide easy access to the podium. They had just arrived when a tall man with a full, black beard ascended the steps and blew a blast on an old brass trumpet. The buzz and murmur of the crowd was immediately silenced.

"Brethren," shouted the bearded man, "we are gathered here tonight to see that God's work is carried on without interruption from the pukes or the damned apostates and unbelievers in our very midst. Several of the brethren have expressed a desire to be confirmed members of our group and to take the secret oath of membership. However, before we endorse these brothers, Elder Samson Avard, leader of the Sons of Dan, would like to address this gathering."

With that, he turned and walked briskly to the steps and off the stand. Immediately a figure detached itself from the shadows and marched in a stately manner to the podium. As Avard stepped to the small log that had been arranged to serve as a podium, John observed that he was a small man with a neatly trimmed beard. He was wearing a fine broadcloth coat and flat-brimmed hat. He walked with a self-important gait that was almost a strut, and when he placed his hands on the podium, he looked out over his audience with a pompous smirk. His eyes glittered in the reflected firelight like jewels set in an obscene bust.

"Brethren," he began, "God has raised up a prophet in these last days, like unto Moses, and it is the duty of this group to obey him in all things and to ensure that others obey him as well. It is our sacred responsibility to report any murmuring against God's anointed and to stamp it out before it grows like the serpent of Satan. If it ever becomes necessary, each and every one of you must be willing to give up your lives in the cause and to protect the mouthpiece of the Lord. It's not our privilege to judge what is right or wrong; we must follow the word of God that is revealed to us by the Lord's own.

"If any one of you sees another of the band in trouble, you must come to his aid. If it requires that you take the life of an unbeliever, this is of no consequence. Return to Far West and we shall protect you, even if we must swear to a lie. We'll take care of each other as brothers. No one will be allowed to speak evil or disrespectfully of the presidency, nor reveal the existence or secret signs and passwords of this society under pain of death. I want each of you to report anyone who breaks the Word of Wisdom or disobeys the laws of the Gospel. No longer will this be allowed in our midst, nor will any preaching of false doctrine or possessing of any printed material that contradicts the teachings of the true prophet."

Avard stopped his harangue to catch his breath and collect his thoughts. John shuddered inwardly; he realized that Avard's band was nothing more than a strong-arm group to enforce the dictates of the church presidency and stamp out nonconformity and free thought. He found that he was agitated and his breath was coming in gasps. Though he was terrified, he knew he must speak out against this travesty, because free agency was one of the principles he was committed to defend, even to his death. He tried to erase this last troubling thought from his uneasy mind, but it stubbornly stayed there like a thorn in his flesh.

Avard raised his right hand with the palm out to signal his audience that he was ready to plunge on. "Brothers," he said in a surprisingly loud voice for such a small man, "now I will demonstrate to you the sacred signs and passwords that we may use to identify a true brother day or night. If one of us is in distress, he will give this sign."

With that Avard clapped his right hand to his right thigh and quickly raised it to his right temple with his thumb behind his right ear. "This is the hand of fellowship," he pronounced. "When giving this sign, ask, 'Who be you,' and if the other is one of us, he will reply, 'Anama,' which in Hebrew means 'friend.'

"Now brothers, know ye not that it will soon be your privilege to go out to the other counties and take the property of the ungodly Gentiles. The prophet has said that the riches of the Gentiles shall be consecrated to the Saints. In this way we will waste away the Missourians and build up the kingdom of God in these, the last days.

"Now comrades," Avard veritably shrieked, "let those who are to take the holy oath come forward."

Immediately, five men stepped forward and walked self-consciously to the stand.

"I would also like Brother Jared Carter, captain general of the Lord's Hosts, to come forward and assist me in administering the oath," Avard said gravely. Carter emerged from the flickering shadows and quickly climbed the steps to the stand.

"Brothers," shouted Avard, "please raise your right hand to the hallowed sign of the square."

Immediately, the five men raised their right hands with the palm out.

"Now I want each of you to think about the oath that I am about to administer and if you cannot, in good conscience, accept it, then don't swear, but step down. 'In the name of Jesus Christ, the Son of God, I faithfully swear that I will uphold the laws of God as revealed by his prophet, Joseph Smith. I further swear that I will obey the First Presidency of the Church in all things, and I will uphold the Presidency of the Church in all things, right or wrong. I also swear that I will never lay a hand on a Daughter of Zion, unless she is given to me by God. I solemnly swear that I will assist the Sons of Dan in the destruction of all apostates in this Church. I will wholeheartedly support the building of the government of Zion on earth in the last days, thus ushering in the return of the Savior. And finally, I vow that I will never divulge the secrets of this holy society on pain of death and I will shed the blood of any brother that I hear divulging these secrets to an apostate or Gentile. So help me God and maintain my faithfulness.'"

The group murmured "I do" in unison.

John couldn't believe what he had heard. Men had actually avowed to steal and plunder their neighbors because they differed in their religious beliefs. They had actually vowed to spill the blood of their brothers in the church if they disagreed with the teachings of the prophet, and they had sworn to perform the grisly ritual of blood atonement if any in this evil society ever divulged its existence or secrets. He knew he must speak out, but his tongue stuck to the roof of his mouth and his mouth was so dry he could not form words.

Avard turned toward the audience. "Are there any here that oppose what has been said?" he demanded in a menacing voice. John saw his chance, but before he could gather his courage, a strong voice came from the darkness.

"What you are preaching here flies in the face of the Gospel; does the prophet know that you are preaching false doctrine?"

Two hundred heads turned toward the speaker. John Corrill mounted a stump in the middle of the clearing and raised his arms in defiance.

"I suspect that the first presidency doesn't know of the existence of this secret society and I don't believe that they would condone your proposal to raid the Gentiles and plunder them to build up the kingdom."

An eerie hush fell over the strange scene.

Avard glared at Corrill with glittering eyes. "How dare you question me?" he demanded. "The prophet and Brother Sidney have both addressed our group on many occasions and have approved every principle that I have expressed here this evening as the will of the Lord. In fact, Brother Corrill, the prophet first suggested that we organize a group such as this to eliminate the hellish apostasy that seems to be rampant throughout the church. I strongly suggest that you hold your tongue lest you be considered among the unbelievers and godless."

Corrill fell silent and skulked away into the dark like a whipped cur. Then Avard turned again to the throng. "Now," he demanded in a menacing tone, "does anyone else want to question my authority?"

John took a deep breath. He wasn't sure if he could force himself to speak. He was so terrified that his throat was so constricted he could hardly breathe. He thought of his promise to himself that he would never again remain silent when men spoke injustice and intimidation. He wished that he could do as Corrill had and slink off into the night like a dog, but he couldn't, and the thought rose to his mind, "To thine own self be true."

What was the purpose of life, if one could not stand up for principle?

John found himself moving forward, shouldering his way through the throng. He was aware of hundreds of hostile eyes turning toward him, but he somehow calmed his rising panic and marched forward to the steps. He hesitated and looked at the rough board stairs and, unbidden, the thought of a gallows burst into his mind like an unwanted guest.

Avard turned toward where he wavered. "Do you have something to say?" he barked.

"Yes," replied John. He slowly climbed the stairs. He realized that his heart was pounding like a steam engine and his breath was coming in little gasps. He wondered if he would be able to speak and then he cursed himself in his mind. "For once," he thought, "you'll do what you know is right and stand up for your convictions and maybe, just maybe, you can ward off a bloodbath."

With that his step quickened and his back straightened and he walked confidently to the podium.

"Brothers," he said in a voice so strong that it surprised him, "Brother Avard tells us that we must not divulge any information about this secret society, but I tell you, any organization that must remain in the shadows does so because what they are doing is evil. If this group was dedicated to doing good, would it have to remain secret? I think not.

"Brother Avard also tells us that the Sons of Dan will soon be privileged to go out among the Missourians and rob and pillage them. By doing this, he says, we'll drive the Gentiles out of this hallowed land and build up Zion with the property of the ungodly. I say to you, if you do this you're no better than the mobs of Independence, who drove the Saints from their homes and stole their property without remorse.

"Brother Avard also says that it is a sin to criticize the church officials, but I say to you, Jesus has said, no man is perfect, and all people sin, therefore the best way to avoid corruption is to point it out. Brother Avard also says that Joseph is the only prophet of the living God, therefore he is beyond reproach, but I say Joseph is only a man and is just as prone to mistakes as any other man."

A murmur went through the throng like a gust of ill wind, but John ignored it.

"In the Middle Ages, John Wycliffe said all authority comes from the grace of God, not from man, and God has the power to speak directly to every man, not just some self-appointed prophet."

Again an angry mutter went through the crowd like the booming of distant surf, yet John was so enthralled with his theme that he was oblivious to the hostile attitude of the Danites.

"Why," he shouted, "would God set one man up as his only mouthpiece? Every man who seeks God in his own way will find the truth, and maybe, just maybe, the truth may take many different forms. Truth is not absolute; truth is relevant and what may be good for one man is not good for another. I say allow each man to seek God in his own way as long as he does not impinge on the rights of another. Sampson Avard says that this group has the right to kill any member of the church who dissents or apostatizes because they have denied the word of God. I say that, if you do, you commit murder, for it is a God-given right for any man—or woman, for that matter—to seek their conscience in their own way. If you really want to show your love of Christ, then forgive all men as he has asked you to do!"

With that, John turned and strode proudly to the steps and into the crowd.

As John tried to make his way through the tightly packed men, he found that they intentionally jostled him and muttered in his ear, "Traitor, antichrist, apostate."

More than once he heard references to "blood atonement." The hostility hung over the rough men like a poisonous cloud, but for once in his life John was proud that he had spoken his mind without considering the consequences. As the murmurs around him grew louder, he realized that he was surrounded by antagonistic men, and fear came flooding back like a cold wind. He found Porter and stood next to him. He looked at Rockwell, but Porter refused to acknowledge his presence or meet his gaze.

Avard walked to the podium with his eyes blazing. "I disagree with Brother Evans vehemently. In this the last dispensation, only those who are baptized, confirmed members and receive the Holy Spirit through confirmation and acceptance of God's anointed will ever be saved in the celestial kingdom. We must deny our selfish, individual traits and follow God's prophet to the letter of the law. However," he said, turning and looking at John, "I would like to discuss this further with Brother Evans. Please make arrangements to ride back to Far West in my buckboard."

John looked at Porter and again he turned away. "Is that alright with you, Port?" he asked.

Rockwell never looked John in the eye; rather he stared at his feet and mumbled, "Ya better go with 'em."

John stared hard at Rockwell, trying to determine what was on the man's mind. He didn't think that Porter would let him go with Avard if he thought he would be in danger, not after all they had been through together. He decided that Porter just wanted to give Avard a chance to talk him out of his heresy. As he was considering this weighty matter, one of the men who had been initiated into the Sons of Dan took him by the elbow.

John jumped at the touch and, turning, he looked into the grim face of the new Danite.

"Let's go," the man said gruffly, and painfully tightened his grip on John's elbow.

He was a big man with huge arms and he seemed bent on taking John to Avard. The grip on his elbow was like a steel band and John knew he couldn't escape if he wanted to. As they walked clear of the crowd, John saw Avard sitting in the front seat of a buckboard. To his apprehension he saw two more of the newly initiated members of the band sitting in the back of the buckboard, and they were as brawny as the man guiding him by the arm.

His big, hairy escort literally lifted him into the seat directly behind Avard and then vaulted into the wagon next to John. Once he had settled into the rough board seat, he grasped John's upper arm as if he thought Evans might try to bolt and escape. Avard turned around and gave John an appraising gaze.

"Well, Brother Evans, I hope you are comfortable. I thought if you rode back with me we could have a little discussion about your views on the Gospel."

"That was my belief, too," John said with a grimace, "but there was no reason to send this thug to get me."

"Well, you dissenters have a reputation for running away in the dark of night, like Cowdery and the Whitmers. It may interest you to know that those sniveling little cowards went to Liberty and retained a lawyer to bring a scurrilous lawsuit against the prophet. And if that weren't enough, the lying traitors published an article in the Liberty newspaper accusing the prophet of adultery, treason, fraud and a myriad of other crimes and heinous deeds. If you think that we're going to allow a group of cowardly apostates to run to the Gentiles and berate the prophet of God, you're wrong! As I said, the next man that tries to sneak away like a thief in the night and spill his guts to the Missourians will end up dead, and the only burial he will get is in a turkey buzzard's gut."

John felt as if his heart had leaped into his throat and his old nemesis, fear, threatened to paralyze him. "John Whitmer is neither a coward nor a liar, and he once loved Joseph and this church, but tyrants like you drove him away," John spat out with a vengeance.

Avard raised one eyebrow and looked at John with surprise.

"Well," he said, "I had been told that you would fold up like a wet shirt when we confronted you, but maybe you've grown a spine."

John returned his glare. "It's not a matter of growing a spine; it's a matter of some in this church trying to intimidate people into following inequitable dictates."

Avard gave John an apprising look. "Brother Evans," he announced, "this church is the only true church on the face of the earth and we are trying to establish the kingdom of God to set the stage for the second coming of the Savior. Do you think, do you even imagine for one moment, that we would allow some malcontent like you or John Whitmer to thwart this sacred work? If you had ever bothered to read the *Book of Mormon*, you would find that Nephi slew Laban, for it is better that one man die than a whole nation should dwindle in unbelief. God will not allow anyone to stand in the way of his work and if they do, it's not murder to slay them to protect the prophet and his work."

John was stunned at the fanaticism of this man. In his heart, he knew that he was in grave danger of losing his life, but he steeled his resolve and silently swore that he wouldn't forsake his passion for freedom of conscience. He had been so engrossed in his debate with Avard that he did not realize where he was. He glanced away from Avard and even in the darkness he noticed that they had left the road and there was no one else in sight. A baleful half-moon provided a dim dreamlike light and he noticed they were passing into a thick grove of cottonwoods, through which a little stream ran.

The driver stopped the team with a harsh yank on the reins. He jumped down and lifted a weight used to tether the horses and snapped it to the bit of the lead animal with a leather strap. Once the team was secured, Avard turned to the big man next to John. "Bring him," he said simply.

The burly escort grabbed John by the collar and unceremoniously dragged him out of the wagon. Nearly lifting John off his feet, he hauled him along, following the retreating back of Avard. John tried to protest, but the man's grip on his collar nearly cut off his breath. He tried to scream, but all that came out was a strangled grunt.

Soon Avard stopped at a pile of fresh soil. Turning to John, who was still dangling from the bodyguard's fist with his feet barely touching the ground, Avard put his nose inches from John's.

"Now then, Evans," he menacingly said, "you've committed a despicable sin. You've encouraged others to speak out against the prophet of God, you've blasphemed, and you've questioned the true Gospel of Jesus Christ. For this you must pay the ultimate penalty, which is blood atonement. God has spoken through the prophet that those who deny the Gospel and fight against God's church can only find atonement through the spilling of their blood. However, I'll give you one more chance: if you swear allegiance to the prophet and God's anointed and pledge that you'll never again question their dictates and become a Danite and accept their vows, this cup may pass you by."

John struggled to understand what Avard was saying. The big man's hold on his collar was cutting off the blood flow to his brain and he couldn't get his breath. He signaled to Avard that he couldn't speak, and Avard nodded to the huge brute holding his collar and he relaxed his hold. John's feet hit the ground and his knees immediately buckled. The thug caught him by the shoulders and held him up. He struggled to speak, but his larynx refused to comply and only a strangled squeak escaped his throat. The man holding him shook him, as if to clear his head. "Do you understand what I just asked you?" Avard demanded.

John nodded his head to indicate that he understood.

"Well then, will you agree?" Avard shrieked into his face.

John tried to think, but his mind whirled. Gradually, his brain cleared and he realized that his life hung by a thread. He thought of all the things he would like to accomplish before he died. He wanted to see his daughter grow into a young woman and marry, perhaps give him grandchildren to edify. He'd always wanted to write a book decrying the travesty of intolerance, and now he was about to become a victim of the most repugnant kind of bigotry. He desperately wanted to live to nurture Jenny until she could care for herself. The personal vow that he'd made came back like gruesome specter and he knew that if he succumbed to cowardice again, he would never be able to respect himself for the rest of his life.

"No!" he croaked through his tortured throat. "I will not become a member of this vile band and I'll never swear to unquestionably follow the word of another man. I'll decide my beliefs for myself and may God forgive you."

"Very well," said Avard in an imposing voice. He nodded at the man holding John, and he grabbed Evans by the hair and jerked his head back. Another burly Son of Dan seized John's free arm and twisted it painfully behind him. John heard the tendons in his neck and shoulder pop under the strain. A bolt of pain shot through his neck and down his spine like liquid fire. He tried to scream, but only a pitiful gurgle came from his throat.

"It seems he's lost his fervor for insolence," Sampson Avard said with a sneer. He pulled a long Green River knife from a scabbard under his coat and raised it to John's throat. Even with his head pulled back at an impossible angle, John could see the wicked blade shine in the pale light of the moon. Avard laid the blade against John's throat and, with a vicious jerk, he pulled it across the man's exposed throat from hilt to tip.

John felt an agonizing, sharp pain in his throat and heard the blade of the knife grate against the vertebra of his neck. He tried to breathe, but a rivulet of blood poured down his windpipe. Mercifully, a humming numbness spread from his throat throughout his body. He could no longer see the pale light of the moon and a soothing, velvet darkness settled around him.

No sooner had the comforting darkness settled over him than he saw what appeared to be a bright light in the distance, which seemed to be rapidly approaching him. He stared fixedly at the light and, as it came closer, he saw that in the center of the undulating, exquisite light was a horse. It was piebald and looked to John like the horses that he had seen the Indians ride on their exodus to the Great Plains. For some reason the horse didn't frighten him; rather he felt a great peace come over him. As the horse swept by him, he found himself astraddle the animal. The horse had no bridle or saddle, yet he found he had no difficulty staying aboard. The light quickly seemed to luminate the entire sky and for the first time in many years, John was totally at peace with himself and the world.

Avard was surprised at the amount of blood that gushed forth from the massive wound in Evan's throat. "Hold him over the grave, so the blood will flow into the soil. It is through the shedding of blood into the grave that he has a chance for salvation."

Both of the jugular veins on John's neck had been cut and his life's blood poured out in an amazing stream. Quickly the spurts became a dribble and the men holding John's body unceremoniously flung it into the freshly dug grave. Three or four of the men quickly grabbed shovels from the buckboard and filled the grave. They cut fresh cottonwood branches and swept the dirt. When that was done, they scattered leaves and grass over the wound in the earth and climbed into the buckboard.

Chapter 20

later that evening, Jenny crawled off her bed and opened the door into the room that served as a kitchen, dining room and living room. As she opened the door, her mother looked up from her *Book of Mormon*.

"Where is dad?" Jenny asked hesitantly.

"I told you, he has supposedly gone to a church meeting with Porter Rockwell, but I wouldn't put it past him to sneak off like the rest of those turncoats," Agnes answered sarcastically.

Jenny looked at her mother with shining eyes. "He wouldn't do that—he wouldn't leave me," Jenny answered in a quavering voice.

"What?" her mother barked, and then continued, "By the way, Brother Jacob Powers came by this afternoon. He said he was representing the high council and he wanted to talk to both of us. He inferred that you'd been sneaking off meeting some Gentile boy and letting him paw you."

Jenny felt a sinking feeling in her stomach, then a flash of anger.

"Has the high council sent their little minions out to spy on me like they do everyone else they suspect of not toeing the mark?" she spat back at her mother. Agnes looked at her daughter with annoyance in her eyes.

"How dare you question the high council? Obviously what they say is true. You've been cavorting with the Gentiles and you've lost your testimony of the Gospel. Well, don't worry, Brother Powers is coming back tomorrow evening and we'll do something about your impudence then."

With that she turned back to her copy of the *Book of Mormon*, signaling Jenny that the conversation was over.

The next morning, Jenny rose early and rushed into the kitchen. She was devastated to see that her father hadn't returned from the alleged meeting. She desperately wanted to talk to him about her relationship with Jake and the upcoming meeting with Powers. She dreaded the meeting because she knew they'd berate her for being friendly with a Gentile and would probably accuse her of fornication.

She understood that if she were called before the high council court, the experience would be demoralizing at best and very much akin to the courts of the Inquisition. The accused had no right to speak up in their defense and had no right to counsel, or even to bring a friend for support. She was aware that if she were found guilty of consorting with the Gentiles or of fornication she could be expelled from Far West. She knew that her mother would never leave and she had no idea where her father was, but there was always Jake and she could run away with him.

Jenny had a nagging fear that something had happened to John. She tried to drive it from her mind but it kept coming back like a bad dream. She desperately wanted to discuss her dilemma with her father. She had always looked to him when she was troubled and they could debate any issue without presumption or unease. She kept telling herself that John had met John Whitmer and left town for a few days, but she couldn't imagine that he would do such a thing without telling her.

Her mother came out of her room looking like she hadn't slept well. She gave Jenny a withering glance and went to the iron cookstove to feed the coals. She deliberately turned her back on Jenny to convey her distaste of her daughter's actions. After she had heated some corndodger and boiled some water for Saint's tea, she finally motioned toward the table with her hand. Jenny sat down, looking across the rough plank table; she stared into her mother's face trying to make eye contact.

Finally, Agnes looked at her daughter with red-rimmed eyes. "I guess you're going to ask me again were your father is?" she said harshly. "I told you before; I suspect the coward has run away. It takes courage to stand up for the truth and he has always been spineless. He never did really accept the Gospel, so it is just as well that he has gone to join the dissenters. The Saints need stalwart men to build the kingdom of God. And by the way," she continued, "you had better prepare yourself to stand before the high council and answer for your sins."

Jenny gave her Mother a disparaging look. "I'll answer for my sins, if they answer for theirs," she said. "The first thing the so-called Saints need to answer for is unmitigated hypocrisy."

Agnes returned Jenny's hostile look. "Just be here tomorrow at seven," she said simply. Then, as if by afterthought, she added, "Also, I don't think it would be a good idea for you to try and run off with that lecher because this house is being watched."

With that, Agnes picked up her books and notes and announced that she was going to the bishop's office to perform her duties as unofficial defender of the faith.

The last thing she said as she walked out the door was, "Remember, the Sons of Dan are watching this house, so don't try and run away."

She slammed the door and Jenny heard a key turn in the lock as she left.

Jenny had never been so despondent in her entire life. She desperately wanted her father to comfort her, as he had always helped her sort out her mind when she was confused. She found she couldn't shake the sinking feeling that all was not well with John. She didn't believe that John would leave Far West without telling her or taking her with him. She had a strange gnawing feeling in the pit of her stomach, as if a worm were slowly eating at her insides. Tears welled up in her eyes and her lip trembled uncontrollably.

Her mother didn't return at noon for lunch, but Jenny had no stomach for food. She lay on her bed and stared at the ceiling through shimmering tears. She felt abandoned. Even though she knew her mother would return before the scheduled meeting with Brother Powers, she found no solace in the thought. She desperately wanted Jake and she frantically needed her father's advice. She toyed with the idea of breaking a window and leaving. She knew little of the secret society that had reared its ugly head in the church, but she did know that the members spoke of it in whispers and didn't dare question the precepts of the church or its leaders. She knew that someone had told her mother about Jake and their clandestine rendezvous. She considered this and thought better of running away. She would wait until her father returned or Jake came for her. Besides, how bad could it be to meet with Powers or the high council? She would live her life as she wanted and Jacob Powers would just have to accept that. Jenny believed that her situation could not possibly get worse.

Agnes came home sometime around five in the afternoon. Jenny heard the key grate in the old box lock; it sounded like the grating of the gates of doom. Agnes burst through the door in her usual brusque manner, as if she always had something critical to deal with. She gave Jenny a condescending look. "It would be in your best interest to dress appropriately for your meeting with the brethren," she spat. Jenny thought of returning her sarcasm with equal derision, but thought better of it and held her tongue. Instead, she turned and abruptly walked into her bedroom.

She emerged a few minutes later, dressed in a plain gingham dress. By the time she was dressed, her Mother had set the table and ladled two bowls of beef stew she had warmed. Jenny sat across the table from her and ducked her head, pretending to eat. She knew her mother was considering berating her for her moral permissiveness and she dreaded the upcoming lecture.

"You should hang your head in shame," Agnes announced self-righteously. "I've learned more about your liaison with that whore-mongering Gentile boy and I'm disgusted. I was told by worthy sources that he was pawing at you and you bared your body. Trustworthy sources informed me that he touched your secret places and you fondled him. Do you realize that fornication is a cardinal sin and you can lose your salvation for your disgusting behavior?"

Jenny looked Agnes straight in the face. "If someone truly loves another, then physically loving them isn't a sin and it is the most sublime form of love—but then you wouldn't know that, would you, because you never touched Daddy, or let him touch you."

"How dare you question my integrity? I know the word of God; I have studied the prophet's writings. Only when we reach the celestial kingdom through the priesthood of a godly man can we propagate worlds through the sacred power to create life."

Jenny looked at her mother incredulously. "You have always lived in a fantasy world. Well, I don't and I plan to marry Jake and have children now, on this earth, and love and nurture them, unlike you—you are totally unable to show love, either emotionally or physically."

Agnes stared wide-eyed at her daughter. Her lips quivered with fury, but she couldn't force herself to speak.

Jenny rose. "When those charlatans arrive, I'll be in my room," she said with malice. She turned and stalked out of the room.

Jenny lay on the little pole bed that her father had made from small cottonwood saplings. The straw tick was supported by hemp rope that crisscrossed between the supporting poles. She lay and stared at the open rafters. John had never found the time to cover the ceiling with lathe and plaster. The joists that supported the walls ran horizontally across the room about four feet above her head. Above those, she could see the rafters supporting the roof and between the rafters and lateral boards, she could see little strips of shingles.

She desperately wished her father would return, but something whispered in her brain that John would never come home again. She turned her head to the side to look out the little four-paned window and hot tears ran down her left cheek. She racked her brain, but she could see no way out of her dilemma. Jake expected her to meet him tomorrow and if she didn't come, what would he think? She wondered if he would come to Far West looking for her. She had serious mixed feelings about Jake coming here. She knew that her mother would try to stop her from leaving, especially with a Gentile, and she had no idea what the church hierarchy would do. With feelings in Far West running high since the apostates had left and with relations with the Gentiles deteriorating, she knew there would be a conflict if Jake came to take her away.

Despite the turmoil in her heart, Jenny dropped off into a troubled sleep. She was standing on the gentle rise above the little valley where they met. She looked across the little swale and saw a solitary figure walking through the tall grass. She knew it was Jake, even at this distance, because she could make out a hound, leaping joyously above the grass by the side of the distant figure. Her heart leaped with joy and she felt odd warmth in her loins. The wind came up and rattled the little cottonwood she was standing under. Her eyes opened and she realized that someone was knocking insistently on her bedroom door.

With a sinking feeling in her chest, Jenny rose and opened the door. Agnes was standing in the doorway and, oddly enough, she gave Jenny a somewhat affectionate look.

"The brethren are here," she said simply.

Jenny rose from her bed and shook her head to clear the cobwebs. She felt a strange melancholy longing to be back in the dream from which she was so rudely awakened. She looked in the little cracked mirror above the basin and splashed a little water on her face. She ran a comb through her tangled auburn hair and, straightening her gingham dress, she stepped out of her room.

Agnes was sitting on a balloon-backed chair and Powers was sitting on the horsehair sofa with another man. Powers's blotchy face brightened when he saw Jenny enter the room. He quickly rose and held out a boney hand to Jenny.

"Good evening, Sister Evans," he gushed. "This is Brother Robert Bowers. He's a counselor to the stake president and is representing not only the stake presidency, but the twelve apostles, the church presidency and the prophet in this matter."

Jenny glanced at Bowers and took his limp, damp hand in greeting.

She found the man as distasteful as his ghastly, clammy hand. Bowers reminded Jenny of one of the old horses that had pulled their wagon from Clay County to Far West. He had a long, horse-like face. His teeth were long and yellow, like those of the old draft horses that had brought them north. However, where the two old workhorses were gentle and unassuming, Bowers was arrogant and self-righteous. When he talked to Jenny, his eyes darted about like two blowflies and they usually settled at the apex of her bodice on the cleavage of her young, firm breasts. Jenny hated the way the man looked at her, for it was not difficult to read his lecherous mind.

"Sister Evans," Bowers began sanctimoniously, "it has been reported to the brethren that you have been cavorting with a young Gentile. It has also been reported that you've engaged in sexual stimulation with this man and the two of you were naked. Our sources say that you may have even engaged in sexual intercourse with an unbeliever."

Agnes audibly caught her breath and held a lace handkerchief to her face as if this news were more than she could bear.

Jenny gave her mother an indulgent look. "Please, Mother," she said, "don't patronize me."

Bowers gave her a surprised look, as if he didn't expect the girl to stand up for herself. "Sister Evans," he stated, "we are trying to determine if a sin has occurred here."

Jenny looked at him as if he were a dog turd sitting on the chair.

"And who will determine if a sin has occurred, you or the hypocrites who think they will judge the world?" she exclaimed.

Agnes leaped to her feet.

"How dare you question God's anointed," she demanded.

"Until God tells me that I've committed a sin, I refuse to be browbeaten by a bunch of self-righteous bigots," Jenny screamed.

"Please, please, Sister Evans," Bowers pleaded, "we're trying to help you to overcome your earthly lusts."

"I really don't need you to tell me about my earthly failings or my sins. I will worry about my soul myself!" she exclaimed.

"Oh, but I think you do," replied Bowers scathingly. "I really don't think you realize the situation you're in," he said menacingly. "Your father has run off and left you, your mother has a strong testimony of the Gospel and supports us in this and you're not in a position to support yourself or to make demands concerning what you will or will not do. Now listen to what I have to say, because it may save your soul and lead to your salvation. The prophet has received a revelation concerning the righteous relationships between a man and a woman.

"It seems that through his priesthood, a man who is faithful in the church may become as God now is. That is, he may create earths and populate them with souls who may work out their salvation, as we are now working out ours. To do this, a man must have multiple wives to populate the earths that he will create. He would populate them as we create our families now—that is, through sexual relationships sanctioned by God. Let me tell you this, Jenny: without marrying a man of faith in the church and without receiving your endowment in the Temple, you'll never be saved in the celestial kingdom.

"What I am saying is that the prophet has received a revelation from God sanctioning a system of spiritual marriage where a man may have multiple wives to aid him in populating the earths that he will create as a God. The prophet has informed me that you have been given to me as a plural wife. Think about this, Jenny. I can assure you that you will receive your salvation and be saved in the celestial kingdom if you but recite the secret vows before the prophet of God. When the Temple is finished, we'll be sealed for time and all eternity in a secret ritual within its holy walls."

Jenny looked at Bowers as if he had just announced that he was the devil incarnate. "What're you talking about? I would rather die on the spot than marry an ugly old reprobate like you!" she exclaimed.

Bowers's blotchy face turned an even more ghastly shade of mottled scarlet. His lips trembled in unrestrained fury, but before he could berate Jenny, Agnes spoke up. "How dare you question an apostle of God?" she shrieked. "If any word from his mouth is preceded by 'Thus saith the Lord,' then it is the word of God. If you deny this or disobey a commandment, you will be cast into outer darkness."

Jenny looked at her mother with absolute disdain. "I would rather spend an eternity in outer darkness than marry someone I don't love, especially someone who has another wife. This is absolutely ludicrous and I'll not agree to it under any circumstances."

Bowers totally ignored Jenny's outburst and turned to Agnes.

"My marriage to your daughter must remain utterly confidential," he solemnly said. "No one must know that she is my plural wife. She can remain here and I'll visit from time to time to consummate the union. Eventually, the prophet will announce the principle of plural marriage, but now is not the time. In the Lord's own good time he will tell the prophet when to publicly announce this holy principle. Until that time we must maintain absolute secrecy."

Jenny looked at the trio incredulously. "Don't I have a say in who I will marry and what I will believe?" she shouted.

"No!" Agnes retorted. Her eyes glittered with passion and Jenny wondered if she had lost her sanity. "You're not old enough to know what is good for you and you don't understand the ways of the Lord. Until you do, I will decide the course of your life for you and that is the end of it."

"No, it's not!" Jenny shouted. "There is no way you can make me do this evil thing."

"Enough!" shouted Agnes. "I am your mother and I will decide. Don't think that you can run away, for there are men who are pledged to protect the church from dissenters, mobs and those who would deny the true word of God. If you try to leave this city, or this house, they'll bring you back and we'll put you in a jail cell."

The two men seemed embarrassed and Bowers donned his hat in a signal that it was time to leave. He turned to Jenny. "Sister Evans," he murmured, "I am acting in what I see as your best interest. Please be assured that I'll treat you with respect as your husband."

Jenny glared at him and noticed that again his eyes were resting on her cleavage.

"You'll never have to worry about that, because I'll never consent to be your wife!" she exclaimed.

Bowers looked at her with a mixture of admiration and rancor. "I know what you think," he said. "But know this: as we speak there are men out there watching this house. They have orders to stop you if you try to leave. They answer directly to me, and if you make any move to leave this city or this house, they will physically drag you back and we will incarcerate you."

With that the two men said good night and left.

After they had left, Agnes turned to her daughter with fire in her eyes. "You're too immature to understand that this is the chance of a lifetime for you. Brother Bowers is a man of substance and he is a man of God. He can take you directly to the celestial kingdom and you'll be a goddess and rule over worlds that he'll create as a god. You will have posterity without measure. Who could want more?"

Jenny returned the haughty stare.

"I want more than that old fanatical reprobate," she declared. "I want the man I love, and I'll have him, despite your interfering."

"No, you will not!" exclaimed Agnes. "I told you, the Sons of Dan will enforce the dictates of the prophet and he has said that God has given you to Brother Bowers as a wife and so it will be!" With that, Agnes turned and went into her bedroom, slamming the door behind her.

Jenny stood looking after her for several minutes, and then she turned and went to her room. She lay on the bed and looked up at the rafters running from wall to wall. Tears stung her eyes and she feverishly searched her mind for an answer to her dilemma. Somewhere along the way, she had come to the conclusion that her father was dead and would never gently prod her toward a logical decision, as he had done countless times when she was searching for an answer to a predicament.

She thought of opening the window and slipping into the night, but she knew Agnes was not lying when she said that a secret society of fanatics was watching for dissidents and runaways. In fact, she was sure that it was this society that had sealed the fate of her father and spied on her and Jake. Besides, now that Whitmer was gone and Luke Rasmussen had taken his place, she knew she would never have access to Molly again. She wondered if Jake would come looking for her if she didn't come to their rendezvous, but she dismissed any chance that he could spirit her away from the authoritarian city of Far West, secured as it was, and he might die trying.

Then, unbidden like a thief in the night, the idea of suicide crept into her mind. She thought of the words of Saint Augustine: "Patricide is more wicked than homicide, but suicide is most wicked of all." She wondered if what she was pondering was wicked and would condemn her to hell. Then she decided the divine being who gave her life probably wouldn't punish her, if she found life not worth living. Her tumultuous mind suddenly dredged up a line from a poem by the English bard, Charles Colton: "Suicide sometimes proceeds from cowardice, but not always; for cowardice sometimes prevents it; since as many live because they are afraid to die, as die because they are afraid to live."

Somehow she found solace in the poet's words and she knew what she must do, but how? She thought about cutting her wrists, but she had heard her father say that this method was not very effective and often resulted in maiming the wrist rather than in death. She thought about shooting herself, but she knew nothing of guns and she didn't know where her father's big horse pistol was. Perhaps he had taken it with him when he disappeared. Her racing mind again touched on a passage she had read: "For the sake of decency, gentlemen, don't hang me high."

She realized that the words were spoken by the English murderess, Mary Blandy, in 1752, just before she was hung for poisoning her father. She looked under the tick mattress and found a coil of rope left over from lacing the frame to hold her mattress. She retrieved the coil and tossed it over one of the rafters. She had no idea how to tie a proper hangman's knot, so she tied a slipknot in the end of the rope. After she had made the rope fast to the leg of the bed, she tested its length and decided if she jumped off the bed, her feet would be several inches off the floor.

She slipped the noose around her neck and then considered the deed she was about to perform. She knew once she stepped off the bed, she couldn't go back. However, after considering all options, she decided she had no other alternative. She wouldn't submit to the foul-breathed Bowers and she didn't believe that God would give her to him without her agreement. She again thought of her father and she knew he was dead. She decided she wanted to be with him, if she couldn't spend her life with Jake, which now seemed impossible. Closing her eyes, she jumped off the bed, hoping her neck would break. The knot slipped tight around her milk-white neck, immediately cutting off her wind and the blood supply to her brain. She immediately panicked when she couldn't breathe and she kicked and squirmed, but soon everything went black.

Jenny was aware of a bright light in the smothering darkness. She stared into the center of the light, which reminded her of a glowing tunnel. She thought she could see the end of the passageway and the sun was shining and there were trees and grass. Abruptly, a horse appeared at the other end of the passage and it was galloping toward her, with flaring nostrils and blowing mane. She thought it was Molly, until she realized that it was a brilliant paint with vivid black and white markings.

It was nearly dark when Agnes stirred from a restless sleep. She had dreamed strange dreams and as consciousness slowly crept over her, she tried to remember what it was she had dreamed. Slowly, she remembered that her dream involved Jenny. In her dream, Agnes was young again and Jenny was a happy, beautiful child. They were walking along a swift flowing stream, and Agnes stopped to pick some flowers that seemed to have a strange appeal to her. She became enthralled in gathering the beautiful blooms and soon had an armful of them.

She soon realized that the flowers, though beautiful, had a vile and strange odor. She threw them on the ground and abruptly realized that Jenny was nowhere to be seen. She ran to the river and found the little girl's shoes lying on the bank. She looked into the wild and swiftly flowing water of the river and realized that Jenny was gone.

Agnes came fully awake in an instant and realized that her heart was pounding. She thought of the strange dream and couldn't make sense of it, but she had a deep foreboding that all was not well. She sat up so quickly that she saw little pinpoints of light before her eyes. She sprang off the bed and nearly passed out. She put her hand against the doorframe to steady herself until the dizziness passed, and then cried out, "Jenny!"

The only sound that she heard in return was a buzzing in her ears. She ran her hand over her forehead and eyes to clear away the cobwebs and called again. She strained her ears in the gathering darkness, but she received no reply. Agnes knew something was dreadfully wrong. It never entered her mind that her daughter might have run away; she knew something far worse had happened.

Nearly stumbling over a little table next to her bed, Agnes steadied herself and her hand came in contact with the cool glass of the oil lamp she kept next to her bed. She became aware that the house was dark and she thought of lighting the lamp. As she reached for the glass chimney of the lamp, she realized that her hand was shaking like a leaf in a gale. Unthinkingly, she grasped the offending hand with her other one and clasped them both to her bosom. She was surprised to find that her heart was pounding in her sunken chest like a trip hammer.

Closing her eyes, she silently called out to her God. "Lord, don't let this happen to me, let her be safe."

Gradually, her hand stopped shaking and she managed to light the lamp and replace the glass chimney. Turning, she opened the door to the kitchen and, holding the lamp high, she carefully stepped over the threshold into the room. Again, she softly called out her daughter's name and again she received no answer in reply. Her heart sank and she found herself praying that Jenny had run away.

With mounting dread she stumbled across the kitchen toward the door to Jenny's room. She placed her hand on the cold porcelain knob, and hesitated, dreading what she might find on the other side of the door. Placing her forehead on the rough pine of the door, she again softly called Jenny's name. She turned the knob and pushed the door slowly open.

The pale, flickering light of the lamp slowly illuminated the little room and Agnes became aware of the gently swaying form dangling from rafters. A heart-rending shriek escaped Agnes's lips and she raised the lamp and looked up into her daughter's face. Jenny's eyes were open wide and appeared to be bursting out of their sockets. Her face was a ghastly blackish green and her tongue was protruding from her puffy lips.

Agnes looked at the pitiful form that had once been a beautiful young woman and a stifled moan escaped her lips. Her feverish mind searched for an answer to why her daughter would have done such a thing. Slowly she backed away from the ghastly swaying figure and turned and ran into her bedroom and threw herself on the rumpled quilt. She desperately fought the feelings of guilt and blame that flooded her heart and stifled her soul.

She silently began to pray and her lips moved in silent supplication. Her mind cast about like a restless bird, and gradually she began to rationalize her position. Obviously, Jenny took her life because she couldn't deal with the vile sin she had committed. The prophet had said time and again that the Saints shouldn't fraternize with the ungodly Gentiles. Despite her warnings, Jenny hadn't only fraternized with a Gentile, she had fornicated with one.

This was a sad and soul-searing situation, but under no circumstances was she, Agnes, responsible for what had happened to Jenny. In fact, this was all for the better—better that Jenny was dead than in the clutches of a morally unclean Gentile. Yes, she was innocent of any complicity in this matter. With that, she matter-of-factly set the lamp on the table and took her coat off the hook by the front door. She would go report this matter to Brother Bowers; he would absolve her of any blame. With that she blew out the lamp, stepped out of the door and turned and locked it. She didn't look back as she hurried down the street.

On the day that he was to meet Jenny, Jake took the gray mule that his father used as a plow animal and bridled the docile creature. He didn't have a saddle, but he didn't mind. He was used to riding bareback and he liked to feel the rhythm of the mule's stride directly through his buttocks. Besides, the warmth of the mule's skin felt good on his legs and he liked the musky aroma of the animal. It was a warm, fair day toward the end of June. The prairie flowers were still in unbridled bloom and the rolling grasslands were alive with color. The gentle breeze caused the billowing grass to roll in waves like ocean swells.

Sam had ridden off the day before on the black mule and left orders for Jake to plow and work the land and begin planting corn and wheat. Jake had gotten a good start on it, but he had to meet Jenny. She was always in his thoughts and his longing for her was like a pain in his chest. The beauty of the day touched his soul and his spirits soared. He nudged the old mule in the ribs with his heel, urging him into a rough trot. The mule was tired from pulling the hand plow for the last three days and he immediately slowed to a more comfortable walk. Jake felt empathy for the beast, for he too was bone-tired from the drudgery of farm work.

Because the mule was reluctant to break into a gallop, Jake was nearly an hour late arriving at the little valley where he always met Jenny. As he crested the little rim bordering the valley, he expected to see her rise out of the bluestem and wave gleefully at him. However, he didn't see her slim figure, or any other living thing. He urgently kicked the mule into a lumbering run and drew him up at the spot where they had made love. The grass was undisturbed and there was no sign that anyone had been there. Jake felt a bolt of concern rise from his gut, but Jenny had told him that if she couldn't get away or obtain a horse, she would come the next day.

He sat down in the grass and gazed out across the waving gama. Nothing stirred, except a flock of crows that flapped across the valley, calling to each other in their raucous voices. He stayed there until the sun was nearing the western horizon, then he reluctantly rose and walked to the mule, which was contentedly munching the succulent bluestem. As he mounted and rode slowly toward the cabin, a little worm of apprehension gnawed at his belly. Jenny had never missed one of their meetings and she had always been there early, eager for his touch.

He was bitterly disappointed and he felt shame when the countryside blurred through hot tears. He hoped that Sam hadn't returned, because he knew the old man would expect the forty acres to be plowed and planted by now. Even though he had worked from dawn to dusk for over a week, he still had several acres to harrow and plant. Besides the backbreaking labor of walking behind the mule holding the handles of the hand plow, he also had his regular chores of milking, feeding and caring for the stock, as well as keeping the family in fresh meat.

He deeply resented the fact that his father rarely helped him run the homestead but always chastised him if he couldn't accomplish the impossible. The old man spent most of his days in Gallatin, drinking, bullshitting, fighting and whoring, and he could never see the duplicity of his ways. Jake looked over his shoulder at the rapidly plummeting sun and again tried to urge the old mule into a gallop. He didn't have the heart to whip the old beast, because after following his rump across endless furrows, he knew how tired the animal must be.

When he rode into the yard, his heart fell when he saw the black mule in the corral. He quickly went about his chores and when he finished milking the red cow, he picked up the frothy bucket of milk and reluctantly started for the cabin. He pushed the door open and was shocked to see his father standing next to his mother with his hand under her dress. Sam turned at the sound of the grating of the door. "Well, boy," he said. The man's tone was good natured, not filled with his typical spite. "How the hell is the plowin' and plantin' goin'?"

"Good, Pa. I am almost done," Jake exaggerated.

"Well, thas good 'cause I heard that them fanatics is havin' a Fourth of July celebration, and I was thinkin' maybe you and I could go and see what they's up to."

Jake's heart leaped. The Fourth of July was still several days away and if Jenny didn't come before then, he could go to Far West with his father and maybe he could find her. The next day, Sam rose about noon and saddled the black mule, Cletus, and rode off toward Gallatin. Before he left, he gave Jake his instructions.

"Boy, ya better have that forty acres harrowed and planted. I expect to have some fresh meat in the larder. I don't expect to eat no buffaler fish and trash like that. Iffen ya don't do what I says, I'll hide ya within an inch o' yer life."

Turning to Bessie, Sam looked at her out of the corner of his eye. "And you, woman! I expect a little more respect when I come back than I got yesterday. And iffen I don't get what I wants, ya kin expect to git your nose broke again, like las' time."

With that he put his foot in the stirrup and swung into the saddle. Jake knew exactly what Sam meant when he spoke to Bessie. He had heard them last night and he knew that Sam had taken Bessie violently. Obviously, she hadn't satisfied his lust to his approval. Jake gave his mother a questioning look as Sam rode away, and she dropped her eyes in shame. Jake knew that if he ever found Jenny again, he would not treat her as his father treated Bessie.

Each day about noon, the usual time that Jake and Jenny had met, Jake rode out to the little basin with hope in his heart, and each day he returned dejected when he found no sign of Jenny. He told himself that she was unable to get out of Far West and as soon as things settled down there she would meet him. He couldn't imagine that anything bad could happen to a woman as young, virile and energetic as Jenny, but that didn't dull the ache in his chest or his longing to see her. He went about his daily chores in a kind of daze. He thought several times of going to Far West to try to find her, but he had never been to the city of the Saints and he remembered his reception at the vile new homestead that had ruined the springfed pond.

Sam rarely asked Jake to go with him on his roaming. The boy could remember going to Fort Osage with his father when he was a child. They had gone there to pick up a mule at a livestock auction. However, Sam didn't want his son to know what he did when he went into Gallatin or some other town, even though Jake had seen his father come home in a stupor many times and had heard his mother bemoan her husband's propensity for loose whores.

Although Sam had mentioned it before, it came as a great shock when he approached Jake one morning as he fed the stock and milked the cow and again asked him if he wanted to go to Far West for the Fourth of July celebration. Sam was involved with a Missouri militia unit commanded by a Captain Samuel Bogart. The good captain had requested some members of his unit to go to the celebration in Far West and spy on the Saints to determine their military strength and taste for war. Sam knew that there would be no drinking or whoring in Far West, and Bessie had meekly asked him to take Jake with him to develop a relationship with his son. So it was that Sam happened to ask Jake to accompany him, just when the boy was thinking of sneaking into the forbidden city alone. Jake despised his father for his violent temper and his abuse of his mother. He had no desire to be around Sam any more than was necessary, but he immediately accepted the offer to go to Far West on the chance that he might see Jenny.

The Fourth of July dawned clear, hot and muggy. Jake had risen long before sunrise to attend to his chores and check some snares that he had set for sharp tails and rabbits. By the time that Sam climbed out of bed, bleary eyed and in a foul mood, Jake had taken care of all the stock and fetched in a bucket of warm milk and four fat prairie chickens. However, the sight of the succulent birds, foam-covered milk and still-warm chicken eggs on the table did nothing to salve Sam's foul mood.

"How come ya ain't got nothing to eat on the table yet, woman?" he demanded.

Bessie looked at him with fear glinting in her eyes. "I got ya an omelet, and bacon a'cookin' right now, and coffee is on," she replied meekly. Sam glared at her and slid a chair out from the table with a screech.

"And you, boy," he demanded, "have you done anythin' this morning but play with yer pecker?"

Jake looked at the old man sitting at the table with a week's growth of salt and pepper stubble bristling on his chin. He considered telling the old bastard that he might get a lot more done if Sam could get his ass out of bed before midmorning and help, but he thought better of it. Why get a beating just for the slight satisfaction of chiding his father?

They ate in silence; neither Jake nor Bessie dared breech a subject lest it send Sam into a tirade. When they had finished, Sam rose from the table without considering the dirty dishes or the smear of egg yolk and bacon grease that he left on the table and floor. Jake looked with disgust at the grease and yellow yolk that surrounded Sam's mouth like a halo, but he said nothing. They went to the corral and Sam threw a rope around the black mule's neck.

"Ya kin run along the side o' the mule," he grunted. "Ah doan want to tire out that gray. Ya still got a bunch o' plowin and harrowin' to do with him." With that he saddled the black and, after mounting, headed off to the west without even a backward glance.

Jake broke into a ground-covering trot. He was lean and thin and was used to running or walking nearly everywhere he went, so it was no problem for him to keep up with Sam astride the mule. They traveled about four or five miles and came to a little grove of trees along a springfed creek. As they approached the grove, Sam put his fingers to his mouth and gave a piercing whistle, which was immediately returned from the grove. A group of about five men emerged from the shade of the trees and rode up to Sam. "Well, Sam," one of them said, "are you ever goin' to get a hoss?"

Sam glared at him and the tall, thin man grinned in return. The man who chided Sam was whip-thin and mounted on a well-muscled bay gelding. He glanced at Jake and lifted his eyebrows.

"I guess this is yer boy?" he said reproachfully. "I guess he has to do all the work around yer place, and walk when ya go to town," he added with a smirk.

Sam gave him a baleful look. "Just shaddup and les' git goin'," he growled.

The temperature continued to rise as the sun rose higher in the brassy-colored sky, but the little group of men continued at a ground-covering clip. The dust kicked up by the horses' hooves choked Jake and sweat ran down his back in rivulets. The skinny man who had mocked Sam looked over his shoulder at Jake. "Doan ya think we should stop and let the boy rest a bit?" he asked with concern.

"Nah, he kin run like that all day," Sam replied. They kept up the grueling pace and within an hour, the outline of Far West rose from the waving prairie.

As the men rode down the main street of the City of Zion, they were amazed at the throng of men, women and children pouring into the city for the celebration. Most of them were Saints from the surrounding areas swarming in to hear what the leaders of the church had to say about the country on this patriotic day. It was amazing how the Saints stood out from the rough Missourians. To Jake, the Saints had a fresh, clean, wholesome, just-scrubbed look about them, whereas the Missourians were dusty, dirty and their clothes were soiled and ragged. The Saints also had a fanatical glint in their eye, as if they were expecting to be quickened at any moment.

The streets were already lined with throngs of Saints and Missourians waiting for the pageant that the prophet had promised to begin. They didn't have long to wait; from down the street they heard the rhythmic sound of drums and soon rank upon rank of the infantry of the Mormon militia tramped by, raising puffs of dust from their marching feet.

The leader of the little group of Bogart's spies turned to Sam. "Gawd," he exclaimed in a whisper, "they is hundreds of 'em and they all got uniforms. I heered that them Saints run ole Jim Avery offen his homestead and took it over; I heered that a bunch of other settlers in Daviess and Caldwell counties been run off, too. If these Saints kin field an army like this, they will run us all out, sooner or later."

Sam looked at the man but said nothing. He was thinking about his own homestead and suddenly, Sam Devine was terrified.

Behind the orderly ranks of the infantry came the church leaders riding in two covered surreys, pulled by matching teams of beautiful black geldings. Joseph, his brother Hyrum and Sidney Rigdon were riding in the first carriage and the prophet was waving his hat good-naturedly to the crowd. As the prophet rode by in the shiny black carriage, the ranks of people lining the street cheered and waved and some even kneeled in the dust to show their allegiance to their beloved prophet.

Sam stared at the tall, handsome form of Smith and fury rose in his guts like acid. He even considered pulling the derringer he had in his pocket and shooting the charlatan on the spot. The only thing that stopped him was the realization that if he attempted to harm this venerated man, the crowd would tear him to bloody pieces. Immediately behind the carriages carrying the church leaders came Avard and his clandestine band of Danites, acting as bodyguards for the prophet and his apostles. Sampson Avard loved the limelight and he carried his polished saber unsheathed as he marched at the head of his band of fanatics.

Jake stared at the man and wondered who he was and why the crowd grew quiet as he marched regally by. He turned to Sam. "Who's that dandy?" he murmured.

Sam put his lips to Jake's ear and in a choking fog of tobacco and whiskey fumes, he replied, "We heered that he is the leader of the Sons of Dan, what guards the prophet and wipes out any criticism of Joe and his councilors. They say they will slit a man's throat fer whisperin' a word against Joe Smith." Jake wondered if the strutting little man knew where Jenny was.

Jake felt alien in the little group of Bogart militiamen. As they whispered among themselves and chuckled or groaned pretentiously at the goings-on, he searched the ranks of people lining the street as the parade passed by. He vainly scanned each intense face, but to his dismay he didn't see the familiar and delightful visage of Jenny Evans.

However, as he studiously surveyed the throngs lining the street, he was amazed when he realized he could discern the Saints from the Gentiles almost every time. It was a subtle thing, but the Saints almost invariably were dressed in somber blacks and grays, men, women and children. He noticed that the Gentiles looked rougher, dustier and unkempt compared to the Saints.

But the biggest distinction between the Missourians and Saints was in the way they interacted with others. Jake noticed that the zealots collected in little knots and didn't speak or even look at the Missourians, whereas the Missourians jammed their elbows into the ribs of those next to them and pointed and guffawed at whatever might be happening in the street. He also noticed that the Saints rarely smiled or laughed and wore a pious look on their faces. It was as if they were frightened to speak out or to enjoy themselves in the presence of the prophet, or perhaps in the presence of the Sons of Dan.

After the church dignitaries passed, a brigade or more of well-mounted cavalry rode by with pennants fluttering. The skinny man who had teased Sam (Jake learned his name was Lucas) asked where all these Saints had come from. One of his comrades remarked that the prophet had sent missionaries to Canada and England and thousands had been duped into joining the church. These converts, he said, were pouring into Far West daily and as their ranks swelled, their military strength grew proportionately. He then opined that if the Missourians wanted to keep their land and live in peace they had better do something about these fanatics before they outnumbered the old settlers.

After the cavalry had passed and the dust settled, the crowd swarmed into the street and followed the retreating horsemen. Sam looked around anxiously and asked a passerby where everyone was going.

"Why, to the Temple site to listen to Brother Sidney Rigdon deliver a patriotic speech," the brother answered indifferently. The little group followed the crowd and soon arrived at an excavation that appeared to be the beginnings of a foundation for a large building.

A pavilion had been erected near the foundation and a rough wooden platform stood under the shade of a canvas covering. Just as they arrived, the crowd began to clap and cheer and they saw a scrawny, hatchet-faced man mount the steps of the platform. He was immaculately dressed in a dark pulpit coat and his graying hair was combed back neatly. He wore a well-trimmed beard that followed the line of his jaw, a style that seemed popular with the Saints.

He mounted the speaker's stand with a confident air that bordered on arrogance. It was obvious that Brother Rigdon was a man who was comfortable before an audience. However, Sidney wasn't a man who considered his words carefully in view of his audience and he could never be accused of being overly diplomatic. He gripped the lectern like a man with a purpose and surveyed the spectators with glittering eyes.

He launched into a monologue exposing the glories of the young nation and the ecstasy of liberty and freedom. Jake breathed a sigh of relief; he had feared that Rigdon might insult the Missourians or give a truculent speech. Jake found that his relief was short lived. After speaking for about an hour with eloquence and moderation, Rigdon launched into a tirade against the Missourians, who he claimed had wrongfully abused the Saints.

He said that the Saints had turned their cheeks again and again to the Missouri mobs and had been smitten time and again for their forgiving and gentle nature; but, he said, that time was over. The Saints wouldn't turn their cheeks again and the mob that came to disturb them would find a war of extermination between them and the Saints. He fulminated that the Saints would spill every drop of their blood in defense of their homes and the City of Zion. If there was another war, he warned, the Saints would carry it to the homes of the mob and they would be as ruthless as any brigands. He paused to catch his breath and he glared out at his audience. Gathering his malice, he thundered his climax: "We this day then proclaim ourselves free, with a purpose and a determination that never can be broken—no never! No never!"

The Saints in the multitude broke into wild cheering that rolled like thunder over the Missouri prairie. A simultaneous cheer rose from ten thousand rapturous throats: "Hosanna, hosanna, to God and the Lamb!"

Jake was shocked and looked around wildly. He believed at that moment if these ecstatic people realized that he was a Missourian, he would be torn to bloody shreds on the spot. He looked at Sam and Lucas, and they nodded toward where the horses were tethered. Silently they crept through the wildly cheering crowd and mounted their horses and rode off to the northeast.

Jake followed despondently behind the others. He had desperately wanted to find Jenny among the throngs of Saints in Far West. As he trotted behind the horses, he felt a nagging fear that something terrible had happened to her.

The news of Rigdon's speech traveled like wildfire across the grasslands of upper Missouri. Joseph the prophet made a tactical error and allowed the text of the speech to be published in the Liberty, Missouri press and the bombastic speech raised a storm of protest among the Missourians. Jake expected upper Missouri to flame into a civil war, but despite the fervor raised by the speech, affairs in Daviess and Caldwell counties continued to simmer but didn't come to a boil—until a minor event in the little town of Gallatin brought things to a seething eruption.

PART SEVEN

Redemption

Chapter 21

❧❧❧

E lder John D. Lee lay in the grass on the town square of Gallatin, Missouri. The day was hot and muggy and Lee was enjoying the shade of a huge sycamore. It was August 6, 1838 and Lee, a devout Saint, was in Gallatin to cast his vote in the local elections. As Lee watched the nearby polling place, he noticed the town square was teeming with men who had come to vote in the elections. Interest was running high because it was well known among the Missourians that the Saints tended to vote in mass and cast their ballot for whatever candidate they were told to vote for by the apostles. The issue of slavery was beginning to rear its ugly head on the American frontier and men were aware of the consequences of electing a candidate who did not represent their views on the issue.

The Missourians also knew that the Saints were dedicated to establishing God's government on earth. With thousands of poor, bedraggled Saints pouring into the Far West area every day, the local residents were terrified that the Saints would displace them and control the local government. To most Missourians, this would be a catastrophe beyond belief. The pukes viewed the Saints as wild-eyed fanatics who sought to force their implausible ideas onto the law-abiding local residents. The Gentiles had heard the "mouthpiece of God" say that those who didn't embrace the Gospel were long-faced dupes who were too evil to accept the truth and should be driven out of northern Missouri so the Saints could establish the holy City of Zion.

Feelings were running high that hot August day in Gallatin. A little group of Saints broke away from the crowd and walked slowly to the polling place. As they approached the voting booth, a local bully named Dick Weldon stepped in front of the lead Saint. "We don't allow no Saints to vote in Daviess County, no more than we let niggers and wimmen vote!" he exclaimed.

The Saint gave him a puzzled glance and tried to step around him. Weldon smashed a huge fist into the man's temple and knocked him senseless in the powdery dust of the street.

Another Saint grabbed a piece of split wood that was conveniently stacked against a building. He swung the club in a wide arc and brought it down across Weldon's head with a resounding thud. The big man dropped without a sound and landed face down in the dust next to the Saint. Immediately, a group of Missourians leaped up to attack the Saints. As Lee jumped to his feet, he saw one of the Saints flash the Danite sign of distress. The man slapped his right thigh with his right hand and immediately lifted his hand to his ear with the thumb extended.

Upon seeing the holy sign, Lee felt a bolt of vigor course through his body and he thought he felt the power of God in his right arm. He sprang to the split kindling and seized a club, which he began to swing with great effect. When it was over, eight or ten Missourians lay in the dirt and the Saints cast their ballots. Though no one was killed in the Gallatin riot, it shattered the fragile peace in northwest Missouri.

The news spread like the plague and was exaggerated with each telling. By time the word reached Governor Boggs, it had grown to monumental proportions. The report he received claimed that several people had been killed and the Saints were planning on plundering the town of Gallatin.

The prophet also received a greatly exaggerated account of the ruckus. He heard from Danite spies that he maintained in the surrounding counties that several Saints had been killed or kidnapped and that the Gentiles were planning on sacking the town of Adam-ondi-Ahman. The Saints considered this town sacred, because the prophet explained it was where Adam dwelt after leaving the Garden of Eden. As was his custom, Joseph went off half-cocked. He immediately recruited twenty well-armed Danites and they rode off to save the town, supposedly under siege from the Gentile hordes.

When they arrived in Adam-ondi-Ahman they found the little town basking in tranquility. The little army met at the home of Lyman Wight to discuss what they should do next. Wight was a firebrand and was sure that a Gentile army was lurking out on the plains, waiting for an opportune moment to pillage the peaceful town. It was decided that the band should scout the surrounding area to determine if any Missouri militiamen were skulking about. In their wanderings, they came across the home of a local justice of the peace, Judge Adam Black.

In their state of alarm, the group stopped at Black's home and pounded on the door, demanding entrance. Black looked out and saw twenty to thirty armed men surrounding his cabin. Although he feared the worst, Black retained his composure and opened the door, allowing the prophet and five or six men to storm into the room. Black demanded to know what the men wanted and the prophet rejoined that he was ordering Black to sign an affidavit stating that he supported the laws of the state and the United States and that he would deal fairly with the Saints. Despite being confronted by a mob of armed men, Black refused to sign the paper under duress. Joseph in turmoil demanded that he sign and threatened to shoot him if he did not. When Black again refused, the mob finally rode away.

However, they returned a short time later with reinforcements. Among the reinforcements was the fanatical Sampson Avard. Avard screamed in Black's face that he must endorse the peace document or he would be cut down on the spot. At this point, Black agreed to draft a statement of his own. With that, he took a pen and wrote a general document stating that he was committed to follow the laws of the country and the state and that he would not take up arms against the Saints unless they molested him first.

Avard again threatened to slit the judge's throat, but Black showed his courage in the face of the armed men and told them they could kill him but he wouldn't capitulate. With that Avard stormed out of the house, taking his brigands with him, and rode off in a cloud of dust.

The Black incident was a serious blunder on the part of both Avard and the Prophet Joseph. Possibly they didn't realize just how fragile the peace was between the Saints and the Missourians. The intimidation of a respected judge was the spark that set the entire Missouri frontier aflame. Immediately Judge Austin A. King issued a warrant for the prophet's arrest. In cooperation, Governor Boggs issued a call for eight companies of Missouri militia to maintain the peace in upper Missouri. Northern Missouri was an armed camp. To ensure that the prophet was not lynched, Joseph's militia and the Sons of Dan put on a major show of force at the trial. Eventually, Joseph was released on a five hundred dollar bond and returned to Far West.

However, northern Missouri was now a tinderbox, and it would have taken great diplomacy on both sides to avoid open warfare. The Saints no longer wanted to compromise—their fanaticism wouldn't let them retreat again. God had told them, through their charismatic prophet, that he had commanded them to establish a holy city and society where there was no sin and debauchery and Jesus could return to a moral society. Now that Far West was growing like a mushroom in the fertile soil of Missouri they were loath to abandon it. In fact, they had announced time and again that they were willing to spill their blood and the blood of their adversaries to hasten the coming of the Millennium.

One way to stamp out evil and build the perfect social order was through the absolute consolidation of church and state. The Saints saw no inconsistencies in allowing ecclesiastical leaders to also serve as political leaders. In fact, the unification of church and state was one of the cornerstones of their Gospel. However, this didn't sit well with the environment of the frontier, where ministers were not expected to become involved in politics. The frontiersmen expected spiritual leaders to deal with spiritual matters and leave temporal matters to political leaders.

The Missourians knew very well how the Saints felt about their "city on the hill," for the Saints were not shy about speaking their mind about defending their church and prophet. Nor were the Saints timid about telling the Gentiles that they would eventually be driven out to make room for the godly. Another bone of contention was the issue of slavery, and as the Saints poured into Caldwell and the surrounding counties, the Missourians saw support for the "peculiar institution" slipping away.

After the incident in Gallatin, the intimidation of Black and the trial of Joseph Smith, the fragile peace in upper Missouri collapsed. The Saints had established a river port city at the confluence of the Grand and the Missouri. DeWitt, as it was called, became a key site in the Saints' plan to develop an economic empire in upper Missouri. The port was intended to be a transportation hub for goods, both coming and leaving the kingdom of God. However, once the delicate harmony was shattered, the Missourians surrounded DeWitt and effectively laid siege to the Saints' supply line.

Once DeWitt was encircled, local millers refused to grind the grain of the Saints at any price. Within days of Joseph's trial, the little sacred site of Adam-ondi-Ahman was raided by a mob and several cabins burned to the ground. Several Saints were captured and trundled out of town astride the barrel of a cannon. When Joseph led a group of men into Adam-ondi-Ahman to bring relief to the raided town, they found that some men had been unmercifully whipped and others had been tied to trees and beaten with quirts and branches. The Saints looked at the raw backs of their comrades and swore vengeance on the ungodly mobs.

The Missourians were willing to raid the homes and towns of the Saints because the church members were only lightly armed. This all changed after the Gentile raid on Adam-ondi-Ahman. The firebrand, Doctor Sampson Avard, heard through his Danite spies that a shipment of arms was being sent to a Missouri militia unit. Avard took a platoon of his Sons of Dan and intercepted the wagons carrying the arms, which he quickly captured as the spoils of war. As he rode into the city of Far West at the head of his militants followed by wagons stacked high with rifles, pistols, swords and bayonets, the entire city turned out to cheer the hero of the day.

Still, hard on the heels of the good news that Avard had captured a major supply of arms, powder and ball came the dismal report that the Saints were forced to evacuate their major source of supply, the river port of DeWitt. The next day, a long line of bedraggled refugees poured into Far West from the fallen bastion of DeWitt. For the most part, the Missourians had allowed the Saints of DeWitt to abandon their town in peace, but with the straggling outcasts came the all-too-common tales of beatings, looting, rape and threats.

The prophet watched the woebegone refugees from DeWitt pouring back into the sacred city and he felt impotent to aid his suffering people. He had promised the Saints that he would call down the wrath of God on the mobs of Missouri, but he had learned that God was fickle and rarely listened to the pleas of his self-appointed mouthpiece. He desperately wanted to tell the stragglers, wearily trudging back to the City of Zion, that he would call down the lightning bolts of a wrathful God onto the heathens who had abused his people. In his heart, though, Joseph knew that his policies alone were to blame for the plight of Israel. In his ambition to expand the holdings of the church, he had extended the grip of the Saints far beyond the original boundaries of Caldwell County that had originally been set aside for the church.

Besides, the Saints and their prophet had learned nothing from the crucible that was Independence. They had been driven from the original sacred city because they sought to control the politics of the area. They constantly lectured the locals that they, the Saints, were a chosen people and God had given this land to them to establish a New Jerusalem to reign in righteousness until the Savior came again. The Saints never missed an opportunity to point out to any Gentile that would listen that only the righteous could inhabit the holy site of the future gathering of Israel, and all those who refused to embrace the strange principles of the church would be burned as stubble. Finally, the Saints never quite mitigated the slavery question. After the destruction of the *Evening and Morning Star* building, Joseph desperately tried to revise his doctrine concerning blacks, but the Missourians saw it for what it was: a feeble attempt by the church to demonize blacks to minimize contention with the slave-owning Missourians.

Joseph watched as the pitiful remnants of his vanguard of settlers streamed back to Caldwell County. Because he couldn't call down the lightning bolts, he did the next best: he called his people to gather at the temple site where he rose to the podium to address them.

As Joseph mounted the raised podium, J. D. Lee felt as if he would swoon. To him, it seemed that the prophet's face literally glowed with divine light. To Lee, Joseph portrayed a regal bearing as befit the only true voice of God. Lee never noticed the prophet's disagreeable ferret-like face or haughty manner. When Joseph grasped the podium in preparation to launch into his sermon, an audible gasp involuntarily escaped Lee's lips in ecstatic anticipation.

"Brethren!" Joseph bellowed. "The time has come for every righteous man to seize his weapon and fight against those who deny the true God. General Doniphan has authorized God's army to act as a regiment of authorized militia. However, I have no regard for the laws of this state, whatever. All who are with me will meet tomorrow to march in defense of Adam-ondi-Ahman. Fear not, for we will trample down our enemies and make it one gore of blood from the Rocky Mountains to the Atlantic Ocean. I will be to this generation a second Mohammed and so shall it be with us, either Joseph Smith or the sword."

A great roar escaped the crowd. "Hosanna to the Prophet, Seer and Revelator," they screamed. "Oh, Joseph, lead us in this righteous endeavor!"

Lee leaped to his feet in unison with two thousand other would-be soldiers of Christ. He felt as if his bosom was on fire and he couldn't wait to do battle against those who would fight against Zion. Like his followers, Joseph was swept away in his own rhetoric. It was then that he was most vulnerable, and he made an appalling mistake. The next day, Joseph dispatched two hundred Danites to Adam-ondi-Ahman to reinforce Lyman Wight. When he found that the city was not in immediate danger of attack, he picked three of his most trusted and fanatic Danite captains to invade Daviess and Ray counties and drive out the hated Missourians.

Until that point, war in northern Missouri might still have been avoided, but once Joseph loosed his feared Sons of Dan on the Missourians outside of Caldwell County, he had crossed the Rubicon and his followers would reap the whirlwind. Joseph picked three of his loyal lieutenants to lead the invasion of the Gentile counties: Lyman Wight, Seymour Brunson and David Patten. He sent Brunson off to attack the town of Grindstone Fork while Wight sacked Millport. Joseph sent his most zealous leader, David W. Patten, or "Captain Fearnaught," as he was known, to pillage the hated hamlet of Gallatin whose residents had impetuously tried to deny the Saints their right to vote.

David W. Patten was a tall, thin man who habitually wore a long, white duster when he was campaigning. The prophet had given Patten the coat and he believed that the garment had the power to ward of the bullets of the Gentiles. On October 22, 1838, Captain Fearnaught donned his magic coat and led four hundred wild-eyed Sons of Dan into Daviess County, Missouri to punish the Missourians for driving the Saints out of DeWitt. He rode into Daviess like a whirlwind and destroyed and plundered every homestead he found on his way to that modern day Gommorah, Gallatin.

The very morning that Patten led his brigands into Daviess County, Sam Devine screamed for Jake to get his "ass outta bed and get down here." Jake was shocked. It was still pitch dark outside and Sam Devine wasn't known as an early riser. He usually returned home from one of the little towns that dotted Daviess County at midday, but never earlier than ten in the morning. This time, however, Jake had heard him come home shortly after midnight. The old man had been in a drunken rage and, through the thin floor of his loft room, he had heard Sam take his mother viciously.

He heard his mother's sobbing pleas when Sam had demanded that she perform some act that Bessie found disgusting. Sam had screamed in his high-pitched falsetto voice that she was his wife and she would damn well do what he asked. He heard her reply in a muffled, pleading voice, then he cringed as he heard the sickening sound of hard fists striking soft flesh. Jake lay quivering in his bed as he heard his father brutally violate his mother. He wanted to rise and go down the little rickety stairs on the outside of the cabin and throw open the door and rescue his mother, but he knew he was no match for Sam, especially when he was fortified with bootleg whiskey.

As he cowered in the dark little room, Jake wondered what could have possibly brought his father home at this time of morning, in a lustful mood. Sam always stayed in town, once there, and got drunk. After drinking himself into a stupor, he would find a whore and satisfy his considerable lust. Jake knew that on those rare occasions that Sam couldn't find a woman in town, his mother would suffer. Sam's sexual tastes ran to the bizarre and violent, especially if he couldn't find a woman who was experienced and depraved enough to satisfy his outlandish desires.

Jake fell fitfully back to sleep before he heard his father call him. At the sound of his father's shriek, Jake sat upright in bed and grabbed his worn trousers. He jerked on his boots and tried to button his shirt as he maneuvered down the rickety stairs by the pale light of a quarter moon. He shoved open the rough slab door and rushed into the gloom of the cabin. There was a lamp lit on the table and Sam was sitting in a rough chair, hunched over a plate of bacon and eggs. Jake noticed that his mother had set a place for him and the plate was filled with steaming eggs and bacon. An equally hot cup of coffee sat next to the plate. When Sam heard the door open, he looked up at his son with red-rimmed eyes. Jake could see by the old man's hollow eyes and lined face that he had been on a bender and was still half drunk. "Sit yer ass down and get some victuals. We is goin' to jine Bogart's militia at Crooked River. Them fuckin' Saints is armin' and threatnin' to invade Daviess County."

Jake's mouth fell open and he looked at Sam incredulously.

At that moment, Bessie turned away from the fireplace and walked to the table with a coffee pot to fill Sam's cup. Jake looked at her face and involuntarily sucked in a great lungful of air. Bessie's face was a swollen mess. Her nose was smashed and dried blood crusted her nostrils. One eye was swollen completely closed and was an angry blue green. She gave Jake a pleading look, begging him with her eyes not to make an issue of her injuries. Jake turned to Sam. "What the hell have you done?"

Sam moved surprisingly fast for a man of his age. Before Jake could continue or even move, the old man produced a huge bowie knife as if by magic and held the gleaming tip against Jake's throat.

"Before ya say anythin' disrespectful to yer father, ya better think about it," Sam said menacingly. "She got what she deserved. I come home las' night, wantin' a little lovin', and she plays high and mighty. A woman has obligations to her husband, and if they don' fulfill 'em, then a man's got a right to kick their ass."

The point of the knife drew a little drop of blood, which rose like an exclamation mark on the soft skin of Jake's neck. Jake was livid, but he knew he could do nothing to avenge the brutal ravishment of his mother. In his heart, he again affirmed his pledge that he would kill Sam Devine.

They ate in silence. Bessie stood in the corner as if tending something in the pot over the fireplace, but Jake knew she didn't want him to see the full extent of her injuries, both physically and emotionally. Sam kept his head close to his plate and noisily shoveled eggs into his mouth.

There was a scraping noise as the door opened a crack, and Rufe squeezed in and curled up at Jake's feet. The old hound had heard stirrings in the cabin and had come to see if Jake was going hunting early this morning. Sam looked at the old hound curled at Jake's feet. "Goin' ta hafta shoot that ol' dog one day," he casually remarked. "He ain't worth keeping 'round."

Jake knew that Sam was trying to hurt him emotionally, as he had hurt Bessie, but he held his tongue.

Sam rose, took his heavy barreled plains rifle from a peg on the wall and, glancing at Jake, he barked, "Come on, boy, we got some fanatics to kill."

With that he turned and walked out the door into the misty light of the waning moon. Jake rose to leave and Bessie turned and ran to him.

"Jake! Don't get killed and don't kill no one if you kin help it. Come back to me," she pleaded.

Jake looked into her one good eye and her swollen, bruised face and he softly said, "Don't worry, Ma, I will come back, but I'll come back alone, and you won't need to worry about being hit no more."

With that he turned and followed his father out of the door into the pale light of early dawn.

Chapter 22

It was a pleasant October day in Far West as J. D. Lee took his place at the rear of David W. Patten's brigade of Danite cavalry. They were forming up to join the invading army of the Saints, who were bent on driving the Gentiles out of Daviess County to make room for the burgeoning population of Saints pouring into upper Missouri.

Lee's heart was beating rapidly as he sat on his old sway-backed mule at the rear of the column. He could hear Captain Fearnaught berating his lieutenants to fight like angels to avenge the Saints who were driven out of the Missouri River port town of DeWitt and for those who had been run out of Adam-ondi-Ahman or whipped unmercifully. Lee was trembling with anticipation and he felt that he was on the verge of a great adventure and a chance to strike a blow for the Gospel. When Patten ordered the column to move out, John vowed in his heart to fight with true courage.

Since Lee was a new recruit and a neophyte Saint, he was assigned to the rear of the column. This late in the fall, the prairie grass had dried up and turned the rolling hills into a dun-colored landscape as far as the eye could see. The monotony of the scenery didn't bother Lee, but the clouds of dust that rose from the dry plains irritated his eyes and filled his lungs with dry, choking grime. He tied an old dirty handkerchief over his nose, but it didn't seem to help much. There was little breeze and the choking clouds of dust hung next to the ground and grew thicker as the columns of horsemen passed. Lee couldn't even see the occasional homesteads that they passed or the cottonwoods, which shone a brilliant yellow with fall foliage.

Although John D. Lee couldn't see anything but the inside of the huge, yellow cloud that the raiders raised in passing, the Gentile spies were aware of the Danite raiders the moment they left Far West. The great cloud of dust was visible for miles and the Missourians had suspected that the Saints would send out marauders to avenge the raids of the outlying towns of the church. When the Missourians withdrew from Adam-ondi-Ahman, they took with them several captive Saints. Joseph had admonished the raiders to rescue the captured Saints.

Patten didn't bother with any of the homesteads he passed on the way to Gallatin. His first priority was to destroy the town. Besides, the spies for the church had long believed that Gallatin was a hotbed of anti-Saint fervor, so he headed straight for the despicable burg. They soon rode down the dusty main street, but they found that most of the businesses and homes were shuttered and appeared abandoned. There were no horses tied to the hitching posts next to the dusty street. No faces peered out of the doors and windows of the hardware store, general store or hotel. Patten halted his troop in front of the saloon and gambling hall.

The place was known as the Jay Hawk Saloon and Social Club. The church apostles had heard from their sources and spies that the joint had an unsavory reputation and that loose women could be had there for a price. In fact, the Jay Hawk was Sam's favorite watering hole and where he usually shacked up on his numerous forays away from the homestead. Luckily for Sam, he was at that moment riding to meet Captain Bogart at Crooked River to reinforce his men and meet the anticipated invasion by the Saints. Patten reined in his horse and addressed the apparently deserted den of iniquity.

"Hail the Jay Hawk," he shouted. "If there is anyone in there, you better come out or we will burn the place down around your worthless heads!" Patten stared at the bat-wing doors of the weathered building. Nothing stirred except a light breeze, which moved the double-hinged doors and caused them to squeak. Every man in the front of Patten's column brought their muskets to bear on the dark entrance to the saloon.

"If anybody is in there, you better come out or you will be fried!" exclaimed Patten. With that, he reached behind the saddle and retrieved a whiskey bottle filled with kerosene from his saddlebags. He wrapped a rag around the bottle and, flicking a match on his thumbnail, he lit the makeshift wick.

Just as Patten pulled his arm back to launch the improvised firebomb into the gambling house, the swinging doors opened and a little, bald, fat man emerged. Josh Walker was not a brave man and he loathed facing the dreaded Danites, but he didn't relish the idea of losing his beloved saloon; neither did he have a burning desire to die in its demise. He stumbled out of the swinging doors and blinked like a toad in the bright sun. His heart fell like a rock when he saw the stony-faced men facing him with muskets aimed at his heaving chest.

"Please don't burn my place. It's all I got and it's my only means of income," he blubbered.

Patten gave him a scornful look. "Step out of the way," he said menacingly. "We are going to rid the world of a den of iniquity."

Walker ran to Patten's horse and grabbed the man's leg. Looking up at the intimidating form, his thick lips quivering, he said, "Please, it took every dime I've got to stock the bar with whiskey, please don't burn it," he whimpered.

Patten viciously kicked the little man in the face, splitting his fat lips and causing a spurt of blood to stain his white shirt and vest.

Patten had seemingly forgotten about the burning rag and bottle he held in his right hand. The flame singed the hair on his hand, and he looked down dumbly at the missile. With that he cocked his arm again and flung the bottle through the doorway. There was a tinkle of breaking glass and almost immediately a dull red glow lit up the gloomy interior of the tavern. Walker struggled to his feet and turned and looked forlornly at the door of his establishment. He wiped his bloody mouth on the sleeve of his shirt and, glancing at the horsemen, he stumbled across the street and disappeared down an alley.

The Danites laughed and cheered as the barkeeper lurched away. Patten was amazed at how quickly the bar burst into flame. The dry pine was full of pitch and it burst into flame like an exploding pine knot. He rose in the saddle and turned to his subordinates: "Take your men and clean out the general store and any houses that have food or guns," he commanded. "Get some wagons and teams from the livery and load them up with all the supplies you can find, and be quick about it before the whole town goes up in flames."

The group broke up into platoons and scurried off to consecrate supplies for the Lord's army.

Bessie Devine came out of the cabin about two in the afternoon and walked to the old pole shelter that served as a barn and shed for the animals. She had an instinctive love for creatures, which she had passed on to her son. She intended to check on the chickens and stock to make sure they had water and feed and that none of them were sick or needed attention. While she was at it, she would gather a few eggs and milk the old red cow. She knew that Jake and Sam wouldn't be back for several days, but she was used to being alone and enjoyed the solitude. The old gray mule that Jake used to work the fields stood patiently in the pole corral and she knew that Sam had ridden the black and made Jake run behind him.

Her heart ached for her son. She loved him more than life and fear gripped her heart in an icy grasp. What if he were killed or injured and didn't come back? She knew that she couldn't face life without Jake, though she didn't give a thought about Sam's well being. She took a bucket and filled it at the well, and then she walked back to the pole corral where the mule was standing. When the animal saw her turn in his direction, his long ears swiveled toward her like antenna and he burst forth with a joyous bray. Bessie patted his velvety nose and the mule nuzzled her apron to see if she might have a carrot there. In her seclusion, Bessie had come to love the critters of the farm, especially this old gray mule and Rufe. They gave her welcome company and kept her from feeling the isolation that she endured.

As she went about her chores, Rufe trotted happily by her side, casually glancing into her face to read her mood. The dog especially brought comfort to Bessie when she was alone, but usually Rufe was out hunting with Jake. It seemed to Bessie that the old hound could read her mind, and when she felt lonely and insignificant after her husband had beaten her or disparaged her, Rufe would lay his head on her knee and look adoringly into her eyes, and his look made her feel loved and worthwhile again.

As Rufe trotted by her side, she suddenly felt a surge of affection and bonding with the hound. She noticed how Rufe's hipbones jutted from his body and she knew his race was almost run. She felt a wave of sorrow wash over her and she wondered what she would do when the dog was gone. She knew that his passing would cause her intense grief and she would miss the dog far more than she would miss Sam if he didn't return from saving Missouri from the Saints.

As she was carrying the eggs and milk to the cabin, she noticed a pall of smoke hanging in the sky like a shroud to the southeast, and she wondered if the Saints were sacking Gallatin. Rumors had been flying among the Missourians that the Saints were planning an invasion into Daviess and Ray counties. In fact, the residents of Richmond in Ray County had already petitioned the governor for troops to defend their city from the impending invasion by the fanatic and bloodthirsty Saints.

The pall of ugly black smoke hanging in the afternoon sky gave Bessie an uneasy feeling, like impending doom. She told herself that it was just a prairie fire caused by lightning or some careless hunter's campfire, but she couldn't shake the tightness in her guts. She kicked open the door and carried the eggs and milk inside, placing them on the rough board table. Rufe followed her in and seemed loath to leave her side. Indeed, he stayed so close to her that she almost tripped over him. She rubbed his long ears. "What is it, Rufe, are you feelin' edgy too?" she asked, looking into the soft brown eyes.

The old dog looked back at her intently and cocked his head as if trying to understand what his mistress was saying. Again, an almost overwhelming feeling of bonding with the animal swept over her.

She wondered if it was a sacrilege to feel this way about a mere animal. After all, didn't the Bible say that man was created in the image of God and that animals were created for man's use? Thus, didn't that mean that the creatures of the field were no more than mere chattel for human consumption?

As Bessie pondered this dilemma, she became aware of a faint drumming sound in the distance. She cleared her mind and cocked her head in an effort to hear the peculiar noise better. Rufe suddenly lifted his graying muzzle and gave a ringing bay and lunged through the still-open door.

Bessie could hear the hound in the front yard baying incessantly; she could picture him slightly hopping on stiff front legs as he pointed his muzzle at the sky and sent the bell-like notes echoing across the rolling hills. She was suddenly aware of what the drumming sound was; it was the thudding of dozens of horse's hooves. She stepped to the fireplace and took her father's old double-barreled, flintlock fowling piece down from the wall. She kept the old gun loaded with nine double oo buckshot pellets in each barrel in case a predator, either man or beast, might threaten her or the chickens.

She cocked the old gun and stepped out the partially open door. There, not twenty feet from the house, sat twenty, well-armed men gazing at the cabin. As she stepped out, the muzzles of ten muskets pointed at her.

"Who are ya and what do ya want?" Bessie yelled. The mounted men were a detachment of Patten's regiment, who had been sent on a foraging mission after sacking Gallatin. Out of the corner of her eye Bessie could see a heavy farm wagon loaded high with foodstuffs, bedding and household items. "Looks to me like ya are a bunch of robbers and looters," she commented. The leader of the group, Elder Robert Watson, grinned and threw a leg over his horse to drop gracefully to the ground.

Watson was a small man, and he exhibited a bad case of little man's syndrome. He strutted across the yard toward Bessie like a bantam rooster. She menacingly raised the barrels of the old flintlock. "I would advise ya to not come no closer. I ain't lettin' ya take our stock or belongin's," she growled. Watson hesitated and then started to walk toward Bessie again. At that moment, Rufe growled menacingly in his throat and the hair on his back rose in warning.

Watson jerked a horse pistol out of its holster and pulled the trigger. Bessie saw a huge puff of grayish-black smoke burst from the muzzle of the pistol and a spray of blood erupted from Rufe's side. The old hound yelped once as the heavy ball sent him flying to the ground where he landed with a thud and lay still, frothy blood bubbling from his mouth and nostrils.

Almost simultaneously Bessie pointed her pappy's old flintlock at Watson and pulled both triggers. A flash of fire erupted from the pan of each barrel and a cloud of black smoke erupted from the barrels. The twin loads of double oo buckshot struck Watson full in the chest and he crumpled into the dust. His shirt was smoking from the load of still-burning black powder that followed the lethal load of buckshot. A huge crimson fountain of blood erupted from his back and chest. The ten mounted men facing Bessie opened fire and five fifty-caliber balls smashed into her skinny sunken chest. The force of the heavy lead balls forced her through the partially open door and she smashed into the rough planks of the floor and slid under the table.

A huge rivulet of blood spread rapidly across the splintery pine boards and began to immediately soak into the thirsty wood. Bessie lay on the floor with her eyes wide open, staring sightless up at the bottom of the table where two days ago she had fed her beloved son and sent him off to war to protect their little homestead from the bloodthirsty Danites. Ironically, it was she that tried in vain to protect the little dirt farm, and she died trying to save an old hound, as he died protecting his mistress.

The sun, though lower in the southern sky this time of the year, was still hot on Jake's shoulders. He had to trot to keep up with the old man astride the black mule. His possibles sack and the long-barreled Kentucky rifle were heavy and awkward, and despite his lean, conditioned body, he was breathing heavily. Sam was anxious to meet up with Bogart's men, who were camped on the Crooked River, waiting to see which way the Saints might attack. They had with them three Danites whom they had captured during their attack on Adam-ondi-Ahman.

Sam wanted to get to Crooked River before Bogart decided to attack some outlying town or homestead occupied by the Saints. Not only did Sam want to get in on the plunder that was sure to be had when the Missourians drove the Saints out of Ray and Daviess counties, but he also longed to shoot one of the fanatics. Sam was basically a coward and he acted as most cowards do. He would slink away from a face-to-face confrontation, unless his adversary was weak or helpless, but he had no qualms about shooting an unarmed adversary or terrifying some poor helpless wretch.

The sun was getting low in the west when they finally saw the line of cottonwoods snaking across the grasslands that marked the course of the Crooked River. From their vantage point on a low hill, it was obvious how the stream got its name, as the line of brush along the stream zigzagged crazily across the rolling country. To Jake, the sight of the wandering stream was a godsend, for every bone in his body ached and his breath was coming in gasps. His homespun shirt was dark with sweat and his face was streaked where the sweat made little lines through the dust on his face. Sam rarely stopped to allow Jake to rest or get a drink from the flax water bag that he carried over the pommel of the saddle. Sam was far more caring of the black mule than of Jake, because he depended on the mule to get him to town for drinking and carousing.

Sam hailed the bivouac and a picket stepped out of the brush and asked them to advance. After Sam explained their mission, the sentry waved them through. They walked toward an inviting campfire, where several men were sitting, drinking coffee and talking.

"I'm Sam Devine, and this here whelp is my kid, Jake," Sam announced tersely. A short, heavyset, balding man rose and shook Sam's hand.

"I am Captain Bogart," he said easily. Jake looked at Bogart and thought that he reminded him of one of the black-and-white hogs they kept on the homestead. His face was framed by large, sagging jowls and beads of sweat glistened on his nearly bald pate.

Jake knew that Bogart was a minister when he was not acting as a leader of the Missouri militia. Bogart viewed the Saints as heathens and heretics and had combed the hills of northern Missouri looking for men willing to drive the Saints out of Missouri. He viewed his mission to either kill or drive the Saints out of Daviess County as a divine calling.

"You two are assigned to Lieutenant Wallace's company. He will show you where to set up. We expect the Danites to attack around dawn. Our scouts report that David Patten intends to attack us at first light and try to destroy our company and free the Danite prisoners. I suspect that we'll have a warm welcome for them wild-eyed fanatics. You two will stand guard duty; Wallace will give you specific orders, but I want you to keep a sharp lookout. I don't want to get caught with my pants down by them fire-eatin' Danites."

With that, Bogart dismissed them with a flick of his hand and indicated the direction they would find Lieutenant Wallace.

Sam mumbled under his breath about being told what to do and standing guard duty at such an ungodly hour. "Bastard didn't even offer us any coffee," he complained. After asking a picket where they would find the lieutenant, they located him sitting with his back against a big cottonwood tree.

"Name's Sam Devine and this is my whelp, Jake," Sam stated curtly.

The sun had dipped onto the horizon, and darkness would quickly envelope the countryside. Wallace was a big man and his biceps bulged under his linen hunting shirt. His face was florid, like someone who enjoyed whiskey a little too much. His eyes were a watery blue and a deep crease ran down the center of his forehead as if he had spent long hours squinting into the sun.

"Good to have you aboard," he declared goodnaturedly. "We really don't know how many men Patten has or how well equipped he is. We've seen some of his scouts so we know he knows we're here. Patten is a religious fanatic who believes that he's fighting for truth and the angels will protect him and his men from our musketballs. We are going to show him that God don't care a fig for him or them Saints. You two get yourselves a cup of coffee and any supplies that you need from my quartermaster, and station yourselves in the brush along the river. Sergeant Watters will show you where. There'll be no talking or any lights of any kind. So see to it that ya don't light yer pipe or show any lights a'tall. When dawn comes, we should be able to see the Danites when they come over that rise yonder." With that, Wallace turned back to the paper he was studying, indicating they were dismissed.

Twenty minutes later, Jake was crouched in the brush clutching his Kentucky rifle and straining his ears for any alien sound. His heart beat like a trip hammer in his chest and he dreaded the coming dawn. He decided he didn't so much fear dying but he was terrified that he would show fear in front of Sam. He knew the old man would watch him like a hawk when the fighting started and any sign of cowardice on his part would be met with disdain from Sam. He pondered what he would do if he had to kill a man and decided he didn't hate these Saints; in fact he loved one of them with all his soul. He cursed himself for allowing Sam to browbeat him into coming on this fool's errand.

The men in Bogart's camp had strutted around like tom turkeys bragging about how they were going to fill them Danites' hides so full of holes that they wouldn't hold corn shucks. Most of them hated the Saints because they viewed them as abolitionists and "nigger lovers" and feared they would steal their land, but Jake realized that most of the animosity these men felt for the Saints resulted from the Saints' belief that they were a chosen people and far superior to the ungodly Missourians. To the frontiersmen, anyone who claimed to talk to God and know his word firsthand was a dangerous fanatic and should be stamped out for the good of the citizens.

Jake wished he could crawl away and wander home to his mother and Rufe and his bed in the loft of the rickety cabin. He knew that his father would ridicule him and call him a "momma's boy" if he knew what he was thinking, but he really didn't care what Sam Devine thought. What stopped Jake from sneaking away into the night like a cur was what the other men would think of him. Jake considered himself a man and men hated a coward.

The night was dark, with no lanterns or campfires illuminating the camp. Although it was late in October, the weather had remained warm, and Jake was surprised to hear crickets singing in the brush along the river. He had always loved the rhythmic, chirping sound of crickets. When he was small, he remembered being sent to his bed because his constant questions and attempts to get attention from his father had resulted in a cursing or a beating. As he lay in his bed in the loft, sobbing, the sound of the crickets seemed to salve his tormented soul.

His heart and mind were in turmoil now, and the soothing song of the crickets seemed to touch his psyche. He knew he was a captive of the mores of others. The entire war in northwestern Missouri resulted from a lack of tolerance on both sides for others' beliefs. He realized that the Saints' sense of conformity ran against the individualism of the frontier, but was it worth killing each other over? Jake didn't think so, but he was a Missourian and he sought the acceptance of his kind. It was this need for acceptance that held him captive and kept him from crawling away in the night, just as if he were chained by the ankle to a post.

As he lay pressed close to the ground, he was startled to feel a distant vibration in his chest as if the Earth itself was shuddering in revulsion at what was coming. He glanced quickly in Sam's direction to see if he had sensed the bizarre pulsation. In the faint light of the quarter moon, Jake could just make out his father's face. His mouth was hanging open and to Jake he looked like a cadaver. But Jake had seen Sam fall into a coma-like slumber before, and when he strained his ears, he could hear the soft gurgling sounds of Sam snoring. He wondered if he should wake him up, but decided if he got flogged for sleeping on sentry duty, so be it.

Jake turned his eyes to the dark, velvet-like sky. The light from the moon was faint and didn't dim the light of millions of twinkling stars. Jake felt a strange sense of intuition touch his soul as if some power were touching his mind. He remembered that Ozzy had told him if he opened his mind, the Earth Mother would enlighten him. He lay face down on the damp earth and spread his arms and legs. Again he felt the Earth tremble as if it shuddered. Something seemed to seize his mind and he saw dancing stars before his eyes.

His mind seemed to drift, as if he was dreaming, but he seemed to be aware of his surroundings. In this surreal state he perceived images as if through a thick fog. Then, he saw Jenny and she was walking away from him toward what had to be a rising sun. She turned and looked at him with love in her eyes, but her eyes were shining as if with tears. She disappeared into the rising fog. He saw nothing then but the gray, drifting mist, until suddenly, a bright light shone through the vapor and seemed to burn it off as he had seen it do a hundred times in the Missouri winter.

He realized that the light was from the sun, which seemed to be setting behind the rolling hills of the prairie. Between Jake and the setting sun was a broad, shining river, which seemed to call to him. In the bright light of the sun a figure appeared, and it seemed to be looking at him intently. The shadowy image gradually became clear, and he saw that it was Blossom. She was smiling at him, and slowly she raised her right arm and unmistakably gestured at him to come to her. Jake awoke with a start. His face was buried in the fragrant earth and he felt as if he were suffocating. He raised his head and looked around. The stars still glittered in the dark sky, but from the position of Orion, he knew that it was about four in the morning.

Despite the cool night breeze that rattled the leafless limbs of the cottonwoods, he was drenched in sweat. He remembered vividly the vision or dream that he had experienced and he wondered what it could mean. The vision of Jenny walking into the rising sun somehow touched Jake's heart and made him excruciatingly sad. Then he thought of Blossom, gesturing to him, and the thought of her alleviated his sorrow. He didn't sleep again that night, if indeed he had slept at all. He lay on the damp earth and pondered his dream. Gradually, the eastern sky began to lighten, touched by the welcoming glow of the still-invisible sun. Jake stared in the murky light of predawn and he thought he saw a glimmer of movement on the ridge above the river. He squinted at the spot where he had seen the shadow and suddenly he was sure it was the outline of a man in a pale white coat, standing on the ridge. He crawled over to where Sam lay, still snoring softly, and he pinched the old man's nostrils together to wake him quietly. Sam awoke with a snort and, looking into his son's eyes, he opened his mouth to curse Jake for bothering him. Jake put his finger to his lips to warn Sam, and pointed to the figure on the hill.

Sam immediately brought his old plains rifle to his shoulder and settled the stock into the hollow of his shoulder. Squinting through the buckhorn sight, he gently set the rear trigger and squeezed the front one, until the heavy rifle barked and jumped against his shoulder. Jake saw the figure in the pale light on the ridge jerk suddenly backward and, throwing one arm skyward, it fell violently. The heavy fifty-caliber ball struck David Patten, Captain Fearnaught, in the hip. It continued on through his bladder and exited his lower abdomen, taking a piece of his pelvis with it.

Though in shock and excruciating pain, Patten struggled to his feet, and, raising his sword, he ordered his men forward toward the Missourians' line. As he struggled to walk, gouts of blood gushed from the dreadful wound in his hip and side. The Danites sprang from their cover along the ridge and ran down the slope toward the hated Missourians screaming "Forward, army of Israel!"

Patten carried on in a stumbling run for about twenty yards, and then he fell into the grass in a pool of blood. His men, though they were loyal to Captain Fearnaught, pressed on, driven by the exhilaration of the moment. Bogart's men managed to get off a ragged volley at the charging Danites. Several men hunched up in mid-stride and fell to the earth, bodies ravaged by the impact of a massive musket ball. However, the charging line of Saints didn't waver, for the men believed that they were fighting God's battle and the Lord's angels would protect them and strengthen their arms in righteousness.

Bogart's men hesitated for a second, then the line broke and they fled in terror from the oncoming army of the Lord. As the Missourians broke, the Saints gave a great cheer and pursued the ungodly Gentiles with renewed fervor.

Jake stared at the oncoming line of screaming yelling fanatics and raised the Kentucky rifle to his shoulder. He centered the bead of the front sight in the V of the buckhorn and then placed the bead on the chest of a Saint charging down the hill. The man was waving a huge sword over his head and screaming, "Follow me, sons of Israel." Out of the corner of his eye, Jake saw Sam desperately trying to ram a ball home in the heavy barrel of his Plains rifle. Sam could see that he wouldn't get the ball seated and a cap on the nipple before the fanatic waving the cutlass reached him. He turned to where Jake was standing and screeched, "Shoot him, fer God's sake, kill the bastard!"

Jake too saw what was going to happen and he thought of the myriad times his father had abused him, Rufe and his mother. He returned his eye to the picture of the attacking terrorist over the barrel of his gun and lowered the rifle and turned and trotted toward the river and the fading line of Missourians.

The Danite closed in on Sam with amazing speed. He raised the huge sword over his head and aimed for the crown of Sam's head. Sam brought the Plains rifle up before his face with both hands to ward off the mighty blow. The sword hit the rifle a glancing blow and slid the length of the barrel. In doing so, it sliced off four of Sam's fingers on his right hand. The old man dropped the rifle and looked at his bloody hand, screaming in agony. The Danite skidded to a stop and raised the sword again. Sam instinctively raised his arm to fend off the blow and the descending blade cut through the bone of his arm, neatly severing it from his body. Sam screamed again and fell into the waving grass, which was already greased with his blood.

Jake, hearing Sam's agonizing screams, looked over his shoulder and saw his father lying on the ground, desperately trying to fend off the blows of the hysterical Danite. Somehow, he felt more disgust than compassion for Sam, and after a furtive glance at the horrible scene, he turned and broke into a ground-covering gallop.

Sam's head was swimming from lack of blood. His life's blood was pouring out onto the parched grassland in pulsing streams. He looked up into his assailant's eyes and in his mist-shrouded brain he thought the eyes had the glint of insanity in them.

The Danite looked down at Sam with unbridled hatred. "Now die, you godless puke," he screamed, spittle spraying from his grimacing lips. Again, he raised the huge, blood-smeared blade above his head and with a grunt of effort he brought it down on Sam's defenseless head. The blade smashed into Sam's face, cutting through his left eye and neatly slicing off his entire nose. Sam gave another piercing scream of pain and terror and the force of his breath sprayed his blood onto his assailant's face and shirt. The religious fanatic gave Sam's piteous form a frustrated look and brought the dripping sword across his body in preparation for a forehand blow. Sam was now beyond any attempt to ward off the blows and he lay in the grass, gore bubbling from his smashed face and arms. The final blow effectively split the old man's skull from the crown to the base of his ears.

The Danite grunted as he pried the blade from the dead man's skull. Wiping it in the grass, he looked down the slope for more victims. Giving the mangled body of Sam a disdainful look, he raised the sword and began running down the slope toward the river.

Bogart's men didn't stop until they ran into a detachment of General Samuel Lucas's men, who had been dispatched to Daviess and Caldwell counties to restore order and subdue the rampaging Saints.

The Battle of Crooked River was a rather mild affair, excluding the dreadful deaths of Sam Devine and David Patten. The captive Saints were rescued and the casualties on both sides were relatively light. Approximately three Danites were killed and two Missourians besides Sam died of gunshot wounds. However, by the time Governor Boggs received word of the battle, the results had been exaggerated to the point that he called out the entire Missouri militia and issued the infamous extermination order, which called for the Saints to be driven from the state of Missouri or exterminated, because "Their outrages are beyond all description." The dreaded General Samuel Lucas was in overall charge of the militia, but General Alexander Doniphan, friend, lawyer and confidant to the Saints, was also in command of one contingent.

Darkness was falling like a velvet veil as Patten's men entered Far West. Captain Fearnaught was lying in a commandeered wagon on a pile of confiscated blankets. Doctor Sampson Avard examined the groaning man and realized that there was nothing he could do for him. The ball had passed through his hip, destroying his bladder and perforating his colon. The brave Patten was in excruciating agony, but he refused to take any whiskey or laudanum to dull the pain. He knew he was dying and didn't want to defile his last moments on earth by taking the poison of alcohol or mind-numbing drugs into his body. He soon screamed his life away on the blood-soaked blankets in the wagon bed.

Agnes stood in the crowd as Patten and the other raiders returned to Far West with wagons piled high with contraband. Her heart leaped with joy to see the heaps of Gentile goods pouring into Far West to build up the kingdom. She lamented the death of the dauntless Patten but rejoiced at the passing of many godless Missourians, and she gloated to think of the dozens of homes and farms owned by the Missourians that had been looted and burned.

She had heard that when the wagons full of loot began rolling back into Far West, the apostles Orson Hyde and Thomas B. Marsh had stolen away into the night with their families. She knew that they would probably bear witness against the Saints and their prophet in the Gentile courts and she silently offered a prayer that God would smite them with some horrible plague. She had heard that when Brother Sidney Rigdon learned of the defections, he had become apoplectic with rage and had said, "The last man has run away from Far West that is going to. The next one who tries it will be brought back and killed."

Agnes agreed wholeheartedly with Brother Sidney. She often thought of John and Jenny, but without remorse. Agnes knew in her heart that the fate of her husband and daughter had resulted from their own failure to obey the word of God. In her mind, "The wages of sin is death." If John and Jenny had followed the dictates of the prophet, they would still be alive today. It was as simple as that. To Agnes life was simple: just read the prophet's revelations and follow them to the letter. Adore the prophet as God's agent on earth and obey his every word. Hate the sinners and unbelievers and do everything in your power to destroy them and work diligently to establish God's kingdom on Earth.

The prophet's scouts and spies brought him disconcerting news. After issuing his infamous extermination order, Governor Boggs had activated the entire Missouri militia and men were streaming to Richmond to join the ranks. Already, over two thousand men under the command of the murderous Lucas were marching to lay siege to the Holy City of Far West. However, many of the Saints weren't alarmed at the idea of all-out war with the Gentiles or the threatened siege of Far West. Many Saints expected Joseph to call down angels to fight the Saints' battles. One Saint, a Brother Winchester, wrote his father:

Now, Father, come to Zion and fight for the religion of Jesus. Many a hoary head is engaged here, the prophet goes out to the battle as in the days of old. He has the sword that Nephi took from Laban. Is not this marvelous?

The prophet kept up a brave front, but the Saints' situation was desperate. There weren't more than eight hundred able-bodied Saints to defend the sacred city and the Missouri militia was growing daily, its ranks swelled by hundreds of recruits pouring in to join and drive the hated Saints out of Missouri. The Saints were poorly armed; many didn't even have muskets and made do with single shot pistols or homemade swords and lances. Even the shipment of arms that they had commandeered from the Missouri militia was inadequate to sufficiently arm the Saints. Joseph realized that he couldn't defend Far West against the advancing horde, but he continually lectured the defenders, telling them that if they kept the faith, the angels of God would fight their battles.

Most of the Saints from the surrounding countryside and outlying villages picked up stakes and fled to the hypothetical safety of the shining city, but one man, Jacob Haun, refused to abandon his newly built gristmill on Shoal Creek, called, appropriately enough, Haun's Mill. The prophet had sent outriders to Haun urging him to abandon the isolated town and flee to Zion, but the stubborn German refused and informed the messenger that he and his people would defend what was theirs.

The next day, a contingent of militia, or just looters, rode down on the little town whooping and screaming like banshees. The residents of the mill fled into the blacksmith's shop, where the militia slaughtered them.

On October 30, 1838, the Missouri militia drove in the pickets, defending Far West and effectively surrounding the Saints in the Holy City. A survivor of the massacre at Haun's Mill managed to sneak through the enemy lines and poured out the lurid story of the sacking of that unfortunate village. Joseph's heart froze upon hearing the dreadful news and he must have realized that the bloodletting at Haun's Mill would probably be a prelude to a much greater slaughter in Far West unless he sued for terms.

Joseph walked along the trenches, reassuring the huddled defenders that God would indeed fight their battles, but in his heart, he knew that if the militia attacked, a slaughter would ensue. He came upon Reed Peck huddled behind a makeshift barrier made from an overturned wagon.

"Brother Peck!" he exclaimed. "Don't let anyone see you, but when it gets dusk, take a white flag and cross the lines. Find General Doniphan and beg like a dog for peace."

Peck found that General Lucas was in command of the Missourians and he wasn't in a mood to be conciliatory. Lucas sent a delegation to parley with the prophet under a flag of truce. The delegation met with the prophet and church leaders to try to hammer out a truce. However, Lucas's terms were so draconian that Joseph was loath to accept them. The Saints were to give up their leaders for trial and punishment for treason, armed insurrection and destruction of property. They were also to surrender all of their arms and property, pay an indemnity to satisfy the claims of the Missourians who suffered property loss during the uprising and leave the State of Missouri within six months under the tender protection of the Missouri militia.

When the prophet hesitated to accept the harsh terms, Lucas's subordinates suggested that the prophet, his Brother Hyrum and Brother Sidney surrender to the militia as an act of good faith. If by morning the Saints still wanted to fight, Lucas would release the prophet and the others. Joseph heard the men hunched in the breastworks murmur when they heard the offered terms and he refused. How could he do anything else? The Saints fully expected to destroy the three thousand militiamen facing them, although they were only eight hundred strong.

All through the night of October 30, 1838, the little band of Saints huddled behind their breastworks watching the autumn sky for a sign from God or evidence of the arrival of angels who would smite the ungodly Missourians. The night was clear but chilly, and John D. Lee pulled his threadbare coat closer around his skinny shoulders in a vain attempt to keep out the biting cold of the night air. He clutched a Kentucky rifle in his bony fingers and peered over the parapets at the flickering fires of the Missourians. He almost envied them sitting around warm campfires with full bellies, drinking coffee. But his mind was convinced he was fighting for the Prophet of God and his bosom burned with fire of truth and right, which drove out the sin of envy. In fact, as he thought about his situation, Lee decided he was most fortunate among men.

He had stood face to face with the man who had communed with God, and that man had shared with him the true word of God. Through that knowledge he would be saved in the celestial kingdom and, in God's own due time, he knew he would create a world like this one and rule over it as Jehovah ruled over this one. He looked out at the flickering fires of the Missourians and he relished the coming of dawn. In his heart he was sure that the coming day would produce a miracle and the evil hosts who were bent on fighting against God's people would be destroyed. He was sure many godless unbelievers would die by his hand.

Lee was to be bitterly disappointed. The morning of October 31, 1838 dawned fair, crisp and clear. It was a beautiful dawn. A few cirrus clouds lay like ribbons in the eastern sky. As the sun rose, as if from the rolling prairie, its light turned the cloud streamers a brilliant pink, which gradually turned into radiant crimson. Lee lifted his head and, through bleary eyes, he vainly searched the fiery sky for some sign of the miracle that he was sure was coming. However, rather than the beating of angel's wings, he heard the distant roll of drums.

He stared to the east toward the Missourians' lines, and through the pale light of dawn he made out row upon row of marching figures all advancing in his direction. With his heart in his throat, he checked his cap box and bullet bag to make sure they were open and accessible. For the tenth time since midnight, he checked the cap and charge in the horse pistol that lay before him on the barricade. He pulled the big bowie knife from the buckskin scabbard at his side and, checking the edge with his thumb, he grimaced as the keen blade nicked his thumb.

He pulled the hammer back on the long rifle and sighted along the octagonal barrel at the dim figures marching over the dry buffalo grass. Just as he was straining his ears to hear the order to fire, a figure mounted the barricades with a white flag and waved it vigorously toward the advancing Missourians. Lee glanced at the figure and was shocked to see that it was Colonel Hinckley, commander of God's army. There was a rattle of drums and shouted commands and the advancing ranks hesitated and then stopped.

Another figure rose and stood majestically on the fortifications. Even at considerable distance, Lee recognized the figure of his beloved prophet. A mighty cheer went up from the ranks of the heathen Gentiles and with a sinking heart, Lee understood that Joseph was giving himself up and was surrendering Far West to the brutal Lucas.

Joseph did, in fact, surrender at the last minute as the Missourians attacked the grossly outnumbered Saints. What resulted was the basic sacking of the Holy City of Far West. The militia, on the pretext of looking for property looted from the Missourians, ransacked the town, tearing houses apart and throwing bedding and clothing out into the streets. There were rumors that women and girls were tied to benches in the meetinghouse and ravished repeatedly by the savage Missourians. Agnes heard these stories and shuddered with concealed delight at the thought of young, God-fearing women being ravished by dirty, smelly sinners. She silently wished that she too could be ravished for her faith.

To her disappointment, the most that Agnes suffered from the profane Missourians was watching a buckskin-clad, bearded lout paw through her underwear looking for valuables or hidden loot. As the Saints huddled in their homes fearing the worst, rumors and news traveled fast. Agnes heard through the grapevine that Lucas intended to summarily shoot the prophet and Sidney Rigdon the next morning at dawn.

General Alexander Doniphan's brigade was assigned to carry out the execution, but Doniphan told Lucas that he would command his men to march to Richmond and if Lucas carried out the execution, he would see him tried for murder. This gave Lucas cause to reconsider his hasty decision to execute the church leaders and he decided to transfer them to Liberty for trial.

The next day, when Agnes heard that Joseph and several other leaders of the church were being loaded into a prison wagon for the trip to Liberty, she rushed to the town square to do what she could to save her idol. When she arrived at the common, she found it crowded with armed troops. She asked one mercenary, who was slouching on his musket, where the prophet was being held, and she received a disdainful shrug in reply. At that moment, a cheer went through the rough militiamen milling around in the quadrangle and Joseph, his brother Hyrum, and Sidney Rigdon appeared, under heavy guard and shackled.

The men emerged from the meetinghouse where they had been held overnight and were dragged by their chains toward a waiting wagon, fitted with an enclosed box with a barred front. When she saw her beloved Joseph in irons and being dragged across the square like a common criminal, a strangled cry burst from Agnes's constricted throat. Ignoring the startled soldiers, who tried to bar her way, she rushed to the prophet's side. She flung herself onto her knees in front of him and implored, "Oh, Joseph, let me go in your place! I would die for you; you must live to receive the Word of God for the church and all the Saints!"

The guards and Joseph's entourage were forced to stop rather than trample over the pathetic form of Agnes kneeling in the dust at their feet. Joseph gave her a startled look and then, as if ashamed of the wretched figure groveling at his feet, he averted his eyes. A burly guard roughly grabbed her by the arm and jerked her brusquely to her feet.

"Git the hell outta the way," he snarled and flung her aside like a sack of meal. As she watched the manacled figure disappear into the crowd, she vowed to God that she would follow him anywhere and honor him until her dying day, and so she did.

Chapter 23

The morning of the Battle of Crooked River, October 26, 1838, found Jake Devine astride Sam's black mule riding aimlessly across the empty grassland. Following the battle, Bogart's men had fled in disarray, leaving many of their mounts and camp to the enemy. Jake had found it easy to find Sam's mule and desert the militia that he had never really joined. He had come to consider the war between the Missourians and the Saints as none of his concern. He really didn't believe the religion that Sam had preached to him incessantly and he considered his father a drunk and a hypocrite. After seeing his mother bruised and demoralized the morning that he and Sam left to join Bogart, he decided that he would kill his father. It was difficult seeing her like that once, but he couldn't stand to see his mother constantly physically and emotionally abused.

He had fully intended to shoot Sam in the back during the battle, but when the wild-eyed Danite had attacked him with the huge cutlass, he sat back and let the fanatic cut Sam to pieces. In his heart, he wondered if he had become as wicked and heartless as Sam, because he felt no remorse at his father's death, nor did he feel guilty for not shooting the Saint and saving the old man. In fact, he felt some satisfaction at seeing Sam die violently and painfully. Unbidden, Jake's mind flooded with memories of his mother, crestfallen and despondent after being used like a whore. Like savoring a succulent fruit, he savored every gory scene of his father's violent death and felt no guilt.

Jake tried to take stock of his feelings, but he felt washed out and his emotions seemed numb. He wondered if this was an indication that he had become uncaring and vile like Sam. He couldn't fathom that both the Saints and Missourians showed such savagery toward each other, all in the name of God. The Saints constantly had berated the Missourians, claiming that they were God's chosen people, but one of them could savagely hack a man to pieces because of his beliefs. His mother had often read the Bible to him and he knew that it admonished men to show kindness to each other and to abhor killing, but both sides killed each other with abandon.

His mind turned to what Ozzy, the old Osage, had told him about how men should treat each other. Ozzy had warned him that the Earth Mother didn't condone killing for pleasure or blood lust. Even when it was necessary to kill an animal for food, the hunter should honor the fallen animal. Ozzy had pointed out to Jake that in the eyes of the Earth Mother, killing another man was a contravention, except if one had been wronged and justifiably sought revenge. He decided that he had not sinned when he watched Sam die, for if anyone deserved revenge it was he, Jake Devine, for himself and his mother.

The day was fair and warm for the end of October. The sun was pleasant and soothing on Jake's face, but he took no pleasure in the flawless day. His mind churned like a whirlpool as he tried to sort out his feelings. He tried to clear his brain of the images of Sam's death, but the unfortunate man's screams seemed to echo down the corridors of his mind. In his mind's eye, he saw Sam raise his arm in a vain attempt to ward off the devastating blow from the huge cutlass. Again and again he saw the gory spurt of blood as the blade severed Sam's arm and it fell jerking into the Missouri dust. He tried to feel compassion for his father, but he could not.

Each time he tried to conjure up sympathy for Sam Devine, he saw Bessie, standing vacant faced, with her eyes nearly swollen shut. It wasn't so much the physical damage that showed on his mother's face that made the rage rise in his chest like bile, it was the vacant stare of a woman who felt she had lost her soul and dignity after being used and cast aside like a dirty rag. He knew, even if it cost him his soul, he would never feel regret for not intervening to save his father's life.

The black mule seemed tense. It flinched each time Jake adjusted his position on its back. Jake realized that the poor creature was also used to Sam's abuse. Jake ran his hand over the quivering animal's flanks, and felt angry raised scars from brutal beatings the animal had suffered at the hands of Sam. Jake decided that Sam's death would spare a lot of unnecessary pain and suffering in the world, but he knew he would never totally come to grips with his part in Sam's demise.

Amazingly, as he rode across the parched prairie, the emptiness of the place seemed to bring solace to his ravaged mind. The gentle breeze touching his cheek like a lover's caress drained the feelings of guilt and inadequacy from his heart. Ozzy's words came to him again. "The Earth," the old man had said, "will heal the soul, if you will just let it." As he matched the rhythm of the mule's cadence, it seemed the rancor drained from his body into the mild autumn air.

His mind turned to Jenny and he longed for her loving touch, but he knew in his heart that Jenny was dead. He wondered if he would ever see her again and if he must become like the Bible thumpers to ensure that he would go to heaven and once again touch her soft, pale cheek. He rejected that idea, after witnessing the culmination of the war between the Saints and the Missourians; he decided Ozzy's creed made much more sense. If one respected the Earth and all living things, then Mother Earth would take you to her bosom when life ended.

Like a bolt of lightning from a sudden summer thunderhead, the image of Blossom standing naked in the shimmering water sprang into his mind. It was so sudden that a little bolt of fear or yearning sprang from his stomach and spread to his cheeks. He wondered if the Indian girl was still alive, and, without thinking about it, he felt sure that she was. He reflected if the abrupt realization that she still lived was wishful thinking or if it was akin to an insight. He knew what he would do, but first he wanted to see his mother.

Jake kicked the black mule in the ribs and then felt guilty for doing it. He thought about what the poor creature must have suffered from Sam's violent temper. He felt deep compassion for the mule and laid his hand gently on the animal's neck. They dropped down into a little valley, cut by a meandering, springfed run. Jake saw a wisp of smoke rising and assumed it was from the chimney of a homestead. He rode over a little rise and his heart leaped into his chest. What had once been a homestead, someone's dream, lay in smoking ruins. A pole corral had been ripped apart and the poles were scattered about like a child's jackstraws. A dead mule lay bloating in the warm sun, twenty feet from the remains of the corral.

The remains of a rock chimney rose like an accusing finger above the charred and ragged remains of the cabin walls. Even the haystack had been torched, leaving a scorched spot and a fluffy pile of ashes where it once stood. Jake dismounted and called, but received no answer. He walked to the house and poked around in the still hot ashes, but he found little to indicate what had happened here. He had heard from other militiamen that the Saints had sacked and burned many homesteads as they pulled back out of Daviess and Ray counties, but he didn't expect this kind of devastation.

He mounted the black mule and surveyed the ruins of cabin and outbuildings and felt a deep sadness, as if he were standing at the grave of a good friend. As he considered the devastation, a bolt of fear shot through his guts and he wondered if the raiders had found their farmstead with his mother home alone. He swung the mule's head around and kicked it viciously in the ribs. There was no thought of compassion for the abused mule now; the only thought in Jake's mind was to get home to his mother.

An hour later he came to the little run that flowed past the Devine farm. He urged the lathered mule into a lumbering lope and strained his eyes to the horizon for any indication of smoke. He saw none, but it didn't ease the anxiety gnawing in his guts. He topped the little rise boarding the swale where the house stood and reined in his mount. His worst fears were realized. The house was a charred ruin; only a remnant of the mud chimney remained. Fearing the worst, he surveyed the outbuildings and saw the ramshackle barn had suffered the same fate as the house. Lying a few yards beyond the charred boards of the barn, he saw the red and white cow lying on her side like a badger mound.

Churning emotion rose in his throat. He had milked that gentle old cow every morning and evening for as long as he could remember. When he had sat on the stool by her side, she had always turned to look at him with soft brown eyes and softly bellowed as if in anticipation of milking. With fear rising in his throat like sour acid, he dismounted and walked toward the remains of the house. As he approached, he saw the body of Rufe lying close to where the front door had been. He knelt by the pitiful remains of his beloved dog and saw that Rufe was lying in a black pool of dried blood. Immediately he surmised that the dog had died protecting Bessie.

Choking back grief and tears, he rose from the body of the dog and, dreading what he might find, he walked to the stone slab that had served as a doorstep. He saw what he first thought were two weathered white poles sticking out through the blackened remains of the doorjamb, but as he stood over them he realized that they were what remained of his mother's spindly legs. Her torso and head lay just inside the entrance and were burned black. He could see his mother's white teeth glistening against the blackened mass that had been her face.

As Jake looked at the remains of his mother, savage rage rose in his heart and he wished that he had killed the wild-eyed Saint that butchered his father. He was consumed with white-hot fury for the fanatics that had done this in the name of God. His mother had never harmed another human being or creature, and she had paid for her compassion with her life. Now all that remained of the loving mother that he had known was this grisly burned thing, lying on the doorstep of her home.

With eyes blurred and stinging from tears, Jake found an old shovel leaning against the pigpen and dug a hole about six feet long, four across and five feet deep. The ground was soft and moist from the autumn rains and the job didn't take him very long. He gathered the remains of his mother, rolled her in an old horse blanket he found near the corral, and gently lowered her into the yawning hole. Once that was done, he found a couple of old burlap sacks and wrapped Rufe in them. Gently, he lifted the bundle in his arms and hot tears gushed from his eyes, falling on the makeshift shroud.

He lay the body of the dog on the chest of his mother and with that he gently filled the hole with the black Missouri soil that he had dug out of it. When he was finished, he pried the doorstep stone up with the shovel and dragged it to the grave. He laid the stone at the head of the grave and thought of carving something in the soft sandstone, but thought better of it. Who would ever stop by here, and, if they did, would they care about the grave of an old woman and a dog? He thought not.

He turned to go, but stopped and turned back to the freshly turned soil. Somehow he could not walk away from the two spirits that he loved most in this world without saying something over the remains. He kneeled on one knee and placed his hand to his forehead. Tears burst from his eyes and fell on the freshly turned earth. He tried to speak, but his throat constricted until he could hardly breathe. Finally, he said in a quavering voice, "Earth Mother, do not forget Rufe and my mother. They both returned love for hate and respected your creations. Send the Pale Horse to retrieve their souls and carry them back to your loving arms." He lifted his eyes as if he were through, then, as if he had a second thought, Jake lowered his head again.

"Earth Mother," he continued, "guide my steps that they may lead me back to Adsila." He spoke the words before he even thought about Blossom, almost as if he spoke a premonition. Then he realized he had nothing left in life, but her. Again, the vision of her brown, glistening skin formed in his mind and he saw her standing in the sparkling waters of the springfed pond. Now he wanted to be with her and listen to the lilting sound of her voice as she spoke her native tongue.

He rose from the half-kneeling position and stood over the grave. Then he stooped and picked up a handful of dirt from the freshly turned surface and, sprinkling it over the dark earth, he muttered, "Hah kon wah sha she I'n tat se tzi sho." In halting Osage, Jake asked the mystery force to receive the spirits of Rufe and his mother and to grant him revenge against the whites who had killed them.

Then he rose and took the reins of the mule and with a graceful move he swung onto the animal's bare back. He turned the mule's head to the west, but this time he did it gently, and patted the faithful animal on the neck. A week later, Jake and Lucifer, as he had come to call the mule, arrived on the banks of the Missouri, at Joseph Robidoux's trading post, which eventually grew into Saint Joseph. Jake knew there was a ferry near Robidoux's fort that served the Indian Territory.

He sat on the mule and looked across the swirling brown waters. The river was nearly a mile wide at this spot and he could just make out the trees and willows bordering the west bank. As he sat there, he reached into his possibles bag and took out a chunk of venison jerky that he had made from a young buck he shot along the Grand. He felt the mule's ribs and was surprised to find that there was a considerable amount of fat covering them and that the critter seemed in good shape. But then, he hadn't pushed the mule or himself, but had hunted his way west toward the Big Muddy.

As he sat munching the jerky, the mule contentedly grazed on the lush grass bordering the river. As he sat there, he heard the crunching of buggy wheels and soon a vehicle rounded a bend in the river. A man and a woman, who appeared to be in their forties, sat on the springseat; unbidden, the man reined in the team and looked at Jake curiously. The man spit a brown stream of tobacco juice into the dust. "Ya lost, young feller?" he asked.

"Don' think so," Jake replied. "I'm a'looking fer Robidoux's ferry."

"Well, it's about a mile north of here, but I cain't imagine why ya would want to cross the river into Injun Territory," the driver admonished. "Ain't nothing out there but redskins and coyotes clear to the Rocky Mountains.

"Say," he continued, "ya ain't one o' them Saints is ya? I heard Governor Boggs called out the militia and drove 'em out of Caldwell County. Good riddance I say; them fanatics wus always a'sayin' that God gave 'em this land 'cuz they was God's chosen people." He eyed Jake again, letting his gaze rest on the long rifle that rested across the mule's withers.

"Naw, I am not one of them," Jake replied.

"Then why do ya want to go out on them dry plains? Like I said, ain't nothing out there but filthy redskins."

Jake gave him a baleful look. "Guess that's why I want to go," he said sullenly.

That evening, Jake led the mule onto the board floor of the ferry. The grizzled old man who ran it eased the ungainly craft into the swirling waters of the Missouri and Jake stared across the roiling brown water at the cottonwoods on the west bank. The old man tried to engage Jake in conversation with questions akin to what the man with the buggy had asked him earlier, but Jake refused to engage in conversation and answered with grunts. The old ferryman finally shrugged and focused his attention on manning the boat. When they landed on the west side, Jake mounted Lucifer and gently nudged him in the ribs with his heels. The boy and mule slowly went down the gangplank and vanished into the cottonwoods above the high-water mark. The old boatman squinted into the setting sun, trying to catch a glimpse of the mule and rider, but they seemed to disappear into the radiance of the setting sun.

ACKNOWLEDGMENTS

I would like to dedicate this book to my parents, who inspired me to eventually give up my irresponsible ways and make the most of my limited abilities. My father was a well-read and intelligent man and I respected him. My mother was a loving and nurturing person, who put her children's needs before her own. I would also like to dedicate this book to my wife, Sylvia, who constantly encouraged me to follow my dreams.

I suspect that this book would never have seen the light of day without the faith and constant encouragement of Robert H. Pruett of Belle Isle Books and his staff. He saw something worthwhile in the original manuscript and constantly encouraged me to press on. I would also like to thank Editor Annie Tobey for her professionalism and commitment. Whatever literary achievement this book may be, I owe to her knowledge of writing and her untiring efforts.

Bill Jensen

www.ingramcontent.com/pod-product-compliance
Lightning Source LLC
Chambersburg PA
CBHW032051260626
47157CB00020B/2704